I love that I can dive into a Masters of The Shadowlands book and get lost and come out feeling warm, safe, and floaty. Just like being in "sub space" ~ Marie's Tempting Reads

Let's liven up our marriage. It'll be fun. Then her husband brought two slaves into the house. That was the end of that.

Divorce achieved, Valerie is working on her goals. Friends: has a new one. Fitness: little muscles! Finances: in the black.

Friskiness? Total. Effing. Fail. So she attends the notorious Shadowlands club's open house. There, a sadistic Dom—a fellow professor--teaches her that she loves pain with her pleasure. He wants to show her more.

Despite the razor edges of his hard face and the authority in his every word, he's careful and caring. He listens, and how tempting is that?

But she knows better. Her heart is off limits.

Retired Special Forces colonel, Ghost has been a widower for long enough. Although he's ready to love again, the generous, caring woman he desires has scars from her past. However, he has hard-won skills, enough to show Valerie there can be a new F on her list—*fulfillment.* Life looks good.

Until his past surfaces, shattering his new life and the love he'd hoped to win.

THE EFFING LIST

Masters of the Shadowlands: 15

CHERISE SINCLAIR

VanScoy Publishing Group

ACKNOWLEDGMENTS

Where do I even start? So many people help to create a story, and I'm so grateful to all of you.

But, you know, it all starts with you—my readers. You're why I'm still plunking my butt down in front of the keyboard. You've offered your ideas and opinions, cheered me on, requested stories for characters I'd never have tried to give a voice to—like Mistress Anne and Master Sam. To all of you, you're amazing and inspiring. Thank you.

So many hugs go to Leagh at Romance Novel Promotions for running the Facebook Shadowkittens group. Herding kittens isn't for the faint of heart.

To my Shadowkittens on Facebook. I adore y'all so much. I love how discussions range from books to real life, how y'all share...ahem...*inspirational* pictures and laugh-out-loud memes, how generous you are with advice and encouragement to other kittens. Blessings on Lisa SK for her generosity and tact as Mama Cat.

As always, my besties and crit partners had my back—even when one of them was only a week from a big surgery. Fiona

Archer and Monette Michaels, thank you! And a huge hug to Bianca Sommerland doing the content editing for this book.

Although, I swear, y'all, I almost pulled my hair out when all of you wanted more sex scenes. ARGH!

Beta readers—Barb Jack, Lisa White, Marian Shulman, and JJ Foster—I treasure you so much. Thank you so much for your time and help in pointing out where something isn't clear and in finding errors in grammar or phrasing that have slipped right past me.

Red Quill's editing team—Ekatarina Sayanova, Rebecca Cartee, and Tracy Damron-Roelle—is simply fantastic, not only catching grammar and punctuation errors, but finding oopsies like characters who miraculously switch clothing in the middle of a scene. LOL!

April Martinez of GraphicFantastic has designed all the covers for the Shadowlands, including this one. Thank you, April!

TIMELINE

Since there is some crossover between the Masters of the Shadowlands series and the Sons of the Survivalist series (Master Z just can't keep from getting involved, right?), I thought y'all might like a chronological order of events.

The thirteenth book in the Masters of the Shadowlands series was: *Beneath the Scars* (Master Holt & Josie's story).

Several months later in the fall comes *Defiance* with Master Z & Jessica. This book takes us to Alaska and introduces the sons of the survivalist.

This book, Ghost & Valerie's story in the Shadowlands series, *The Effing List,* occurs the following spring.

Before the end of their story, the first book in the Sons of the Survivalist, *Not a Hero,* begins.

AUTHOR'S NOTE

To my readers,

The books I write are fiction, not reality, and as in most romantic fiction, the romance is compressed into a very, very short time period.

You, my darlings, live in the real world, and I want you to take a little more time in your relationships. Good Doms don't grow on trees, and there are some strange people out there. So while you're looking for that special Dom, please, be careful.

When you find him or her, realize they can't read your mind. Yes, frightening as it might be, you're going to have to open up and talk to them. And you listen to them in return. Share your hopes and fears, what you want from them, what scares you spitless. Okay, they may try to push your boundaries a little—they're a Dom, after all—but you will have your safeword. You *will* have a safeword, am I clear? Use protection. Have a back-up person. Communicate.

Remember: safe, sane, and consensual.

Know that I'm hoping you find that special, loving person who will understand your needs and hold you close.

And while you're looking or even if you have already found your dearheart, come and hang out with the Masters of the Shadowlands.

Love,

Cherise

PROLOGUE

N*ovember*

Happy fiftieth birthday to me. And it was time and past time to make some decisions. Valerie Winborne rolled out of the narrow bed in the bedroom that had once been her daughter's. And was now hers.

Two weeks ago, when her husband invited a second slave into their bed, Valerie had moved to this small, very bare bedroom. Who would have thought she'd miss her daughter's garish posters on the walls?

In the tiny bathroom, she frowned at the sad-looking woman in the mirror.

A purpling bruise was obvious on her cheek. Yes, she had decisions to make.

Pudgy. Limp, dark blonde hair. Sallow complexion. Pitiful.

Removing her nightgown exposed the tiny red wound and bruise on her right breast. A lump on her mammogram resulted in a biopsy a few days ago.

The findings were negative. She was all right.

But the days of thinking she might have cancer—might *die*—had shaken her world. And today, she was fifty—and her husband had hit her.

She tilted her head to the ceiling. *Listen up, all of you gods, I really don't need wake-up calls like this. Right?*

Once out of the shower and dressed, she retrieved her briefcase from under the bed and unlocked it. There were student papers to grade before the community college's Thanksgiving holidays next week.

She started to set it on the desk and stopped abruptly.

Oh, wonderful. There was a sludgy puddle in the middle of a pile of papers. A pungent orange scent wafted up.

Someone, undoubtedly Kahlua, had dumped orange juice on the desk.

Anger roused...and faded to frustration.

No harm done, after all. The jealous, petty slave had vandalized things before. It was why Valerie kept her paperwork in the locked briefcase. All Kahlua had destroyed *this* time was years-old unclaimed homework that had been left out as a decoy.

From the kitchen, Kahlua's shrill voice rose. "It's not my fucking turn, you bitch!"

"You slut, it is your turn. I cooked yesterday," Alisha yelled back.

Something shattered. Probably a plate.

Barry yelled, "Keep it down."

As cupboards slammed in the kitchen, Valerie started to open her briefcase, then shook her head. The essays needed to be graded, but if she didn't have coffee first, she'd probably mark every paper with an F. With a rueful laugh, Valerie rested her head in her hands, feeling the onset of a low-grade headache.

A morning person she was not.

Food would be good, but neither Kahlua nor Alisha liked to cook. After tasting their grudging efforts at making suppers,

Barry had decreed that Valerie would cook in the evenings, despite working a fulltime job.

She would have refused, but she preferred her food to be edible.

It just wasn't fair the two slaves brought in no money and didn't do much of anything around the house.

Yet their presence was partly her fault. When Valerie had mentioned how a colleague talked about the fun in exploring BDSM, Barry'd been interested since his friends often boasted about their kinky lifestyles.

She'd thought trying something new might be fun too. After all, they'd been married for years; the children were raised and gone.

And the sex was, face it, *boring*.

They'd joined a BDSM group. She'd learned something about herself—like how she reacted to pain and domination and sex.

Unfortunately, all Barry learned was he liked having someone serve him. At the end of summer, when he wanted someone totally submissive to him—a slave—she'd reluctantly agreed to let Alisha move in. To give polyamory a try. In the BDSM group, some of the poly Masters had two or three slaves, and the women were all very happy. Sister slaves they called themselves.

She'd always wanted a sister.

Instead, she'd hated the whole thing. Two weeks ago, after the agreed-on three months trial, she told Barry it wasn't working, and Alisha needed to leave.

Instead, he'd added Kahlua.

Valerie had almost walked out right then.

But she'd been married to him half of her life. Wasn't this merely one more storm to weather?

No, no, it isn't. She shook her head. Barry's slaves would never be like sisters to her. In fact, she didn't like them at all.

Valerie pulled in a breath. Why was she putting up with living in misery and anger and resentment? Had the gods given her a scare to force her to answer the hard questions? *If your life ended in the next few months, what would you be pleased about?*

What would you regret?

Pulling a pad forward, she started a list of things that made up a balanced life.

Health: Before the biopsy results came back, the doctor had mentioned her weight and lack of exercise could be a contributing factor to getting cancer. Well, she sure didn't want to go through this again, so she'd fix it.

Exercise? *Ugh*. But she'd do it.

At least menopause hadn't reared its ugly head quite yet.

Friends: Ha! That'd be nice. She liked people, but Barry always oh-so-subtly discouraged her friendships with other women. And when Alisha moved in, subtle disappeared. *"Vanilla people don't understand us, Val. You don't need other friends; you have Alisha now."*

Spiritual: Got it covered. Meditation kept her sane and from murdering the other two women.

Financial: There was a mess. Barry's construction contractor earnings fluctuated with the housing market, but her community college job brought in stable wages. They should've been doing all right but not when supporting two other people. Not when Barry kept buying the slaves expensive presents and alcohol. He'd decimated their joint savings account.

She tried to be a generous person, but nope, not any longer.

Work: Teaching her classes—world religions and philosophy— was her crack. What better way to utilize her experience of growing up in the Middle East?

She'd hoped to apply for a university job after earning her doctorate in philosophy last year, but Barry had discouraged her. She frowned. Had he viewed her success as competition?

Family: They'd been partners, raising their two children, loving each other, supporting each other.

And there was the crux of it, why she hadn't acted before this.

Instead, for months, she'd refused to believe that what they had was gone. That love had...died.

All she was to him now was a...housekeeper. Tears welled in her eyes.

And he was no longer the man she'd married. Before the children were born, he'd promised to abstain from drinking and had kept his promise.

Then Kahlua had arrived, bringing in more than attitude—she'd brought in alcohol.

Barry was drinking every day now, and his behavior had changed.

Last night, when Kahlua deliberately broke Hailey's ceramic handprint from preschool, Valerie had sworn at her, using the Arabic insults she'd learned as a child.

Barry had turned on Valerie. Yelled at her. *Slapped* her.

She gingerly touched her bruised cheek. In all their years of marriage, he'd never struck her.

Straightening her shoulders, she rose and walked into the dining room.

Kahlua was serving Barry a plate of pancakes. Her husband looked good for a guy over fifty. During a mid-life crisis and with a receding hairline, he'd shaved his scalp. Being in construction, he'd stayed muscular.

Once upon a time, she'd loved his body. Had loved *him*.

At the table, Alisha was sipping coffee. The petite, slender redhead was in her thirties, a good fifteen years younger than Valerie. She wore shorts, a blue sleeveless shirt, and a thin leather collar.

Because Barry wanted his slaves to be collared.

Valerie had refused to wear a collar. Or to be called a slave.

"Oh, look what the cat dragged in." Kahlua picked up her own plate from the counter. Her shorts barely covered her ass cheeks; her tank top was skintight, and her collar bright red. She smirked at Valerie. "Sorry, I didn't make you any. But pancakes would make your ass an even bigger mass."

"Morning, babe." Barry stuffed a bite of pancake in his mouth.

No one asked how she was feeling. No one wished her a happy birthday.

All right. Time to get this done. This...confrontation. She could do this, even though her childhood memories of her parents' insults, shouting, and screaming seemed far too close these days.

"Good morning, you all." She forced her lips into a smile. "And happy birthday to me, actually.

Barry blinked. "Oh, hey, I—"

"Sorry, Valerie," Alisha said in her snotty voice. "We didn't get you anything."

"Not a problem. All I want for my present this year...is a divorce."

CHAPTER ONE

M *arch*

Humming to herself, Valerie entered the small Vietnamese restaurant near campus and breathed in the heady aromas of lemongrass, mint, herbs, and fish sauce. Thankfully, the sound of her stomach gurgling was drowned out by the clattering of tableware and conversations in various languages.

She was so hungry. It was good her careful budget would keep her from ordering everything on the menu.

Was Queenie here yet? She swept her gaze around the crowded room.

"Excuse me, please." The deep, raspy voice came from behind her.

Oops, she was blocking the doorway. "Sorry." She edged sideways, bumped into a chair, and started to trip over someone's purse.

The man caught her upper arm in a firm grip. "Steady there."

Grace in motion, that's me. "Thank—" She looked up, and her mind went blank.

He was six feet of lean and deadly. His clean-shaven face was darkly tanned. Short, curly, steel-gray hair and weather-beaten skin indicated he was about her age. His green eyes held a keen intelligence.

As all his attention focused on her, her breathing tried to stop. *Honestly, woman, you've seen men before.* "Thank you for the save."

"You're very welcome." With an unexpectedly charming smile, he released her.

Giving him a friendly nod, she stepped out of his way. Her arm still tingled from where he'd held her. He certainly was strong.

Especially for a professor. She'd seen him at a couple of faculty receptions...and the man totally demolished the stereotype of an amiable, forgetful professor.

"Here!" The high-pitched call and raised arm pinpointed Queenie's location near the back. The English professor was a friendly sort—and another person who loved the wonderful variety of Asian restaurants near campus.

"Happy beginning of March. Sit, sit." Pushing her red and purple streaked hair back, Queenie motioned to a chair. "I already ordered your usual for you."

"Perfect, thank you." Valerie took a seat across from her. "I'm past ready for something uplifting like good food and conversation."

Queenie's eyebrows shot up. "What's happened? Student problems?"

"Nothing so serious. My ex-husband called. He wants me to pick up the boxes the children left there."

Queenie's eyes narrowed. "He has your old house, and you mentioned once you're in an apartment, but he's going to make you store the boxes?"

"I might have objected, but he has"...slaves... *"guests* who are snoopy and destructive." She wasn't going to let Kahlua ruin the things her children wanted to keep.

"Ugh. No wonder you need feel-good food." Queenie grimaced. "At least your kids are grown. Dickface and I battled constantly about custody, vacations, and child support until ours were gone."

"Ouch. I hope my ex and I don't come to bickering over holidays. Thankfully, at Christmas, he and my son went ocean fishing so I could spend the day with my daughter and the most adorable grandbaby in the world."

Queenie grinned, then shook her head. "You were lucky. I predict problems for future holidays."

A dismal thought. Because when it came to conflict, Valerie would lose. Or give in. Or run.

Change the subject.

"How are your classes going?" Valerie had mostly upper-level students in her philosophy and world religion classes. They were actually interested in the subjects.

Poor Queenie's English composition lectures were filled with freshmen.

"I hate eighteen-year-olds." Queenie rolled her eyes. "One of them was still drunk from the weekend, and the fumes rolling off him turned my stomach."

Valerie grinned. "Ah, the sweet bouquet of hungover freshmen, hmm?"

Queenie laughed.

As the waiter arrived and set their food out, Valerie recognized him as one of her students. "Jamail, everything looks wonderful."

"It is. In fact, I can personally vouch the food is excellent here." His smile stretched across his face as he gave a small bow. "Thank you so much for helping me get this job, Dr. Winborne."

"It was my pleasure. I'm sure they're delighted to have you." And they were feeding him well, she was happy to see.

As he strode away, Queenie lifted an eyebrow in inquiry. "You found him this job?"

"He kept getting skinnier, so I called him in for a talk and learned his part-time jobs didn't pay enough for food and rent. I suggested a restaurant job where he'd get free food, then told the owners here he was a hard worker. It's a good match."

Queenie shook her head. "Most of us think we're doing an excellent job if we counsel students about course material and grades. You take it a step further, don't you?"

"It's all part of the whole." Valerie moved her shoulders in a half-shrug. "If starving, how can a child study?"

"There is that." Queenie turned to her food, letting the subject drop.

Valerie gazed fondly at the redhead. The two of them would never be besties—their views on the world were too different—but Queenie was a fun colleague and lunch date.

After a few minutes of contented eating, Queenie eyed Valerie speculatively. "Hmm."

"*What?* Did I forget to wear makeup or something?"

"You never wear makeup. Very funny." Queenie nibbled on a shrimp spring roll. "Remember when a group of us were talking about the *Fifty Shades* stuff, and you said you and your husband tried it?"

Valerie winced. Post divorce in January, she'd had too much to drink at one of Queenie's parties. The alcohol hadn't helped her depression and neither had oversharing. "And?"

"You see there's this club—"

Hastily, Valerie held up her hand to stop her. "I'm not a member of any clubs."

"No, no, that's not what I mean. So, this place, it's not a swinger's club where there are people watching and jerking off. This one is supposed to be classy, like, in a mansion, and all BDSM. It's really private and exclusive, but they're having a night when visitors can see what it's all about. Even get a kind of sampling of what they do."

"Like a taste test?"

"Exactly." Queenie waggled her eyebrows. "Don't you think visiting a BDSM club sounds interesting?"

More like avoid-at-all-costs. In a way, BDSM had destroyed her marriage. Or maybe it was merely the final blow.

"A club, hmm?" She and Barry had considered trying a club, but they were all expensive. Instead, they joined a small group who played in one guy's house. And it'd been fun, at first. Especially when one Dom showed Barry how to spank her...

No, don't think about that.

After Barry brought in Alisha, they'd quit the group. Probably because someone had criticized Barry's techniques and offered pointers.

Barry didn't take criticism well.

"What do you think, Valerie? I really don't want to go by myself." Queenie gave her an appealing look.

"No, going alone wouldn't be wise." They were friends...well, lunch friends, anyway. And Queenie had gone out of her way to introduce Valerie around on campus, show her where things were, and generally help her figure things out. Teaching in a small community college had been quite different from being a university professor.

Valerie pursed her lips. "I'll admit, I've never been to an actual BDSM club."

"See? I'm really curious. Most of my hookups are jump on, pump away, jump off. A BDSMer must have a more extensive repertoire." Queenie wrinkled her nose and made Valerie laugh. "Although I'm not exactly a nubile young thing anymore."

Queenie was only around forty. Valerie shook her head. "Try being fifty." Probably no one would even notice her.

Barry had certainly lost interest.

But this wouldn't be like a real BDSM night. How could she turn Queenie down?

"All right. Let's do it."

Later in the afternoon, Valerie slid out of her car and faced the house where she'd lived for twenty-five years. On each side of the entry, bird-of-paradise plants stood as sentinels. Vibrant pink flowering azaleas were bright against the white front. Butterflies danced above the white flowers of the viburnum.

When they'd moved in, the front yard had contained only grass. She'd worked hard to make the yard colorful. Welcoming.

But there was no welcome here for her.

Not my home. Not my house. Not my family.

Despite the painful squeezing in her chest, Valerie repeated the words under her breath and pushed the doorbell on the ranch-style house.

"A Country Boy Can Survive" rang out. Barry had been so pleased when she had the new doorbell installed with his favorite song. It'd been their twenty-fifth wedding anniversary.

Their marriage hadn't made it to the twenty-seventh.

The briny air from the Gulf of Mexico swept through the small residential neighborhood, making the palm trees sway, easing the warmth of the March afternoon. Not having gone home to change after her last class, she was still in khaki pants and a button-up shirt.

Footsteps sounded inside.

Relax. I'm only here to pick up boxes, and I won't let their snarking get to me.

Alisha opened the door. "Oh, it's you. Come for your shit?"

"I did." Valerie walked past and flinched at the sight of the filthy carpet, dirty dishes on side tables, and dust everywhere.

Even when the children were small, the place had never been such a mess. She'd been gone for only three and a half months and...

Not my home. Not my circus. Not my monkeys.

Alisha's expression turned ugly. "Master Barry doesn't care what the house looks like. He wants other things from us. It's a shame you never figured that out."

Valerie smiled politely in response.

Because she had figured that out. Dabbling in BDSM had briefly invigorated their dull sex life. The couple of times he'd spanked her before sex, they'd both been surprised at how hard she'd climaxed.

But Barry wasn't into exerting himself when it came to the bedroom. Especially when he'd found two submissives who hung on his every word and serviced him without him having to do a thing.

Valerie was no young babe. And being a slave? *Not my thing.* "Where are my boxes?"

"Against the wall there." When Alisha turned to point, vivid scratch marks on her neck were visible. Kahlua had probably been drinking last night.

Valerie shook her head. Even *her* peacekeeping skills weren't up to dealing with the belligerent drunk. Thank goodness she didn't live here any longer.

Six boxes were stacked against the wall, more than she'd figured. Family albums, baby books, the kids' precious art projects. Probably even some stuffed animals to hand down to Luca. Valerie's heart turned mushy. Her two-year-old grandson was the smartest, sweetest, most adorable child in all the world.

Valerie picked up the first box and suppressed a grunt. Not stuffed animals in this one. What had Hailey packed—rocks?

She carried it out to the car.

Returning, she heard a long groan from the master bedroom to the right. Undoubtedly, Kahlua had pushed Barry to have sex right when the ex-wife was scheduled to show up. Because that was how Kahlua operated.

Alisha smirked.

Don't react. Let the ugliness simply pass through into the floor. She picked up the next box.

Back when Alisha became Barry's slave, Valerie had been jealous—oh my gods, she'd been jealous. And felt so cliché—the older wife whose husband was chasing after a younger woman. But she'd tried to overcome her feelings, only Alisha had been even more jealous.

Then, when Barry brought in Kahlua, the two slaves had joined forces against Valerie.

Valerie took the second box to the car and drew in a long breath of the sultry Florida air, cleansing her lungs of the toxic stench of the past.

Back inside, there was Kahlua, naked and stinking of sex. "Hey, it's our pal, Val. The ex who never gets sex." She ran her hands over her oversized, abnormally high breasts, gifts from a previous lover. "I'm sorry. I should have dressed. I know it bothers you to see someone getting some when you can't get anything."

Responding to nitwits is an exercise in futility.

Valerie picked up the next box and carried it out. Three more to go.

Kahlua and Alisha were talking amiably when she returned, obviously having united against a common enemy.

"So, *Val, babe.* Got any since you left?" Kahlua asked in a simperingly sweet voice.

Valerie picked up the next box, her arms aching.

"Please. You know no one would want her if she even had a sex drive left." Alisha shook her head in pseudo pity.

Valerie carried the box out. Returned. Two left.

"You should take that paycheck you're so proud of," Kahlua

sneered, "and buy yourself a fun night with a man. Man-hos aren't picky."

Alisha choked on the beer she was drinking.

Barry walked out of the bedroom, fastening his jeans. "Val, babe. You're here."

Valerie turned. And felt...nothing. What they'd built together —raising children, making a marriage—was gone.

Kahlua was right in a way. Sex with Barry had been only so-so. Once in a blue moon, he'd go down on her so she could get off. He wasn't inventive or one to exert any effort.

"I'm here for the boxes." Valerie motioned to the wall.

Still naked, Kahlua handed him a beer. Leaning against the doorframe, he put an arm around her. "You're looking...good, Val."

Good, hmm. After all the snark from the two women, Valerie had to clamp down on her urge to let loose, to sound like the sarcastic heroines in her favorite romance novels. But why bother?

She picked up the box.

"I miss you," he said.

She froze. In December, she'd longed to hear those words. It'd been her choice to move out, but the first month alone had almost broken her. If he'd said something then, she might well have returned.

Not now.

"I'd take you back, you know." Ignoring Kahlua's angry gasp, he moved close enough to stroke Valerie's hair. "I might even toss in a spanking or two."

The memory blanked her mind. Being laid out on the bed, his hand coming down on her butt with a loud smack, the warmth of an orgasm, the...

No.

"Sorry, but no." Arms encumbered with the box, she couldn't shove him away, only retreat a step. "We're done."

His mouth tightened, then he nodded. "Have you heard from Hailey or Dillon recently?"

Dillon had been in China since January, setting up a manufacturing plant. Last week, he'd called, and they'd talked for over an hour. Even men in their twenties could get homesick, it seemed. "Dillon won't be back for another six or seven weeks. And"—no, she wasn't about to serve as an intermediary between him and their children—"you have a phone, Barry. Call them if you want to know how they're doing. Or maybe you should invite them over."

"I'll call them both." He scowled...because he had been avoiding having the children over to visit since Kahlua and Alisha moved in. He couldn't avoid telling them forever.

She sighed. It was bad enough she'd acquiesced when he'd asked her not to tell the children about the slaves. Although, really, how in the world would she have ever found a way to explain? Hailey and Dillon believed Barry could do no wrong.

"Hey, this box is heavy, and I need to go. Good seeing you all." Such a lie.

As she lugged the box out the door, it occurred to her he hadn't offered to carry it.

Had he always been such a jerk and she hadn't realized?

She drove to her apartment in the "New Tampa" area. Near I-75, the complex was just far enough from the university the place wasn't filled with students.

After storing the boxes in a closet, she forced herself to change into running shorts, sports bra, and a loose tank top. Because exercising was part of her new life.

Ugh, ugh, and ugh.

I can do it. I will.

Once out of her apartment complex, she walked to the Flatwoods Wilderness Park, feeling the heat surround her. Up north, people considered March a springtime month, but in Florida, summer was here already. She should probably jog in the early mornings.

What an awful thought.

Old-growth pines and oaks lined the paved trail, filling the air with their tangy fragrance. After stretching out, she started off at a slow jog. Admittedly, her speed was barely faster than a walk, but, damn, she was proud of herself. *Jogging—go, me!*

She pulled in deep calming breaths and started to relax. The ugliness of being around Alisha and Kahlua had tensed her whole body.

Conflict was something she avoided. Cruel words and loud voices brought back how her parents would shout at each other... and her...so loudly everyone in the neighborhood heard. It didn't matter where they were living—Doha, Qatar or in Riyadh, Saudi Arabia or in Muscat, Oman. Mom and Dad never cared what the locals thought. Valerie had been the one who interacted with the Arab housekeepers, and she'd felt humiliated by the sympathetic looks and whispered gossip. The other children, already inclined to dislike her because she was a foreigner—an *American*—jeered at her.

Even so, she'd managed to make friends with the nicer locals. And learned to create her own safe place, deep inside her mind.

But meditation couldn't help everything, and insults hurt more when they were true. She hadn't been a cute child...as her parents had, all too often, complained about.

In her twenties, finally outgrowing her chubby cheeks and awkwardness, she'd been astonished when men found her attractive. When Barry found her attractive. Those had been nice years.

Unfortunately, part of growing older was...growing older. And, admittedly, she'd gained too much weight.

She nodded to another jogger, then smiled to herself. Some of those pounds were gone now, and everything had tightened up.

But no matter how much she exercised, she'd never be a fresh-looking twenty-year-old.

At one-and-a-half miles, she turned around and headed back at a nice pace. A motion in the brush caught her eye. Wild turkeys. Then she caught a glimpse of a deer with last year's fawn. This was such a lovely park.

As she passed a water station, a man jumped off the bench. "Hey, hey, you. Lady. I could use a buck."

"No money, sorry." She increased her pace, but he caught up easily.

"Gimme a buck, woman." His clothes were dirty, his hair greasy. His fingers twitched. And his eyes looked mean.

Oh spit. "Leave me *alone.*" *Don't show fear. Be loud and firm.*

"Money, dammit, bitch." His long legs kept up easily.

She veered away from his hand into the path of two young men who were passing her. "Hey, guys," she called. "Could you escort me?"

They slowed, stopped, and turned.

"Fucking cunt," the guy spat out before veering into the underbrush.

One of the men motioned to her. "C'mon, we'll get you out of this area and let the cops know there's someone harassing women."

"Thank you so much."

When out of the park, the men resumed their run, and she slowed to a walk, still shaking.

Nonetheless, she wasn't going to give up her jogging. She simply needed to figure out how to defend herself.

Would pepper spray work? Or she could take self-defense courses? Something.

At least the two men had been nice.

It'd been embarrassing to be panting like a bellows and drenched with sweat trying to keep up with even their reduced speed. She sure couldn't blame them for not looking at her twice.

Although...could Alisha and Kahlua be right, and *no* man would be interested in her? That she'd have to pay for sex?

Heavens, how insecure could she get? Then again, after the months of them tearing her down and Barry not disagreeing, of course she was. Who wouldn't be?

But she wouldn't let herself stay caged and afraid. They were wrong, and she needed to prove it, not to them, but to herself.

Her shower left her smelling like jasmine rather than sweat—a vast improvement. Picking up her dark red planner, she walked out onto her small balcony that overlooked the preserve.

Settling into a chair, she put her feet up on the railing and flipped past the pages with her goals for the week.

The next page held her goals for the year. She'd started the list on the day she asked for a divorce.

Then when her divorce was final, she narrowed the goals down to what she really needed to work on. Didn't it figure the list turned out to be all F-words?

And, of *course*, the first item on the *effing* list was *effing* fitness.

Fitness
Friends
Family
Finances
Fun

Two weeks ago, she'd added: *Friskiness.*

How nice that neither lover nor husband started with F and thus couldn't be part of her list.

The thought was bittersweet because she really missed having someone to talk with in the evenings. And, sometimes, she wanted to be touched so badly she ached with it.

But loneliness was better than betrayal.

She didn't need to love anyone or live with anyone. The risk wasn't worth it. However, in this century, women could do hookups as easily as men could. Maybe she'd consider that...eventually.

After all, "fuck" started with the right letter.

Laughing under her breath, she studied her list.

Fitness. Doing well there. The jogging helped—and the weights. Too embarrassed to use the campus gym filled with young hard bodies, she'd bought elastic straps and weights and worked out at home. It was paying off. She bent her arm and actually saw her biceps flex.

Friends. Well, she had quite a few friendly colleagues. Real friends would be better. Still needed to work on this one.

Family. The children were doing well, although they still hoped she and Barry would get back together. There was nothing she could do about their wishes, except maybe tell them about the slaves and his drinking.

Should she ever reveal he'd hit her?

Just the thought was uncomfortable. A good parent didn't destroy a child's image of their father. Maybe telling the children the truth would be easier on her, but that didn't make it right, especially since Barry would, hopefully, see the mess he was making and turn things around.

Finances. Better. An adjunct's pay was dismal and less than what she'd earned teaching at the community college, but this fall, she'd be an official assistant professor.

Fun. Ouch. She worked. Worked some more. This goal needed attention.

Then the last goal: *Friskiness.* Total fail. She'd tried flirting but hadn't really been interested in anyone.

Maybe if a guy had offered to spank her?

Amused at herself, she glanced toward the bedroom where there were two new toys in the bedstand. Toys didn't spank either. They did deliver orgasms, at least.

Okay, maybe she needed to work harder on this goal, too.

CHAPTER TWO

In his pickup, Ghost—or as his mother called him when he'd screwed up royally, Finlay Kamron Blackwood—rolled the windows down to savor the humid air of the Florida countryside. Pine and grass, and nearby wetlands added a sulphury hint.

Stretches of hardwoods and conifers vied with marshy areas. Red-winged blackbirds and yellowthroats perched on fence posts. *Nice.* It'd been too long since he'd escaped the city.

He frowned. How long had it been since he'd visited the club?

A month? Two? He'd been so busy recently it was a wonder he found time to breathe. Hell, he wouldn't be here this Sunday if he hadn't volunteered for the open house way back in the fall. He'd completely forgotten it until the calendar reminded him.

Turning, he drove through the iron gates that had been left open for this event. The setting sun reddened the graceful palm trees lining the long drive up to the stone mansion.

Once parked, he swung out of the pickup and glanced down to be sure the leg of his pants hadn't hung up on his prosthetic. He didn't particularly care, but no need to startle people who weren't used to seeing a metal shaft where a lower leg should be.

After locking up, he strode up the sidewalk to the three-story building that stood alone in the wide acreage. Probably wise, considering this was the home of the notorious Shadowlands BDSM club.

Pulling open the heavy oak door, he walked inside and frowned. An unfamiliar security guard was at the reception desk in the entry room.

How long had it been since Ghost's ass had been planted in that chair?

When he'd arrived in Tampa—damn, was it two years now?—a military buddy had needed someone to relieve him at his receptionist-slash-bouncer job here. Ghost had nearly refused. He'd left the West Coast for a reason, abandoning his past, his friends...and the lifestyle.

But Ben had needed time to pursue a Domme, and yeah, Ghost'd been bored after only a few months of retirement. Besides, sitting in the club's entry wasn't technically participating in BDSM.

Ben should have warned him about the owner, Zachary Grayson, known as Master Z. The renowned psychologist took far too much interest in his dungeon staff and the regulars.

Z had first manipulated Ghost into assisting in the dungeon, then pushed him into more activities, then made him a full member. Hell, Z and the members had even nailed Ghost with the title of *Master*.

Ghost grinned. The Machiavellian Shadowlands owner—*the bastard*—was a credit to the Green Berets, although Z had been with Special Forces less than a decade.

After signing in at the desk, Ghost studied the security guard, assessing him with the skill forged by over twenty years in the military—and nearly as long in the lifestyle.

The man was six-two, maybe two-twenty. Bouncer-sized, but his muscles were flabby, his gut big. His mandatory dark pants and button-up shirt were rumpled. The two-day-old stubble, bloodshot eyes, and the stink of a previous night's bender completed the picture.

Z hadn't hired the man. Wrecker, the club's new manager, had. In Europe, on New Year's Eve of all things, Z's mother had broken her leg. Z took his family overseas to help, planning to return in two to three weeks, but then Madeline had caught pneumonia. Realizing there'd be no quick return, Z had done a long-distance hiring of a manager for the Shadowlands.

Meanwhile, all through January, the Masters had been at the club constantly, trying to cover for Z's absence.

But a couple weeks after being hired, the manager had seemed to have gotten the hang of things. Near the end of January, he'd hired dungeon monitors.

Good thing, since all of the Masters were burned out at that point.

Ghost rubbed his jaw. It would be interesting to see how the club was doing without Z's supervision. Had to say, when he first met Wrecker, he hadn't been particularly impressed.

"The club is open to guests tonight." Ghost eyed the guard. "Do you know how to process them?"

The guard straightened from his slouch. "Yeah, I've been told. Get names, check IDs, have them sign the paperwork."

"Very good." Ghost started to leave and stopped. No, he couldn't ignore this idiot's appearance. "In the restroom, there's a locker labeled VISITOR with disposable razors. Use one and get cleaned up and presentable. You're the first person people see when they enter. I'll watch the desk until you're back."

"Jesus, are you serious?"

Ghost gave him a hard stare, one that worked as well on civilians as it had in the military.

Flushing, the guard rose. "Right. I'll be back in a few minutes."

With a sigh, Ghost rested a hip on the desk and prepared to greet visitors as they arrived.

From the number of cars in the lot, the club members who'd volunteered for demonstrations had already arrived. Thanks to a batch of homework to grade, Ghost was running late. The perils of being a professor.

As the door opened, Ghost smiled at the wide-eyed couple. "Welcome to the Shadowlands."

Ghost had turned the desk back over to the adequately presentable guard and set up his demo area.

For the next two hours, visitors trickled in and out. It seemed Wrecker hadn't done any advertising, since there weren't as many people as normally attended an open house. But the ones who came were enthusiastic. They watched the demonstrations, asked questions, and participated.

In half an hour, the visitors would be escorted out. It did seem strange to be here on a Sunday, didn't it?

Rising from his chair, Ghost shook his head at the hopefuls grouped outside the roped-off scene area. After answering nonstop questions in the noisy room, his voice was rasping worse than normal. "Sorry, but I need to take a break and get some water to keep my voice from disappearing."

As the group gave him sympathetic nods, he smiled at the two probable Doms who had stopped to watch the spankings. "Never forget to hydrate yourself and your submissive." Turning, he spoke to the handful who appeared to be submissive. "If your Top doesn't make sure you get fluids, find a better Top."

Such wide eyes.

Innocence could be deadly in the lifestyle. "When you're under orders, whether for a scene or a lifetime, if your health isn't important to your Dom, then you're with the wrong person. Don't take up with a slacker."

Slightly puckered brows indicated they'd heard and were considering what he'd said.

As a professor, as a commanding officer, as a Dom, he was pleased.

Stepping over the rope, he turned the signpost "SPANK-INGS" to face the wall, then headed for the food and drink tables.

Around the perimeter of the room, the scene areas were busy. Like Ghost, the Masters and Mistresses who'd signed up last fall to help hadn't forgotten.

It was good to see them again.

Silver-haired Sam was treating people to a taste of a black snake whip—and the sadist undoubtedly savored the occasional yelp.

Anne was using a cane on a young man. Ben, her submissive, handed her various sized canes as ordered. Ghost was glad his buddy had caught his Domme—although Mistress Anne probably thought it was the other way around.

Visitors were wandering around, lining up at the various stations. Getting into the spirit, several had stripped off shirts and blouses to better enjoy the sensations.

In a sleeveless black top and black jeans, Olivia demonstrated wax play by dripping candle wax on visitors' forearms and backs. When a hopeful young woman offered her breasts, Olivia smiled slightly and shook her head.

Ghost studied the British Mistress with the aggressively spiked golden-blonde hair. Her fair skin revealed dark circles under her eyes, and her stocky, muscular frame appeared thinner.

Earlier, Anne had mentioned Olivia had broken up with quiet little Natalia sometime in January. Although the Brit didn't appear happy, she was a very reserved person. It was doubtful she'd welcome anyone's help.

With a bottled water in hand, Ghost wandered down the back hallway to see who was in the theme rooms.

Wearing white lab coats, the former Feds, Galen and Vance, had taken over the medical room. Vance was showing a drawerful of enema bags to the visitors—and Ghost chuckled at the shocked exclamations.

In the office theme room, Cullen role-played a billionaire to the hilt. Ghost grinned since there were as many male "secretaries" in there as there were women. Submission had no gender.

The end room—the one Ghost thought of as "orgy central" had been transformed into a giant pen for Saxon to supervise puppy and kitten play. With painted-on whiskers and headbands with furry ears, guests yelped and meowed, batting balls around with furry-mittened hands.

The Shadowlands was a special place.

Wasn't it a shame Saxon hadn't provided anyone with furry, anal plug tails?

Smiling, Ghost headed back to his area, swinging by the wall of paddles to pick out a few.

His hand was getting sore.

"Ghost, it's been a while." Bottle of water in hand, Nolan slowed to talk. "Connor and Grant drafted Beth and me into coaching their soccer teams. We didn't make it in last month at all."

"Same here." Ghost shook his head. "At the end of January, the university dumped an extra class on me—and I've been scrambling to catch up ever since." In addition, his trialing a new lower leg prosthetic had required a fair amount of time.

"Teaching." The building contractor grimaced. "I'd rather have a scaffold collapse underneath me."

Now that seemed excessive. Ghost grinned, then sobered. "We're not the only ones who took a month off. Cullen's been tied up with some serial arsonist. Galen, Vance, and Anne...well, their company got busier than they have staff for."

"The downside of being too good at finding shit."

"So, it seems." The retired FBI agents and Mistress Anne

specialized in locating missing people, money, children, and anything else that was misplaced.

Nolan frowned. "I'd hate to think we all disappeared the minute we were relieved from duty."

"Hell, even Josie was gone." The Shadowlands bartender had married Holt, one of the Masters, the last day of January. "She and Holt took February and the first week of March for their honeymoon. I think they get back this week."

Frowning, Nolan looked around. "The place is still standing, at least."

"The Masters aren't essential; we just like to think we are."

"True enough." Nolan eyed the paddles in Ghost's hand. "Your hand getting tired, Colonel?"

Ghost grinned. "Age must be catching up with me. You ready to take over?"

"My Beth would have a fit if I put some submissive over my lap." Nolan's smile said he didn't have any problem with his woman's possessiveness. "Your demonstration is popular tonight... even though spankings can easily be done at home."

"Confused me, too, until a lady told me she wanted to see if she liked it before telling her husband. I guess after being married a decade, it'd be tough to say, 'Hey, honey, could you spank me tonight?' "

Nolan rubbed his jaw. "Good point."

"If they like the spanking, most head over to your flogging area."

"Yeah? Then thanks for warming them up for me." Laughing, Nolan headed back to his scene space.

Ghost took a final sip of water, tightened the lid, and tossed the bottle onto his toy bag. The paddles went onto a table stand.

After turning the SPANKINGS sign back around, he took a seat on the comfortable armless, leather chair.

Open for business.

His first takers were three women who'd waited for him to

return. The first two got paddled. The third wanted his bare hand. She offered to drop her pants and pouted when he said no. After he was done, she slipped her phone number into his pocket.

Jesus. She was young enough to have been his daughter if he'd ever had one.

He spanked a trans woman, then a gay lad, and two more women. The next—a masochist—asked about joining. Ghost pointed her toward the table set up near the front and then frowned.

Wrecker should have been there to handle applications and answer questions. Instead, there were a few scattered forms on a table. And no manager.

Lazy bastard.

Ghost rubbed his chin, realizing he hadn't been contacted last month to teach classes or do demonstrations. Who was doing the educational work Z considered so important?

Which made him wonder... If Z hadn't arranged this event last fall with the Masters to staff it, would the open house have even happened?

As the masochist left, Ghost noticed a couple of women who looked familiar, one with eye-catching red and purple hair? Was her name Queenie? He'd seen her at the few faculty receptions he'd been unable to avoid.

The other woman was a lush blonde around his age—the same one he'd saved from a fall the other day.

She'd been so appealingly soft.

She had a fascinating face—pointed chin, laugh lines on each side of her mouth, and a slightly upturned nose. Her blue eyes were a shade lighter than true navy and gorgeous.

He wouldn't remind her of their meeting, though. BDSM courtesy meant the vanilla world remained outside the club—and what happened inside stayed inside. So, he simply asked, "Who's next?"

. . .

Standing beside Queenie, Valerie still couldn't get over the shock. It was the professor—the man she'd bumped into at the Vietnamese restaurant.

And he was administering the spankings.

She and Queenie had been moving around the room. They'd experienced hot wax on their forearms, a lightweight flogging, much like a tapping massage, a scratchy vampire glove, a stinging cane. They'd been headed for the cropping demo when Queenie spotted the professor.

A chime rang through the room and a voice announced, "The club will close to visitors in twenty minutes."

"Oh no. I wanted to try being a puppy." Queenie gazed yearningly toward the back.

"We can always come back some other time on the guest pass." The guard had handed them each a FREE NIGHT ticket for use in the future.

"I don't know if I'd ever come back, so I need to try this now." Queenie patted Valerie's arm. "Meet you at the front in twenty minutes."

"B-but..." Valerie's mouth dropped open as Queenie hurried toward the smaller rooms. "Well, honestly."

With a sinking feeling, she turned toward the scene area.

Yes, the professor was watching, a smile quirked on his firm lips. "Abandoned?"

"So, it seems." She took a step back.

He studied her for a moment. "You were in the line. Did you not want to be spanked?"

"I...uh..." She could feel telltale heat rise into her face.

Because the professor was a hot guy, Queenie had decided they'd join this line.

Valerie hadn't protested too much, because the two times Barry had spanked her, she'd loved it. The thought of getting that pain again, of feeling those sensations was...

But how could she get a spanking from someone who was

basically a colleague? And now, Queenie had left.

Gods help her, she really did want to try it again.

The professor's sharp gaze caught hers. A blind man would have been able to read her desire, and this man, no, this *Dom*, was far from blind.

His lips curved. "Well then. Come here."

Her whole body yearned to do just that.

Her head said, no, absolutely not.

And her feet moved her forward.

"Brave lass." He took her hand, pulling her down and over his knees, and she didn't try to resist.

"Ah, you're a comfortable size for me, aren't you?" he murmured, the gruff rasp of his voice almost palpable against her skin.

His muscular thighs were under her belly—and a second later, his hands closed around her waist, and he shifted her, so her butt tilted up.

Fingers spread, she braced her hands on the floor with her feet on the other side of his legs.

His hand caressed her denim-clad bottom, and she tensed. "Easy, lass. I simply need to ensure I won't hit a cell phone or wallet and to see how much padding you have over those bones."

"More than enough," she said under her breath. She'd seen the young things he'd had in his line earlier. What must he—

"Just the right amount in my opinion. It's no fun when a good smack might fracture a bone."

Oh...to think a big ass had advantages. The approval in his voice was obvious, and she relaxed.

He liked her butt.

He slapped her bottom lightly several times as he talked. "Since there's no one waiting, I'm going to take my time. Do you have a name you like to be called?"

"Valerie is fine."

"Valerie, it is. Now, tell me on a scale of 1-to-10, where ten is excruciating and one is barely there, how much does this hurt?" He slapped her harder.

A bare sting. "Two."

"Mmm, you're going to be delightful." He delivered three more powerful spanks.

Her blood started to hum.

"Number?"

"Five."

"Very good, we'll stay with this for a while and see how you like the burn." He started smacking her, strong, even blows, one cheek, then the other, then several in one spot.

The sting of each radiated out, through her whole body. Rousing everything inside her and heating her blood.

Unlike the flogging, this wasn't impersonal; in fact, when he stopped and rubbed her bottom, it was the furthest thing from impersonal. She was lying across his legs; his bare hand was on her ass.

And she was growing aroused.

Could he tell? Face flaming, she tried to push up.

"No, pet. There's no shame here in the Shadowlands," he said. "Actually, we're much alike. Giving pain to a willing recipient makes me hard—and receiving pain excites you."

His hand in the center of her back held her down. "You're in a place that celebrates this kind of kink, so you're going to relax and enjoy it."

At the firm command, everything inside her melted into a total puddle of goo.

"Very good." His chuckle was low and deep. "Say 'stop' if you truly want to quit; otherwise, I'm going to hold you here and give us both what we want."

His left hand kept her still against his legs as he increased the impact of his right, although the blows stayed even. He paused long enough for each burst of pain to transform to simmering need.

Pleasure took her over, roaring through her, filling all the pockets of need that had existed for so, so long.

He halted. "Number, Valerie?"

"Seven, a marvelous seven."

His laugh was deep and wonderful. "I'd have to agree. Hang on, then, pet."

As if she could go anywhere.

The firm control he had over her body, the authority in his voice was like turning up the heat under a pot of water. Her blood was starting to boil...with need.

"Brace for the next batch, lass." He smacked her hard, did some softer ones, then stingingly hard again.

Like an ancient chorus, the pattern repeated until her bottom was aflame. Such an amazing burn.

"Oh my god, he's hitting her too hard. He's hurting her. Stop him." Queenie's voice was loud and clear.

When Valerie stiffened, the professor eased off. His blows slowed and lightened, even as he grumbled under his breath, "*Vanillas*."

She choked on a laugh.

"We've been busted, lass. I'm going to help you stand and will hold you until you're steady." He eased her to her feet, even as he rose and gripped her waist.

Her ass stung, and if she weren't an adult—or in public—she'd have rubbed her bottom like a child. Instead, she pulled in a breath and faced him.

Taller by several inches, he smiled down at her, then tucked a strand of hair behind her ear. "Thank you for the most fun I've had in"—he frowned—"in an exceptionally long time."

She swallowed, unable to look away from the hard face, the attentive gaze. Unable to not respond to his honesty. "Me, too."

"Good." He stepped back slightly and ran his hands up and

down her arms as if to restore her circulation. "Next time, we'll do this without the jeans."

Heat swept into her face, and his smile widened. How many times had he made her blush in the last few minutes?

"Are you steady on your feet? Dizziness? Pain? Aside from your ass, of course." A grin flashed white in the tanned face.

She half-snorted, then moved another step away, far too conscious of Queenie. "I'm good to go. I...thank you."

The sharp green eyes softened, and he ran his knuckles over her cheek. His voice dropped to where only she could possibly hear. "The nice part of when sadists and masochists interact is no thanks are needed. We both enjoyed me beating on your ass."

Her mouth dropped open, because...it *was* obvious he had liked spanking her. How different this had been from Barry's begrudging two spankings.

"Come back, and we'll do it again," he said softly, before turning to Queenie. "Here she is, all right and tight."

CHAPTER THREE

O n campus, Ghost sat in the mid-sized lecture hall and barely kept from sighing.

Yesterday, he'd thoroughly enjoyed his lecture because his class covering World War I held students who truly were interested in military history. The discussion about the Battle of Somme had really kept their interest. Of course, how could it not? The clash of forces had been a total bloodbath.

He loved seeing young minds at work, spurring them into thinking. Some of those men and women could well be the leaders of tomorrow.

Made a professor feel good.

Unfortunately, on Tuesdays, he had this class that'd been dumped on him after the regular professor suffered a heart attack.

All freshmen. At least it was Tuesday, so most of them weren't suffering from hangovers.

They did try his patience.

He flipped on the projector switch to display the homework assignment since some still hadn't figured out how to use a syllabus. "Homework is due the beginning of next class."

"Nooo," one young man whined. "No homework. I have a hot date tonight."

Ghost raised an eyebrow. "Does that mean you'll have to write with your other hand?"

As the nearby students burst into laughter, the young man reddened.

Ghost tossed his lecture notes into his briefcase. *Bad colonel.*

His self-control had been frayed by the lack of sleep last night. He'd dreamed of his wife and the gut-wrenching weeks where she'd slowly wasted away.

Damn, he missed her.

She hadn't been perfect—what person was? But she'd been a strong woman, sticking with him through moves and deployments and the ugliness of post-combat stress. They'd laughed and fought and made-up. He'd have given anything if she could have beat back the cancer and won her own victory.

That war they had both lost.

He shook his head. Kelly had been gone over four years now. Perhaps her loss felt closer today because, for the first time since she died, he'd truly *seen* another woman. Had wanted to be with her.

And damned if he didn't feel guilty about wanting someone. About not being able to keep Kelly alive.

But her fight with cancer hadn't been his to win or lose. He'd given her all his support and love. During her last month of life, she told him, over and over, that he'd better live his life to the fullest and find someone to love, or she'd come back and kick his ass.

He hadn't been ready to hear those words then. Now he saw the truth. If he'd been the one to go first, he wouldn't have wanted her to mourn him all her days. Well—he smiled ruefully— for a while, yes, but then he would expect her to put her life back together.

So, lose the guilt, Colonel.

The students filed out, chattering about their next classes, exams, and, of course, hot dates.

He stopped one young man with dreadlocks and piercings. "A moment, please."

"Professor?"

"You had a good argument on whether prejudice was involved in the number of Irish who died. I look forward to hearing more from you in future discussions."

The student's mouth dropped open. "Uh..."

Suppressing a chuckle, Ghost tilted his head toward the door, releasing the student...who fled.

During the discussion, the light of battle had filled the freshman's face, yet the diffident student rarely spoke in class. So, Ghost had singled him out and goaded him to talk. The youngster had an excellent mind, and it was Ghost's duty—and honor—to encourage him to use it.

For the next hour, Ghost held office hours. He advised a student about study habits, another about what was expected in essay questions. And, oddly enough, another one about a possible military career. Apparently, his past in the service was common knowledge, and the lad wanted information a recruiter might not provide.

After buying a coffee in the Marshall Center, he enjoyed a quiet break by the lake next to the Fine Arts building. A few of the green and brown mallards waddled up, and he tossed out a handful of cracked corn.

Bread wasn't good for them. Wasn't particularly good for him either, but at least his morning PT kept his gut within bounds.

Brushing off his hands, he checked the time, then headed inside and down a hall, checking lecture room numbers. *Here.* He entered the room silently and chose a place in the shadows in the back.

At the front, Valerie Winborne was talking about Middle Eastern cultures. Her hair was pulled back in a tidy French braid.

She wore tan pants and a white top with dark red embroidery. Professional...and, even when lecturing, she had the most beautiful voice he'd ever heard. Her vibrant contralto was somehow peaceful and sexy at the same time.

Curiosity had spurred him into searching for more information. Conveniently, very few professors were named Valerie. She held an interesting mixture of degrees and minors—philosophy, economics, world religions—and had been hired as an adjunct to replace a tenured professor who'd retired early.

Of course, the university had jumped at acquiring a teacher who'd written a bestselling book about the commonalities of various religions and philosophical practices. She'd tried to show how most people believed in something more, whether they called it god or gods or a great spirit or life force—and the beliefs, if followed, led people to create a better world.

Oddly enough, he'd read the book last year and enjoyed it.

Now he could see she taught as brilliantly as she wrote. Her fresh way of viewing the world captivated her listeners. Even better, she sprinkled her lecture with illustrations from her own life.

Apparently, she'd asked her class about home remedies their mothers had used. Students offered up the usual—chicken soup, mentholated ointment on the chest, 7-Up for nausea.

She laughed. "Now, see, when I suffered from a sore throat, the housekeepers made me drink thyme tea rather than taking a pill. Like here, 7-Up is popular for stomach aches. But if I got an earache...or a backache, olive oil was the go-to. I never did figure out how olive oil could help a backache."

The class laughed.

Interesting. Her examples were pulled to show the intriguing differences—and down deep, the similarities. The remedy might not be the same, but caring for children was universal.

As Ghost headed back into the hall, he frowned. Wasn't it a

bit odd Valerie hadn't mentioned either of her parents when she'd spoken of being ill?

He had a feeling there was a lot to learn about her.

On the USF campus, Valerie sat beside Queenie at the umbrella-shaded table.

Rain earlier had left the air sparkling clean with a hint of brine. On the stones underfoot, gulls strutted back and forth, hoping for generous diners to toss a tidbit.

Valerie opened the lunch she'd brought from home.

"Brown-bagging it, girl?" Queenie asked, setting her bag from Subway on the table.

"Mmmhmm. Tuesdays are ham 'n' cheese days." What with deposits for rent and utilities, she'd spent a lot setting up on her own.

"Didn't you score anything in the divorce?"

Valerie's laugh was only slightly bitter. "What with raising children, then helping them out with college, we hadn't saved much." And Barry had spent what there was on his slaves.

"The house, though?"

"He owned it before we married. Really, I was happy simply to be gone." At least, he hadn't been able to touch her 401k.

Her money was now all her own.

Independence didn't make up for an empty bed. She sighed. "Although we gradually grew distant, and the final year was ugly, our early years were good. I miss those times—and having someone to cuddle up to in the evenings. Sharing laughter over silly things. Even someone to be grumpy with in the early morning before breakfast."

Somewhere along the line, the man she'd loved had disappeared. Or maybe he'd merely stopped putting any effort into the marriage. Or the sex.

"I feel you. Indeed, I do." Queenie nodded in sympathy. "I've also noticed a decided lack of orgasms, post-divorce."

There hadn't been many before the divorce either. Valerie grinned. "Guess we have to do it ourselves, like all the magazines say. They're all about sex toys and *masturbating.* Have you ever heard a less appealing word?"

Tapping her chin, Queenie nodded, face serious. "True, true. Men get much more interesting terms. Handjobs and wanking."

Laughing, Valerie pointed at her. "Exactly. Beating the meat, stroking the salami."

"Oh, oh, my turn. Yanking the crank."

"Good one." Valerie thought for a second. "Burping the worm."

Queenie sputtered her coke and had to mop the front of her shirt.

Opening her thermos of coffee, Valerie frowned. "Really, the guys not only received better terminology, but their anatomy is a better design. After all, a man's dick is right there, ready at hand, so to speak."

"Ah, yes." Queenie waved her sandwich in agreement. "No fumbling around to find the good stuff."

"Exactly." Barry had sure enjoyed sex more than she ever did. Her orgasms had been in short supply, and even then, nothing to write home about. Except for the two after being spanked.

But spanking her hadn't turned him on, so that was that.

"Really, if life were fair," she muttered, "I'd find a man skilled in the sack so I could indulge in tons of glorious sex." And spankings.

"I hate to tell you, my friend, but life isn't fair." Queenie opened her sack.

"I know." Valerie scowled. "Have you noticed every guy past his forties just wants a readymade cook and housekeeper?"

"Well, he has to find someone to replace his wife who probably divorced him for that very reason," Queenie said cynically.

"Ladies, how are you doing?" Dr. Wang, a Communications professor pulled a chair out. Short and balding, Paul loved working lunches. "Queenie, I brought the schedule you asked for."

As the two of them started discussing a project timeline, Valerie settled in to enjoy her meal. And to muse about spankings and sex.

The professor at the Shadowlands who'd spanked her said she was a masochist. He'd acted as if being aroused by pain was normal. And said some people were simply wired that way.

If he was right, did it explain why she'd found sex so boring?

The self-knowledge wasn't useful, however. She sure couldn't tell some date she'd like sex with a side helping of pain.

Besides, she was still recovering from the damage Barry and his women had inflicted, and from feeling betrayed. It was best for her to avoid the dating scene entirely.

Celibacy was good for a girl, right?

Overhead, a gull flew past, its screech sounding like the word *sex*.

Valerie rolled her eyes. *I'm being mocked by the gods.*

Deservedly so since she was lying to herself. It'd be awesome to have good sex.

But nothing more. No relationships. Nope. Never again would a bastard decide she wasn't enough for him and wring her heart like a dirty washrag. *Never, never, never.*

Not even if there were spankings involved.

A shiver ran through her as she remembered the previous weekend at the Shadowlands. The skilled hands caressing her bottom, the stinging smack of a hard palm, the pain flowing through her like honey, and rousing every nerve in her body.

She'd never been so excited—not even when Barry had spanked her.

She could go back to the BDSM club. Along with the free guest pass, the application for membership to the Shadowlands was sitting on her table. Staring at her as if it had eyes. She could be a member.

No. Be practical. A membership wasn't in her budget.

Let alone having to walk into the place all by herself. The BDSM Sampler night was over, which meant she'd have to get a... what was it called...a *Top* interested in doing a scene with her.

Face it, what were the chances any of them would be interested in her?

Zip. Nada. None.

It wouldn't be worth putting out all that money to be ignored. Although the professor Dom had been nice.

More than nice.

But tempting potential members into joining was part of his job. He wouldn't be nearly as interested in her on a regular night.

No, she couldn't afford the Shadowlands membership—or the potential blows to her already fragile ego.

She bit into her ham and cheese sandwich. It would be best to stay away from the sexy professor, too, whatever his name was.

With a choked-off laugh, she shook her head. She'd let a man whose name she didn't even know spank and rub her ass.

He'd invaded her sleep for the last few nights, his deep, rough voice fueling hot dreams that left her teetering on the pinnacle of coming.

Yes, she'd had dream sex with the professor.

And if she ever saw him, she'd undoubtedly turn so red her blood vessels would explode in her head.

As the discussion between Queenie and Wang turned to an argument, someone slid into the empty place beside Valerie.

"Excuse me." That voice. Exactly as she remembered...and so much more.

She turned—it really *was* him—and choked on her coffee.

"Careful, woman." He thumped her shoulders a couple of times. "One pipe is for air, the other for liquid. Don't mix them up."

41

She sucked in air and laughed.

He grinned back at her, his teeth white in a lean, tanned face, and so devastatingly masculine, he could stop a female's heart. He held out a hand. "I don't think we've met. Dr. Blackwood—Finn. History."

"Right. Um, hi." She took his hand, feeling the calluses, remembering how he'd touched her, fondled her ass. Spanked her ass. As she feared, her face burned with embarrassment. "Dr. Winborne—Valerie. World religions and philosophy."

"Fun combination. As it happens, I read your book last year and enjoyed it very much."

Seriously? "Uh, thank you."

"Will you be writing another?"

She shook her head. "Not anytime soon. That one happened because I had things to say."

"An excellent reason to write a book." He eyed her necklaces with the various religious symbols and grinned. "Why the mixture?"

Today she was wearing a cross, a pentagram, a dharma wheel, and a yin-yang symbol.

"To make a point. Like most mothers, I didn't care if my children called me mom or mommy or mother. I worried more about them being compassionate and honest. And I can't think any god is more small-minded than a human."

"So you quietly wear the necklaces in hopes you can get your students to think." His approving smile sent a wave of warmth through her. "Do you have one you prefer?"

"Nope. I wouldn't want any deity to feel left out." She patted the necklaces. "I tend to swear by all the gods—or the generic 'all-that-is'."

A crease appeared in his cheek. "Generic, hmm. I like it."

Noticing the professor, Queenie broke off her argument. "Well, hello." The woman was totally unfazed at where she'd seen Finn the last time.

Valerie smothered a laugh. "Queenie, have you met Dr. Finn Blackwood. He's in the history department. Finn, this is Dr. Queenie Gundersen—English."

"Good to meet you, Queenie."

Before Queenie could reply, another professor pulled out a chair and sat down. After greeting the women, Pohl turned to Finn. "Blackwood, I wanted to see you. Heard a couple of students discussing your lecture on the Battle of the Somme. Do you think the Brit commanders were incompetent?"

As the two talked military history, Valerie noticed Queenie watching Finn. Turning her gaze to Valerie, the redhead waggled her eyebrows before returning to her argument with Paul.

Crazy woman.

The sound of Finn's deep voice and easy conversation sent an odd unrest tap dancing through Valerie.

Trying to ignore the feeling, she unwrapped her dessert and took a bite of the sweet date-filled cookie. *Mmm.* The citrusy-fennel taste of cardamom brought back memories of childhood holidays.

Finn glanced at her dessert, and his steel-gray brows lifted. "Is that *kleicha*?"

"Good eye. Yes, I make it when I need a sweet treat."

The longing look he gave her cookie made her regret she hadn't brought more. With a smile, she handed him half.

"Generous woman." He popped it into his mouth. "Mmm, this is excellent. I used to buy these all the time when I was stationed in Baghdad, especially on their holidays."

"Stationed?"

"In the army."

Well, that explained the military-straight shoulders and air of command. Add in being a Dom, and it was no wonder he exuded authority.

She tapped a finger on her half of the *kleicha*. "I grew up in the Middle East. No matter how old I was or in what country, every

43

housekeeper wanted to teach me to make their traditional foods."
Kitchens were happy places where she'd been liked for who she
was. Really, it was surprising she hadn't grown up to be a cook.

"Since my talents don't extend to much more than simple
meals," Finn said, "I won't ask for the recipe. But if you ever have
extras..."

She laughed. "I'll remember."

His smile lightened his eyes. "We'll have to compare notes on
our travels. I bet you saw an entirely different world than I did."

In every city, she'd run with the local children in neighbor-
hoods and the bazaars, been scolded by housekeepers, and turned
brown from the sun and dirt. In many ways, she'd enjoyed a
wonderful childhood. "Probably so. I'd enjoy talking about it."

About the Middle East or probably anything at all. He was
intelligent, articulate, and had an interesting sense of humor.

And hard hands, too.

As he held her gaze, she felt her body soften, warm.

A glint appeared in his eyes.

"Valerie, girl." Queenie waved her hand to catch Valerie's
attention. "You were going to tell me how the self-defense class
went."

Disappointed—and relieved at the interruption, Valerie
turned. "It didn't. The students were all young and energetic and
far above my skill level. But I did pick up pepper spray, so if it
happens again, then—"

"If *what* happens again?" Finn asked in a dark voice.

"Nothing. Only a minor alterca—"

"Some skeezoid where she jogs wanted money," Queenie interrupted, "and wouldn't back off until a couple of male joggers
helped her."

The protective anger in Finn's hard face made her stomach
quiver.

"It wasn't that serious," Valerie said.

"Were you frightened?" he asked in a level voice and saw the answer in her face. "Then, yes, it was that serious."

"I bought pepper spray."

He nodded. "Good choice. But if he's too close or the wind is against you, pepper spray won't help. You need the ability to get free of an attacker, if nothing else."

Well, damn. "I understand."

"Perhaps—"

"Pardon, Blackwood," Pohl called. "But, if you have the time, let's see if admin will go for an addition to the schedule."

"Of course." Finn rose and bent to say quietly to her, "It was good to talk to you, and I hope to see you soon. Here or elsewhere."

His smile left no doubt of what he meant. He wanted her to return to the Shadowlands.

The guest pass came with a free night.

Maybe...

CHAPTER FOUR

On Saturday night, Ghost spent some time simply wandering through the Shadowlands. Pausing to watch a violet wand scene, he breathed in the unique scents—leather, sweat, perfumes, citrusy cleansers...and sex. In BDSM clubs where sex wasn't permitted, that heady fragrance would be absent.

Not all clubs held the enticing smell of leather, either. But, here, Z had filled the place with expensive leather furniture and hung a myriad of floggers and whips on the walls.

Unfortunately, although the smell was right, the Shadowlands didn't feel the same. It took him a while to identify the subtle difference.

The sense of community had disappeared.

Why? Was it something Wrecker was doing?

Or was it because, as he and Nolan had discussed, most, if not all, the Masters had been absent for a month or so? Quite a few had been out of town or, like him, swamped with work. Others had taken February off after being here every weekend in January to help cover Z's absence.

There would probably be a hell of a lot of them here tonight.

Last night with her honeymoon over, Josie had returned to her job as Shadowlands bartender—and had been appalled.

Earlier today, Holt had called everyone to share her concern at the state of the club.

Ghost would've been here last night if an old military buddy hadn't arrived in Tampa. Instead, he'd given Josie and Linda a description of Valerie and asked them to keep an eye out.

Yeah, he'd been intrigued with the pretty professor, and his interest had grown with their second meeting.

She was...captivating. He did love intelligent women, ones who could stand on their own two feet. And the hints of insecurity she'd revealed made him want to scoop her up and reassure her.

Come on, Dr. Winborne. Be brave and show up tonight.

If she didn't, they'd undoubtedly run into each other on campus. He could ask her out for coffee. She'd be worth taking the time to get to know...and patience was one of his strengths.

"Ghost. How is the evening finding you, sir?" The overly loud, edgy music playing over the speakers almost drowned out Marcus's slow Southern drawl. Impeccably dressed in a silver-gray suit, the Master had his arm around his wife, Gabi.

Gabi smiled, but as a good submissive, she kept silent.

Betting her docile behavior wouldn't last long, Ghost smiled back, then answered Marcus. "Actually, I've been unpleasantly surprised this evening. And you?"

"The same, I fear." Marcus appraised the room, then shook his head. "We have much to discuss."

"I plan to collect more information tonight. Let's plan on getting everyone together." Because it appeared they had a mess to fix.

"Agreed."

A few minutes later, Ghost stopped when greeted by Wendy and Smith. The bulldog-faced burly trucker had a rough manner... and the sweetest submissive.

47

"How are you two doing these days?"

"Hauling is good." Smith glanced around. "Club's not doing so well, gotta say."

The Dom and his wife tended to pop in once or twice a month for a scene but always seemed oblivious to anything else. If they were concerned, things really had gone to hell. "Can you put your finger on what's bothering you?"

"Eh, part of the problem are the dungeon monitors the manager hired. Lazy bastards. Spend their time drinking at the bar, so shit happens."

Ghost felt his jaw tighten. Shit happening meant scenes were going bad. People—submissives—were being hurt. Rather than cursing, he nodded. "We're assessing what needs to be fixed. Anything else?" He looked at Wendy.

"Go on, baby. Tell him," Smith prompted.

"We have a lot of new members, and their behavior is..." Wendy leaned against her Dom. "Master Z didn't tolerate disrespectful submissives, but he also came down hard on Dominants who were pushy or rude. People in the club used to be polite. Respectful to everyone. That's changed."

Fuck. Ghost tilted his head. "I think you've put your finger on what's been bothering me, too. Thank you for your honesty—and clear vision."

Her soft smile was probably part of why the brusque trucker was so in love with her.

With a nod, Ghost continued his stroll around the room, making mental notes of what he saw.

Like the two DMs at the bar talking with Wrecker.

Ghost paused to interrupt a scene where the bottom was obviously panicking, and the newbie Top wasn't paying attention.

A DM should have been closely monitoring the scene.

Dammit.

Z was supposed to be back any day now. But even if he showed up tomorrow, then what? Ghost shook his head. The Shadowlands owner's clinical practice was probably screaming for his attention. He had a pregnant wife, a toddler, and they'd moved into a new home. Z wouldn't have time to breathe, let alone deal with this mess.

Well, if nothing else, Ghost would help organize the Masters to—

"Hey, Colonel. You're back!"

Ghost turned. "Evening, Cameron. What's up?"

The young man approaching him was perhaps, early twenties, reminding Ghost of the soldiers he'd commanded. And he had a newer Dom's enthusiasm. He'd mentioned how he spent all the years since puberty not understanding the urges simmering under his skin. Here, he'd found a place where he was understood.

"You'd said once you'd show me how to use a cane."

"Of course." Ghost eyed him. "That was a while back..."

Cameron's expression was disgruntled. "Yeah, I'd hoped to attend a class, but there haven't been any or even demos for maybe a month or more."

It appeared Wrecker had abandoned the teaching Z considered to be one of the club's main functions. Not being here, the Masters hadn't realized. Z rarely scheduled classes—he'd simply draft whatever Master or Mistress was at hand when he wanted something taught.

Here was another way they'd let the club down.

Cameron gave him a hopeful smile. "Maybe, if you have time now..."

"Absolutely." Ghost tilted his head. "Do you have a volunteer?"

Cameron flushed. "No. I haven't met many of the submissives."

Ah. "Let's see who we might find. How sadistic are you?"

"Uh, I like fairly hard, but not to the point of blood."

"All right. We need one who likes some pain." Turning, Ghost led the way to the sitting area near the bar where the unattached submissives tended to hang out in hopes of being approached by a Dom. He checked them over.

There was a nice variety of young to old, with various genders and orientations. A few nearly vanilla types. Two who wanted to be dominated, not hurt.

Three were masochists.

One called herself a pain slut. Being on the old-fashioned side, he'd never been able to embrace the term.

He glanced at Cameron. "I'd suggest the lady in the red corset. Angelica likes pain and domination both. You two might suit for a scene."

Cameron firmed his shoulders—good lad. He was an attractive man, and the young woman brightened when he approached.

After a few minutes, they both returned to Ghost.

He smiled at her. "Did Cameron explain we'll be using you for a lesson on caning?"

"Yes, Sir."

Ghost went through his usual negotiations, finding out if she had any triggers, physical problems, things to avoid. From her expression, Cameron had already covered most of the questions.

The lad listened carefully, obviously adding a few more items to his own mental list of questions.

Good, this was what mentoring was all about, after all.

Taking the two over to a bondage table, Ghost pushed a box step close to the foot. "Stand on this and bend over the table, Angelica."

Once she was situated, he let Cameron take the lead in restraints and reassurance, pleased the young man was careful about circulation and comfort. He left the woman's thong and corset in place.

Done, Cameron returned to Ghost. "Now what?"

"Go ahead and warm her skin up. There's no hurry—and the impact from a cane isn't something to jump into unless punishment is what you're after." Ghost retreated to one side.

With more confidence, Cameron ran his hands over the submissive's ass, working his way into a light spanking, checking in on pain levels frequently.

Ghost nodded to himself. The Dom wasn't a newbie. Learning caning was appropriate for his skill level.

Once her skin reached a nicely flushed state, Ghost started on the lesson. First, where not to hit. The spanking had shown Cameron knew the basics, so Ghost just added a few cane-specific warnings, like avoiding the sciatic nerve with heavy canes, and positioning to avoid wrapping where the cane might bend around a side.

"Parallel strikes are best, since you can cause damage if the spots intersect." He demonstrated the light wrist action used and started tapping his way up. "You can flick, taking the cane away instantly for a stinging sensation, or rest the cane on the skin right after impact for a thuddier—and more painful—pleasure."

Ah, he did like canes. And Angelica was a nicely responsive bottom, reacting with small squirms and inhalations.

"Your turn." Ghost handed the cane over and took his seat.

The young Dom showed excellent control, and as Ghost watched, fell into Top space, totally oblivious to anything except the scene, his actions, and the bottom's response.

Very nice, indeed.

Not having anything urgent to do, Ghost stayed. He stepped in only when Angelica hit subspace to remind Cameron that her responses were no longer a reliable indicator of the amount of pain or damage she could take. It was time to lighten up and work back out of the scene.

Mentoring complete, Ghost did a quick tour of the club, hoping to see Valerie.

No such luck.

He paused to watch Olivia using a flogger. The Mistress had discarded her leather jacket, leaving her in a sleeveless latex shirt and pants. Her honey-colored hair stood up in short spikes, and her forehead was damp with sweat as she flogged the bottom.

Ghost frowned. Although the Domme was extremely skilled with a good awareness of the bottom, the scene lacked energy. The submissive was fine, already falling into subspace, and probably didn't even realize the Domme wasn't especially into it.

Like a skilled computer operator, Olivia was inputting the right commands to get the machine's response, but she was not emotionally involved.

It was a shame.

He'd seen Olivia scene with her previous girlfriend, Natalia, and the energy between the two had been heady, like the thundering of an artillery barrage.

This was more like a few rounds of a .22.

Shaking his head, he walked away.

Out of the corner of her eye, Olivia noticed Ghost moving away. The tall, gray-haired Master was frowning and shaking his head.

What was his problem? Her mouth tightened. She hadn't thought him prejudiced against Dommes. Or maybe he didn't like lesbians? Not unusual. Even the Shadowlands had always held a few haters. In the past, they'd been unobtrusive.

Tonight? The club seemed filled with intolerant bastards, especially the new members, although she'd been shocked by a few she'd thought were good people. Not any longer. Bigotry was apparently now accepted here, and the knowledge rubbed her raw.

But she hadn't thought the Colonel would be prejudiced. She liked the guy, bugger-it-all.

Pushing the annoyance aside, she tried to get her head back into the scene, knowing if she'd really been into it, she'd never have noticed Ghost at all. But the scene was flat—at least, for her.

With a sour taste in her mouth, she continued the session,

getting Chelsey into subspace, then bringing her back out with a slow warm-down.

Finally, she finished and shook out her aching arms.

Her heart hurt, as well. This hadn't been a scene where a Domme and her submissive connected on a soul-deep level; it'd been more like a pleasant tennis match. A nice workout and nothing more.

She bundled Chelsey in a blanket, gave her a bottle of water, and started to clean the equipment.

"Please hold me," Chelsey whined. "I need to be held. Can we go upstairs?"

Upstairs. To have sex. It sure wouldn't be making love.

Olivia had found out how love and sex could combine into something glorious—and then that joy was gone. For a couple of weeks after breaking up with Natalia, Olivia had tried to bury the heartbreaking memories with other women. With sex. Including with Chelsey.

The hollowness of the act had only depressed her further, and she'd stopped coming to the Shadowlands.

Now, she was back. Tonight she'd indulge her need for topping, give good aftercare...and be done.

She'd made her conditions clear to Chelsey before they started. "I need to clean the area so someone else can use it, then we'll go sit and get your cuddles in."

No upstairs.

After the equipment was disinfected, Olivia took Chelsey to a quiet sitting area for chocolate and more water and hugs. Told her she was a good girl and a pleasure to flog.

Provided the submissive with what she needed.

And felt even emptier. Why did it seem as if she gave and gave and never received anything in return?

Eventually, she left Chelsey with her friends, pleased at how they supported each other. Much as she and Anne had stuck together in earlier days. But Anne had Ben now—and the most adorable son.

Olivia had crickets.

Bollocks, what was with this self-indulgent whining? *Stop. Now.* Shaking her head, she headed for the bar. She'd get a drink and chat with Josie, the bartender, a rather adorable submissive who, unfortunately, preferred men. Holt was a lucky guy.

"Mistress Olivia, what can I get you?" Josie's short, sassy hair was the color of her freckles. In black pants, black vest, and white shirt, she was the epitome of a professional bartender...although her soft Texas accent made it seem as if she should be wearing a cowboy shirt and jeans. "You seem tired. Maybe coffee instead of alcohol?"

"How about both?" Perhaps the vodka and Kahlua would help her sleep. "I'd like an espresso martini, please."

"Coming right up."

"How was the honeymooning?" Olivia asked. The wedding had been beautiful, with Josie escorted down the aisle by her grandaunt and her twelve-year-old son.

"Spain was amazing, and then Greece..." Josie patted her chest. "Oh my heart. We came back early enough to take Carson and his friends to Disney World for a long weekend."

Olivia snickered. "A way to say *I'm-sorry-we-abandoned-you-to-go-off-and-have-sex-in-exotic-places?*"

"It so was. The trip to Disney World earned us all sorts of forgiveness." Josie grinned. "It's great to be back...well, mostly great. The club feels off, at least to me. I know Holt called y'all in, so what do you think?"

"I'm glad Holt called." Olivia tapped her fingernails on the bar top in irritation. "The club has changed...and not in a good way."

"Hey, look at the lez flirting with our bartender." The voice came from the other side of the oval bar.

Another male voice. "She's one of them muff divers, huh?"

Seriously? Olivia glanced over to see a batch of men. Late

twenties to thirties, around her age. New members. White male Doms with attitudes. The kind of arseholes Z would never have let set foot in the Shadowlands.

And, bloody hell, the manager, Wrecker, stood with them. Tall, fair-skinned, and good-looking, he reminded her of a scheming politician. He was laughing at what his arsehole friend had said.

If the manager was a homophobe, no wonder prejudice was thriving.

She put her back to them and watched the people near the front trying to dance to the sucky music. Z had favored variety, from heavy metal to Gregorian chants, but during prime scene hours, there was always a solid rhythm to enjoy while flogging. Wrecker's grindcore mixes and bands like Anal Cunt were worthless.

Turning away, she noticed, off to the left, three Doms surrounding a newer, young submissive. Trying to intimidate her.

Olivia jumped off her barstool and—stopped.

Already moving, Ghost pulled the submissive out of the circle, tucked her behind him, and turned on the three men. "Your behavior is unacceptable, a disgrace to Doms everywhere. I don't know what rock you were raised under, but in the Shadowlands, everyone"—the Colonel's dark rasp sounded like the wrath of God—"*everyone* is treated with respect. If you pull this kind of stunt again, I'll wipe the floor with your asses before I throw you out the door."

"Shit, what's the old bastard doing?" came from Wrecker. The manager hurried over to the group. "Ghost, what the fuck? They were only having some fun. You're not a DM; you're just a—"

"Just a Master of this club, which gives me an even higher authority than a dungeon monitor." The Colonel directed a pointed stare at Wrecker and the Doms. "Along with the obligation to correct behavior that goes against the club's rules."

Olivia winced. He was right. As a Mistress, she held the

same responsibility. Rather than ignoring verbal abuse, she should have dealt with it, whether or not the manager was involved. If the arseholes spoke so insultingly to a Mistress, they'd undoubtedly been even nastier to untitled members. Other lesbians and gays might be more fragile. She'd been a bloody coward.

I'll do better.

With a low curse, Wrecker stomped away, steaming from the ears. Two of the Doms retreated quickly.

One didn't. The one who resembled—and acted—like an aggressive ape stood with his hands in fists.

Bad choice, you muppet.

Ghost moved like British SAS operators did. The younger Dom might manage to land a punch or even two, but then Ghost would put the arsehole in hospital—or a grave.

Apparently making the same calculation, the Dom said something ugly and retreated.

Ghost put his arm around the submissive and led her toward a sitting area.

The young woman had tears in her eyes, and Olivia's heart ached. That's how Natalia had looked when Olivia sent her away.

And no matter how deceiving and lying the little submissive had been, Olivia missed her with all her heart.

Okay, she could do this, Valerie thought. Really. *I'm not some teen who can't go anywhere without a bunch of friends.*

Off in the distance, thunder rumbled over the Gulf. Rain was coming, and the air was hot and humid. Valerie pushed her damp hair off her neck. She'd left it down because...well, her dark-honey blonde, shoulder-length hair was one of her best features.

As she walked up the sidewalk from the parking lot, she felt as if she'd forgotten her purse. But she hadn't. Using common sense, she'd locked it in the trunk. Her car keys and ID were in her pockets...and why she'd worn jeans.

Jeans companies weren't as misogynistically pocket-unfriendly as women's suit and dress manufacturers were.

At the front, she stared up at the three-story mansion. It was much more intimidating after dark. The black wrought-iron lanterns on each side of the door didn't help.

She could barely hear any noise from inside other than a thin thread of music. The soundproofing must be amazing. Well, it would have to be, right?

Here goes. Reluctantly, she reached for the door handle.

"Hi."

At the sound of a woman's voice, Valerie startled.

Two people strolled up the sidewalk.

One was a silver-haired man with icy blue eyes and a lean weathered face.

His companion was a full-bodied redhead. She smiled. "Could you be Valerie?"

"Well..." Valerie hesitated, having never seen the woman before in her life.

"Sorry, I didn't mean to scare you." The woman laughed. "The other day, one of our friends said he hoped a blonde named Valerie would join the club."

Valerie blinked. The only Dom she'd given her name to had been the professor. Finn. The thought he'd mentioned her set up a warm glow in her stomach.

"I'm Linda, and this is Master Sam." The woman seemed only a few years younger than Valerie, and how reassuring was that?

"You're right; I'm Valerie." She gave them a wry smile. "I was trying to find enough courage to open the door."

"In that case, missy, allow me." Master Sam's rough-timbred voice reminded her of the actor whose gravelly voice was so well-known. Finn sounded much the same although his voice might be a bit rawer, a bit deeper.

Sam stepped around her and held the door open.

The same guard as on the BDSM Sampler night sat behind the desk, obviously bored. "Here. Sign in." He pushed forward a paper.

"I'm not a member." Valerie held out the FREE NIGHT ticket.

He took it, ripped it in half. "Okay. You're good."

Sam's eyebrows went up. "What the hell is a free night?"

"I got the coupon during the open house." She gestured to the guard. "From him."

The guard nodded. "Yeah. Like the manager said to do."

"I haven't heard anything about free nights." Sam's eyes narrowed, and he turned to Valerie. "Did you get any instruction about the rules? What you can and can't do? Fill out any forms? Have bloodwork?"

"No."

"Dammit." Master Sam looked furious. "Sign in and put 'free pass' beside your name. Show the guard your ID." His glare hit the guard like a baseball bat.

Paling, the guard sat up straight.

"Check that her ID and name matches," Sam snapped. "The rules are in the top drawer. Give her one. Make sure anyone else with a free pass gets the same."

After she signed and showed her ID to the now-anxious guard, he handed her the list of rules.

"Since you don't have a purse, Valerie, you can leave your shoes in the cubbies here." Linda put her flats into an empty slot in the shelves against the wall. "If you're submissive, of course."

She might as well own up to it. But... "I can't wear my shoes?"

"Master Z prefers for submissives to be barefoot unless wearing seriously stunning footwear." Linda eyed Valerie's attractive, but nowhere-near-stunning sandals.

There were certainly a lot of rules to getting in this place.

Master Sam's chuckle indicated her frown had made it onto her face.

With a sigh, she shoved her sandals into a cubby, then stood there in her bare feet. To her relief, the hardwood floor was polished to a satiny smoothness. At least she wouldn't get splinters.

"Very good, missy. Now, you're ready to go in."

Gazing up at Master Sam, she knew she'd lost an inch in height and more in...what would she call it? Power? Authority?

Shaking her head, she followed Linda and Master Sam through the door into the club.

Harsh music assaulted her ears. To her right, a few people were on the dance floor. Five younger men and women wearing cat and dog ears, fuzzy mitten-paws, and tails gamboled off to one side.

People sat in various conversational groups. About half of the roped-off scene areas around the perimeter were being used.

There was a big oval bar in the center of the room and a dance floor to the right. In fact, the layout resembled a nightclub's... except she'd never seen a bar with chains dangling from the rafters above it.

And no one dressed like this in any club she'd been in.

Look at all the fetishwear. Lots of skintight latex, PVC, and leather. One woman wore hot pink leggings and a tunic with strategically placed holes. Two women were bare from the waist up. She could see mini-skirts, fishnet stockings, corsets, and bustiers.

Men were wearing chain and leather harnesses, vests, or went bare-chested with suspenders. One had on a kilt. A guy wearing only a loincloth danced with a man in motorcycle leathers.

Valerie tugged on her black bustier with thin shoulder straps. "I'm under-dressed."

"What you're wearing is perfectly acceptable," Linda answered. "When you're more comfortable with the place and people, you can explore more options...or not. The Shadowlands is more relaxed about the dress code than many other clubs."

Valerie nodded. "I did check the internet for information. Some places won't allow jeans or T-shirts or even normal suits."

"They want to establish a sense of community—and keep out gawkers. But since it's not easy to get a Shadowlands membership, we don't have looky-loos. A lot of members, like this one"— Linda nudged Sam—"prefer to feel comfortable when they play. But since dressing up is fun, the club has theme nights now and then."

"Theme nights?" Valerie almost laughed. The essays she assigned her students often had themes.

"Basically, kinky costume parties. The Western Nights are Master Sam's favorites."

The Dom laughed, not at all insulted.

"Let's sit at the bar while you get your bearings, then we'll wander around." Linda motioned toward the dark wood bar.

A huge male bartender filled drinks at one end; a female bartender with a pixie-cut worked the other end.

"Master Cullen, you're working," Linda said as she took one of the high wooden stools.

"I wanted to bartend with Josie tonight. Best way I know to get a feel for what's going on." The rough-hewn man behind the bar had a grim expression, but then he smiled. After nodding at Master Sam, he studied Valerie with green eyes darker than Finn's. "Welcome to the Shadowlands, love. And you are...?"

A hint of an Irish accent danced in his voice.

"Thank you." She settled on the barstool. "I'm Valerie."

"Good to meet you." He glanced at Linda. "Andrea's working, but Rainie and a couple other subbies commandeered a sitting area near the back if you want to introduce her."

"I do, thank you. But first, we'll sit and admire the costumes." Linda winked at Valerie. She undoubtedly knew how overwhelming the place was.

"Valerie." The rasp of Finn's deep voice had her turning. And had her wayward heart rate increasing.

When she met his green eyes, the stool beneath her seemed to shiver. Or had that been her? "Hi. I made it." *Such brilliant conversation, idiot.*

Linda nodded at him. "Ghost, it's good to see you. It's been a while."

Ghost? Oh, of course. Some people used different names in places like BDSM clubs.

She'd need to remember to call him Ghost.

As he greeted Linda, Valerie sat back.

He'd adhered to the Dom-standard of black and more black. His cargo pants were in a Goth style, with D-rings and buckles. A long-sleeved Henley fit snugly, outlining hard muscle. Black leather belt and boots. A gold band circled his biceps...and *hmm,* Cullen and Sam wore them, too.

As the men talked, Valerie whispered to Linda, "What do the gold bands on their arms mean?"

"Means they've received the club honorific of 'Master' for experience, power, and service. The Shadowlands doesn't hand them out like lollipops."

Master, huh. Valerie wrinkled her nose. "My ex thinks he should be called Master."

"What to call your Dom is an internal relationship choice." Linda shrugged. "After all, a Dominant can tell his submissive to call him anything he wants, right? But he can't force anyone else to use his title. Inside the club, we all call these Doms the "Masters" because they've earned our respect."

"Although *some* of us try to dodge any title." Cullen grinned.

Finn gave him a displeased frown. "I'll stick with simply Ghost, thank you."

Linda smiled slowly. "As it happens, the Shadowkittens heard Ben calling you Colonel. Since you hate 'Master', we decided to use your rank. Because we're nice that way."

At Ghost's grunt of displeasure, everyone burst out laughing.

"It works," Sam said. "Everyone knows colonels are sadists."

"There is that." Ghost held Valerie's gaze, then grinned and bent to whisper, "It's lucky for you I didn't achieve the rank of general."

Oh gods.

"Valerie."

She jumped when Master Sam said her name.

"Um, yes?"

Ghost chuckled.

Sam tapped the paper in front of her. "Study those rules before you leave the bar."

"Right." She set the page under the brightest spot of light.

"What rules?" Ghost moved forward to read over her shoulder.

He smelled like a Florida morning in winter—all sea breeze with a hint of citrus. *Mmm.* She barely resisted leaning back against him.

Sam scowled. "Apparently, Wrecker had the guard hand out "free night" tickets at the open house, and those guests are walking in with no supervision, no warning to the members, no intro to the rules."

Valerie hunched slightly. Had she done something wrong?

"Not your fault, girl," Sam said. "We've discussed free tickets in the past, but there are too many liability and legal issues."

Gripping her shoulder, Ghost turned her to face him.

"You didn't get anything to read or have to take a class?" he growled. "No one was assigned to watch you? No special collar or—"

"No."

Those were two unhappy Doms. No, all three. The bartender appeared just as displeased.

"The night keeps getting better and better." Ghost kept his

hand on her shoulder. "Cullen, give me one of those supervision collars we store behind the bar."

"Good plan." Bending down, Cullen rummaged, then set a golden leather collar on the bar top with a marker. "What name goes on the tag?"

Both Sam and Ghost spoke: "Mine."

Cullen laughed. "You have a woman, Sam. I'm giving this one to Ghost." He wrote, "GHOST" on a tag and inserted it under a plastic cover on the collar.

"I don't understand." Valerie stared at the collar, feeling like when she was five and got lost in the winding alleys of a souk.

She really should have stayed home.

"Now, lass, don't fret." Ghost showed her what was written on the collar tag.

"Permission to play must be cleared with: GHOST."

He continued, "Anyone scening with you needs to know you didn't get the background and medical checks required for members. Since you didn't attend an orientation class, I'll vet your play partner and help you negotiate if needed."

She frowned. "The regular members go through all that?"

"We do." Linda tapped a finger on the bar. "Remember, though, simply because someone passed a background check doesn't mean they're good people. The club does try—"

"*Did* try," Sam muttered.

"—but there aren't any guarantees. Not in here, or in regular dating, or in life, for that matter."

Huffing out a breath, Valerie smiled. "A disclaimer is reassuring, actually. I wouldn't trust a place promising utter safety."

Ghost chuckled, then lifted the collar. "You'll wear this. Anyone who wants to play with you needs to find me and get permission first. Agreed?"

In answer, she gathered her hair and moved it out of the way, then lifted her chin.

He buckled the collar around her neck, his hands competent

and warm. The collar had a soft fleece lining, and rather than being terrifying, felt almost comforting.

"Ever worn one before?" Ghost asked softly.

"No." Barry made his slaves wear them. She'd never agreed, despite his annoyance. Because she wasn't a slave.

She frowned, and the question spilled out. "Do you have slaves?"

He stood close enough she felt the warmth of his body. "No, lass. I'm single and unattached." Sadness dimmed his eyes for a moment, then he pulled her hair out of her grip and let the strands fall over her shoulders. "The collar looks good on you."

Shouting sounded from the back, catching his attention. Brows together in a dark frown, he glanced at Cullen. "From what I've seen this evening, Wrecker's hired DMs are worthless."

"Agreed, buddy. You going to check on whatever's happening?"

"What else?" Ghost nodded to Sam. "She's with you."

"Got her."

Ghost squeezed Valerie's arm. "I'll find you in a bit. Enjoy your night."

Limping slightly, he walked away, his shoulders wide and military-straight.

And the tingle from his touch lingered. "A DM is a dungeon monitor, right?" She remembered that much from the group she and Barry had joined.

"Right. They're *supposed* to make sure things run smoothly and according to the rules." The irritation in Sam's voice left no doubt about how he felt. "Josie was right about things having gone to hell. When's Z flying back?"

"Just arrived home a few hours ago," Cullen told him.

Sam grunted.

Who was Z? Well, not her business, now was it? "Is Ghost a DM?" Valerie asked.

"Not these days, pet." Cullen started mixing a drink. "However, for some men, duty is a calling. Even being discharged doesn't release them."

She gazed after Ghost, seeing his firm stride, head up as he disappeared into a hallway at the back of the club. "Apparently not."

"Time to show you the place. If you want to be introduced to a Dom, let me know." Linda slid off the barstool.

Did she want to meet Doms? Not really. Yet that *was* why she'd come.

Or had she come just to see Finn again?

"Stay with at least one other submissive, missy." Master Sam gave Linda's hair a tug. "Or I'll tan your ass." Delivered in a low growl, the threat sounded too real.

In a husky voice, Linda responded, "Yes, please, Sir."

Valerie blinked. Well, wasn't that an interesting answer?

Laughing under her breath, she joined the redhead for a leisurely stroll.

Most of the scene areas were against the walls. St. Andrew's crosses were popular. So were the luxurious spanking benches with padded surfaces for the torso, elbows, and knees. They appeared far nicer than the cheap sawhorse ones her small BDSM group had used.

At the very back, down a hallway, was a room Linda called the dungeon. On one side, a sex swing was being used vigorously enough the chains to the rafters clanked slightly with each thrust. Only, rather than a man fucking a woman, a female Domme wearing a strap-on was penetrating a man's ass.

The guy climaxed with a happy moan.

Uh, right. "Sex is allowed in BDSM clubs?" Valerie kept her voice low.

Linda smiled. "In some. It depends on city and county regulations and the club itself. The Shadowlands does. For a lot of people, pain is tied to arousal, and it's nice to be able to act on it."

"Not for you?"

"Oh, sometimes. I'm a 24/7 masochist, one of those people who likes most kinds of pain, and I get cranky if I don't get my endorphins. But Sam can easily turn a few whacks into a sexual frenzy."

"There are different kinds of masochists?" Frowning, Valerie stopped by a fire cupping scene.

Leaning her hip against a couch, Linda laughed. "Probably as many kinds as there are people. Are you the sexual arousal type?"

"Um. Maybe?" And wasn't that embarrassing to admit? "I haven't had much experience."

"A lot of masochists get aroused by pain, depending on the Top and the scene. Sadists are just as variable."

What was Ghost? Not wanting to show her curiosity, she looked away.

And noticed interested gazes from a wide variety of people—women and men, including some around her age.

In fact, as she surveyed the population, she spotted several middle-aged couples. Not everyone reached their fifties and traded out their wife for a younger one.

Linda headed down the other side of the room with Valerie beside her.

"Hey, it's the old bag with the sag. The frump we got Master to dump." The piercingly high voice and the hackneyed rhymes were all too familiar.

Barry's slave was sitting with two young women who'd convulsed in laughter.

Spit. If Kahlua was here, so was Barry. Yes, this evening had taken a quick right turn right into hell.

Was Alisha at the club, too? Doubtful. She didn't particularly like people.

Bad enough Kahlua was here.

Spirits sinking, Valerie kept walking.

"Seems like she found someone her age to hang out with," Kahlua said loudly. "Like two hags in a bag."

"Shut up," one of the young women snapped. "The redhead is Master Sam's submissive. Do you know what that sadist could do to you?"

Linda didn't lose a step although she wrinkled her nose as if she'd stepped in dog poop. "I assume the mouthy one isn't a friend?"

"Not even close. She's one of the slaves my ex brought to live with us." After getting out of sight of Kahlua, Valerie stopped. "I should go. I really don't want to run into my ex. He's the kind to make a scene."

Linda shook her head. "Are you going to let your ex-husband dictate all your choices? Permit him to ruin any fun you might have?"

The blunt words had Valerie straightening. "Put like that, the answer is obviously no."

"Let me introduce you to some people for a buffer if you need one. And I might have a word with the manager. Disrespect to other members is frowned upon." Linda moved forward again. "You said the mouthy one is *one* of your ex's slaves. How many did you end up with?"

"Two. Kahlua was the second—whom I didn't agree to—and one of the reasons I left."

"Ah, I see. Polyamory works for some people, but I'm glad Sam isn't interested."

"What would you do?"

"I'm not sure." Linda pursed her lips. "Discuss it. But it would change things. How I see him. The trust. I can intellectually think that loving another doesn't diminish what we have, but my emotions don't agree."

The relief of Linda's understanding and sympathy was so profound, Valerie couldn't keep walking. "That's how *I* felt. Barry said I was selfish and insecure."

"Maybe. Or is *he* selfish and insecure, instead?"

The question was a startling light in the darkness. Valerie stumbled. "Why didn't I ask myself that?"

Linda frowned. "Have you talked with anyone like a counselor?"

The idea made her laugh. "BDSM and counselors don't belong in the same zip code."

"Not for most counselors, true. There *are* kink friendly ones. Ask Gabi for recommendations."

"Gabi?"

"I saw her..." Linda scanned the area, then motioned toward a St. Andrew's cross where a tall Dom in a suit was restraining a woman with strawberry blonde hair. Streaks of blue and green showed in her bangs when she turned her head. From her expression, she was sassing the Dom.

"That's Gabi."

Valerie grinned. "Her attitude doesn't seem like a healthy choice for a submissive."

"It certainly wouldn't work for me—not with Master Sam. Gabi's different. Her over-controlling parents never let her speak her mind. Master Marcus encourages her, partly to break the programming they did, and partly because they both enjoy the consequences of her sassing him. *Punishments*."

"Oh. Hmm." Being punished for fun? *Interesting*.

"If he's walloping her, they're having fun. She says if she does something that really bothers him, his disappointed expression is far more painful than anything physical he could do." Linda slowed as she neared three barefoot women in a conversational area.

"Linda, you made it." The first jumped up, and then all three were hugging Linda. "It's been too long."

"Sam got overloaded with the harvest—orange season, you know?—and he wouldn't let me come to the club without him." Linda pointed to two of them. "He thinks you two would lead me into trouble."

The three were laughing as they took their chairs again.

"I hear none of us have been here for over a month," the one with her hair in pigtails said. "Vance and Galen were really unhappy when they realized that."

"Sam, too." Linda motioned to Valerie. "I want you to welcome Valerie. She was at the BDSM Sampler event, and this is her first night here. Hopefully, not her last."

With the chorus of welcomes, Linda added, "I wanted her to see how nice we are, but would you believe one of her ex-husband's slaves is here and was incredibly insulting to her?"

The one with colorful hair and gorgeous tats over her pale breasts and shoulders gave Valerie a sympathetic smile. "That sucks."

The slender woman with a sweet expression confirmed. "Submissives should support each other, not tear each other down."

Wearing a boarding-school uniform, the woman with her hair in pigtails pointed to the couch. "Join us, guys. The floor is hard on bare feet."

Linda pulled Valerie down on the couch beside her. "Adding injury to insult, the witch rhymed her putdowns."

"How nasty." The woman with tats frowned. "A rhyme would stick in your head even worse than a normal dissing."

"It did. It does," Valerie said ruefully.

"I'm Rainie." She patted her rotund belly and winked. "I've heard my share of rude comments."

"People can be mean," the brown-eyed submissive with light brown skin agreed. "Being different is like putting a target on your back. I'm Natalia."

The brunette in the school uniform rolled her eyes. "Want me to go over and slap some sense into the slave? Oh, I'm Sally."

Spirits lifting, Valerie laughed. "No need for violence; it's nothing new. I was simply shocked to see her here. Actually, I don't know how my ex afforded the membership fees with me gone."

CHERISE SINCLAIR

Sally's eyes brightened. "His budget tightened when you left?"

"Definitely." Valerie snorted. "Neither of his slaves work full-time. Truthfully, I resented supporting two people I didn't even like. It was...well, destroying my mental health."

"Oh, sister, supporting a husband's slaves? That would burn my butt," Rainie said.

Natalia nodded, brown eyes filled with sympathy. "Especially if you don't like them."

The warmth of having her outrage understood ran through Valerie. As her eyes stung, she pulled in a breath. "Thank you, all of you. I couldn't exactly talk about this with people. Not—"

"Not with vanilla friends." Linda patted Valerie's leg. "I had the same problem before I joined. It's one of the reasons I love this place."

"Exactly." Rainie pointed to Valerie. "You have to join us for a subbie evening out. We have them now and then, basically to whine about our Doms."

"Or whine we don't have one," Natalia said under her breath, her gaze downcast.

Sally bumped her shoulder against Natalia's. "You'll get another one. A better one. Promise."

CHAPTER FIVE

After chatting a while, Linda needed to return to Sam.

"I'll escort you back to him so you don't get in trouble," Valerie grinned, "since he might not dispense a fun kind of punishment."

"You're a true friend."

At the bar, they got paper from Cullen, exchanged phone numbers, and agreed to get together sometime, then Valerie continued her tour.

Alone.

Eventually, she might grow accustomed to being on her own in a place like this. Sometimes, right after her divorce, she'd look around for Barry, feeling as if she'd forgotten something—much like when she didn't have a purse.

She laughed under her breath. Much like her purse, a husband was a weight she could do without.

After watching a stunning scene where the Top used a variety of knives without ever drawing blood, she headed for the restroom. A familiar-looking man caught her eye.

Tall and handsome with thinning, sandy-blond hair. Big-boned —and with a gut. Scott Hicks?

The patchy beard—which she'd figured he'd grown to hide the lack of a chin—confirmed his identity. Yes, it was Scott. Barry was good buddies with the realtor, although she never understood why. The guy was a creep. However, it explained why Barry was here. Scott had boasted about being into BDSM and been disappointed when Barry hadn't wanted to join an expensive club.

Shaking her head, she opened the door to the restroom. *Nice.* Spacious. Opulent. In cream and gold colors, the floor and counters were marble. Sinks were on the near wall, showers and toilets on the far wall. To the right, a second exit door probably led to the reception area. On the left, a dividing wall sectioned off a dressing area with built-in lockers and a cushioned bench.

After doing her business, she walked into the dressing area to unfasten her bustier, give her ribs a scratch, and let her skin breathe.

Oh yes, much better.

A few deep breaths later, she re-did the tiny hooks—what idiot invented this contraption anyway?—and adjusted her breasts.

Checking herself out in the wall mirror, she had to laugh. *Cleavage, I have it.*

On the other side of the divider, the music from the club grew louder for a moment as a door opened and closed.

"Fuck. Just fuck," a young voice whispered loudly. "This place is fucking scary. Did you hear the woman screaming?"

"I know." This voice was also young with a southern accent. "Should we sneak out? Maybe he wouldn't notice?"

"Dream on. His friend is waiting for us. And how would we get home anyway? Fuck, what if they want to—you know. Did you see the way his friend, like, drooled, when he saw us?"

"We shouldn't've done this, Alexis. I'm so stupid! I thought it'd be the ult, getting into a place like this. Like we'd be the stars of the class. I'm sorry."

An ugly feeling tightened Valerie's stomach. The *class*? College students didn't show off to their class—maybe to their sorority or dorm buddies.

High schoolers did. But high schoolers couldn't get into a BDSM club...could they?

"I'm scared, Chloe. I don't want to be here."

Valerie started around the divider—slowly—not wanting to frighten them away.

The choice was taken away.

The door to the restroom whooshed as it opened, and someone called, "Hey, Valerie. Are you in here?"

"I'm here." Valerie stepped out.

Two young women stood by the sinks. A quick glance told her they certainly weren't twenty-one. More like seventeen or eighteen.

Seeing her, they edged toward the door, then stopped. Afraid to leave.

"Hold on a minute, please, ladies," Valerie said.

Natalia waited just inside. "Hey, Valerie. Linda said—"

"Can you bring Ghost here, please. Quickly," Valerie interrupted.

Wait, if the men waiting for the girls were outside this door, then having Ghost—a man—waltzing into the women's room would be too obvious. "Bring him through the entry door, not this one."

"Oh." Natalia obviously heard the grim note in Valerie's tone. "I'll get him right away."

Now what?

Valerie smiled at the girls. "Hey, I'm Valerie, and I'm a professor at the university. Sounds like you have a problem. Maybe I can help?"

As the lanky redhead stood petrified, the short blonde burst into tears. Pulling the crying one close, Valerie took the redhead's hand and guided them around to the dressing area. She sat down with them on the long bench.

"There, now, it'll be all right. We'll get this straightened out."
How many years had she spent offering the same reassurances to
her two children?

"Are we going to get in trouble?" the blonde asked.

"*Weeeell*, I might have to lecture you a smidgen—I *am* a professor, after all."

The crying one gurgled a slightly hysterical laugh, and the
redhead leaned in, letting Valerie wrap her free arm around her.

The way the girls were trembling sent fury through Valerie's
veins. If the bastard who'd brought them here had been in reach,
she'd kick him so hard, he'd curl up like a worm around his
ruptured testicles.

With a bit of persuasion, she established the girls' names.

Alexis was the slender, f-word-loving redhead.

The crying blonde was Chloe, originally from Georgia.

The sound of the door opening made them all freeze. Footsteps sounded on the marble floor.

Ghost strode around the corner, bearing erect. Mouth stern.

The girls relaxed, then Alexis frowned. "Can a guy come in the
girls' room?"

What the fuck?

Ghost pulled in a slow breath. Natalia had said Valerie asked
him to come quickly. He'd been expecting an upset professor, not
two young women who clung to Valerie like toddlers who'd lost
their mama.

They looked so young.

He frowned. Too young. He'd be damned if they were older
than nineteen. If that.

And he was scaring them. *Bad colonel.*

Deliberately relaxing his muscles, he smiled. "Good evening,
ladies. As it happens, I'm one of the Masters here, so I'm allowed

to poke my nose into every room. Even in here when someone asks for me." He lifted an eyebrow at Valerie.

"Thank you for coming. We have a bit of a problem." Her warm voice was so comforting the girls leaned in closer.

He had to appreciate her wording. *"We"* showed she was standing with the girls. And they had only *"a bit"* of a problem. One he'd been summoned to fix. "Let's hear it."

"Someone named Wrecker told Alexis and Chloe he could get them into the club since he's the manager here. Now they're here, he said they'd all go have a good time upstairs. Him and one or *two* of his friends. Privately."

Jesus. Ghost forced his voice to stay calm. "Can I assume they're not twenty-one?"

"No. Eighteen, barely, and seniors in high school. They've figured out this isn't a good place for them, but they have no transportation. The manager drove them here."

Don't blow your stack, Colonel. "I'm glad you realized the danger, ladies. Good job."

The compliment reassured them.

With a shuddering breath, the petite blonde wiped her eyes.

Now, what to do? Hadn't he seen Max playing in the back dungeon with Alastair and Zuri? *Sorry, Max.*

"First, I'd like you to talk to one of our members. He's a cop—and no"—he held up his hand to forestall the protests—"you're not in trouble with the law. We want to make sure this doesn't happen to another girl, maybe even one of your classmates."

"But, but..." The blonde was shrinking back.

The slender redhead was made of stronger stuff. "He's right. We were fucking stupid, but we're okay. Only, maybe someone even dumber, like your sister, wouldn't be."

A flash of worry crossed the blonde's face, and her chin went up. "Okay."

"You got this?" Ghost asked Valerie.

"I do. However, if you could walk in here, can't the manager? Apparently, he was called away to deal with a fight in the dungeon and left them with one of his friends—who might be getting antsy."

"I'll handle it. Sit tight." Leaving through the entry, walking quietly so as not to wake the snoozing guard, he entered the club, spotted Olivia, and motioned her over.

She gave him an unreadable look. "What?"

Whatever her problem with him was, he'd deal with it later. "I could use some help. Wrecker brought in a couple of high school girls to play with."

Olivia's face darkened. "The bloody wanker."

"Exactly. They're hiding in the restroom with Valerie—a friend of mine. I want them to talk with Max."

"Good plan. And me?"

"While I find and brief him, will you take guard duty?" Ghost motioned to the restroom behind them. "If Wrecker or his conspirators poke their head in, can you tell them you're the only person in there?"

"I can and I will." She smiled tightly. "It'll be a pleasure."

Ghost left her to it. At the bar, he sent Cullen in search of Max and pulled Josie over to fill her in. Having a lookout might be wise.

On the way to the loo, Olivia spotted a man by the munchie section, who was keeping an eye on the door. *Hmm*. He was one of the new members who'd joined shortly after Wrecker had been hired.

When he turned to assemble some food from the buffet, she slipped into the restroom. As the door closed behind her, she glanced around. The Masters and Mistresses had their own locker room, and she hadn't been in here in years.

No one in sight. She poked her head around the divider. Yes, there were two terrified girls tucked against a blonde about

Ghost's age. "Good evening. I'm Olivia, serving as your guard dog while you're in here."

Ghost's friend relaxed. "Thank you so much for helping out."

"It's my pleasure. Sit tight and quiet, and I'll fend off the bad guys." On that note, Olivia headed back to take up position just inside the doors.

Hmm. If Wrecker invaded the restroom in search of his missing girls, she should provide a reason for him to leave quickly.

Smiling slightly, she unclipped the flogger from her waist, then undid her corset about halfway down.

A thought made her stiffen. She'd seen Natalia earlier—and had crossed to the other side of the club to avoid her. What if the subbie came in here?

Talk about awkward. She didn't have a chance to worry, though.

The door was shoved open. And there was the manager in his black vinyl pants and sleeveless shirt. *Aren't you all shiny, you dodgy git?*

He stopped dead, the door half open. "Olivia."

Hands on her hips, she gave him the haughty glare she'd learned from Anne, a warning that indicated the male's balls would be in danger if he continued in his stupidity. "I believe you're in the wrong room. This is the loo for the feminine oriented. Or was I mistaken about your gender identity?"

The way red rolled into his beefy face was quite rewarding. "Yeah, no. Just searching for a couple of friends of mine. They in here?"

She glanced at her flogger. It'd be so satisfying to whip him right out of the room.

Instead, she rolled her eyes. "You have no friends in here, Wrecker. Now sod off—and close the door. I'm not putting on a strip-show for the club."

For a long moment, he stood there, his gaze on the toilets behind her. The doors were open; no feet showed in the stalls.

Without another word, he turned and left.

Her eyes narrowed.

After Natalia moved out, Olivia had tried to erase her memory with meaningless play for a couple of weeks. Failing miserably, she'd given up and stayed away from the club. Until this evening after Holt called.

Apparently, the other Masters and Anne hadn't been here either. Hadn't *anyone* been around to see what the bloody wanker was doing to their club?

At the bar, while filling Max and Cullen in, Ghost saw Wrecker enter the restroom—and exit rather quickly.

Good job, Olivia.

After Wrecker spoke with a Dom near the food tables, they both walked out the door.

Leaving during the club's busiest time? Hell of a manager. Despite his disgust, Ghost nodded in satisfaction. Now, Max would have time to talk to the girls.

Cullen gathered some sodas and cookies, then joined Ghost and Max as they headed toward the restroom.

"Thanks for helping," Ghost said to Max. "Sorry about disrupting your scene."

The cop shrugged. "Interruptions come with the job. We were wrapping up the session anyway, and Alastair will enjoy giving Zuri aftercare. Hell, he'll probably drag her upstairs and taunt me about it later."

Cullen grinned. "The doc has a mean side."

In the restroom, Olivia was hooking up her corset. "If you're going to talk with the girls, I'll continue to stand guard."

"Thanks, Olivia," Ghost said.

Her short nod made him wonder if she was angry at Wrecker —or at him?

As the girls started on the food and drinks Cullen had brought, Max introduced himself and showed his badge. He took a knee on the hard floor, putting him at the level of the girls. He was a big man with the hard expression of someone who'd seen the worst of humanity, and Ghost was impressed at his ability to appear nonthreatening.

Under his gentle questioning, the complete story came out.

At the beach, the girls had been sighing over the *Fifty Shades* movie, and Wrecker heard them. He'd said he could show them all kinds of BDSM stuff, but they—*smart girls*—said no. So, he told them about the Shadowlands and said he could get them in, no problem.

Fucking bastard. Z was going to... Hell, there were no words.

Olivia stepped around the corner. "Josie sent word that Wrecker is back in the club and doing a search."

Ah, the asshole and his buddy must have been driving up and down the road, hunting for the girls...without success.

At the news, Chloe and Alexis started clinging to Valerie again.

"Right, then." Max closed his notebook and turned off the recorder. "I'll take you two home."

The girls jumped up. "That's it?" Alexis asked.

"That's it. He's our problem now." Max handed them each his card. "Let's go."

After giving Valerie long hugs—and smiling at Ghost—the girls followed the detective out the door to the entry. The guard might report their escape to Wrecker, but it would be too late.

On the drive, Max intended to discuss the law, the dangers, and would probably manage to talk with their parents. He was a good cop.

"Ghost, I'll wait for you at the bar," Cullen said.

"I'll be right there." Ghost turned to Valerie, who was still sitting on the bench.

Her brow was puckered with worry. Because she cared.

Because she'd stepped in. Alexis and Chloe hadn't asked her for help; she'd involved herself anyway.

"Nice work with the girls, Professor. I'm glad you were here." He took her hand and pulled her to her feet. "Not the way you thought the evening would go, I bet."

Her laugh was a beautiful, husky contralto. "Not even close. Thank goodness you were here."

"I'd like to settle you at the bar to unwind while Cullen and I deal with Wrecker."

He saw the objections in her eyes, but then she showed him her trembling hands. "Unwinding might be wise."

"Good answer." She'd handled everything with admirable calm. Not until after the crisis had she started to shake.

He really did like this woman.

As he led her into the dim interior of the club, the thrumming music washed over him. He tucked an arm around her soft waist and curled his fingers over one pleasingly round hip. She fit against him exactly right.

She gazed up at him. "When Wrecker spoke to Olivia, his voice sounded familiar. Would his real name be Scott Hicks?"

"It is." Ghost eyed her. "Do you know him?"

"He's one of my ex-husband's friends." Her nose wrinkled. "I always thought he was a creep, but perving on high school girls is past disgusting."

"I'd have to agree with you there." He studied her for a moment. "How long have you been divorced?"

"Separated since last November, official in January."

Fairly recent then. "Children?"

"Two and one grandson." The way her voice softened told him her family hadn't lacked for love. Lucky kids.

At the far end of the bar, Cullen was talking with Saxon, one of the younger Masters. He and Jake, another Master, ran a veterinary practice.

Hips swaying to the music, Josie was mixing drinks. "Colonel, what can I get you?"

He shot her a look that made her laugh.

"Hey, *colonel* isn't so bad," she said. "Jessica told me about a club in San Francisco where the submissives call the owner *My Liege*."

"God help me," he muttered.

Valerie had her hand over her mouth, but her eyes were laughing.

"I am *no longer*," he said with emphasis, "in the military."

"Right you are, Sir," Josie said with a tiny salute.

"I'm going to tell Holt to beat you more often."

Valerie stiffened. "No, you shouldn't."

The professor was quite the defender of young women, wasn't she? Ghost leaned down and whispered, "It's an idle threat. Holt is a gentle Dom."

"Oh. Oh, that's good."

He tugged on her hair. "I, however, am not."

To his delight, she swallowed, and her body leaned against his.

"So, you two. Orders?" Josie held up his bottle of Elijah Craig bourbon.

He shook his head. "Nothing for me. Valerie?"

"I'm fine. Really."

He eyed her. No purse. No wallet-sized bulges. "There isn't a charge for drinks, lass. Why don't you two figure it out while I deal with business?"

She touched his arm. "Be careful."

"Of course." He stroked his hand over her silky hair, then collected Cullen with a glance.

Indicating that Cullen had filled him in, Saxon came too. The veterinarian was almost as big as Cullen and moved like a fighter. Good enough.

Any one of them could toss Wrecker out, but the manager had friends here. If he called for help, a brawl might erupt. Hopefully, a show of overwhelming force would intimidate the bastard enough he'd leave quietly.

"He's over there, Ghost." Cullen jerked his jaw toward the munchie corner where Wrecker was sitting and watching the restroom door like a cat at a mousehole.

"Probably still hoping the girls will reappear."

Saxon grinned. "We'll make a good substitute. I have really nice legs, after all."

"You do. I've noticed that myself." Ghost coughed as Saxon's elbow hit his ribs.

As they approached, Wrecker scowled. "I don't have time to deal with your problems. Come back later."

"You're our problem," Cullen said. "We're going to show you to the door. Z will be in touch."

Face darkening with anger, the asshole jumped to his feet. "What the fuck. I'm the fucking manager here and—"

"We spoke to the high schoolers," Ghost said in a low voice. "You can leave quietly, or I'll make a call, and you'll be in handcuffs with a police escort."

Wrecker took a step back, then shook his head. "I don't know any high—"

The bastard. With a growl, Ghost took his arm, ready to dislocate it if he put up a fight.

When Saxon slapped a big hand on the asshole's shoulder, and Cullen stepped closer, Wrecker caved.

The guard watched them walk out without speaking.

In the black night, they walked silently down the sidewalk. The parking lot lights were haloed by the fog rolling in off the Gulf. Thunder boomed in the distance, echoing Ghost's anger.

At his convertible, Wrecker opened the door. "The owner's not going to put up with your crap, you self-righteous bastards. He can't run this place without me."

"Yada, yada, yada," Saxon muttered.

"Leave and don't come back." Ghost shoved Wrecker into the

car, then joined Saxon and Cullen on the sidewalk.

After glaring at them through the windshield, Wrecker sped from the parking lot.

"You know," Saxon grumbled, "I really wanted to hit him a couple of times."

"This was better." Ghost headed back up the sidewalk. "Cullen, I know Z's overseas, but can you call him to make the firing official? He'll want to change the locks and security codes."

No matter what Wrecker thought, Ghost hadn't a doubt Z would want the bastard gone.

"Guess you hadn't heard—Z and family arrived home a few hours ago. It was getting close to the cut-off date for Jessica being able to fly." Cullen scowled. "And why is it me drafted to tell an overprotective, jetlagged shrink how his manager was preying on teens?"

Ghost's lips twitched. "Seems like that kind of heartening news should come from an old friend, don't you think, Saxon?"

Saxon grinned. "Absolutely."

"Assholes." Cullen pulled his phone out of his pocket. "He's going to blow his stack over this mess."

Knowing Z, Ghost had to agree.

Stepping inside, Saxon stopped, gaze on the security guard. "Seems like those youngsters should've been stopped here before setting foot in the club."

"You're right." Anger rising again, Ghost fixed the guard with a stare. "You're fired. Clear out. The owner will be in touch if you have any wages due...or maybe to discuss charges for ignoring the law about the age of entry."

The guard rose. "You can't—"

"Bet?" Ghost asked softly and took a step forward.

"Shit. Fucking shit." The guard sidled toward the exit. "I just did what Wrecker said. But I'm gone, no problem. I don't want no fighting."

The door closed behind him.

Saxon slapped Ghost on the shoulder. "Bet you terrorized your poor troops.

"My operators would have eaten him and Wrecker for breakfast." Yeah, there were days he really missed his SF comrades.

"Yeah, I'll call back in half an hour," Cullen said into the phone, tucked it into his pocket, then frowned at Ghost. "What about a guard for tonight?"

Ghost settled into the guard's chair. "I'll hold it down for now. If one of you can relieve me in a bit, I have a pretty submissive who might never return after seeing the dark side of the lifestyle."

"Valerie, hmm?" Cullen nodded. "She's got a way about her. If those girls had been small enough to climb in her lap, they would have."

He understood. The woman simply radiated serenity. Being with her was like experiencing those rare early mornings in Baghdad when there was silence—no shouting, no shooting, no explosions—only a sunrise and the chirping of birds. When a man could remember what peace meant.

"We can be grateful she found them," Ghost said. "And was able to reassure them enough they'd talk to us."

"She sounds like good people," Saxon said.

As the two Doms headed back into the club, Ghost leaned back in the chair.

The manager would be fired. They'd need a new guard. Even worse, there was a problem with the actual atmosphere of the club. Like those three Doms who'd been trying to intimidate a submissive. That should never happen in the Shadowlands.

Guilt swept through Ghost. He'd let the club down. Sure, he'd been buried because of the extra university class and the new prosthesis he'd been testing requiring fittings and formal evaluations. Yes, he'd been busy.

But his presence—any Masters' presence—might have kept Wrecker somewhat in check. They'd fucked up, all of them. Had let Z and the Shadowlands down.

CHAPTER SIX

Since Valerie doubted she'd ever return to the Shadowlands, she decided to make the most of the night. She smiled at Josie who was waiting for her order. "I don't think alcohol in here would be wise for me, since I'm still learning my limits."

Josie tilted her head. "Now, you have me curious. Learning your limits?"

"In a way. My ex's parents were alcoholics. After a couple of blackouts, we realized the dangers, and he stopped drinking at all. I did, too, to keep him from being tempted."

And then, despite Valerie's protests, Kahlua had brought in beer and hard alcohol—and Barry had given in.

Josie's gaze dropped to Valerie's ringless hands. "Divorced?"

"Recently." The dent left by her wedding ring had gradually disappeared over the winter. Her thumb still searched for the metal band now and then. "Afterward, I fell prey to the entice-ment of strawberry daiquiris—and regretted it. My tolerance isn't what it was."

"You're not the first person I've heard complain about losing their tolerance." Josie started mixing a drink.

"Good to know." Valerie waved toward the room. "So, instead of drinking, I'll—"

"Wait." Josie emptied the blenderized drink into a glass. "Why don't you enjoy this while you stroll around. It's a strawberry daiquiri without the alcohol."

Valerie sampled it. Thick and sweet, and filled with crushed strawberries. "Wow. It's wonderful. Thank you."

"Have fun."

Sipping her drink, Valerie headed for the back, figuring she'd see everything and work her way forward again.

Most of the people she passed were friendly, and a few Dominants came close enough to read Ghost's name on her supervisory collar.

One extremely handsome Dom with a long scar down his face checked the collar. "Ghost, hmm? Good choice."

"Um, thank you?"

Chuckling, he moved on...and she realized he had a gold band on his arm. Another Master.

As she was watching a flogging scene—and wincing at the welts the Dom was inflicting on the poor woman's back—someone joined her.

"Hi, there." The Dom was tall, thin, and wearing a black shirt.

"Well, hi." She smiled, slightly startled at being approached. But this was why she was here, after all.

"You look like you're new. Are you enjoying the club?"

"Yes. Everyone seems very friendly." Why was it so much harder to talk to a man than to chat with her students?

"We are, really. Are you interested in participating at all tonight?"

Went right to the point, didn't he? But he seemed pleasant rather than pushy. And wasn't it splendid she'd attracted someone's interest? In fact, he was the second one who'd asked her.

Unfortunately, as with the first man, she wasn't interested. After Ghost, they all seemed rather bland. There was no...sizzle.

"Not tonight but thank you. Really." Because, maybe...once she stopped reacting to being around Ghost, she might be interested. Maybe. "But I do have to be going." She gave him her best smile, left her glass on a table, and headed for the exit.

Disappointment slowed her feet. After her hopes for sexy times, the evening had been rather a letdown. Time to go home to her cozy apartment and a good book.

Near the front, Natalia was also heading out.

Valerie waved at the short Hispanic woman. "Thanks for the help with rounding up Ghost. Did you find someone fun to play with?"

"Sure, I did. There are a couple of Tops who think I'm cute, and one gave me a nice flogging." From her unexcited expression, the scene hadn't been particularly rewarding.

In the brighter light by the door, Valerie noticed Natalia had used nipple clamps with silvery chains to lace her black sleeveless crop top to her cheeky panties. The crop top displayed: PUNISH ME with a paddle below it. "I love your outfit...and the print design."

"Thank you." Natalia grinned. "I'm kinda quiet, and this way, Dommes have something to...you know, start a conversation?"

"It's a great idea." Would it be a good way to find men who were interested in spankings? "I especially like that somehow you found a cute top instead of a baggy T-shirt."

"I know, right? I print my own with special ink." Natalia tugged at her shirt. "Actually, I started selling some for extra money."

Perfect. "We totally need to talk. I'd love one."

"Really?" Natalia bounced on her toes. "I can bring in a list of designs and prices next time."

Valerie winced. "I...I'm not sure I'll be back. But I'll walk you out, and we can talk."

The way she'd reacted to the interested Doms had affirmed her decision to not join the club. The dues were high, even if the people were welcoming. Well, most of the people. After all, her ex and his slave were members...as was Scott who was manager.

"Valerie." The deep rough voice halted her in her tracks. *Ghost.* He strode toward her, a bag slung over his shoulder.

"Oh, hi." She flushed.

Natalia grinned. "You know, I really think you'll be back. Catch you next time." With a wave, she continued out the door.

"Um. I was just leaving." Valerie swallowed.

"Were you?" He studied her, then moved closer and tucked a strand of hair behind her ear. Merely a small casual touch, but intensely intimate when all his attention was focused on her. "I can see you haven't had a scene with anyone."

How would he know?

Then again... She remembered how messy and red-faced she'd been after he'd spanked her. "Well, no. But everyone was nice."

His mouth curved slightly. "I don't think you're looking for nice, lass. Come with me."

Tingles of excitement raced across her senses as he led her to a couch, set his bag down, and sat beside her. "Normally, with a new member, a Dom would be able to pull up her file."

At her horrified stare, he grinned. "Those files don't include private data like addresses or phone numbers, no more than information about medical problems and a soft-and-hard limits list. Information about what you like or want to try—or never want to do. It's a place to start when negotiating a scene."

"Oh." She stared at her lap, unsure what to say.

"With you, we'll start from scratch." His hand closed over hers, warm and strong. "I know you like being spanked. Are you interested in doing a scene where we'd take it a bit further?"

How could she possibly explain to him her liking for pain depended on—

"Hmm." He ran a finger down her cheek. "There's usually only one thing that turns a submissive this color of red. You get aroused by pain and want to explore it as well?"

Her mouth dropped open, and she sputtered. "How can you just say such things?"

His deep, masculine chuckle resonated in her bones. "Between the military and the lifestyle, I don't have much modesty left. Although I don't mind handing out pain alone, I prefer when sex and pain are inextricably combined. Are you open to having that kind of experience with me?"

Oh, she did love intelligent men who could say words like inextricably. "Um. Yes. Yes, I am."

"In that case... Since we don't know each other well, how about sticking to the basics for a first scene? Maybe an erotic spanking where I can strip you down and use my fingers. Fingers only, and we'll go to what's known as third base."

She laughed and relaxed, even though the room was growing steadily warmer. "That sounds like it's something I'd enjoy more than you would."

"This time, you will." He tilted her chin up, his gaze level. "If things continue, rest assured I will take my pleasure when the time comes."

The sheer self-confidence in his tone made her shiver.

"Any triggers or fears or injuries I should be aware of? Any blood-thinning meds?"

"No."

"Do you like being restrained?"

Her breathing caught, and deep inside, the quivery anticipation heightened. "Yes," she whispered.

"Have you ever had a problem with being tied up?"

"No. It's only been a couple of times and only my arms."

"Excellent. I can see we'll have some new experiences for you." As he ran his hand down her arm, his gaze stayed on her face. "Since we don't know each other well, you can choose whether to play in public or private. Some people feel safer down here where there are people, but others, especially when new, don't like getting off in public. The rooms upstairs are private, but monitored, so if you shouted the safeword, 'Red', a DM would come running. If we use an upstairs room, I won't use any restraints you can't get out of with a bit of work."

The way he carefully considered her fears and laid out her choices was amazing. Wonderful.

So...private or public. She considered the nearest scene area and thought about being touched intimately where people could see. Thought about possibly being seen by Barry or Kahlua. "Private."

He curled his fingers around hers. "All right then."

She tensed, expecting him to rise and pull her toward the stairs.

Instead, he just...studied her. After a few seconds, he lifted her hand and kissed her fingers. "Lean forward for me, please."

Frowning, she obeyed.

"Put your arms behind you with wrists crossed above your ass."

"But—"

At the slight tilt of his chin, she followed his directions.

When she looked at him, he slowly pressed her shoulders back against the couch cushions until she was leaning against her arms. It was a type of unbound restraint, she realized.

"As it happens, Professor, I'm not only a sadist, but also a Dom," he said softly. "I'm quite pleased you're submissive. Are you comfortable giving up control to me tonight?"

She *was* submissive. It was simply the truth. And the command in his voice reduced her to helpless jelly. "Yes."

His finger ran over her cheek, leaving warmth behind it. "Did you learn any languages when you were in the Middle East?"

There was an odd detour. "Yes, a couple. I'm fluent in Arabic with some Persian-Farsi."

"Well, then." As his finger traced down her jawline, under her chin, down her neck, he asked her how she was feeling. In Arabic.

Filled with gutturals, the language was a warrior's language.

Spoken by the warrior who was watching her, it brought back a childhood spent in the souks—the marketplaces in Dubai, Riyadh, Muscat....

Her mouth dropped open, and she asked in English, "Where did you grow up?"

"South Dakota, actually." He switched back to Arabic. "Special Forces soldiers are required to learn at least one language of interest, if not more."

She stayed in Arabic. "Why?"

"Ah, of all the armed forces, we're the ones who interact with a foreign country's population the most, working with the locals and training their soldiers. Our medics help the sick and injured in the villages. It's how I came to have a fondness for the food there."

"I had no—" Shocked to realize her lacy bustier was halfway open, she tried to sit up. "What...?"

A crease appeared in his cheek, amusement in his eyes. With a hand between her breasts, he gently pushed her back. In English, he said, "We're also good at multi-tasking."

He leaned forward, kissing her slowly, his lips firm. His breath held a hint of mint. He cupped her chin, holding her as he took it deeper, coaxing her to respond to his slow invasion. Her bones melted like the snow in the first spring sun.

Lifting his head, his gaze held hers as his fingertips brushed the swell of her upper breasts.

Her nipples budded, and her body roused, making her far too aware of his hard face, his knowledgeable hands.

And how her arms were pinned behind her back.

Even as he nipped her jaw, his fingers were unhooking the rest of her bustier to expose her breasts. Only the shoulder straps kept it from falling off.

"What are you doing?"

"Aside from thoroughly enjoying myself?" His smile flashed white in the tanned face. "Before we go somewhere private, I want to see if you're comfortable with my hands on you." He cupped one breast, weighing it, molding it.

His palm was warm; his touch curled her toes.

"Comfortable isn't the word I'd use," she muttered.

She'd heard his quick laugh before, but now his laughter was open and hearty. Two people walking past paused and grinned.

He dropped another kiss on her lips before rising. Gripping her around the waist, he easily lifted her to her feet, even though she certainly wasn't a lightweight. Under his shirt, his biceps bulged enough to strain the fabric.

After slinging his bag over his shoulder, he put his arm around her. As they walked, she started to fasten her bustier, and he put his hand over hers. "On a scale of one to ten, how uncomfortable will you be if it's open? Ten is embarrassed enough to run."

Such *questions*. Leave the bustier open? Her breasts sagged. Her stomach was certainly not lean and ridged.

Ten.

But there were lots of women here, all ages, all body types.

He was watching her, and the masculine appreciation in his gaze made her feel...beautiful.

So, maybe five?

Some of the people here were walking around completely naked. She'd only have her corset open. "Three, maybe?"

He ran his fingertips over her breast again. "Then leave it open. We'll give the members a lovely treat. You have beautiful breasts."

The compliment made her flush, and...almost...alleviated the embarrassment of walking past people and their gazes dropping to her chest.

To her surprise, only approval and pleasure showed in their expressions.

With his arm behind her, they climbed the spiral stairs to the second floor. A long hallway showed door after door, each with a tiny, shuttered window. Some had red lights glowing above the frame.

As they passed the ones with doors ajar, she'd glance in. She'd expected only beds and dark walls, like the stereotype of a low-rent brothel. Instead, the first room was decorated in southwestern reds and blacks. The next looked like a dark Gothic nightmare. One resembled the deck of a pirate ship with wall murals of the sun setting over an endless expanse of ocean.

Most of the way down the hall, Ghost pushed a door fully open for her. "I thought you'd enjoy a royal welcome."

The opulent, decadent décor was reminiscent of the reign of Louis XIV. Lavish red and gold tapestries hung on the right and left walls. A sofa was over to the right. The far wall held a...

"A throne?" Elaborately carved and cushioned with red leather, the throne stood on a raised dais in front of gilded gold wall panels. But the center of the seat was missing.

He made a guttural sound of agreement. "Mmmph, it's called a queening throne. This is a popular room with female Dominants who like to be worshipped in a carnal fashion."

As in the submissive would lie beneath the throne and... "Oh. Right."

Great, now she was blushing again.

Everywhere in the room, there was gilt and gold, from the panels behind the throne to the wall of mirrors around the doorway to the candleholders.

A dark wood cabinet inlaid with gold and silver filigree stood open, revealing a myriad of BDSM implements.

In the room's center, beneath an extravagant chandelier, was a luxurious spanking bench with extravagantly carved legs and padded with golden leather. The straps were gold studded.

A sensual floral fragrance drifted through the room.

One arm around her, Ghost turned to adjust a wall rheostat. The tiny lights in the chandelier grew brighter.

No, no, no. She didn't have a twenty-year-old body. Turning, she put her hand over his and lowered the lights.

Tilting his head, he regarded her for a moment. "This time, I'll allow you to have your way...with the lighting. Another time, it will be different."

Her mind simply emptied at the casual authority in his voice. "Thank you."

After closing the door and setting his bag down, he gripped her hair, pulling her head back for another kiss, molding her against his hard frame. He was all muscles and sinews, and a thick cock strained against his pants.

Smiling slightly, he said in Arabic, "Here we have the proper place to indulge in a spanking. Do you want to try being restrained on the bench, or should I put you over my knees?"

Oh gods, how could she ever decide?

Ghost smiled down at the little professor. So pretty with her flushed face and the silky hair he had mussed. He slid his hand under the open bustier. Her breasts weren't the perky ones of youth, but instead, incredibly soft with large pink nipples. The best kind of nipples for clamps.

Her body quivered each time his fingers brushed over a peak.

This was going to be fun.

And frustrating. His throbbing dick would have to settle for a handjob later. This time around, it would be all about her.

Biting her lip, she looked from the sofa to the spanking bench. Her longing to try the bench obviously vied with her need for the familiar.

The Shadowlands was all about exploring limits.

"The bench it is." He tried to smother a laugh as her shocked gaze shot to him.

"But..."

With one arm still around her, he led her to the bench and slid the bustier's straps down to remove the garment. Standing behind her, he closed his hands on her lush breasts to keep her immobile as he nibbled on her shoulders. Her skin was like satin beneath his lips.

"Ghost..."

"Shhh." Still behind her, he reached down to undo her black jeans, then bent and tugged them and her briefs down.

He squeezed her soft waist between his big hands, then slid his palms lower. He curved his hands around the beautifully full hips and squeezed. "This is how I'll hold you in place when I take you," he murmured and enjoyed the tremor that ran through her.

Lifting her, he laid her on the bench, belly-down. When she wiggled, he swatted her ass lightly. "Stay still, lass."

Her face was turned to one side, and he saw the flush pinken her skin. And how she didn't move a muscle.

"Very good." Smiling, he tugged her jeans and briefs all the way off. Having the submissives shoeless in the club made stripping them so much easier. He wondered if Z had taken that into consideration when creating the rule.

Gripping her right knee, he set it on the horizontal padded board, then did the same with the left one. "Rest your forearms on the board here, too, pet." He adjusted her breasts to dangle on each side of the top cushion.

She turned her head to watch him, eyes slightly wide, breathing fast.

Intending to reassure her, he bent and kissed her lightly. Her yielding response brought out the Dom in him, and he deepened it into an erotic possession.

Damn, she was intoxicating.

Straightening, he ran his hand down her bare back and up. Someday, her beautiful skin would serve as a blank canvas. Not today.

Control, Colonel.

Instead, he pushed her hair out of her face. "Are you comfortable, Valerie?" He traced the tiny frown line between her brows. "I want you comfortable before I beat on you."

A snort of laughter escaped her. "I feel like an idiot."

"Sex really *is* one of the silliest sports ever." He touched her, learning her skin, the muscles beneath, the tiny quivers. Accustoming her to his hands. "You'd think someone could have come up with a better schematic for the human body. Breasts and balls get in the way and bobble during activities. Such a poor design."

Her eyes closed when he didn't do anything startling. Her frown was gone. "Good point."

Oh, now, mustn't have the pretty subbie get too relaxed.

He bent and cupped one of those beautifully heavy breasts... and her eyes popped open. And when he rolled her nipple between his fingers, her pupils dilated.

So very responsive. He was looking forward to seeing her all flushed and sweaty from pain and arousal.

First things first.

He restrained her right and left legs by running a strap over each calf.

After testing the restraints, she tensed as obvious worry set in again.

He almost grinned. She was a delight to his sadistic heart. But this was a balancing act—and in the beginning of this scene, the emphasis needed to be on comfort.

"Easy, pet." He stroked her hair. "I'll leave your hands free. If needed, you can always reach the straps."

"Oh. Thank you."

Valerie couldn't believe she'd thanked him. For leaving her hands free. Her legs sure weren't. She pulled at the calf straps again. There was no give.

With the tilt of the bench, her butt was slightly higher than her head and stuck out past the end of the table. He'd drawn her knees a short way toward her shoulders before strapping her legs down, and it felt as if he'd painted a bullseye on her ass.

His warm hand ran over her no-longer-taut bottom. The calluses on his palms lent an intriguing abrasion over her skin, as he kneaded and slapped her ass and thighs lightly.

Over hidden speakers came the faint sound of music—one of Bach's Brandenburg Concertos, maybe—still in the slow build-up. Taking his time, he spanked her harder, then paused to run his palms over her thighs, her ass.

A burn started in her skin, echoed by the one in her core. She started to tremble in anticipation of where else he would touch.

"I love this, seeing you laid out for me, for my enjoyment," he murmured. "You're wondering what I'm going to do to you. Hang in there, little professor, you'll find out soon enough. Remember, your safeword is *red*."

When she shivered, he laughed—and his hand smacked down on her ass. Gently, at first, several times.

"You're turning a nice light pink. Do you bruise easily? Should I try to make sure you don't have any lingering marks?"

"I'm pretty normal, I think, and I don't care if there are some bruises."

"Perfect." He delivered several more slaps, and then...oh gods, he explored between her legs. His finger slid between her folds, up and around her clit.

She was quite wet.

"Nice, very nice." The next set of spanks were harder and faster, and her bottom was burning. Somehow, each blow sent more blood to her pussy, making it pulse with need. After rubbing the sting away, he ran his hands up and down her thighs, then...there. Sliding over her clit with the lightest of touches.

She squirmed, wanting more.

After pressing his hand against her pussy, he wiped the damp-ness off his palm onto her bottom—and slapped that spot.

The sting was much more pronounced on wet skin, and she squeaked.

His deep laugh rang out in the room.

Moving forward, he stroked her hair and gave it a hard tug. "I intend to hear more of those squeaks," he whispered, then kissed her hard and deep.

She sank into the bench cushions.

For a minute, he nibbled on her lips, even as he caressed her breasts, his hands gentle...then rougher. Squeezing and tugging. Taking possession.

Heat swept through her body, top to bottom, as everything grew more sensitive. As she fell into an abyss of desire.

"These are too pretty to leave unadorned." He pinched her left nipple, making her gasp.

From his bag, he pulled out nipple clamps and fastened them on her lightly, then tightened the clamps, one, then the other.

The pain turned to liquid heat in her veins. She started to pant.

"There now, aren't those nice?" His voice, despite the amusement, sounded deeper. Huskier. "Your breasts are perfect for clamps, you know."

No, she had no idea but couldn't find the words to say so. Her brain wasn't working quite right. Only his voice and the sensations he created penetrated.

His hand trailed down her back until he reached her bottom again.

And he spanked her more. Softer, then harder. Slowing to play with her pussy, tease her clit, then spanking again. Sometimes, he used a cupped hand, making the sound explode in the room; sometimes, he struck the tender crease between her buttocks and her thigh, making her yelp.

His fingers touched her, so very intimately, and she heard a rumble like a big cat purr, as if he enjoyed fondling her as much as she enjoyed being touched.

Her clit engorged to a needy ache. When he pressed one big finger up inside her, her back arched at the burst of pleasure.

"Oh, ohhhhh." The sound came from her, a long-drawn-out sound.

"Next time, sweetheart, you'll get more than my fingers." He pressed in another digit, pumping slightly as his other hand played with her clit.

Everything down there tightened as she neared an amazing peak—and then he pulled away. Her moan was drowned out by more smacks on her ass.

Her orgasm lurked, just out of reach, turning the pain into shooting stars of excitement.

"Let's add to the fun." As she tried to catch her breath, to protest, he picked up something from his bag and played with the nipple clamps.

She couldn't see, but as he straightened up, something still tugged on her breasts. "What?"

"Weights, my dear. So, when I do this"—he smacked her bottom— "they'll swing."

And they did. Every time he hit her hard, she rocked enough to make the weights pull. Her attention became divided among her throbbing breasts, her burning bottom, and her aching, needy pussy.

He swatted her harder, lighter, varying the blows. Kneading her stinging skin, then teasing her clit until she teetered on the precipice of coming.

Each time, he'd back off again.

He was driving her *mad*.

"Pleeeeze," she finally whined. "Why are you doing this?"

He chuckled. "It's called edging, sweetheart, something sadists love to do to poor strapped-down submissives."

"You are a *monster*."

He laughed again. The next flurry of blows hurt enough to bring tears to her eyes. He pressed his fingers deep inside her, filling her, as he slid his other fingers over her slick clit. Over and over.

She held her breath as the exquisite pleasure grew, and this time, he didn't stop, and oh gods, as the first incredible wave of pleasure bloomed inside, the world disappeared. She fell off the mountaintop into an ocean of sensation.

His low purr sounded again. "Mmm, that was nice. Again." His fingers pressed inside, driving in and out.

The spasms of pleasure started up again, rolling over her like warm surf.

When he finally stopped, she lay limp, gasping for air, heart hammering.

Keeping one hand on Valerie to reassure her, Ghost used the other to undo the restraints. Her skin was slightly damp under his fingers, and her breathing still fast.

Damn, he hadn't had so much fun in an exceedingly long time. Earlier, he'd wondered if the quiet professor would be too inhibited to climax, but once past her initial worries, all her responses were open. Genuine.

"Up you come, lass." He lifted her off the bench, wrapped her in a blanket, and guided her the three steps to the gold and red upholstered sofa.

Steadily, he pulled her onto his lap, adjusting her so her right shoulder was against his chest, and her legs lay on the cushions. "Comfortable?"

She blinked at him, her cheeks still adorably flushed. "Um. Yes. Thank you."

"So polite." He removed one nipple clamp and waited for the blood to return to the abused tissue. "Let's see if you know any curse words."

"What?" Her light brown eyebrows drew together. "I don't—"

Her eyes widened as the pain hit. "Owww. *Ya Ibn el sharmouta, ayuha alwaghd!*"

He grinned at the language a pissed-off, street vendor might use. "Oh now, lass, my parents were married."

She glared at him.

"Good choice though. Let's try for more." Avoiding her grab for his hands, he removed the second clamp.

A hiss escaped her like an angry cat. *"Ayreh feek, hemar."*

Laughing, he covered her breast with his hand, preventing her from rubbing the ache away. "A warning though. In here, cursing is fine. Downstairs, you might use caution about calling a sadist— or a Dom—a donkey. Or saying, fuck you. The Shadowlands can be fairly strict."

Now, there was an adorable pout. "No one would understand me."

His lips quirked. "I would." He emphasized his warning with a pinch to her undoubtedly aching nipple.

To his delight, she not only squeaked—but color swept into her cheeks. She really did like pain. Sexual pain.

So, he massaged her tender breast—damn, but he loved the softness. Gripping her hair with his other hand, he kissed her deliberately hard, owning his territory in the same way he'd owned her ass.

Marked her ass.

Colonel, don't get carried away.

Yes, the tug of desire was there, the urge to let this be more than an enjoyable scene and evening.

However, it wasn't fair to ask a submissive anything after flooding her with endorphins. He could wait.

After a while, Valerie cleaned up in the tiny bathroom as her body hummed with satisfaction. She already felt the loss of Ghost's rough, callused hands on her skin. How could his touch turn her willpower into jelly?

Was it the easy authority he wielded? Or the confident grip? Or the pain... She checked the mirror to see the red marks on her butt.

Was it utterly weird she wanted to show them off?

By the time she'd dressed, Ghost had wiped down the equipment and was stowing away the cleaning supplies.

"I could have helped," she protested.

The way his smile lit his green eyes was amazing. "I'm used to it."

"You're a Dom. Shouldn't the submissive do the cleaning?" Because she wanted to. Totally wanted to do something, anything, for him.

Tucking an arm around her, he guided her out the door, flipping a "check room" light switch.

"Not always. We sadists enjoy turning our victims into quivering messes who aren't up to anything more demanding than sitting on the floor."

Valerie stopped short. "Really? You didn't do that to me."

"We don't know each other well enough, and you're still new to pain." His smile deepened. "I'm not sure if your expression is of hopefulness or worry."

She wasn't sure either. Her legs still felt like jelly, and her muscles like boiled noodles. What would she do if he gave her...*more*?

As they continued down the stairs, he held her close enough she could feel he was limping. "Are you all right? Did you hurt your leg?"

"I'm fine. The limp is nothing new. I lost my lower leg in combat, and the prosthesis I'm wearing today doesn't flex well enough for going down steps."

"I...I didn't know." Then she winced. Her words had sounded rude. "I mean—"

"It's all right, lass. It's hardly a secret and rather obvious when I wear shorts."

"Oh." She shook her head. What does one say to someone who'd lost part of a limb? "I'm sorry, Ghost. I can't imagine the adjustment that must have taken."

"Life is full of adjustments." He tugged her hair. "If you get angry with me, don't kick my left leg, or you'll break a toe."

Her mouth dropped open, and a laugh escaped. "Thanks for the warning."

At the foot of the stairs, he paused. "Can I talk you into a drink?"

Sorely tempted, she hesitated, then shook her head. "I need to get home. I have grading to do tomorrow."

He snorted. "My students complain about *their* homework. They should see ours."

"Truly."

He took his arm from her waist and turned her to face him. "In that case, how about meeting me for lunch on campus this week?"

Everything inside her surged with happiness before her brain turned on and shut it all down.

She retreated a step, then met his eyes. "Ghost. I like you, and if I were at a different point in my life, I wouldn't hesitate to agree. But right now, I'm not interested in anything other than... than what the kids call quick hookups. What we just did."

Still holding her shoulders, he studied her, his thoughtful gaze drifting down her body and back.

She realized her arms were around her waist and forced them to her sides. "I'm sorry."

"I am, too, Valerie," he said softly. Bending, he kissed her gently. "Drive safe, then."

. . .

Hell of a night, eh? From finding out about the damage Wrecker had done to the club, discovering the high schoolers, tossing the asshole manager out, and then...

Well, he'd never anticipated how much he'd enjoy being with Valerie.

He'd missed that sense of connection with a submissive during a scene.

With a sigh, he took a seat at the bar. He was ready to head out now, but he should give her time to leave so she wouldn't feel he was stalking her.

She'd been honest with him—and damn, but he'd appreciated the way she told him how she felt and the straightforward way she met his gaze.

He shouldn't have been surprised by her rejection. She was divorced, after all, and might even have been burned a time or two in past relationships.

Would she even be interested in a man who was missing part of his leg? Some people couldn't deal with it. But she hadn't seemed revolted.

He listened to the harsh dungeon music for a minute, preferring the baroque concerto playing in the Versailles room.

Damn, she'd been beautiful when she'd come.

The bartender noticed him. "Colonel, what can I get you?"

"A beer would be good, Josie. Thank you." He probably had some of his Scottish ale still there.

She moved to the fridge.

He eyed the row of bottles and notepad on the bar. "What are you working on?"

Handing him a bottle of Dark Island, she scowled. "Last night, I poured Edward a shot from his private bottle of Balvenie 21, and he said his bottle had gone down faster than it should, considering he'd only had one shot from it."

She pointed at the wall behind her. The sadist's bottle was barely half full.

"There's quite a bit more than a shot missing." And it was an expensive alcohol.

"Exactly." Her lips quirked. "I happen to know Edward keeps a rather close eye on his Balvenie. I wanted to see if his Balvenie was the only one coming up short, so I've been asking anyone else who keeps a bottle here."

To avoid selling alcohol, drinks were included with a membership. If someone wanted more expensive alcohol, they'd bring in their own, and the bottle would be reserved for their use only.

Josie scowled. "I know Master Z's bottle of Glenlivet was mostly full, and now it's down to a quarter. He certainly hasn't been here drinking it."

Damn. "Someone's stealing the private stock."

"So, it seems. I haven't been here for a month, so I don't know what's been poured. However, none of the Masters were here while I was gone, so their bottles are the ones I'm checking."

She caught his raised eyebrow and held up his Elijah Craig. Half full.

"I bought it after New Years when everything was on sale." He tapped his fingers on the bar. "I had, at most, two shots from it."

Aside from the open house, he hadn't been in the club at all in February, and not in March until tonight.

The notepad in front of her was almost full, and he frowned. "It seems I have a lot of company."

"Most of the private bottles are down at least half of what they should be.

Ghost rubbed his neck. Another problem. The club was a mess, dammit. "Who has access to the alcohol when no one is around?"

She frowned. "When the bartender leaves, the club closes, and Wrecker locks up. He said his friends took over bartending while I was gone. Aside from them... Well, it used to be Andrea and her cleaning crew who came in during the week, but she's proud of her work and keeps a close eye on her people."

Andrea was Cullen's submissive, and Josie nailed her sense of honor. "Used to be?"

"Wrecker fired Andrea right after I went on vacation, so we have a new cleaning crew."

"Fired her?" *What the hell?* "Did Cullen know?"

How was Wrecker even still alive?

Josie moved her shoulders. "I don't know who knows what. I only found out because I called her today."

"Ghost, I'm glad I caught you." Saxon walked up to the bar. "Z wants a meeting tomorrow afternoon in his office here. You good for then?"

Hell of a way to spend a Sunday. "I'll be there." Ghost tilted his head at Josie. "Are you planning to tell Z about the missing alcohol?"

"I hate to add to his problems, but yes. I'll call sometime before your meeting. He needs to know."

Ghost rose and clapped Saxon on the arm. "Tomorrow looks to be a regular clusterfuck of a day."

CHAPTER SEVEN

The next afternoon, Ghost shut off his pickup in the Shadowlands parking lot. As he swung his legs out, he was once again grateful it was his left lower leg he'd lost and not his right. At least his driving hadn't been impacted by the amputation.

No whining, Colonel. Two men had died during the extraction in Afghanistan. He could have stayed at the base like the rear-echelon motherfuckers he'd despised as a young grunt. Not about to be one of the REMFs, he'd jumped on the transport. During the firefight, he'd carried two injured onto the helicopter before getting shot himself.

A foot was a small price to pay for two young men's lives.

Striding up the sidewalk, he pushed the memory away and grounded himself with the scent of freshly mowed grass. A freshening breeze rustled the palms lining the long drive. The sky was a heady blue with bright white, round clouds. Everything around him felt like a celebration of life.

Sure, his days were more complicated, what with lacking a lower leg. The loss was why he'd left the military after the twenty-two years he'd put in, rather than going for thirty.

Life is change.

Working as a professor was interesting. So was testing different prostheses for a prosthetics company.

But he missed the sense of fulfilling his duty, of being responsible for others. Being needed. Helping change the world for the better. The military had given him that in spades.

The Shadowlands door wasn't locked, and Ghost entered to see Ben at the reception desk, reading a book. Behind him, portable play panels created a kid-space where a toddler ruled.

Ghost grinned. "I swear each time I see him, he's bigger."

Wyatt's dark brown hair and big blue-gray eyes came from his mama. The boy was a few months past his first birthday now and looked as if he'd grow to be a goliath like his father.

"Go-es!" Wyatt made it over to the panel and lifted his arms. "Go-es."

"Go-es, now, hmm?" Ghost lifted the boy and bounced him to get a rolling toddler laugh. "I do have another name, you know."

"Too late to change." Ben's New York accent was always a shock here in Florida. "Besides, I'm not sure anyone here even knows your real name. When did you get stuck with the label, anyway?"

"Mmmph. Way back around 1990. Sneaking around in Panama during the invasion." He'd had the handle a long time.

When Wyatt waved his toy hammer in the air, Ghost held out his palm to get pounded on. "Excellent swing, lad. You're a good carpenter. What are you working on down there?"

Letting the boy down to show off his work, Ghost turned to Ben. "I see you're back to holding down the desk."

"It's like old home week, too." Ben motioned toward the door. "Z said to swing by the bar and grab a soda or beer from the fridge if you want. Beth and Gabi sent cookies with their men. Seemed to think you'd need a good sugar high."

Thinking of the mess, Ghost rubbed his neck. "They could be right."

With a Coke in hand, Ghost entered Z's office. The couch and chairs had been pushed to the perimeter, leaving room for long, modular tables to form a square with an open center. If one couldn't have a round table, this was the next best thing.

Damned if everyone hadn't already arrived. He checked his watch to find he was still a few minutes early.

Nearby, Z broke off from talking to Marcus. "Ghost, I'm pleased to see you."

"Welcome home, Z." As they shook hands, Ghost assessed him. Tall, leanly muscular, in his mid-forties with black hair silvering at the temples. "You look rested for a change. How is your mother doing?"

"Well, thank you." Z smiled slightly. "We flew back with her and helped set her up at her home in Sarasota. Not that she appreciated what she called being mother-henned."

Ghost laughed. He'd met the indomitable Madeline. He'd give her a general's five stars any day of the week. "She'll be all right?"

"She can walk with a cane, her lungs are clear, and the exhaustion is lifting," Z said. "We arranged help for her for another couple of weeks."

Overhearing, Raoul made a disbelieving sound. "Madeline accepted *help?*"

Z's jaw set. "It was either a nurse's aide or stay with us here in Tampa."

"Compared to that discussion," Cullen called, "I'm guessing today's meeting will be a piece of cake."

Doubtful.

Ghost sat down with Vance and his partner Galen, both retired FBI to his left. On his right was slender, brunette Anne who'd been a bounty hunter and now worked for Galen and Vance's firm.

Jake and Saxon, the veterinarian partners, and Doc Alastair held down the right table, with Marcus, Olivia, and Sam across from Ghost.

"Ghost, try some of these." Marcus pushed a plate of cookies across the table.

Oatmeal cookies were always welcome. "Thank you—and thank Gabi for me."

"I will."

Z took a seat between Cullen and Nolan, with Raoul at the end. "Dan and Max were called out on a homicide, but everyone else is here. Let's begin."

Conversations stopped; when Z spoke, even the Masters listened.

"First"—Z folded his hands on the table—"please accept my apology for abandoning the Shadowlands over the winter."

Shrugs and variations on "Life happens" came from the Masters and Mistresses. They were all experienced Dominants, none of them younger than thirty.

"Z, *we* could have done more. Should have done more," Nolan said.

"People, I know you all put in extra time during the first month I was gone. It's why I hired a manager. My mistake was in not asking you to oversee him. But you all have lives—and limited time."

"Now, see, there's your weakness," Cullen said. "You rarely ask for help. Hasn't Jessica taught you anything?"

"Not enough, apparently." Z's faint smile was rueful. "You're correct about asking for help."

Very few Doms liked delegating.

"But even though I'll be around more than in the past months, I can't be here every Friday and Saturday. Not with a pregnant wife and a toddler." Z shook his head. "The same applies to many of you. Families come first."

Ghost glanced around the table. Nearly all the Masters and Mistresses were in solid relationships. Quite a few had children.

Z continued. "Which is why I still feel having a manager is

essential. Unfortunately, the one I hired created more problems than anticipated."

Ghost understood. Stuck in Europe, Z had taken recommendations for people who'd do well at the job, but none had wanted part-time work. After all, the Shadowlands was only open on Friday and Saturday nights. So, Z ended up settling for Wrecker.

And Ghost had heard the asshole looked good on paper.

"Ghost," Z said. "Since you were here last night, can you tell us about the girls? Not everyone has heard the complete story."

As if to illustrate his point, Vance leaned forward. "Girls? *Girls?*"

"High school seniors, barely over eighteen," Ghost told him. "It's lucky Valerie happened on them."

"Who's Valerie?" Jake asked. "The name's not familiar."

"A submissive who was here on the free-night pass given to people attending the open house."

Several *what-the-fucks* came from Masters who hadn't heard about the guest passes. It was another few minutes before Ghost returned to the high schoolers.

"In the restroom, Valerie heard two girls talking..." Ghost explained what had happened with the girls and with Wrecker.

Anger suffused the atmosphere. Good Dominants were protective, and the Shadowlands Masters and Mistresses were some of the finest he'd ever known.

"Is the asshole still alive?" Sam asked Z in his sandpaper voice.

"Unfortunately, yes." Z's expression held cold annoyance. "Dan said he'd be pissed-off if he had to arrest me for murder."

"Law enforcement. Always so fussy," Anne said and caught frowns from Galen and Vance, as well as Cullen, a fire investigator.

Ghost exchanged a smile with her, because in his opinion, she wasn't wrong.

"Scott Hicks—Wrecker—expressed himself quite virulently about being terminated. As a precaution, the Shadowlands' locks and security codes have been changed." Z shook his head. "Josie discovered there is expensive alcohol missing. Some smaller items have also been stolen. Nonetheless, I'm disinclined to prosecute. Sorry, Marcus."

Marcus, an assistant state attorney, inclined his head. "I do understand, sir. Discretion is part of what we owe to our members."

"Precisely. However, Scott Hicks will no longer be welcomed in any clubs in the state—or wherever I have influence—which will curtail him targeting those in the lifestyle. Dan and Max—and their colleagues—intend to keep an eye on him, too."

Last night, Ghost had wanted to pound the bastard into the ground. Today, after some thought, he'd arrived at the same conclusion as Z. The girls and the Shadowlands members wouldn't be helped by trying to arrest the bastard.

"Going forward..." Z glanced at some notes in front of him. "I've terminated anyone Hicks hired—the dungeon monitors, the guards, the cleaning service, and the two women who replaced Peggy."

Peggy had worked during club hours, cleaning scene areas if the participants weren't able for some reason. A kind woman. Maybe she could be persuaded to return.

"The cleaning service? You mean Andrea's company?" Marcus turned to Cullen.

"Aye, he fired Andrea and her crew at the beginning of February." The big fire inspector's face was dark, although, after a month, surely his anger would have faded some.

Unless he'd just found out?

Ghost pressed his lips together to stifle a laugh. That explained why Wrecker was still alive.

"Unfortunately, catching up with my patients will take the majority of my time, which makes hiring a new Shadowlands manager imperative." Z leaned back and steepled his fingers. "Hiring from outside the club was a mistake. We need someone who already belongs here and has the same high expectations for the club and the membership as we do. Someone who is comfortable being in charge."

Now that wasn't going to be an easy person to find. Ghost rubbed his chin, trying to think of someone.

Z's gaze met his. "I'd like the person to be you, Finlay."

The statement hit Ghost's gut with the impact of a .50-cal bullet. *What the hell?* "No." *Surely not.* "There are others who would do a better job and who have been here longer."

Cullen's hearty laughter echoed off the walls. "You're not going to get out of this, me boyo. We're all in favor."

Ghost swept his gaze around the table. Aside from Olivia, each person wore a shit-eating grin. "You bastards. You started the meeting before I got here. This is a set-up."

Raoul swore, dug out his wallet, and handed Marcus a five-dollar bill.

The attorney smirked. "He's as smart as a fox. I knew he'd figure it out."

Z cleared his throat. "Finlay, I know you're a professor at the university. Still, I think you could handle the added commitment."

Ghost eyed him. "Because you managed to balance the club and your job for years."

"Balancing wasn't difficult until we had children." Z rubbed his face. "Part of being a parent is simply being present. During my first marriage, I was in the military, then college, and my boys grew up mostly without me. I want to do better this time around."

Easy to understand—and appreciate.

Kelly couldn't have children, but... "My tours of duty were why my wife and I decided against adopting. Her health was poor enough she wouldn't have been able to handle parenthood with me deployed so often." There were times he regretted their decision.

In the military, he'd enjoyed working with young soldiers. Now, teaching helped fill the need.

As if Z had heard his thoughts, he said, "We all want to help the next generation along. The university is one way." Z paused. "So is mentoring new Doms."

Ghost sipped his Coke as he thought.

He didn't need the money. The question was: Could he do the job and do it well?

Probably.

Did he want the job?

Hmm.

Z held up a hand. "I do have a condition: the manager must live on the premises. Upstairs. Rent-free, of course."

"Is there a reason?" Ghost asked.

"Indeed. There has been vandalism in the Capture Gardens and in the private gardens."

"Isn't there a security system?" Holt asked.

"There is, and the alarms were set off. Unfortunately, the property is quite distant from the nearest police station. Having someone living here again might eliminate the problem."

"That's logical." However, the main reason for being the manager was the club, and it wasn't a job he could do alone.

As attention shifted back to Ghost, he considered them all. "I would have conditions." He spoke to the Masters and Mistresses, not Z. "The hired dungeon monitors weren't invested in the club and did the minimum necessary."

"We sure saw their lack of involvement last night," Nolan grumbled.

"More than that, our members should learn there's a give-and-take in belonging to this club. The Shadowlands isn't a nightclub, it's a community."

Nods showed him they were following.

"But people need examples of how to give back. I'd like you all to take dungeon monitor shifts again. I'll hold DM classes to grow a volunteer pool. You'll get apprentices for hands-on training. Eventually, the time I need you to put in will decrease."

"Fair enough," Marcus said. "I'm in."

The rest agreed.

One down. "The second condition is much the same. I want you each to teach a class every other month and to mentor less experienced Doms when you're here. Our newer Doms need role models—which means all of us need to show up more often."

Galen nodded. "He's right. It's what we owe to the club."

After glancing around the table, Cullen said, "We're in for your second condition, as well. Z?"

"I approve." Z smiled. "We have a consensus and a good start. Thank you, Ghost."

Ghost eyed him. "You're not off the hook, *Master* Z. You don't have to be a dungeon monitor, but you'll make up for it by giving extra demonstrations. Jessica will enjoy some time in the dungeon, I'm sure."

The room burst into laughter because Z's adorable submissive hated being put on display.

Ghost rubbed his lips and wondered how Valerie would feel about it.

He'd undoubtedly see her on campus, and then the ball would be in her court.

Unless—and until—she handed it to him.

CHAPTER EIGHT

Monday afternoon, Valerie spotted Ghost walking across the campus.

The entire world seemed to get brighter, and wasn't that crazy? She wasn't some naive sixteen-year-old with a crush.

Honestly, her heart really *was* beating faster. Holding her breath, she waited for him to notice her.

The sun glinted on his gunmetal gray hair. Her fingers remembered how the short curls were smooth and slightly springy.

Resilient, much like his personality. Whatever disaster overtook him, he'd bounce back.

He already had. Now she knew what to look for, she could see his left leg wasn't as flexible as the right. Yet, his stride was balanced and powerful.

Her hands clenched with the desire to touch him.

Noticing her, he paused.

When she lifted her hand to acknowledge him, he veered her way, and oh, she really did like his easy smile. "Valerie. You appear well."

"Thank you." She glanced around. No one was within hearing

distance. "Were there any problems with the manager? Did he get fired? You didn't get in trouble, did you?"

"Let's see. No problems, he was terminated, and on the contrary."

She laughed, trying to remember her last question. "What can be contrary to getting in trouble?"

"I ended up saddled with his job." He grinned, obviously not worried about the responsibility. Then again, if anyone was born to take charge, it would be this man.

This Dom.

"Well, there's an improvement. Are you resigning from the University?"

"No, I like teaching. But I only work part-time as a professor, and the manager position is also part-time."

"I thought you had a full load of classes."

"Actually, I had only been thinking about going fulltime. Then, at the end of January, a professor had a heart attack, and the administration drafted me to teach one of his classes." He gave a wry laugh. "He was already behind. Between catching up with his students' ungraded exams and homework and preparing lectures, I was swamped all through February."

"Oh dear. Those kinds of surprises are never good."

"And thus, I learned I enjoy free time too much to sacrifice it all to teaching."

"With managing the club, your free hours are going to be a fantasy."

"I don't mind spending time at the Shadowlands, and honestly, having seen the mess Wrecker created, I'm itching to fix it. In fact, I'm interviewing new security guards tonight."

"Ah, new security because the girls shouldn't have been able to get in if the guard had been conscientious?"

"Exactly." A crease appeared in Ghost's cheek as he smiled down at her. "As it happens, I also talked the owner into offering one-month probationary memberships. The application process

CHERISE SINCLAIR

will still be in force, the orientation class will still be mandatory, but the either side can back out during the first month."

"The Shadowlands is already able to terminate a membership at will."

"I might have known you'd have read all the contract verbiage." He tugged a lock of her hair. "Very good, Professor. Unfortunately, quite a few people don't read what they sign and are upset when their membership is canceled. But the probationary time will make it clear there's a trial period. Maybe it will entice more people like you into giving the club a chance."

She snickered. "Instead of handing out free night tickets?"

"The coupon was a disaster waiting to happen, letting newbies into the club with no precautions or explanations of the rules. However, it's good to offer a way for new members to back out if the place doesn't meet their needs."

"Linda said the owner never enforced the year-long contract if someone wanted to quit."

"He doesn't and still won't. But this will let people sample the place with an easy out."

She frowned. "I suppose so."

"Tempted?"

She was. She'd filled the application out already. The membership fees were what had given her pause. A month would give her a chance to see if she liked it enough to make it fit into her budget.

Only...

"Will it bother you if I'm a member?" And what a stupid question. Why would he even think twice about her?

Ghost could probably have any submissive in the club simply by snapping his fingers.

He moved closer, the smallest amount. Just enough to invade her space. "I'd be very pleased. I won't harass you to play with me if that's what you were obliquely asking. If you want another scene, I'll be delighted, but you'll have to ask me. Or simply

118

fetch me whatever paddle you'd enjoy being used on your pretty ass."

Heat flashed through her, rousing her. Making her long for exactly that.

In a casual move, he squeezed her shoulder, then his grip tightened to the edge of painful, reminding her of his powerful hands, his touch, the burning of her ass.

That he was a sadist who could fill her needs.

All her needs.

Damn the man.

"You'll start Friday night. I'll see you then." Later, at a second desk that had appeared in the Shadowlands office, Ghost shook hands with the young man and escorted him out.

A transgender man, Fyodor Koslov was in the process of transitioning, which might cause some absences, but he had the right experience and sense of professionalism that Ghost—and Z— wanted. Ex-military, black belt in Krav Maga, working at a gym in Tampa.

Yes, he would do.

Re-entering the club, Ghost saw Andrea perched on a barstool. Noises from the back hallway indicated her cleaning crew was still at work. "Were you waiting for me?"

"Yes." She smiled. "I'm so glad you've taken over the management."

The sentiment from Cullen's submissive was a fine compliment. "Thank you. With everyone's help, we should be able to bring the club back to what we all love. Is there anything I can do to make things easier for your cleaning crew to get back up to speed?"

One of the first calls he'd made was to re-hire Andrea's cleaning service.

"We're good. I need to talk to you about something else." Her smile disappeared. "When Wrecker came on as manager, he and his friends were using the Shadowlands as their personal dungeon during the nights it was closed. I warned him that equipment was being broken and the rooms left dirty. The next morning, he ended our contract and hired a different cleaning service."

Having seen Cullen's face in the Masters' meeting, Ghost couldn't resist. "I'm surprised your Master didn't get involved."

She averted her gaze. "I...um...didn't tell him?"

Guilty submissives were so adorable. Already knowing the answer, he set his hand on her shoulder. "Please, tell me he knows now."

"*Sí*, he does. I told him Saturday night." She flushed. "I just didn't want *mi Señor* upset over something he couldn't fix, but he didn't agree."

"No Dom would." Ghost tried to hold his laugh in and failed.

Her glare made him laugh even harder.

She took up a paper from the bar and slapped it into his hand. "This is a list of missing items and broken equipment, damaged flooring and carpets, and plumbing problems. Most of the locations are the private rooms on the second floor."

Her *list* was a spreadsheet. Date, location, problem, when reported and to whom, follow-up dates. The damages she'd reported to Wrecker back in January hadn't been fixed. And she'd added a hell of a lot of new problems today.

Wrecker had truly abused the management position.

"Give me a second, please." Ghost pulled out his phone and added a note to call a plumber as well as Z's repair guy. Some repairs he could handle himself; others required more expertise. "I'll get these taken care of. Thanks for the detailed list; it makes things easier. I'll give a copy to Z if you haven't already."

She shook her head. "I didn't want to add to his worries."

"You're thoughtful, but now he's back, he needs to know." Ghost smiled at her. "He looks good, Andrea. I'm sure he was stressed, stuck in Europe with an injured and ill mother. But he was also away from his practice and basically forced to rest."

"I'm glad he's caught up on sleep—since they'll have a new baby all too soon." The worry in her expression gave way to a grin. "Jessica is whining about resembling a watermelon."

A snort escaped him. Z's submissive was adorable...and very short.

"Since we need you to survive and be the manager, I won't tell her you laughed." Andrea grinned.

"Thank you," he said, quite sincerely.

As she returned to work, he headed for the private rooms upstairs to do his own inventory. Halfway up, his cell rang.

A check of the display showed "Drake." Excellent. It'd been a while since he'd spoken to the owner of Chains, a Seattle BDSM club. "Drake, how are you?"

"I'm doing well, thank you." The smooth, deep voice still held a touch of a French accent. "Congratulations on your added responsibilities. Zachary picked wisely. And I'm pleased he managed to get you back into the lifestyle."

Ghost snorted. "His rep as a shrink is well-earned—as are his manipulative talents. How'd you hear about the management position?"

"Max and I talk, now and then."

"Ah. He's a good Dom, although he and Alastair chose a challenging submissive. Zuri keeps them on their toes." Ghost grinned.

Last month, Max had angered her, and she'd squirted blue food coloring into his showerhead, thinking he'd have time for it to fade in the two days he was off. Unfortunately, the detective got called in for a homicide.

Gave new meaning to the phrase: *the boys in blue.*

"Sassy subs are the best kind." Drake hesitated. "Speaking of submissives..."

There was only one submissive Drake might hesitate to speak of. Uneasiness lodged in Ghost's chest. It'd been over two years. Had she followed through on her threats? "Go on."

Drake, being a perceptive Dominant, probably heard Ghost's worry. "*Non, non,* I have been clumsy. I simply wanted you to know Faylee is healthy and happy."

The young woman was all right.

Ghost shook his head to regain his balance. "Thank you. It's good to hear." He'd never forgiven himself for the damage he'd done. The mess hadn't been all his fault, but that wasn't something a man weighed out on a scale. Damage was damage.

"And you, too, are moving on from the past. Soldier to professor. Now manager after having been awarded Z's infamous Master title, *hein?*"

Ghost laughed. "Infamous?"

"But this means you are playing again, because the title indicates both power and experience, not something to be measured in a void. Are the Florida women more beautiful than our northwest beauties?"

Drake, for all his elegant sophistication, loved gossip as much as the nosiest of neighbors.

Ghost smiled. There were days he missed Seattle. "Yes, they are. Have you found yourself a submissive yet?"

"*Non, non,* not me. And you?"

The thought of Valerie came to mind. The feel of her in his hands. The sounds she made when he hurt her, as she slid into arousal. As she came. Willing and responsive and warm. "No, the one I'm interested in wants no relationships."

"Ah, one of those." Drake clicked his tongue. "Have hope, my friend. As you have learned, wounds do heal, and life will balance out again. Don't give up on her."

"No," Ghost narrowed his eyes. "Giving up isn't in my vocabulary."

CHAPTER NINE

U nder a beach umbrella, Valerie sat on the sand and played with her grandson, the love of her life. Out in the water, her daughter was swimming and splashing and undoubtedly enjoying a few minutes to herself.

Valerie remembered when her two were toddlers. Alone time didn't happen.

"Did!" Luca's big brown eyes lifted, and he waved his shovel in the air with a crow of accomplishment.

"Is your bucket full?" Valerie smiled. "It *is*. Excellent work, my man. Shall we dump it together?"

The damp sand in the bucket went on top of the growing pile, and they patted it to smoothness.

Valerie glanced at the sun and sighed. Her time with Luca and Hailey was almost over.

Such a lovely afternoon. Her daughter had driven over from Orlando for a computer programming class, and Valerie had volunteered to babysit Luca.

After class, Hailey, a total beach girl, had wanted to take Luca to wade in the Gulf of Mexico.

Happy for more time with her precious daughter and grandson, Valerie agreed.

Smiling, she checked in the cooler and pulled out a baggie of orange wedges from her daughter's backyard tree. She ate one and grinned when Luca reached out a sandy hand, remembered, and opened his mouth like a baby bird.

"You're such a smart boy," she praised and popped a slice in his mouth.

Bouncing a time or two, he chewed, accepted another orange wedge, then started filling the bucket again.

"You're a very hard worker. Just like your mama," Valerie told him.

Drops of cold water splattered down on them as Hailey arrived and shook her hair. Luca burst into giggles, the most infectious sound in the world, and Valerie laughed.

"San'," Luca pointed to the pile.

"Yes, it is. You have a most awesome pile of sand," Hailey said solemnly as she pulled on a cover-up. "Mom, we need to get going, I'm afraid."

"Of course." Valerie rose and started gathering everything together. "I'm so happy you were able to leave Luca with me—and to have a beach trip after."

"Me, too." Hailey frowned. "I'm sorry Dad was too busy with work to see me and Luca today. It's been quite a while since we visited him."

"Mmm," Valerie said noncommittally.

"It's still weird you're not together. Do you ever talk or anything?"

"No. I haven't spoken to him since the day I went over to get your boxes."

"Oh. Right. Thank you for picking them up." Hailey shook her head. "I can't remember the last time I was at the house, actually. Then again, without you there, it's probably a mess. Dad was never much of a housekeeper."

And neither were Barry's two slaves.

Valerie could feel her daughter's gaze.

Her soft-hearted child wanted her parents to get back together. Unlike some children of divorce, neither Hailey nor Dillon had seen Valerie and Barry fighting. The vague explanations of "*We grew apart*" hadn't satisfied either child. Barry certainly wouldn't tell them about his slaves—and had asked Valerie not to.

Last fall, on the rare occasions the children came over, Alisha spent the evening with her family in St. Pete. Kahlua, though, had thrown a fit at leaving the house to hide her presence, so Barry's solution had been to avoid having the children visit at all.

Apparently, he hadn't changed his method.

Ah, well, not her problem.

With Luca chasing the seagulls, the trip to their cars didn't take long, although there was a brief interlude when a man walking in front of them was berating his wife. Both parents forgot their crying toddler who had sat down in the sand.

Valerie picked up the girl and waited. The two kept walking. *Honestly.* "Excuse me! I believe you forgot someone?"

At her shout, they turned.

The woman went white. "My baby!" Tears running down her face, the woman ran back and reclaimed her child.

Valerie turned to the man. "As someone who raised a couple of children, I suggest you postpone fights until your child is safe and out of hearing."

The man scowled at her, glanced at his crying wife and girl, then scowled again. "Yeah. Right."

As the two hurried away, Valerie gave way to her feelings in a flurry of Arabic.

"Uh, Mom? Translation, please?"

Ouch. What she'd said hadn't been nice. But Luca was occupied with watching a beachcomber with a metal detector.

"Roughly, I called him a ringworm-ridden, dickless, son of a donkey then compared him to a filthy, turd-soiled shoe."

"Spot on, Mom, spot on." Hailey's laughter could lighten any irritation.

Valerie smiled. The gods had blessed her with two magnificent children...and a grandson, as well.

At the car, she gave Luca a big hug before fastening him in his car seat. "After all the bird chasing and fresh air, he'll be asleep before you reach the highway."

"Maybe before we even get out of the parking lot." Hailey hugged Valerie.

When Valerie didn't get in her own car, Hailey gave her a confused look. "Aren't you leaving now?"

Valerie motioned toward the stores on the boardwalk. "I'm going to visit a friend who owns one of the stores."

"Ah-hah, and there's the reason you wanted Foggy Shores."

"Exactly. It's also quieter than the big beaches."

"It was great. Good choice." Hailey grabbed a last hug. "Love you, Mom." She popped in her car, and then they were gone.

Valerie felt the ache as the distance increased. "Nope, don't even start with whining." The goal of a parent was to raise his or her offspring to be happy, productive adults, which meant the children eventually left the nest.

There were times she wanted a culture where three generations lived under one roof. Then again, she'd fled her parents as soon as she possibly could.

Life was full of odd balances, wasn't it?

Boxing up mugs behind the counter of Linda's small beach store, Natalia breathed in the spicy scent of potpourri, the lighter fragrance of sand candles, and, best of all, the wonderful briny air off the beach.

I love this place. The store carried handcrafted items made by Floridian artisans and was always full of sunburned, cheerful tourists. The only dark spot in all the brightness was knowing she owed her job to Mistress Olivia.

Back in January, after Uncle Bartolo had shouted at Natalia for what seemed like hours because she was slow at doing the accounting books, Olivia had found her in tears. After the Mistress made a phone call, Linda had offered Natalia a job.

"There you go. They should be safe for your trip home." Natalia handed the Canadian shopper a well-padded box containing two etched coffee mugs.

"Thank you so much." The woman joined her friend.

Natalia glanced at the few people scattered through the store. Two were considering the beach tote bags. Near the right wall, a blonde woman and a couple were checking out paintings of Florida beaches.

A Tampa woman made the next purchase—a beautiful sea grass basket Linda had woven. "It'll hold my yarns and be lovely in my living room."

When she left, the man and woman took her place. The man held...one of Natalia's paintings from the wall.

She barely contained a squeak. "Um, you chose a pretty one."

"Isn't it though?" The woman's smile was so happy. "We're from North Dakota, and when we're snowed in next winter, I'll enjoy this and remember there really are warm places on this earth."

The man tucked his arm around his wife and kissed the top of her head so lovingly a pang of longing ran through Natalia. "We'll make it back here someday. Maybe not next year, but someday."

"And, in the meantime," Natalia cleared the hoarseness from her throat, "you'll have a lovely memory of the beach to look at."

"Exactly."

As they wandered out, holding hands, Natalia stared after them, heart full. They'd bought her painting.

She'd sold other paintings—and every single time, she experienced the heart-stopping surprise that someone valued what she'd painted.

Her family never had.

She shoved the dismal thought away. Wasn't it wonderful her painting of a pelican resting on a dock above sunlit water would give someone happiness during a cold, dark winter?

"You *can* tell the customer you created the painting," Linda said from behind her. "People would be thrilled to meet the actual artist."

Natalia turned. "Not a chance. No way. Uh-uh."

In her forties, Linda had a sociable nature—and a confidence Natalia could only hope to achieve someday. "No pressure. I won't out you to your fans."

"Too late. She's outed," someone said from the other side of the counter.

Natalia spun.

The woman had caramel-colored hair pulled up on top of her head. She wore shorts and a sleeveless white top with deep blue embroidery the color of her eyes. What interesting cross-stitching. "Whoa, Valerie, I didn't recognize you at first."

She laughed. "No one looks the same when out of a corset, right?"

"No lie."

Linda was laughing. "Valerie, welcome to my slice of heaven on the beach."

"You have a lovely shop." Valerie turned to Natalia. "And your impressionist paintings, Ms. Natalia Rosales, are amazing."

Linda beamed. "It's what I keep telling her. In fact, she's one of the featured artists in a gallery opening coming up. You need to come—it'll be fun."

"Congratulations," Valerie said. "And I will."

Natalia studied the woman. In the Shadowlands, Valerie had

seemed somewhat nervous. Then again, who wouldn't after being verbally attacked by an ex-husband's new girl?

Today, she was perfectly self-confident. As Linda showed her around the shop, they chatted comfortably, and Valerie's compliments were both sincere and knowledgeable.

When she and Linda returned to the counter, Natalia sighed. "Can I be like you two when I grow up?"

"You lost me," Linda said.

"I get it." Chuckling, Valerie glanced at Linda. "She's like my introvert of a daughter. Ask Hailey to create a computer program and she's right at home. Ask her to attend a party and chat with strangers? One traumatized girl. In elementary school, she hid in closets to avoid attending birthday parties."

"Oh, wow." Natalia straightened slightly. "I'm not that bad."

"Not even close." Valerie's expression held approval. "We worked on her social skills, and she can hold her own at a party now, but she'll probably never be entirely comfortable with people-centered activities. Which is okay. After all, I can't program computers. And if you handed me a brush and canvas and said, 'Paint something', I'd panic."

The reassurance was like...like standing in a warm rain on the beach, feeling it clean the gritty sand away. Natalia sighed. "That's what Linda keeps telling me."

What Mistress had been working on with her. "And I know it, but sometimes I forget."

Especially since Olivia had shoved her out the door, ripping all her hard-won self-confidence to shreds.

Valerie's smile was rueful. "Don't we all?"

Linda moved behind the counter. "Let me get you checked out. The store is closing early since we have a moving-in housewarming party to attend."

Valerie handed over a pair of blue handcrafted earrings and a matching set of Natalia's paintings where she'd been playing with sunset tones. One showed Spanish moss hanging from a tree. The other was of a delicate blue heron in the wetlands.

"Being in a small apartment, I don't have much wall space, but these will fit perfectly with what I have," Valerie said. "They're beautiful."

Would she ever get tired of hearing compliments? No, never. "I love trying to capture sunlight and shadows."

After ringing up the earrings, Linda held them up. "The rich blue is definitely your color." She gestured toward Valerie's shirt. "Your embroidery looks almost like Tatreez, but I don't recognize the designs."

"Some of the motifs are my own," Valerie ran a finger down the cross-stitch. "I learned the Palestinian designs when I was growing up, but I wanted designs from my own heritage. Tatreez is one of my meditations."

"No way." Natalia leaned forward. "Meditation stitching?"

"In a way." Valerie chuckled. "The motifs can tell a story, and I like the way it makes me consider my life as I pick the symbols and colors for what's happened. What stiches should be repeated or adjacent to something else. When I embroider, I can let the world go and simply focus on that stitch and the related aspect of my life."

"How awesome," Natalia breathed.

"Sweetheart, I've seen you paint. You do much the same thing," Linda said, then clapped her hands. "All right—let's close up and get this show on the road. Valerie, unless you find a really good excuse, you're coming with us."

"I...what?"

Natalia nodded. "Yes, you should come. Totally."

"You can't just drag a stranger to a party. I mean, yes, maybe to a party, but housewarmings are for friends."

"You'll know some of the people. Cullen and Max will be there. And so will Sam who'll be unhappy if I fail to get you to show up."

Natalia snickered. "Ooooh, good threat. Don't make the sadist unhappy, Valerie."

"Really, this is a work party to help unpack," Linda added. "The move was a hasty one, and we could use some extra hands."

"Oh. In that case, I'd love to help." Valerie smiled. "I'll follow you there."

Natalia followed Linda to the back to get their purses. "You are a very sneaky woman. I noticed you didn't say who the party is for."

"No, I didn't, did I?" Linda smirked. "Have you seen the way Ghost watches her? He *likes* her, and it's our duty as submissives to give the Masters what they want."

"There's an interesting way to look at a set-up. But I'm in." Wouldn't it be fun when Valerie realized who the housewarming was for?

Following the other two out of the store, Natalia sighed. Linda sounded so positive about knowing how to give a Master what he wanted.

So...how did a subbie give a Mistress what she wanted? Because Natalia sure had failed in that endeavor.

CHAPTER TEN

Humming to himself, Ghost wandered through his new place...*flat...quarters*. Hell, what *did* one call a living space on the third story of a mansion?

A home?

Not yet.

Relocating after only two years in his apartment was sure a pain in the ass.

But Z was a friend, and being an overworked shrink with a pregnant wife, toddler, and new home, the man didn't need any added stress.

So Ghost had put out some extra cash to expedite a move and ease Z's worry about the property.

Admittedly, the three-story stone building was beautiful. In front, the long palm-lined drive led to the parking lot on the left. Behind the mansion was a screened lanai, gardens, and pool for the private quarters—his, now. The larger area on the other side of the mansion held the club's Capture Gardens.

The Shadowlands took up the first floor. The second floor housed the club's private theme rooms.

And the third floor was now his living quarters, which held

more than ample space. And was beautiful. The tall arched windows let in light—and the scent of tropical flowers blooming in the extensive private gardens below.

The living and dining areas had brownish walls—what Jessica had called cappuccino—with white crown molding and trim. The deep red Oriental carpets he'd brought home from his tours of duty looked good on the polished hardwood floors. Since he preferred oversized, deep-cushioned furniture, his beige chairs and couch filled the big room nicely.

However, the boxes piled high around the room detracted from the ambiance. The moving crew earlier had unpacked the bigger items—and barely made a dent.

"Yo, you home?" Cullen's bellow from outside the mansion would have echoed off the mountains...if there were mountains in Florida.

What the hell? He walked through the kitchen and out the door that overlooked the patio and gardens. "I'm home."

"C'mon down, Colonel. You have company," Cullen yelled.

Company? More than Cullen—who wasn't expected either? Hell, he hadn't been expecting anyone.

Since his leg was aching, he took the steps slowly, stunned as people flowed in from the parking lot.

The tough Brit Olivia and tall, slender Anne were first. Anne had brought her submissive, Ben, who tossed Ghost a friendly salute.

Cullen and Andrea were already inside the screened-in lanai.

Z was carrying two-year-old Sophia and helping Jessica who scowled at the assistance. Z did tend to hover over his pregnant wife.

Max, Doc Alastair, and their feisty submissive, Zuri, carried in a stack of pizza boxes.

"How's the moving going, Ghost?" Anne asked as he approached. The Mistress planted a kiss on his cheek.

"The movers unpacked the big stuff, but I still have boxes

piled everywhere." Ghost frowned at Ben. "I'm holding you responsible for the mess my life has become."

His friend, a retired Army Ranger, had the size and appearance of a pro wrestler...and was a world-renowned photographer. Not something most people would guess from seeing him. He scowled. "And exactly why am I to blame?"

"I was enjoying a well-deserved retirement when you talked me into helping you out as a Shadowlands security guard."

Ben snorted. "Colonel, you were bored out of your mind. Besides, if you'd been smart enough to stick to being a guard, you wouldn't have these problems."

"There you have it, Ghost," Cullen agreed. "We all know *someone* waggled a crop and a couple of masochists in front of you"—everyone looked at Z—"and lured you right into the dungeon."

Jessica giggled. "You sadists—so easy to entice."

Ghost laughed—and who wouldn't? Z's half-pint submissive was rounder than hell with the unborn baby and had the glow and assurance of a well-loved woman.

It was odd Valerie didn't have the same confidence. As a professor, she obviously knew her worth. She was an excellent lecturer, vibrant and interesting with a good understanding of her students.

Had the divorce sabotaged her self-assurance when it came to man-woman interactions?

As Sam sauntered through the gate, Ghost considered the growing crowd. "Am I having a party?"

They laughed.

"A housewarming one, yes, to celebrate your moving in so quickly." Z pulled out a chair and seated Jessica. "You're getting help with moving furniture, hanging paintings, and hauling boxes away. Also, Olivia needs to orient you to the security system here, since it's different from the one in the club."

Olivia gave him a cold nod.

"Good thing Wrecker didn't have the codes to the security system on this side," Nolan muttered.

After seeing the mess in the club's private rooms, Ghost was grateful for that small favor.

"Start thinking of what you need done." Cullen slapped his shoulder. "You got railroaded into being manager, and we appreciate you taking the job on. Don't even try fighting us; you're getting our help."

Ghost noted the determined expressions. "Be like trying to fight a Bradley tank. While on foot. And armed with a .22."

"Now you're getting the idea." Cullen's laugh boomed out.

Ghost grinned. "In that case, thank you all."

"Drinks are here!" Beth held open the gate as Nolan wheeled in a chest-sized cooler.

A second later, Linda and Natalia walked in.

Followed by Valerie.

The evening was looking up.

How did she affect him this way? She wore no makeup, made no effort to appear sexy, and yet she was. The way her streaky golden-brown hair gleamed in the sunlight brought back the memory of its silky weight. Her shorts hugged a soft ass designed for a man's hands—*his* hands—and her sleeveless shirt showcased full breasts that were—

Mind out of the gutter, soldier.

"Let me help you there." He took the paper sack from her and set it on a table.

"Happy Housewarming Day, Ghost." Linda started pulling paper plates out of the sack. "When we closed down the store, we dragged Valerie here with us."

A frown creased Valerie's forehead. "Um, I hope it's all right..."

He took her hand. "I'm very glad you came, Professor."

Her eyes were as deep a blue as he remembered. Simply lovely. When her lips tilted up, he couldn't help remembering how she'd responded to his hands, his mouth...

She flushed pink.

Although he released her, his smile and words might perhaps have been warmer than discretion called for, considering the speculative stares he was receiving.

Hell. He didn't give a damn, but Valerie might.

At a pat on his thigh, he looked down.

Sophia held up her arms. "Gose, up."

"My favorite bundle of trouble." Bending, he picked up the cutest two-year-old who ever walked the earth. She had Jessica's fluffy light hair, Z's gray eyes, and her very own dimples.

When the mini-Domme patted his cheek approvingly with her tiny hand, he grinned at the two Mistresses. "You two are going to have serious competition from the next generation."

Anne laughed...because everyone knew she was firmly under Sophia's thumb.

"Where are the rest of the munchkins?" he asked Anne and Ben, then glanced at Nolan and Beth.

"Our two have Boy Scout activities this evening," Nolan said, "so we're free to help."

"Wyatt's with the babysitter." Anne snorted. "Ben and I wouldn't get any work done otherwise."

"A shame. I could have played with the kids while everyone else worked," Ghost said. Best of all worlds.

"We have Sophia because we can't stay. A contractor's coming to the house in a bit," Jessica said apologetically, then pouted. "Z wouldn't let me lift anything, anyway."

"Good. I'd hate to have to hurt him for being a negligent Dom." Ghost received a scowl from Jessica and a quick grin from Z. "No, seriously. There are a lot of heavy boxes up there. I'm still not sure how I accumulated so much considering I divested myself of almost everything when I moved from Seattle."

"Speaking of Seattle..." Scowling, Max leaned against a table. "I'm still pissed-off I walked past you every weekend for a year before I finally realized I knew you from Chains."

It *had* been rather funny.

But Ghost had been content as a security guard and uninterested in being ousted from his *responsible-for-nothing* cave. "It's not my fault you're blind, detective."

"Gotta say, you sure didn't act like a Dom." Ben snorted. "You even sounded horrified I planned to actually go into the club rather than be a guard."

Ghost raised an eyebrow. "Ben, I didn't care if your vanilla ass got lured into the club. I was horrified you were planning to offer up your junk to the club's most sadistic Domme."

As Ben guffawed—and folded his hands over his groin—Anne snickered. "Why, what a lovely compliment, Colonel."

Grinning, Ghost rubbed his clean-shaven jaw and told Max, "Back in Seattle, I was still in service and flying in and out of the sandbox, so I had a full beard and long hair. I don't look the same now."

"No wonder," Max muttered.

Z frowned. "You weren't still a team operator, were you?"

Because combat was for the young. "No. Back when I joined Special Forces, I was honored to lead a team for far longer than is allowed nowadays before getting dumped behind a desk. But, even as a desk jockey, I went overseas to check things out, so I kept my beard."

He checked for Valerie and saw Linda had introduced her to Jessica—and all three appeared to be enjoying their conversation. Excellent.

"Ghost, I can't stay long either," Olivia said in her clipped British accent. "Could we do a quick security tour first?"

"Of course." Ghost considered her expression. He'd always considered her at least a friendly associate, but the last couple of times he'd seen her, she'd been quite cool. Damned if he knew why.

"Why are the two security systems different?" Ghost asked Z.

"The club's older system has been in place for years." Z said.

"When Sophia was born, an old friend who owns Demakis International Security installed one for the third floor and grounds as a baby present."

Jessica laughed. "So many people were interested in the system that Simon opened an office here and stole Olivia away from where she worked. This summer, her crew will upgrade the club's system to match this one."

"We do need to get going," Z said. "Thank you for moving in here, Finlay. I hope you enjoy the place; we had many happy times here."

Ghost believed it. The quarters felt as if they'd been filled with love. "I'm glad you found a house that suits your growing family."

Reluctantly, he set Sophia down.

Rather than letting Z pick her up, the toddler beamed and trotted over to pat Valerie's leg. "Hi."

Laughing, Valerie bent to shake her hand. "Hi to you."

"Hug." Sophia held her arms up in a demand no one in the world could possibly deny.

"Anytime you want, sweetie." Valerie picked her up and received a neck-squeezing hug with a big kiss on the cheek.

Anne, the sadistic mistress who still terrified Shadowlands submissives actually whined. "I didn't get a hug."

As the rest of the Masters teased Anne, Sophia babbled to Valerie about her day.

The professor seemed to understand every garbled word...and answered appropriately.

"Amazing." Jessica shook her head. "She's been going through a shy phase, especially with women. Are you wearing some child-attractant perfume, Valerie?"

Valerie touched foreheads with the little girl, making her break into peals of laughter, then smiled at Jessica. "For some reason, children seem to like me."

"Now, why would that be?" Z murmured and lifted an inquiring eyebrow at Ghost.

Ah, Z hadn't met her. Ghost lowered his voice. "She feels like sunshine and peace. Of course, children like her."

"Indeed." Z moved forward. "Sophia, we need to return home so you can show Galahad where his food is."

"Kitty," Sophia explained to Valerie.

"Yes, it's good to make sure kitties eat on time," Valerie agreed.

Z took his daughter, set her on his hip, and held his hand out to Valerie. "Valerie, I'm Zachary Grayson, Sophia's father. It's good to meet you."

She shook his hand. "And you."

Laughing, Max said, "What he's not saying, darlin', is he's the owner of the Shadowlands."

Valerie's eyes widened. "Oh. Well, you have a fine club and a wonderful daughter."

Z chuckled...and released her hand. "Thank you. I'm sure with Ghost in charge, the club will be even better soon."

Turning back to Ghost, Z rested a hand on his shoulder. "Thank you again for taking over management—and the quick move." He glanced at Valerie. "Very accurate assessment."

Ghost smiled at the psychologist's agreement—*sunshine and peace.*

As Z left with his family, Linda started introducing Valerie to people.

Ghost turned to Olivia and motioned toward the stairs. "Shall we?"

"Yes, let's get this over with."

Upstairs, she showed him the security panel, went through the codes, and displayed the log. "Recently, there have been a couple of alarms, although the police drive-bys showed nothing. Also, a security camera near the pool went offline. I'd like to see which camera is out and what needs to be replaced."

"Sounds good. I haven't had a chance to walk the grounds—perhaps you could point out the cameras as we go." Ghost sighed. His leg was swelling inside the prosthetic sleeve and starting to ache. Damn stairs.

After flowing around the inside of a screened enclosure, an artificial stream splashed into the swimming pool with the melodic sound of falling water. Filled with flowering shrubs and tropical plants, the setting was like a slice of paradise.

He held the door for Olivia, stepped inside after her, then stared down into the pool. Clothes and shoes lay at the bottom.

"It appears someone went skinny dipping and forgot to dress on the way out," Olivia scowled as she picked up pieces from a broken security camera. "Probably one of Wrecker's good buddies who didn't realize the security system would call the police."

"Seems likely." Unfortunately, the automatic pool cleaner was tangled in the mess. Ghost flipped off the switch to the robot. "Something else to do."

With a snort, Olivia motioned. "Get in and hand the stuff up to me."

"Thanks, no. I'll deal with it later."

She gave him a cold stare. "I've seen naked men before."

"I rather assumed that. I'm simply not—"

"Listen." She braced her legs and folded her arms across her chest. "If you have a problem with lesbians or female Dominants, your new job is going to be difficult. There are quite a few of us in the club."

For fuck's sake. He reined in his irritation. Just because he was achy and tired didn't give him license to be rude. "Why would you think I have a problem with lesbians?"

"I saw the way you looked at me when I was doing a scene. The way you shook your head in disgust."

He couldn't remember being disgusted with any of her scenes. "When exactly was this?"

"Last weekend—I was with Chelsey."

Ah, the scene in the dungeon. Hell of a leap she'd taken, though. "Olivia. I don't have a problem with lesbians or any of the LGBTQ+ community. Or dominant women. I shook my head because I've watched your scenes before, and the one with Chelsey lacked any energy whatsoever."

She flushed slightly. "Maybe. I suppose." Her gaze went to the pool, then she gave him another somewhat-less belligerent stare.

Fine. She apparently thought he was unwilling to bare his dick —to be vulnerable—to a lesbian or Domme.

"My flesh-and-blood junk can survive being exposed to a Mistress. However, my *metal* junk won't survive an immersion in water." He pulled up his pant leg far enough to expose the prosthesis.

The color rose and fell in her face. "Bloody hell." Swearing under her breath, she averted her face for a moment, then turned back with a rueful expression. "I'm sorry. I was out of line. Last weekend, Wrecker's buddies threw a lot of homophobic and other insults my way. I was overly sensitive—and jumped to the wrong conclusion with you. Then and now."

Here was the Olivia he'd grown to like. Honest. Blunt. Insightful and not sparing of herself.

The tightness in his jaw relaxed. Death had stolen friends from him often enough. It'd be a shame to lose one over a misunderstanding. "Considering the crap I heard being dished out, I'm not surprised you over-reacted."

After a second, he added mildly, "Or was some of your sensitivity because it's tough to scene after losing a regular partner?"

He remembered that raw feeling all too well.

Her scowl would've been intimidating...if he'd been submissive. "Maybe. Some."

He opened his mouth, and she cut him off. "No, I don't want to talk about it. Why people assume a person wants to share her woes just because she's female is bloody annoying. Or why it's assumed because I have tits, I'm naturally nurturing and should offer a shoulder to anyone who wants a good cry. Or I'm awesome with children because I have ovaries."

The rant was the last thing he'd expected from the normally controlled Domme.

He grinned. "Don't hold back. Tell me how you really feel."

For a moment, he thought she'd punch him—right into the pool—but after a second, she snorted. "It seems I let the pot simmer long enough to reach a boil. Sorry."

"Not a problem." Ghost motioned toward the house. "This isn't the time, but when you come back to replace the camera, I'd like your help in locating the rest of them. You can use the walk to educate me about assumptions."

She narrowed her eyes, evaluating him with her quite considerable skills. "You mean that, don't you."

"I do. I was Special Forces, surrounded by men. My knowledge of your problems isn't as good as it could be. If nothing else, help me for the sake of your less...forthright...sisters."

A corner of her mouth pulled up. "Fair enough. A lecture you will have."

A weaker man might quail.

He wasn't weak.

Or stupid, either. He'd wait a while before raising the topic of her love life again.

After Ghost disappeared with Olivia, Valerie watched the Shadowlands people make themselves at home as if they'd been here many times. But, of course, they had. The owner of the club had lived on the third floor.

Linda might have mentioned it was *Ghost's* housewarming she'd be crashing.

Honestly, her heart had almost stopped.

And not only was Ghost here, the place was filled with Dominants who radiated power like high-voltage lines. Here was the top of the Shadowlands hierarchy.

Yet everyone was so nice.

Such unique relationships, though.

Beth was kneeling beside her Master, who she openly called Master Nolan. The mean-looking, scarred-up Master had dropped a cushion onto the paving so his submissive wouldn't scrape her knees.

Andrea was helping Cullen serve the pizza—and Valerie knew enough Spanish to recognize the rude names she called him when he snuck a bite.

Mistress Anne bossed her giant submissive around but laughed when he pushed her into a chair.

Zuri was bouncy and fun, giggling when her two Masters yanked her down between them on the long patio swing.

Linda didn't defer to her rancher Master. However, when he snagged her with a long arm, pulled her against his side, and slapped her butt—hard, she simply melted into his side.

Valerie sighed. *Envious, much?*

Pushing the thought away, she sat at a table beside Natalia, the only other unattached submissive.

A minute later, Olivia and Ghost strolled out from a section of the grounds, chatting about needing more Mistresses since someone named Catherine had left.

After gazing longingly that way, Natalia rose and busied herself getting drinks for the new guests—a Hispanic-looking Dom and his black-haired, blue-eyed submissive accompanied by a gorgeous German shepherd.

Valerie bit her lip as Natalia kept glancing at Ghost and Olivia after they joined Linda and Sam.

Natalia and...Ghost? On Valerie's first night in the club, Natalia mentioned a relationship not working. Could she have been Ghost's submissive?

The young woman couldn't be even thirty. A bitter taste

invaded Valerie's mouth. But really, why was she surprised he'd go for a much younger woman? Look at Barry and *his* slaves.

Don't be judgy, Valerie. Natalia was a sweetheart. Any guy would want her, no matter how much older he was.

Valerie sighed. The urge to order Ghost to choose a woman closer to his own age was both shallow and pitiful.

Shaking her head, she rose. "Natalia, I can get the drinks if you want to talk with Ghost."

Natalia gave her a funny glance. "Why do I need to talk to Ghost? I mean I'm here to help, but..."

"Ah..." Valerie frowned. She'd misstepped, hadn't she? "You...I saw you watching him, and I guess I misunderstood."

Natalia turned toward Ghost and Olivia, and the longing look crossed her face again. She saw Valerie watching, blinked, then sputtered. "Oh, *noooo*, do I have hearts in my eyes? I'm so *stupid*." She banged her head on Valerie's arm.

Valerie rubbed the young woman's shoulder. "No, c'mon, he's a good guy. It'll be all right."

"No, it won't," Natalia whispered. "It's not Ghost I want. It's the heartless Brit."

The Brit. "Olivia? Oh. *Oh*." Valerie slung an arm around Natalia's shoulders. "Well, you might be stupid, but I think I'm stupider. Is that a word? That's a word, right?"

They started giggling themselves...stupid...and now everyone was watching, which made it worse.

Valerie tried to hold it in, letting out tiny hiccups of laughter. Natalia had her hands plastered over her own mouth, and they caught each other's eyes and exploded again.

"M-maybe we should—" Valerie waved her hand toward the parking lot. Turning, she bumped right into a hard chest.

Natalia's giggles grew louder.

"Seems like you keep running into me, Professor," a guttural voice whispered in her ear. "Now you caught me, what shall we do?"

Heat streaked through her, melting her laughter into pure arousal. Into longing. And she lifted her head. "I..."

Firm fingers closed on her chin, and he held her still enough to plant a kiss on her lips. A perfect kiss—not hard, not soft—just right.

"And there's how you silence a submissive, ladies and gentlemen," Cullen announced to a wave of cheering.

Oh...great. Talk about being the center of attention.

Ghost tucked an arm around her, turning to face the group. "Laugh away, fools. When you've finished eating, I intend to put you all to work."

His attempted diversion got a chorus of "what do you need done?" but didn't stop any of the interested and speculative glances.

The sound of Natalia's soft giggles had set up an ache in Olivia's chest and brought back way too many memories.

The first time they met, the subbie had been suffering from subdrop because a Domme had abandoned her after an intense scene. Bad form. Unless a submissive didn't need help after a scene or other arrangements were made, a Top was responsible for aftercare.

But Olivia had quite enjoyed providing the shaken submissive with the cuddles and soothing the other Domme had neglected.

She'd left it at that, though. Until the club's cops-and-robbers theme night where Olivia had been dressed as an English bobby, and shy Natalia had stolen a bag of gold coins off her belt. The little subbie had fled, giggling so hard it was a wonder she could run.

Who could resist those giggles?

That had been the beginning.

Olivia ran her fingers through her short hair and sighed. Every year it grew more difficult to be around her fellow Masters and

Mistresses. So many of them had found wonderful, satisfying relationships and were making families.

She'd thought she had something with Natalia, but, wrong once again. The proof had been unmistakable—her beloved submissive had cheated on her.

Bloody hell, why? Olivia had never been unfaithful in her whole life. Why couldn't she expect the same?

Her throat closed, hurting. Couldn't her lovers at least break up with her first before jumping into bed with other women?

She swallowed against the lump and turned her gaze to Ghost and the blonde he'd kissed. The expression on the woman's face was charming, really.

Olivia studied the woman with a Mistress's eye. A year ago— before Natalia—she'd have been interested in Valerie herself. The submissive was comfortable with everyone from Sophia to Master Sam. Intelligent. Soft-spoken with an incredibly sexy voice. She had a lovely self-confidence...right up until Ghost spoke to her.

How could a Dominant resist such endearing insecurity? The Colonel certainly couldn't.

Because Dominants wanted to help.

Olivia had with Natalia, who wasn't worried about being attractive but was simply timid when it came to strangers. They'd been working on her confidence. She wasn't shy with friends—or eventually with Olivia.

Nats always woke up first, and when Olivia would grumble and start to move, the little subbie would pounce on her like a puppy.

Mornings were a lot colder these days.

Ah, well. Olivia felt a bittersweet longing as she watched Ghost and Valerie in the beginning of a D/s dance. They looked good together, and even if her heart ached, Olivia hoped his woman would be more loyal than hers had been.

Because when love went away, pain was all that was left.

The evening had arrived, and people were heading home.

After seeing Max, Alastair, and the irrepressible Zuri off, Ghost walked through his new quarters. The enthusiastic volunteers had accomplished an amazing amount of work, and the rooms had become homelike. Furniture was in place, paintings hung on the walls, his TV and stereo system were set up.

Blackmore's Night drifted through the room, adding a Celtic feel.

His bed was assembled and even made. Towels hung neatly on the bathroom racks.

"More livable now, isn't it?" Sam flattened a final box and called to Linda, "Time to head out, missy. There's stock to feed."

Valerie beside her, Linda emerged from the kitchen and smiled at Ghost. "Everything is put away in here, but it'll probably take you a few days to orient yourself."

"Bless you both. I am clueless when it comes to kitchens." He shook his head. "My wife always unpacked that room after the one time I tried, and she ended up rearranging everything."

Linda motioned toward Valerie. "She directed. I followed orders."

Blue eyes alight, Valerie laughed. "It was fun. I had kitchen unpacking down to a science before I reached my teens. I even created my own protocol with rules like: pots and pans live by the stove."

Created, hmm? He eyed her. "Your mother didn't teach you?"

Her expression darkened, then the cloud blew away, and she shrugged. "No, she had work. Since it usually took several days to hire a housekeeper, unpacking was my job."

As a child?

She'd learned to cook from the housekeepers...who'd also treated her illnesses. Had her parents been involved in her life at all? "Your experience is to my benefit. Thank you."

After seeing Linda and Sam out the door, Ghost stopped Valerie from following by curling his hand around her arm. "If you have a few minutes, I'd like to talk to you about our scene at the club. I would have called before, but I don't have your phone number."

She hesitated. "I... Um, of course."

He ran a finger down her cheek. "It's not an exam, Professor. There are no right or wrong answers."

With a low laugh, she relaxed. "In that case, ask away."

Better. Now to ease into what he wanted to know... "First, at lunch, you mentioned you had an interest and maybe a need for learning self-defense."

"Well, yes."

"If you don't mind private lessons, I can show you the basics."

"Really?" Her blue eyes lit. "I'd love it."

"We'll tackle the essentials: how to break free, how and where to strike. It won't make you a contender in martial arts, of course. But I'd like to improve your chances of getting to safety."

The thought of her in danger was one he simply couldn't tolerate.

When she nodded, he smiled. "Good." He dug into his pocket and pulled out one of his cards. "Here's my number. Give me a call, and we'll work out times."

She was smiling. "I will. Thank you."

Now to move into trickier territory.

She'd said she didn't want to be involved with anyone. However, as an experienced Dom, he could read body language and knew she also felt the chemistry between them.

So...he'd invite her to explore more while leaving her room to retreat if she needed.

"You have a beautiful place here," she murmured. "Beth showed me some of the hidden spots—she calls them garden rooms."

He chuckled. She'd given him an excellent opening. "There are many things about this place that aren't immediately noticeable." Arm around her waist, he leaned on the railing over the patio and pointed down. "Like the steel eyebolts in the lanai posts and beams."

She leaned forward. "There are a lot of them. Did Jessica have a fondness for hanging plants?"

A laugh escaped him. "No, they're for dangling submissives. The eyebolts are anchors for restraints."

Oh gods. Valerie's eyes widened. Who would have thought? Master Z would restrain Jessica right out there on the patio? She swallowed hard. "I suppose someone who owns a BDSM club would be interested in bondage."

"No question about it. Then again, a lot of people enjoy bondage." Finn tugged on her hair. "How about you? Did you enjoy being strapped down?"

Aaand as if he'd flipped a switch, she was far too aware of the rock-hard arm around her waist. Of his fresh aquatic-citrus scent that made her want to burrow her face against his neck and sniff.

No. Remember, Valerie, no involvement. Then again, she'd decided simple hookups would be all right.

What would this Shadowlands Master do if she admitted she'd loved being tied down?

Under the impact of his keen green eyes, hers dropped. "I did. Yes."

"Sweetheart, look at me."

She lifted her gaze.

He wasn't smiling, but a crease appeared in his cheek. "Everything we did—including my restraining you—was fun. Isn't enjoyment the point?"

It was, and she should get over feeling wrong about having sexual feelings. Blame it on her upbringing. Too many men in both American and Arabic cultures pushed their beliefs that "good" women shouldn't like sex.

But she was old enough and smart enough to see past those biases. To identify—if not conquer—her insecurities.

Really, she'd been fine when she and Barry visited the BDSM group parties. Her loss of confidence had started when he wanted a slave. When he said she wasn't meeting his needs. Then came Alisha and Kahlua with their constant put-downs—and Barry's delegating her to only being his housemaid and financial support.

Her mouth firmed. It was going to take work, but in time, she'd get past her lack of confidence. After all, she'd managed to overcome the feeling of being worthless instilled by her parents. At least until this past year.

"You're right." She pulled in a determined breath. "In fact, I hope you'll feel like doing it again. Doing more." Her words were firm, although inside, she was shaking. What if he—

"Now, I was hoping you'd say that. Especially since I saw—and approved—your application for membership in the Shadowlands." He pulled her closer and kissed her temple. "I won't ask you to stay tonight since you don't know me well enough. But Friday or Saturday, I'd like to see you at the club. We'll find out what else you're interested in."

She stared down at the eyebolts on the post and felt the quiver of excitement. It was why she'd joined the club, right?

But...no relationship. She hesitated. *Be clear so you don't lead someone on.* "I want to play, but, Finn, I haven't changed my mind about...anything more."

"I understand, pet." He pulled the scrunchie out of her hair and the strands fell to touch her shoulders. He combed his fingers through, then tugged, tilting her head back. "What day?"

"Saturday. I'll be there Saturday."

CHAPTER ELEVEN

Arriving at the Shadowlands shortly before opening, Zachary stopped in the entry to evaluate the guard behind the desk.

Dressed in a dark red, button-up shirt and black jeans, he had short dark hair with a mustache and trimmed beard scruff. Intelligence and determination gleamed in his brown eyes.

Very good.

"Welcome to the Shadowlands." The guard smiled. "I'm new so I don't recognize everyone yet. Are you a member?"

Behind Zachary, Finlay entered, obviously catching the question. He laughed. "In a manner of speaking, he is. He owns the place. "Master Z, this is Fyodor Koslov, who goes by Koslov. He'll be here most weekends."

The guard rose. "Sir."

Zachary reached across the desk. "It's good to meet you, Koslov."

As they shook hands, Zachary noted the firm grip. The locations of calluses on the hand implied martial arts...and guitar. The posture suggested military.

As Finlay stayed to talk to the guard, Zachary headed into the club, pleased with not only the guard, but the manager, as well.

The Colonel was an excellent judge of character.

When Jessica arrived a couple of hours later, he took her on a walk through the club. Zachary had already made the rounds once, talked with the members, and assessed the changes in the atmosphere. It'd been difficult to rein in his temper at the damage done to the Shadowlands community.

But Jessica soothed his ire as only she could do. Was there anyone more beautiful than his wonderfully pregnant submissive?

"What did Nolan's babysitter say about adding Sophia to her charges tonight?" Zachary asked. Their new home was not far from Beth and Nolan's, so Jessica had dropped Sophia off there and caught a ride with them.

"Like Beth said, she loves children and was disappointed Sophia was sound asleep. I warned her Grant and Connor would probably sneak out of bed to try to play with our girl."

Nolan and Beth's boys adored Sophia.

"They'll be delighted when you give them a new baby to dote on." Smiling, Zachary put his hand on Jessica's rotund belly, enjoying the return kick from their unborn child. This time, he hadn't coerced the obstetrician to learn its gender.

Jessica patted his hand. "Another month to go."

"Jessica, you're back. Finally!" The squeal of joy came from a submissive with green-streaked brunette hair. Previously a trainee, Tabitha had dropped out after discovering she didn't enjoy a high level of submission.

After a glance at Zachary for permission, Tabitha gave Jessica a warm hug. "Look how pregnant you are!"

Behind the submissive, a lanky Dom in shiny black leather shifted impatiently.

Releasing Jessica, Tabitha motioned to the Dom. "Master Z, this is Dogget who joined about a month ago. Dogget, Master Z owns the Shadowlands."

Dogget's expression closed.

"How are you, Dogget?" When Zachary shook his hand, the

man's resentment was quite apparent. He was likely a friend of Scott Hicks.

His animosity would undoubtedly increase if his membership fee was one of Hicks' unauthorized discounts. The reduced dues and free memberships were for people providing services. No service, no discount.

Well, he'd let Finlay handle the problem children. The Colonel was well up to the task.

At eleven, Ghost heard a soft chime of three notes over the intercom system—the Shadowlands' heads-up to gather for announcements. Of course, Z had already prepped everyone with an advance email.

Scenes ended, and members congregated on one side of the bar.

"People." In his usual black silk shirt and black pants, Z stood by the bar. "As you can see, Jessica and I are back from Europe. Finally. If you hadn't heard, my mother broke her leg while in France. Jessica and I went over to care for her—and then she contracted pneumonia, so our stay was longer than anticipated."

"Poor Jessica," someone behind Ghost muttered and added, "I've met Madeline Grayson. She's scarier than Master Sam."

Z continued, "I wasn't able to keep up with what was happening here in the Shadowlands. I want to thank you for your patience—and promise we'll try to get things back to normal."

The pleased murmur was punctuated by a few disgruntled snorts.

Off to one side, a man grumbled, "What the fuck is he talking about? Shit's been good."

"To that end"—Z's voice grew louder—"I have asked Ghost to take over as manager, effective immediately."

Rather than the stunned silence Ghost had anticipated, a hell of a lot of people cheered, and he was slapped on the back enough times to please a damn masochist.

The enthusiasm felt good.

Z motioned for him to come forward. Didn't it figure the man would make a production of this?

No problem, though. After two decades of army life, Ghost was an old hand at enduring pomp and circumstance.

With a hand on his shoulder, Z said, "In case you haven't met him, Ghost is one of our Masters, although he apparently dislikes the title."

Jessica snickered and said loudly, "We decided to call him Colonel, instead."

Laughter ran through the crowd along with agreement. He'd never escape the title now.

The little brat.

He had a feeling Valerie had a bit of brat in her, too. And how fun would that be?

Focus, Blackwood. "People, it's an honor to be chosen for this position. I'll do my best for you—and I ask that you come to me if there are any problems or concerns."

When Z took a step back, Ghost continued, "There will be some changes coming. For one, dungeon monitoring will return to being done by the Masters for now rather than hired personnel."

The announcement collected another cheer. He wasn't the only person to notice that the hired DMs had been a waste of space.

"The hired waitstaff is also gone. Once again, submissives who want to serve drinks can sign up for a shift at the bar and receive a discount on their membership fees accordingly."

More happy sounds and not merely for the cut in dues. Waiting tables was an easy way to meet people.

"Since we need more DMs than we have Masters, in April, we'll offer training classes to expand the DM pool. As you know, the only way to get discounted membership fees is to be of service to the club—and this is one way. Applications and information about the requirements will be at the bar."

There were interested nods. *Good.*

Time to give Wrecker's cohorts a warning. "Anyone who's gotten a discount recently, I'll be in touch to see what service you plan to provide."

He heard Z's low chuckle. Because there were several Doms with sour expressions, giving *what-the-fuck* growls. Wrecker's friends.

"My turn," Z murmured, then addressed the members. "People. I created the Shadowlands to give us all a safe and nurturing community in which to enjoy the lifestyle. A place to learn and share, where safe, sane, and consensual—or risk-awareness —applies."

Unlike Ghost's rasp, Z's voice was resonant and compelling. "Here is where tolerance is practiced. We enjoy different kinks— as well as different lifestyles, relationship dynamics, sexual preferences, identities, and backgrounds. I want to be clear: intolerance is a crash-and-burn offense in this club, right along with not obtaining consent before touching or playing. So, to all of us...let's be mindful and respectful."

Ghost let Z's polite warning percolate through the membership before grinning and adding his own growled threat, "Or I'll be pulling you aside for a polite...*chat.*"

Yep, from the laughter, his timing was good.

Olivia gave him a smile and a nod, as did Alastair who stood with Max near the center. Andrea gave him a thumbs-up.

The bigots hadn't ruled for long. Now it was time to repair the fractures and restore the community spirit.

CHAPTER TWELVE

Valerie had never started an evening so late in her whole life. But Linda had said Ghost, as manager, would be occupied during the busiest hours—and likely to be free after midnight.

Even better, Barry probably wouldn't be here this late. Not that she'd let him drive her away if he was, but since construction crews started early, he rarely stayed up late.

Smiling, she looked around. The atmosphere in the club felt different this Saturday night.

To begin with, rather than a surly, disheveled mess, the guard at the door had been welcoming and efficient.

And she was an actual member now, too.

Before coming, she'd read the club emails and watched the video of Master Z and Ghost from last night where they'd spoken of the change of management.

She'd watched it a second time because...Ghost.

Why, oh why, did she have to lust after him? Especially now he was manager. For submissives, a man in power was a lure all its own, even without adding in his hard body and firm jaw. And air of command.

She sighed. Would he even remember she was coming to the club tonight?

Maybe. After all, he'd probably seen her name on the orientation class signup.

It'd been an interesting two hours, filled with information about safety, proper behavior, and the various rules and traditions. Master Jake had been very thorough.

Pausing, she studied the room, spotting quite a few Dominants wearing a Master's gold bands.

In a dungeon monitor vest, Olivia nodded at Valerie.

Farther down the room at a St. Andrew's cross, Mistress Anne was laying out toys from her bag. Off to one side, Ben saw Valerie and winked at her.

She smiled back and kept smiling. It was so different this time. Knowing who the people were helped her relax and be comfortable. Moving so often as a child had taught her how to be comfortable with strangers and turn them into friends if provided the opportunity. Linda had given her that chance. *Thank you, Linda*.

She noticed a higher percentage of people her age here tonight. So wonderful. A few were even older, like a white-haired man who must be in his seventies—with his equally senior wife. And, wow, the Dom was a wizard with a soft-stranded flogger.

After a minute, she recognized the music was from Razed in Black—*Master*—and quite a few of the people with impact toys were using the driving beat.

In a roped-off area, a submissive was swaying his hips to the rhythm very enthusiastically. Losing patience with hitting a moving target, his Top delivered a fast flurry of cane strikes across the sub's well-padded ass.

When the submissive squeaked and held still, Valerie—and several other onlookers—had to muffle their laughter.

Then a spate of ugly words caught her attention.

"Look, Piers, it's a brown subbie, all alone with no lezzie lover."

"Aww, maybe she needs some dick to bring her back to the right side."

Valerie turned.

Natalia?

Two obnoxious Doms had cornered the slender Hispanic woman.

The flabby blond man yanked on the submissive's dark hair, as the big muscular ginger crowded her on her other side.

"Go away, Uttley," Natalia said to the blond. "You, too, Piers. Or I'll call for a DM." The words were good, but the shakiness in Natalia's voice was like raw meat to starving dogs.

"Shit, lezzie, you know you want this." The ginger-haired man ran the back of his hand down her breast. "Want some man-meat."

"Leave her alone." Valerie spoke in the tone she'd used with her teenagers when they'd exceeded her tolerance. "Back off."

Both men froze.

Turning, they saw her bare feet, marking her as submissive. Their expressions turned mean.

"Bitch, you're my mom's age." The muscular Dom named Piers shot her the finger. "Should you even be here?"

The remark about her age brought the familiar wave of doubt, but she pushed past it. Reaching between the two, she grabbed Natalia's arm and pulled her close.

Both men moved in, looming over Valerie and—

"Is there a problem here?" Ghost's rough, deep voice made the pushy bastards jump and spin.

"Nah, just talkin'." Blond Uttley edged back a step.

The muscle-bound redhead crossed his arms over his big chest, flexing his biceps. "None of your business anyways."

"Since he's the manager, it is," Valerie said calmly and turned to Ghost. "These two cornered Natalia." She pointed to Uttley.

"He pulled her hair. After she told them to go away or she'd call a DM, the other one touched her breast. They also said, and I'm quoting"—Valerie thanked her excellent memory— " *'Look, it's a brown subbie, all alone with no lezzie lover. And aww, maybe she needs some dick to bring her back to the right side.'* "

Ghost's face held as much softness as a stone wall. "Thank you. I appreciate the information." He smiled at Natalia, then said to Valerie, "Please stay with her while I speak with the men."

"Of course."

Ghost turned to the jerks. "Let's chat in the entry where it's calmer."

"Yeah, no," Uttley spat. "Get 'im, Piers."

Even as terror froze Valerie, Piers lunged forward, swinging at Ghost.

Ghost blocked and delivered one, then another punch to the solar plexus. With a gut-wrenching sound, Piers dropped to his knees.

"Fuck. Shit." Expression contorted with pain, Piers was folded in half, even as Ghost pulled him back up.

He tried to yank away.

"Don't fuck with a sadist, boy," Ghost growled.

"You asshole." Uttley moved forward.

Letting go of Natalia, Valerie sucked in a breath and lifted her fists.

And someone slapped a big hand on Uttley's shoulder, yanking him to a stop.

Valerie blinked at the size of the new arrival. He was as big as Cullen with shoulder-length white-blond hair.

"Thank you, Saxon," Ghost said quietly to the blond. "Escort him out, please."

"Aye, aye." Saxon turned an icy cold blue gaze on Uttley. "Let's go."

Smoothly, quietly, the two *effing* jerks were herded to the front and out the door. Piers would have fallen if Ghost hadn't kept him moving forward.

The Colonel was scary.

Valerie pulled in a long breath, then smiled at Natalia. "Well, they handled the creepers quite efficiently, didn't they?"

Natalia stared at her.

"Easy, honey." Valerie put an arm around the young woman and could feel her shake. "It's over. I don't think those guys will be allowed back in. Let's go sit somewhere."

As she guided Natalia toward the quieter area in the back, two women hurried up.

Valerie recognized the strawberry blonde with blue and green streaks in her hair as the submissive Linda had pointed out. Gabi, the one who liked to sass her Dom.

Carrying a tray with drinks, the other was slender and black-haired with startlingly blue eyes.

Wait, she'd been at Ghost's housewarming. She'd been with the very muscular Hispanic Master. And had the sweetest big dog. Ari.

Wasn't it embarrassing to remember pet names better than people names?

"Hey, you two." Gabi took Natalia's hand. "Josie sent me and Kim over as comfort crew. Let's find a spot to recover."

So, Kim was the black-haired one. She led the way toward the quieter back of the room where tall containers of plants created a secluded sitting area.

Gabi plunked down in a chair.

Since Natalia had a death grip on her hand, Valerie seated them both on a couch.

"Valerie, in case you don't remember everyone from the housewarming, I'm Kim and she's Gabi." Kim handed out drinks. "Josie said you'd probably prefer non-alcoholic."

"She's an amazing bartender, isn't she?" Valerie took a sip of the orange and cranberry juice mix. The soda water had added a refreshing fizz.

"Me, I'm ready for alcohol most definitely." Natalia took several hefty gulps before letting go of Valerie. "I'm such a clinging vine. Thank you for the rescue."

"You stood up for yourself; you were simply outnumbered." Valerie patted her hand. "And we were both outweighed. It's good Ghost showed up."

"They're all watching for this kind of bullshit. I bet Ghost is delighted he has the authority to deal with it now." Gabi grinned. Adorable baby bat tattoos on her upper arms went well with her slinky black top and shorts. "He sure has an effective punch. Did you see the way Piers went down?"

Kim shook her head. "For a nice social worker, you sure have a brutal side. I like how quietly he and Saxon escorted the creeps out."

Valerie shook her head. "I don't think I'd argue with either Ghost or the huge blond."

Gabi laughed. "Saxon's mama must have known he'd grow up to resemble a Viking warrior."

Natalia nodded, then pulled in a breath and gave Kim a some-what wavery smile. "So how was Cuba? Master Raoul was designing some fancy bridge in Havana, right?"

"It's so beautiful there." Kim's eyes turned dreamy. "Only I got carried away and spent so much money on souvenirs that Master started cursing...in Spanish, which is a really bad sign."

Her happy expression showed she hadn't fallen into too much trouble.

"I want to be a tourist," Gabi whined. "How'd I end up with a lawyer who only travels to the courthouse and back?"

"*Neener-neener*, my Master's better than yours," Kim sing-songed. Her smug expression spoke of long friendship. After snickering at Gabi's muttered, "Is not," she turned to Natalia.

"When I left, you were with Mistress Olivia, but she would never let you wander around alone. Are you..."

When Natalia's eyes filled with tears, Kim faltered.

"She broke up with me," Natalia whispered.

Gabi frowned. "That's what I heard, but I'm still surprised. From the outside, you two looked really good together." The question of what had happened hung in the air.

When Natalia slumped, Valerie wrapped an arm around her. The young woman couldn't be more than a few years older than her daughter.

"I don't know why Olivia... I thought we were happy, that she was happy." Natalia's breathing hitched, and a tear spilled over. "I don't know what I *did*."

Oh, now that didn't sound right.

Gabi rose and brought back tissues from one of the service stands located throughout the club.

Natalia wiped her face and pulled in another breath. "Everything was fine, and then one day, she came home, and I had supper ready since it was my day, and she stared at me, all cold and hard, and told me to pack my stuff and get out. It was over, and she was done. While I was asking her why, begging her to tell me what was wrong, she walked out. I waited and waited, but she didn't come back, so I moved my stuff out. She doesn't even talk to me now."

"For heaven's sake," Kim murmured. "I always thought Olivia was the reasonable one of the Dominants."

Gabi frowned. "This doesn't sound like an *I'm-bored-and-over-it* breakup. Her rant sounds more like a *you-hurt-me-and-I'm-furious* one."

"Hmm." Valerie's own breakup hadn't been sudden. Despite her dislike of quarreling, she *had* at least let Barry know she was unhappy. He'd been surprised about the divorce, but it hadn't come out of the blue. "She sounds as if something unexpected set her off."

"B-but I'd never hurt her." Natalia cried silently, tears streaking her face. "I wouldn't. Couldn't."

It was perfectly clear she still loved the Domme.

"You deserve an explanation, at the very least." Gabi tapped her finger on her leg. "I know all that authority is difficult to confront..."

"Not difficult for you, maybe." Kim snorted. "The rest of us, yes."

Gabi wrinkled her nose at her friend and continued, "The Mistress isn't being fair."

"But she won't talk to me."

The blunt statement silenced them all.

What could they do to get Natalia an answer? To get Olivia to speak to her?

Would Ghost know? He certainly had experience in this stuff. Although, relationship problems were probably not within his managerial duties. Still, Olivia was one of the club's big shots. A Mistress. "You might..." Valerie bit her lip as she tried to think of the ramifications.

"Might what?" Gabi encouraged.

"Might tackle Olivia here at the club in front of the other Masters and Mistresses—especially Ghost."

The three women stared wide-eyed at Valerie.

"Wait, no, I don't mean physically tackle, right?" Valerie waved her hand in the air. "I mean *verbally confront* Olivia."

The three were still staring at her.

"Bad idea, huh?"

"Actually, no. Although the vision of Natalia actually wrestling the Mistress to the ground was priceless." Gabi grinned. "But verbally...yes. Do it in front of Master Z, too."

Kim snorted a laugh. "God, yes. Seriously, do it. If she doesn't talk to you right away, Master Z or Ghost will have a *chat* with her. I don't know the Colonel very well, but something tells me he might be as meddlesome as Master Z."

Natalia's eyes were wide. "Are you all crazy?"

"No, not at all." Kim tapped her chin, calculating. "When there's a group of them at the bar—especially Ghost and Master Z—walk up and talk to her. Make your voice loud enough that others can hear. You won't have to shout. The Masters are all nosy, I swear."

"I..." Natalia's brown eyes showed a hint of hope. "I might. Maybe. I'll think about it. She's not here right now, anyway."

As Gabi turned the conversation to something mundane, Valerie heard a voice she'd been listening for. The raw, deep voice of Ghost.

"...how to add an extra kick to impact play? Certainly. Makes it more fun," he was saying from the closest scene area.

She moved to her left, and yes, there he was, talking to a younger Dom who held a flogger. A female submissive was tied to a St. Andrew's cross. After Ghost talked to her for a minute, the woman nodded.

Getting consent?

He motioned to the other Dom, who started flogging the woman in an unchanging pattern up and down her back and ass.

Then Ghost took the flogger and...Valerie's eyes widened as the pattern disappeared. The flogging was still rhythmic, but the intensity varied, lighter here and there. A big whap on the ass sent the submissive up on her tiptoes. Harder, harder, and back to a light rhythm. Then he stopped and rubbed the reddened areas and scratched his fingers down her back. He resumed the flogging for a while, then sprayed her with something that made her scream.

Both Doms grinned.

Valerie swallowed hard, feeling the prickle of arousal deep inside. How could it be so sexy that he liked to hear someone scream?

Ghost picked up a cane, using it on the submissive's thighs, her ass, and *dear gods,* ran sandpaper over the marks before starting again.

The bottom was moving, trying to escape even while making needy sounds.

"...him work, too," Gabi was saying.

Valerie startled, realizing she'd totally lost track of where she was. "Um, what?"

Gabi grinned. "I love watching the Colonel work. He's really good."

"Definitely has a sadistic edge to his play, though," Kim noted as Ghost lifted something resembling a tiny pizza cutter with spikes on the wheel.

When he started running it over the submissive's back, her voice rose higher.

Valerie swallowed, appalled at what he was doing...and even more appalled at the way her own skin grew sensitive.

And dammit, she was definitely damp between the legs.

Smiling, Ghost clapped the Dom on the shoulder and turned.

His eyes met Valerie's.

Caught. Totally caught staring at him.

His gaze swept over her, and one corner of his mouth turned up.

Anticipation shivered over her skin as he headed straight for their group.

Stepping into the sitting area, he was totally at ease. "Ladies. Might I steal Valerie away?" He caught sight of Natalia who was wiping her cheeks, and his dark brows came together. "Natalia, is—"

Natalia held up her hands, palms out. "No, no, I'm fine. Just talking. That's all. Go, Valerie. She's coming, Sir."

"What?" Valerie widened her eyes. "You're tossing me under the bus?"

"No, wait." Natalia looked horrified. "No, I didn't mean—"

"Kidding." Laughing, Valerie nudged her shoulder. "It's fine. We'd planned to talk tonight."

"Oh." Natalia let out a long, relieved sigh while the other two women snickered. "Okay. Good."

"It's late, and we're all leaving in a few minutes anyway. Marcus and Raoul should be finished with their dungeon monitor duties, and we'll walk Natalia out," Gabi said. "See you next time, Valerie."

"Drive carefully." Taking Ghost's outstretched hand, Valerie let him pull her to her feet...and tried to ignore her shiver at his strength. He kept her hand in his as he led her away from the group.

"Is Natalia all right?" he asked quietly when they were out of hearing.

"The tears weren't from being picked on by the Doms. And... it's not my story to tell. Sorry."

After a moment, he nodded. "Fair enough. I'll keep an eye out for her."

Of course, he would. Because that was who he was. "Thank you."

"I'll keep an eye on you, for entirely different reasons." Ghost ran a finger down her cheek. "Want to play?"

His light touch set off fireworks inside her.

"I...I didn't think you'd be able to." Or would still want to. "Aren't you supposed to be on duty as manager?" Hope rose inside her.

"I am, but I joined the club to enjoy the lifestyle. There are only a few people left, and Holt and Jake are comfortable closing up." He smiled. "Holt likes to stay so he and Josie can go home together. So, I'm off duty."

Valerie swallowed, her mouth suddenly dry. "Well, if you want..."

"Yes, Professor. I definitely want." He kissed her fingertips, then his assessing gaze swept over her. Slowly. "Ready to explore more?"

Uh-oh. The words sounded like a Dom who was also a sadist. Barry hadn't been interested in pushing her. But the burbling heat in her veins said she wanted to try. Except...he'd hurt that woman and enjoyed it. "Yes?"

Stopping in a quiet spot, he chuckled. "The certainty in your response is lacking, pet."

His certainty wasn't. "Well..."

"Tonight, I'd like to stay down here so I can secure you better and use some different implements, not just my hand. Will you be comfortable with being more public and having your arms restrained?"

She'd seen others stripped and restrained. Not only young slender bodies, but every size and shape and age. It was time to let go of her insecurity.

"If you ignore my blushes, I'd like to try it."

He moved close enough she had to tilt her head back. "I like seeing you blush, Valerie, and more.... I want to see your skin turning red, your eyes wide, maybe even a few tears and whimpers. Begging to come, mmmph, that, too."

So much pain? The idea was frightening, yet her insides melted into a puddle of need. "I..."

He ran his hands up and down her arms, standing so close she could feel his body's heat. "One more time, I need to ask if anything in your past would cause you distress if you're restrained, hurt, or touched intimately."

The intent look in his eyes was careful. His jaw showed a taut line of muscle.

"No, nothing." She touched his cheek. "Really, Ghost."

"All right." He shook his head as if throwing off the tension.

"You really do worry a lot."

He stilled, then a faint smile lifted his lips. "Noticed, did you?"

Rather than answer, she tilted her head.

He bent and kissed her lightly, then with a hum, returned to plunge and plunder, demanding a response.

Even as she melted against him, her body craved more.

He lifted his head. "This is also the time to ask if you'll stay with me after the scene. In my bed"—his hand covered her breast, sending shivers of need through her—"with all that implies."

Sex was what he meant. She licked her lips. "Yes. I'd like that." After a second, she frowned. "You wanted to give me lots of warning?"

He chuckled. "Simply, I wanted your consent while your head is clear. Because I intend to fuzz it up."

To...what?

"Come, let's begin." He led her to roped-off scene area with an interesting stand she hadn't seen before. The man-sized cross wasn't completely vertical but tipped slightly backward. A metal ring around the bottom stabilized the stand.

"Where did it come from?"

"Master Z ordered custom furniture, and it was finally delivered. This is perfect for what I want to do to you tonight." He positioned her at the foot of the cross. "It'll support a bit of your weight, while keeping you at a nice angle for a flogger."

Her mouth went dry. "Oh, well, it's good I'll be positioned right for your convenience."

His laugh made her knees weak.

Slowly, he drew one finger down her cheek. "I know you better this time, sweetheart. I won't go past what you can take—and you also have a safeword."

His hand was warm as he cupped her cheek. "I'll check in with you to make sure we're on the same page."

"Okay." She pulled in a breath. Was she really going to do this? Yes, yes, she was. "Okay.

"Very good." His gaze swept over her. "You're stunning in that corset, but take it off now, please."

But, but, but...

He smiled. And waited.

Oh gods. At least they were near the quietest area of the club. And the rationale didn't relieve her embarrassment one bit as she unhooked the corset. With lace on the top straps and extending down into a thigh-length skirt, it made her feel very feminine.

Biting her lip, she removed...everything, and now, she felt very, very naked.

At his leisurely perusal, she grew all too aware of everywhere that sagged or dimpled where it used to be firm.

"You're so pretty." His growl of appreciation let her breathe again.

He pulled a wide rolling table closer and set out two floggers and a cane. "Come over here, please."

She silently joined him, feeling every single waft of air on her bare skin.

"These are what I plan to use on you. A few of the basics."

He took her hand and ran her fingers over the suede falls of one flogger, then another with thicker strands. "Floggers are fun, don't you think?"

What would that feel like—with him using it? With the submissive earlier, it...

"Then there's the cane." He stroked her fingers over the smooth, cool surface, studying her closely.

"I don't know what a cane feels like," she admitted.

"All right. I'll take it easy to begin."

Her gaze focused on the stuff still inside the bag. Even one of those spikey pizza cutter things.

He followed her gaze. "This is a Wartenberg wheel."

"It looks...sharp."

"The better to tease you with, my dear...sometime in the future. On your back, your ass. And it's an interesting sensation for here." He cupped her breast, rubbing his thumb over her tightening nipple.

Something so sharp on her breast? She almost stepped back,

but his arm behind her back kept her in place as he fondled one breast, then the other, the kneading increasing in pressure until the tissue swelled. His green gaze stayed on her face as his fingers rolled her nipples, pressed and loosened, tugged to where the pain started to slide into pure heat.

His smile appeared, then he took fleece-lined cuffs from his bag and fastened them on her wrists and ankles.

The sensation of something wrapped around her wrists was... appallingly carnal. As if he was already holding her down. She ran her tongue over her dry lips. "I thought all you Dom types used leather and buckles and padlocks."

His laugh was deep and masculine. "I have those, too. But for inexperienced subbies, I prefer something I can release quickly."

He turned her to face the cross. "Lean into the support and relax, Valerie."

The padding was cool against her stomach and between her breasts. Unlike the St. Andrew's cross, she had a place to rest her cheek as he snapped her wrist cuffs to the horizontal arms.

The upright cushion was narrow, letting her breasts dangle, and he adjusted them, openly enjoying himself in the process.

"I want your legs open, pet," he said, a moment before he pulled her right leg out to the side and secured it to a chain on the cross's bottom stand. "Because I like to touch...everything."

He did her left leg. "Perfect." He took a scrunchie from his bag and secured her hair on top of her head.

She closed her eyes and pulled in a breath as anticipation and anxiety bubbled like froth on a heated lake of arousal. It didn't help that he was running his hand up and down her bare back. "I'm good."

"Yes, you are." He kissed her again, making her world spin as if the lake had a whirlpool at the center. What would she agree to, just to have more of those kisses?

· · ·

Valerie's body hit every hot button he had, Ghost thought. Her legs and arms were tanned, but her torso was paler, perfect for showing red marks. Full breasts with big nipples with the faint striations that showed she'd nursed her children.

Her lush hips were made to be squeezed by a man's hands. Her belly was soft and rounded, and he looked forward to flattening her under his weight.

To taking possession in the most basic of instincts. How many wars had the desire for a woman started?

He moved forward to cup one heavy breast and enjoyed the faint gasp she gave as he touched her. "Damn, I like your body."

Her eyes lifted, disbelief obvious.

He rather thought he might know how she felt in a way. Age, wear and tear, and war had caught up with him, too.

"Valerie." He weighed her breast, thumb teasing the jutting nipple. "You're softer than you were, I daresay, but I enjoy softness. Very, very much."

Knuckles under her chin, he lifted her head so he could enjoy her mouth, her response, and the slight gasp as he squeezed each breast.

He stepped back.

Wasn't she a lovely sight? Bound to the cross, legs open for his enjoyment.

He did a quick check to ensure the Velcro wrist and ankle cuffs weren't cutting off her circulation. Then, taking his time, he ran his fingertips up and down her inner thighs, enjoying how her legs started to tremble.

"Such delicate skin," he murmured. He'd have to take care. Her skin would be thinner, easier to tear, than if she was twenty.

He slapped the backs of her thighs, then her ass lightly, warming her skin, before moving up to check positioning. Yes, perfect. Her cheek rested against the upright cushion, and her arms were supported by the cross-pieces.

"Are you comfortable, Valerie?" He kept one hand on her,

above her ass. Reassuring her. "You'll be in this position for a while."

She was still almost upright, tipped only slightly forward on the cross. "Yes, Sir."

"Good answer." He kissed her gently, then took the kiss deeper. Pain would feed the arousal in a masochist like her, but it all started with awakening the sexual response. Once they knew each other better, he'd be able to do it with a tone in his voice, with a look, but now, especially with her nervousness and self-doubt, he'd have to waken her deliberately.

He couldn't think of anything he'd enjoy more.

Kissing her again, he nipped her lips, introducing the first sting of pain, before taking her mouth again. Possessing. Dominating.

Gripping her hair, he tilted her head back and enjoyed the sweet yielding response of a submissive. "Look at me."

Her eyes lifted to meet his.

Keeping her hair fisted, he held her immobile. "I'm going to hurt you now," he whispered. "And when I'm done, we're going to find a bed, and I'm going to take you until I'm satisfied."

Her pupils dilated with heat—and longing.

"What is your safeword? The one that stops the scene immediately." He waited for her to remember.

It took her a moment. "Red. It's red."

"Use yellow if you want me to change something, but not stop the scene entirely."

A tiny nod said she understood.

But her hesitation in remembering her safeword indicated it didn't come automatically to her lips. For now, he'd have to be careful. Observant. Remind her.

"Let's start with your favorite kind of pain." Because she needed the intimacy of his bare hand.

He started light, working up to what should be a comfortable sting, before leaning his weight against her and pausing to enjoy her breasts. As he squeezed, tugged, and rolled those full nipples, he could feel how her breathing sped up. Her clean scent was like the fragrance of a garden at dawn as he kissed the lovely curve between her neck and shoulder. When he bit down, her nipples peaked in his palms.

"There's a good girl," he growled in her ear. He kneaded her breasts roughly, with his chest pressing hard enough against her back she couldn't move away, letting her feel her helplessness as he hurt her.

Her body was warm; a faint sheen showed on her face.

Moving back, he picked up his warm-up flogger. Starting slow, he ran the soft suede strands over her shoulders, her breasts, and her ass. Letting her steep in the sensuous smell and feel of leather.

Then he slapped the falls against her back in a comfortable figure-eight pattern, going for a light pattering sensation. The tune "Half God Half Devil" playing over the speakers determined his rhythm as he flogged her shoulders and down to her ass, avoiding her spine and kidneys.

The club, the people, everything disappeared as his focus tightened, as every motion of her breathing registered, every twitch and shiver, the color of her skin, the light glow of sweat.

Only the music existed with what she gave him—the hitch in an inhalation, a moan.

Soon there would be more.

With each circuit, he increased the strength of the blows until her skin roughened, pinkened, showing it was ready for more.

But was she? Laying the flogger aside, he leaned against her again, nipping her earlobe.

The sharp bite of teeth on her ear pulled her from the pretty haze, from the lovely mild burn that covered her back like a heated blanket, a contrast to the cooler cushion on her front. His belt buckle was a cold circle against her lower back. When he cupped her breasts, his palms were hot.

"Okay, pretty professor." The low rough voice felt like the flogger had, dancing over her skin. "You with me here? Open your eyes."

When had she closed them?

She lifted her lids.

His green gaze was assessing, careful—and hotter than the center of a flame.

"You like this," she said in wonder.

His deep laugh was openly amused. "Absolutely. So, do you, it appears."

"Yes. Yes, I do." She managed to stop herself from saying, "More." The memory of Barry's disgust had never completely disappeared.

But he must have read the request in her face, this too-perceptive Dom. "We're nowhere near done, pet."

He kissed her, even as he caressed her breasts. Stepping back, he trailed his hands down her back, over her ass, and between her legs. Discovering she was wet, he made a low appreciative sound. With slow, deliberate strokes, he slid his fingers over her clit and around her entrance, until the bursts of pleasure were entwined with the burning of her skin.

With a low laugh, he moved back. Something struck her back, a different flogger. This one felt less like raindrops and more like the slapping of a myriad of hard hands. He worked from her shoulders to her ass, slowly increasing and decreasing the blows, occasionally hitting hard enough to take her breath.

And it started to hurt as the heat turned to a burning ache.

Just before she was ready to speak, he stopped. His weight pressed against her again. Her skin was so hot and tender, she could feel every strand of thread in his shirt and pants. His clothing was wonderfully cooler.

Then his hands found her breasts and *oh*, the feeling. As if she'd been waiting forever to be touched.

"You still with me here?" he rumbled in her ear as his fingers teased her, hurt her. The pain was sweet, blooming in cascades of pleasure, leaving her gasping for air. "Valerie, look at me."

She opened her eyes and met his gaze. So hot and amazing and... "Um. Yes. I'm good."

He huffed a laugh. "You're going to be an easy one to toss into subspace, aren't you? Let's get you off first, then we'll enjoy some mutual play after you recover."

"Right." Play sounded amazing.

He laughed and pinched her nipples until the burn ran like a stream of molten lava straight to her core.

As he moved away, his hands ran over her back and ass, then between her legs. He teased her until she was squirming, and all she could think about was being touched.

Being taken.

He flogged her again, slower, bringing her back to a mindless place where she was simply...taking.

Until it all changed. The pain was different, harsher, stinging lines walking across her ass and upper thighs. The cane? Not quite unbearable, pulling her deeper, until—

There was a pause and the cane struck harder. The pain was a burning line and then sank into her, blended with her somehow, and then he struck again. Again and again.

He stroked his hand over her butt. "Breathe, Valerie. Ride the pain."

She pulled in air through her nose, breathed it out, as if preparing to meditate. The ache receded like the surf pulling away from the sand.

His gaze was on her, waiting, giving her a chance to quit. And she wanted to—it hurt!—only she didn't, because the pain had turned into the slow surge of waves with the turning of the tide.

Her lips formed the word. *More.*

A crease appeared in his cheek, and she could almost feel the pleasure radiating from him, the enjoyment of what he was doing.

He'd given her this—and she'd given him the same.

The pain started again, startling another squeak from her, and his deep chuckle swept over her like a hot wind before it disappeared into the pool of sensation.

"You deserve a reward, sweetness."

She blinked, realizing he'd stopped. His chest was against her, and then his fingers under her chin tilted her head back against his shoulder. His hand curled around her vulnerable, exposed throat, pressing lightly in the most primal of threats.

The fingers of his other hand slid between her pelvis and the cross, then down over her mound. With her legs wide, nothing was denied to him, and he slid two fingers over her clit and inside her. Out and over again. And inside again.

Overwhelming pleasure swept through her, making her shake, but her arms were restrained; his body pinned her, his hand still pressed against her throat.

She could only tremble as the tension, the need to come spiraled out of control.

His chin rubbed against her temple as he whispered, "You feel good, pet." His fingers pressed in and out. "Later tonight, my cock will be here, buried deep inside you for my own pleasure."

His slick fingers swept over her clit, paused, and circled, slower and slower as her whole body went rigid, waiting for the next touch.

It came, and *gods*, everything inside her contracted and then released in billowing waves of sensation. "Ah, ah, ahhhh."

He was chuckling, still holding her in place, and before she'd come down, he slid his fingers inside, his palm on her clit, sending her over again so hard all she could do was gasp.

"Nice, very nice, pet."

He stepped back, and then he was spanking her ass, sending her back up, the pain—the not-pain—resonating with the orgasm, and she sank into a whole new space. Deep under the waves, there was no pain. She could feel each impact like a quivering of the heavy waters.

Then he was flogging her again, only lighter. A patter like rain on the ocean danced over her skin, and she sank even deeper.

A low chuckle broke into the rhythmic rocking of the waves. "Eyes open, sweetheart," he said.

His eyes were so green, his face so hard. Such a warrior. So safe.

"Come on back to the real world, Valerie. I'm taking your restraints off now."

Restraints? She blinked as he pulled her legs together.

Bracing herself on the cross, she tried to stand on her own. He kept an arm around her waist as he undid her wrists.

Even as her legs wobbled, he wrapped a fluffy blanket around her and sat her down on the floor.

Taking a knee, he lifted her chin.

She tried to focus her eyes.

"You went a bit deeper than I expected for a newbie, pet. Let's get some fluid into you." He put a bottle into her hand, curling her fingers around it, then helped her raise it to her mouth.

A sip of cool sweetness slipped down her throat, and she swallowed. *So good. More.* She drank, and after a minute, he let her hold the bottle on her own. "Thank you."

Why did she feel so shaky inside?

He studied her for a long moment, then leaned forward and kissed her. His touch and attention on her settled the quivery feeling.

When he pulled back, all she could do was look at him, falling into his eyes.

He kissed her again. Slow and sweet.

When she sighed, he chuckled, then rubbed his slightly scratchy cheek against hers. After removing the scrunchie from her hair, he massaged her scalp.

It felt amazing. Was it possible for her muscles to go even limper?

Giving one lock of hair a tug, he smiled at her. "Sit and get hydrated while I clean up."

"I can—"

"No, sweetheart, you will stay where I put you." His smile deepened. "I warned you what happened with sadists, didn't I?"

"...we sadists enjoy turning our victims into quivering messes who aren't up to anything more demanding than sitting on the floor."

Good grief, he'd done exactly that.

CHAPTER THIRTEEN

G host used the elevator to take his blanket-wrapped submissive upstairs to his own quarters. To his bedroom. Still glowing and pink, she was a lovely sight.

She'd look exactly right in his bed.

Stopping near the doorway, he dimmed the hanging Moroccan lanterns to a golden glow.

Leaning against him, she was staring at the king-sized canopy bed he'd bought when he returned to the lifestyle. Rather than wood, the steel frame was of twisted black metal. The Celtic scrollwork on the head and footboards—and corners of the upper and lower posts—made excellent anchors for bondage without being obvious.

He set Valerie's clothing on the dresser and dropped his bag at the end of the bed.

After stripping off her blanket, he sat Valerie in the center of the satin comforter. The black and dark blue arabesque patterns set off her fair skin. Her hair was tangled, her big blue eyes wide, and even as he watched, she flushed under his gaze. "What?"

"You are so pretty," he murmured, and bent to kiss her.

As he straightened, she whispered, "I'm not, though."

"What?"

She shook her head, and he could see her thought processes were still running slower than her usual blinding speed. "I'm old and—"

"Stop." Wasn't it interesting how subspace and the aftermath could dredge up worries a submissive might never say aloud otherwise? "Valerie, self-disparagement wins you a punishment prize," he said.

"Punishment?" Her soft pink mouth dropped open. "What?"

"We're going to discuss your self-image later." Holding her gaze with his, he slowly unbuckled his heavy leather belt and pulled it slowly from the loops. "But for now, I'll give you a taste of what happens when you disparage yourself."

Her eyes widened. "You can't punish me—not without talking about it or anything."

"Well, then we won't call it punishment, but a continuation of the scene downstairs." He grinned. "However, I'll know—and you'll know, it's for talking like that about yourself."

And after a few good swats, he really would continue the scene and slide her back into a fine erotic space before taking her.

However, it'd be good to discover if discipline domination turned her on.

Because he enjoyed the hell out of it.

Pushing her onto her back, he gripped her ankles in one hand, and lifted her legs up into the air, slightly toward her shoulders. Her ass tilted up in an excellent vulnerable position.

"But—"

Her ass cheeks were still reddened from the flogging and cane —although he'd gone easy on her. Poor subbie.

"This, woman, is going to hurt," he said in Arabic.

He smacked her with the folded over portion of his belt, left cheek, right cheek. Powerful enough to sting. Discipline, right? The sound was most pleasant.

Although, he'd been half erect for an hour, her adorable

squeaky-squeal hardened him like a rock. "Nice. Let's hear that again." He slapped the belt over both cheeks of her pink ass and got the response he wanted.

Her scream was even louder, and even as her eyes filled with tears, her nipples contracted into hard peaks.

Setting the belt down, he brushed his palm over the new pink stripes on her ass, then, pulling her legs even farther up, he checked her pussy. Very slick. "Sweetheart, you like being punished."

"No, you're wrong. Of course, I don't."

Such a weak protest.

"Your safeword is red. Because I'm going to make sure you think twice before saying you're anything but gorgeous." Gripping her ankles more firmly, he picked up the belt and gave her three more stinging blows.

She sobbed but...the look in those tear-filled eyes held pure submission.

Beautiful.

Letting her legs down, he set her feet on the bed, widely apart, opening her to his gaze. She was bare for him, her pussy glistening with arousal. "Now, this is another warning. If you exceed my patience, there are other targets than your pretty ass. Like here."

Holding her gaze, he ran a finger around her clit, feeling her shiver under his touch.

Her eyes dilated and...yes, she was holding her breath. Someone was turned on by the idea of pussy spanking, was she?

He wouldn't, surely, he wouldn't. Valerie's bottom already stung, the burn from earlier re-ignited by the belt—and the pain had already turned into an urgent need for more.

But her pussy? She put her hands right over the target. Her clit was aching with need to be touched. But not slapped, surely not.

His lips curved into a terrifying smile.

"You should have a sample, don't you think?" He reached into his bag and pulled two lengths of something out. One went around her left thigh, and he clipped her left wrist cuff to it, then did the right side the same way, leaving her hands pinned to the outside of each thigh.

Leaving her pussy open and unprotected.

Her heart started hammering, and she pulled in air, even as her body shivered with a dark need. "Wait."

"No. I think we're both going to enjoy this." He lifted his hand, paused, and then slapped right on her mound.

The shock reverberated through her a second before the stinging burst through the tender area. She tried to move—and couldn't. Her whole body went rigid as pain—and heat—surged outward, bringing her right to the edge of coming.

"Oh, you really are a delight," he said softly. He struck again, slightly harder, and, oh gods, she *came*. Sobbing and gasping—and coming.

He opened his pants, released his long, thick cock, and covered himself with a condom.

Setting a wedge-shaped cushion on the edge of the mattress, he slid her ass up onto it, so her pelvis was tilted up. Setting her feet against his stomach, he stroked his callused palms over her legs. "Eyes on me, Valerie."

She met his gaze.

"Still green and good to continue, sweetheart?"

"Yes. Green." Her voice was hoarse. "More."

As he lifted her legs onto his shoulders, she realized the cushion put her pussy at just the right height for...

His cock pressed at her entrance, sliding, making her realize how wet she was. Her legs were on his shoulders, her hands pinned at her thighs. She pulled in a sudden breath at the vulnerability.

His green eyes met hers again, and he paused there at her

entrance, giving her a chance to change her mind.

She lifted her hips toward him, only an inch. *Yes.*

"All right then." Gripping her hips, he thrust, hard and deep, taking her in one devastating movement. He was *big*, and as she stretched around him, everything inside her burst in a glorious wave of sensation, and wave after wave of pleasure exploded inside her as she came again.

He was laughing as he hammered into her, and her orgasm kept coming, more and more. As he bent forward, her hips tilted up, letting him get almost painfully deep. The angle let him reach her breasts, and his hard hands caressed her, tugged and rolled the swollen nipples, sending more exquisite sensations through her.

Straightening, he gripped her hips again, holding her immobile. "Look at me, pet," he growled.

Her gaze met his. His face was rock hard, the muscles standing out. Thrusting hard and fast, he held her gaze as his hands tightened, and his shaft jerked inside her.

And she could remember the first time they'd really talked and him saying in a rough deep voice, *"...be assured I will take my pleasure when the time comes."*

He had. And the knowledge was incredibly satisfying.

After disposing of the condom, he lay down on the quilt and pulled Valerie into his arms. She squirmed closer, resting her head on his shoulder. It was a fine feeling to hold a sated, soft woman. And wasn't it nice she was a snuggly one?

The air was cool against his still heated skin and smelled of sandalwood and sex—the finest of fragrances.

Eventually, she sighed and sat up. Seeing him watching, she flushed and wrapped the throw blanket from the end of the bed around herself. "I really should go. Thank—"

He gripped the blanket between her breasts. "Stay."

"But..."

"No, pet. Although I'll admit I want to hold you longer and make love again later, I really do need to know you won't drop after the fun we had earlier."

When she appeared confused, he clarified, "Subdrop—when the endorphins disappear."

"I've heard about that." Her voice still held a sexy huskiness. "Ghost, I'm not sleepy, and I don't want to keep you up."

"I'm wide awake, too. Want to shower, have a glass of something, and see what happens?"

The tiny line between her eyebrows really was adorable. "Well... Are you sure?"

"I'm very sure. You can have the first shower while I get us something to drink. Beer, wine, juice or water?"

"Wine would be lovely." She didn't move.

He stroked a hand down her soft hair, remembering how difficult it had been to return to socializing—and sex—after his wife died.

Valerie had been brave to get this far. "Let me leave out some things in the bathroom."

"Um. Right."

After laying out towels, a robe, and a spare toothbrush, he bowed slightly. "All yours, pet."

In the kitchen, he pulled out wine for her and a beer for him and left them on the coffee table.

When she left the bathroom, he went in. Time to deal with his leg.

Once his prosthesis was off, he took a quick shower and washed the liner, leaving it hanging to dry. After pulling on his robe, he set his knee on the iWalk knee crutch and strapped it to his thigh and upper calf. He left his prosthesis beside the bed with his second liner.

He was trained to be prepared for emergencies—and the amputation sure did fuck with his response time. He could no longer jump out of bed and run to deal with a problem.

But he was an expert at donning his prosthesis quickly—and if it took too much time, he had crutches and the iWalk.

In the living room, Valerie was curled at one end of his couch, wine glass in hand. Seeing him, she raised her eyebrows. "What a cool device. Almost like a peg leg."

He smiled. He'd hoped she wouldn't be the type to react poorly. Curiosity, he could handle. "It's useful for getting around after I take my prosthesis off and beats using crutches. I like having my hands free."

He unstrapped the device and set it to one side, then sat beside her.

Checking out his residual limb, she caught his gaze and flushed.

"It's all right to look, sweetheart. I don't mind."

To his surprise—and delight—she took him up on the offer. Leaning forward, she ran her hand over his left knee and down over the stump. Unhappiness showed in her expression, but no revulsion.

"You handle the sight better than a lot of people do." He picked up his beer. A sip of the icy cold brew went down well.

"Ah, well," she went back to her wine, "I was an analyst in the Department of Defense"

Interesting. "Somehow, I wouldn't have thought you the type for warfare."

Had she startled the Colonel? Valerie almost laughed. "I'm not. I wanted to go to college and—" She winced. She really didn't want to talk about her mess of a childhood.

"And...?" He'd turned so he could watch her face, and after a second, took her hand in his big warm one. Staying in contact.

How did he know it would loosen her tongue? "And my parents were consulting with American businesses in the Middle East. They wanted me to continue tending the house, planning their social events, doing the shopping. When I refused to stay, they cut me off." They'd shouted she was a worthless, ungrateful child and thrown her clothes in the street and told her to never come back. "It took almost all my savings to fly back to the US."

"How old were you?"

"I turned eighteen that day." She gave him a rueful smile. "I was an unplanned pregnancy and not especially wanted until I was old enough to be useful. Then again, maybe it was good for my character."

When she sighed, Ghost put an arm around her shoulders, pulling her close. "Feeling unwanted isn't good for anyone," he growled, "especially a child."

"Well, being broke is how I ended up in the DoD. I spoke Arabic, so they snatched me up as a linguist."

"Ah, excellent choice." He toasted her with his beer. "Then you managed college and grad school?"

"Mmmhmm. Marriage and a couple of children, teaching in a community college, working on a doctorate and a book. That's pretty much my life."

He ran his fingers through her hair. "I somehow doubt that, but it gives me a timeline, at least."

She laughed. The wine had started a lovely buzz in her veins. She was warm and comfortable, and his hand in her hair made her want to purr like a contented cat. "What's your timeline, then?"

"My father wanted me to get an MBA and handle his manufacturing company, but I disliked business. I switched to history, earned my master's, taught for a couple of years, then wanted some adventure. So, I joined up, did officer candidate school, and worked my way into Special Forces. Got married. I was in a bit over twenty years, mostly based in Seattle, and picked up my doctorate and did some teaching while in."

He hesitated before adding, "No children, my wife died of cancer." His voice had gone rough with the last sentence. He'd loved his wife. A lot.

"Oh, Ghost, I'm sorry."

"Thank you. It was four years ago, so it's not fresh." He tugged her hair. "As you've probably learned, it takes a while to recover from losing someone. And to being alone."

"Don't I know it." She sighed, then frowned. "My children are only a couple of hours away, and I drive over to see them fairly often, although Dillon is overseas right now." She had to admit her children's worries over how their father was doing occasionally made for awkward conversations. "Do you have any family here?"

He chuckled. "Not even close. My father died a few years ago. When I was a teen, my parents divorced. My mother returned to Scotland and later married a good Scottish man. You remind me of her sometimes—your ability to pick yourself up and get on with what needs to be done."

That...was an amazing compliment. "Thank you."

He continued, "I have a few half-siblings, and they've given me plenty of nieces and nephews to spoil whenever I get over there."

His hard face softened as though he was picturing those rolling hills and the laughter of children.

"I bet they adore their uncle," she said softly.

"It's mutual. They're great kids."

As he sipped his beer, she said tentatively, "It's a long way from Seattle to Florida."

His mouth tightened. Not with anger, but something more unhappy.

"Did...something happen to make you move?"

He rubbed the back of his neck, then sighed. "In a way. My wife had died. When I tried to get back into being social, I had a scene go bad, and then"—he motioned toward his leg—"I left the military. Seattle no longer felt like home at that point."

"Well, you certainly chose to move a long way," she said, then rubbed her head against his arm. "I'm glad you're here, Finn."

He pulled her closer. "Me, too."

CHAPTER FOURTEEN

The new tech on the prosthesis Ghost had trialed had some excellent benefits, but the device had been unbalanced enough he'd strained his hip trying to compensate.

It was the downside of testing new equipment. Although he received a discount on anything he wanted to purchase, if something didn't work, the guinea pig—him—suffered for it.

Then again, it was better if *he* discovered any problems. An older amputee might not bounce back as well from an injury the prosthesis might cause.

Back in his usual work prosthesis, Ghost rubbed his hip as he walked toward his military history class. This was a fun one with a fair number of ROTC students as well as upper grad history majors. Their questions and arguments kept him on his toes.

He smiled as he set the box on his desk and opened it. The scent of *kleicha* drifted out, catching the attention of his students. Young people were always hungry.

"We've been discussing the wars in the Middle East, and I was reminded today how easy it is to label someone we're fighting against as 'other', to see them as lesser humans or even as evil. It's more difficult—but more accurate—to realize we all have reasons to fight, and their reasons are, to them, as compelling as our reasons are to us. It's even more difficult to remember that soldiers—or terrorists—are only a small percentage of a population."

The frowns showed they were thinking.

"Hoffman, you're from a small town. Let's say you got sucked into some manipulative politician's warmongering and went out and slaughtered a bunch of people. Would it be right for the world to blame your town? To think the residents had all agreed with you? To condemn them all because *you* were an idiot?"

His insult won laughter, then more frowns, then several students muttered, "No."

"Excellent. One of the questions on the upcoming test will relate to the blame game, so keep your eyes open for examples you can pull from your reading. And in the future, remember soldiers on the other side also have families, have sisters and children. They have their special holidays and favorite foods."

More nods. This really was a good class.

He grinned. "To drive home this lesson... One of the professors here grew up in the Middle East and was taught to cook by the local housekeepers. She made *kleicha* and gave me enough to share with you all. Like our Christmas cookies, this is a holiday cookie, and when I was in Baghdad, it was one of my favorite treats."

The students surrounded his desk, and the cookies disappeared like magic. Homemade sweets, who could resist? Even better, the sweet professor had made enough he could keep some for himself.

After putting the quiz questions up on the display, he sat back and nibbled on his own cookie. In reality, he'd forgotten the half-joking request he'd made of Valerie.

She hadn't.

Because she was an intelligent and caring woman, a combination he found far too compelling. She was also damned determined. The way she had buckled down to learn self-defense was impressive.

After her lessons, he could usually talk her into joining him for supper and then into spending the night.

At least at his place. When she'd cooked him a meal at her apartment, they'd made love, and then he'd gone home rather than stay over. Their relationship wasn't at the point when she could tell him she needed time alone. At his place, she knew she could just depart when she was ready. Asking a man to leave was often difficult for a woman, especially a submissive one.

But he'd hated to leave. He liked waking up with her. Cooking breakfast with her, or if they had late morning lectures, they'd go out for breakfast.

Face it, he simply liked her company—and they'd spent much of last week's spring break together.

To find a submissive whose kinks matched his own was damn rare. Kelly had enjoyed a minimal amount of pain for a minimal amount of time. At the clubs, with her permission, he'd occasionally flog or whip the masochists who begged, but the satisfaction for him was minor and mostly from knowing he'd helped someone who'd needed the relief.

He'd far preferred the deeper bond of playing with Kelly, even if she was a lightweight.

With Valerie? Being able to play longer, to fill all her needs for pain, submission, and arousal...that was heady stuff.

It was way too damn easy to fall for her.

But she'd been burned in the past. He was going slow, letting her get used to being with him. To sex with a Dominant.

She was worth the slow pace.

Natalia finished cleaning her brushes and put everything away neatly. When she'd moved in with Olivia and kept this tiny apartment as an art studio, she hadn't worried about being messy.

But now she was once again living and working here, she had to keep it tidy.

For a moment, she studied her latest painting of a marshy area by the Hillsborough River shrouded in a thick fog. The hues were a mournful blue, and the cypress trees almost gray.

The image captured her spirits perfectly. Here was loss; here was loneliness.

Her doorbell rang, and she jumped and spun around as her hopes lifted...and died. The Mistress wouldn't be at the door.

After checking the peephole, Natalia opened the door. "Mama, what are you doing here?"

"*Mija*, the neighbor caught a huge tarpon when he was on a fishing charter. He gave us most of it, and I thought you'd enjoy some, too."

Any little bit would help her budget. "I really would. Thank you." She hugged her mother.

Her mother tucked the wrapped fish into the fridge, then sniffed the air. Despite the open windows, the turpentine scent lingered from cleaning the brushes, as did the much nicer fragrance of oil paints. "You're still drawing, I see."

"Of course. It's what I do." Even more than before since she no longer had anything better to do most evenings.

Her mother sat down, frowning at her. "I know you'd like to make a living from your art, but Natalia, you're not being realistic. Painting isn't a career choice—it's a hobby."

How many times had they had this conversation? "It's a career to me, Mama. This is what I do and what I want to do with my life."

"Bartolo is still willing to take you back. You'll have a job in a nice clean office, regular hours, and he'll give you the time and money to take accounting classes. He wants you to work for him, *mija*."

"I know he does." Natalia tried to keep her disgust out of her voice and failed. "Because he can employ family cheaper than he can get a real accountant."

Even worse, she'd have to listen to her uncle and cousins bring out their tired homophobic jokes about lesbians and gays. Cousin Tadeo would drag in guys to hit on her in hopes of turning her straight. For her own good, of course.

"I won't work for him. However, I *am* taking a couple of college classes." She smiled brightly. "Art classes."

"Art won't put food on the table."

"Eventually, it will. I *believe* that." Why couldn't her family believe in her? Because she was the youngest, so they all had to tell her what to do? Because she was too quiet to make a scene like her older sisters?

Her defiance hadn't been a loud one. Instead, when Bartolo began pressuring her about her choices and her family deliberately interrupted her painting time, she'd simply found this apartment and moved out.

"However, I'm also working as a clerk in a beach store. It's really fun." She gave her mother a straight look. "Oddly enough, it pays just as much as Uncle Bartolo was paying me."

"Natalia..."

"No, Mama. I'm sorry he's harassing you about my choices, but they're *my* choices. I'm an artist and a lesbian. I'm not going to change to make your brother happy."

Her mother sighed tiredly. "No, you shouldn't have to change. A child must go her own way. And a mama will worry. That is our prerogative, *sí*?"

Natalia laughed. "I suppose."

"Are you still seeing Olivia?" Mama walked over to the wall, studying the paintings.

"No." The word was a smeary black stripe across the day's brightness. "We're not together any longer."

"Oh. I'm sorry. She seemed nice."

Even that small amount of sympathy made Natalia's eyes prickle with tears.

Moving jerkily across the room, Natalia picked up one of the gallery brochures. "By the way, an art gallery in Ybor is having an opening next month for four *emerging* artists who are painting in the modern-impressionist style. I'm one of them. Here's the information."

She handed over the publicity brochure. "If you want to come."

"A gallery? In Ybor City? Oh, *mija*, of course I'll come." No hesitation, simply a wide smile.

Natalia's throat clogged. In the club, Olivia had told Ben Haugen about Natalia's art—and the renowned photographer had recommended her to the gallery owner.

So, even this she owed to Olivia...who wouldn't attend her special night.

But maybe she'd have someone she knew there. "Thanks, Mama."

CHAPTER FIFTEEN

The bar stank of spilled stale beer and sweat. But the drinks were cheap, something Barry had to consider these days. Dammit.

At the table, Piers was on his left, Scott across from him.

"It still pisses me off how Ghost stole your manager job." Barry took a hefty swig of his beer.

"That meddling, stick-up-his-ass bastard." Scott slammed his fist on the table hard enough to rattle the glasses ...and silence the other customers. Wrecker was a perfect scene name for him. "My fucking wife's giving me crap about losing the job, and I have to grin and take it."

Piers shook his head. "It's rough when a bitch holds the purse strings."

"Yeah." Or when the purse disappeared entirely. Barry scowled. Valerie had brought in a steady paycheck, managed their accounts—and kept his contractor business organized.

He stared at his drink. The bank account was at zero and the credit card maxed out. Wouldn't be anything coming in, either. He'd lost another job this morning when a finicky old fart of a client had backed out.

"It'd be nice if you could get the club manager job back." Piers tapped his fingers on the table. "Did I tell you me 'n' Buttley got tossed out of the Shadowlands?"

Barry half-smiled at Uttley's nickname. Then frowned. "Tossed out?"

"What the fuck happened?" Scott straightened.

"We were giving the lezzie-lover spic some shit, and an older bitch tries to stop us. And then your good buddy Ghost and Saxon kicked us out. Said not to come back." Piers glared at Scott. "You said we'd run that place. And get a lot of pussy, too."

"Jesus, it's not Scott's fault GI Joe caught you. Or that the owner came back from Europe," Barry said loyally.

"Not my fault, but I know who to blame for me losing the job." Scott's eyes darkened with anger. "Fucking Ghost."

Piers curled his fingers into a fist. "I owe him somethin' too. Want to ambush him?"

"Yeah, but not in the way you're thinking." Scott looked at Barry. "You're still a member, so how about a whisper campaign? The bastard has a file in the Shadowlands; there's some good shit about why he left Seattle."

"Spread gossip?" Barry grinned. "Sure. Me 'n' Kahlua will be all over that."

CHAPTER SIXTEEN

In a sitting area, Valerie glanced around the Shadowlands, trying not to be obvious as she watched for Ghost...and hoping *not* to see Barry or Kahlua.

Linda joined her, then bouncy Sally came over with her friend Zuri, and Valerie was flabbergasted to learn Sally lived with two Doms, and then Zuri said she had two Doms, as well.

"Seriously?" Valerie shook her head at Zuri. "I saw you at the housewarming with two men, but I thought you were only playing around. Both of them?"

Zuri burst out laughing. "Both. I was so not ready for them, but they're far better than Sally's. Can you imagine a trouble-maker like her hooked up with two former FBI agents?"

"Not a problem." Sally buffed her fingernails on her shirt. "I have them properly tamed now."

A black-haired, olive-skinned Dom leaned over the back of Sally's chair. "Are we discussing taming techniques, baby girl? This should be fun." The low voice held a pronounced New England accent.

Sally stiffened like a cornered rabbit. "Um, Master Galen, this is a new member, Valerie."

With what looked like a very firm hand, Galen gripped his submissive's shoulder even as he smiled at Valerie. "Good to meet you."

"Galen." A big fair-skinned Dom walked up. "Did you know Ghost changed up the office room in the back?"

"No. Into what?"

"He's calling it a fuck-machine festival."

"Wicked good." Galen straightened. "As it happens, we have a little pet here who needs taming."

"Do we now?" Laughing, the bigger man plucked Sally right off her chair, slung her over his shoulder, and the two strolled away.

Despite being upside-down, Sally managed to wave goodbye.

Zuri shook her head. "Bet she'll be walking bow-legged tomorrow."

"And I thought *one* Dom was intimidating," Valerie murmured.

"One is usually more than enough," Linda agreed. "By the way, you look great tonight."

Zuri tilted her head, giving her what seemed like an almost professional appraisal. "Agreed. That's a perfect style for you." She grinned at Valerie. "I'm a women's clothing buyer at Brendalls, and my friends all call for help with choosing outfits. You nailed it."

"Thank you." Valerie ran her hands over the red vinyl cheer-leader-style skirt she'd bought this morning. Although short, it covered her full butt and upper thighs. The black bustier hauled in her tummy. She felt...sexy.

When she'd walked through the club, some of the Tops cast appreciative glances her way. And wasn't it shallow to admit she loved the attention? "It's fun to dress up."

"Unless it's a sadist who dresses you." Linda's lacey gauze pants were topped by a blue waist-trainer corset. "I think my internal organs have been rearranged. My lungs gave up and died an hour ago."

"Ouch," Valerie said in sympathy.

When Zuri snickered, Linda frowned at her. "You're supposed to feel sorry for me. And he's planning to flog away the dents the whalebone leaves in my skin."

"Good grief." *Remember not to let Finn ever pick out clothing.*

But he wouldn't. That wasn't their kind of relationship, although admittedly, during spring break, when she wasn't out of town to visit Hailey, they'd spent a lot of time together.

Nonetheless, they had a *friendship*—with benefits, yes—but it was casual. Sometimes, he'd stop by her office to chat or to take her to lunch. Or she'd bake him cookies or a meal.

After work, he taught her self-defense, and sometimes she'd stay over. There was the time she'd cooked him supper at her place and teased him about something. He'd called her a bad subbie and spanked her. When she'd yelped, he made a tsk-tsk sound, said she couldn't scream in an apartment because the neighbors would hear. The sadist had gagged her.

Which was good, since he'd made her come twice before he'd taken her, hard and fast.

But then he'd left.

Because what we have is a sexy friendship, not a relationship.

She didn't want a relationship.

Girl, you're lying to yourself.

A sigh escaped. No one had ever made her feel like he did. Protected. Cared for. Sure, the sex was amazing—okay, yes, he totally aced the sex stuff—but even better, he listened to her. Understood her. Nothing could be more devastatingly wonderful.

Listening to Zuri teasing Linda about Sam, she watched the flow of people in the room. And spotted Ghost.

Her breath caught in her throat even as her heart rate kicked into high gear. All the confusion disappeared under the wave of pure wanting.

With that distinctive military bearing, he strolled through the room, slowing to assess each scene. Members instinctively moved out of his way, merely from the authority in his presence. But he was liked. He was getting smiles. Questions. People simply wanting to talk. The younger Doms kept stopping him to ask questions.

The women...

Valerie's lips pressed together. Submissives also stopped him, wanting to talk. Wanting more. The one now was fidgeting with her hair, not quite daring to touch him, but leaning in.

"Ah, there's the Colonel." Linda had followed her gaze. "Sam says he's an incredible Dom—and a good man." Her tone lifted suggestively.

"He is. But I'm not ready for anything other than"—Valerie shrugged—"than some fun times."

Zuri lifted her eyebrows. "Does he know?"

"Yes, of course. I told him the first time we played."

"Mmmhmm." Linda's lips twitched. "I have a feeling he can be as determined as Sam. Good luck to you."

Zuri burst out laughing.

Valerie frowned. It was true both men were sadists. But... Linda's comment seemed to imply something more. Why exactly did Valerie need luck?

Her thoughts were derailed as a beautiful redhead blocked Ghost's path. When he shook his head no and started to move away, the woman dropped to her knees, holding her hands up in a plea.

He motioned for her to rise, and they stayed there. Talking.

Valerie's spirits sank. She knew all too well the power of nubile young flesh.

"Valerie, I have what you ordered." Natalia dropped into a chair and handed Valerie a bag. "Hey, Zuri, remember the top you recommended? It works great with printing."

"Ooooh, I want to see." Zuri leaned forward.

"Certainly." Valerie held up the garment. The off-white, short-sleeved shirt had such a deep V-neck it needed a fabric strip across the front to keep the shoulders from falling. "SPANK" was printed on one side of the V-neck, "ME" on the other. Below the neck were the words: "I've been good."

"Valerie." Zuri fanned herself. "If you wear it in here, you won't be able to sit down for a week."

"I think that's the idea." Natalia snickered. "Let me know how it works out for you, okay?"

"Absolutely." Valerie tucked the top back in the bag. If she wore tight jeans, she could knot the shirt at the waistband and—

"See, I told you she was here." Kahlua's shrill voice stabbed into her ears. "A hag in a bag, right? A fat toad carrying a wide load."

Valerie stiffened and almost groaned. Barry was with his slave.

With Kahlua clinging to his arm, her ex stalked over. "Val, what the fuck are you doing here?"

Like she was any of his business? She forced a smile. "Ladies, this is Barry, my ex-husband. Barry, this is Natalia. And Linda. Master Sam belongs to her."

Linda stifled a laugh, undoubtedly at the "belongs to" phrase.

Maybe the mention of influential Masters would keep Barry and Kahlua from being rude—at least to her friends. Valerie motioned to Zuri. "This is Zuri. Master Alastair and Master Max belong to her."

Oh dear, it seemed she'd left Kahlua out of the introductions. *Oops.*

"Good evening, Barry," Linda said in a chill voice. She ignored Kahlua.

Natalia nodded, and Valerie felt a twinge of unhappiness at subjecting the shy young woman to Kahlua's nastiness.

"Hi." Narrow-eyed, Zuri studied the two...and Valerie felt a tremor of worry. Ghost had mentioned Sally, Rainie, and Zuri were known as the Terrible Trio. The brats.

"It's good to meet you all," Barry said dismissively and turned his attention back to her. "Why are you here?"

Seriously? "Why, I come for the food, of course. It's excellent."

A small sneeze came from either Natalia or Zuri. Linda had more control.

Barry's face darkened. "Don't give me that bullshit. You're here for...for sex."

"And what if I am?" Unable to help herself, she glanced at Ghost.

Kahlua followed her gaze and snorted scornfully. "You and the silver fox? Get real. He wouldn't waste his time on a pity fuck."

The dismissive insult penetrated Valerie's armor and wedged in painfully.

Pulling in a breath, she tried to shake it off. Ghost had taught her self-defense, but she could hardly ram her knuckles into Kahlua's throat. Not for a verbal attack.

Barry made a scornful sound. "You don't belong here, Val. No one is going to play with you. I'd hate to think of our children knowing how desperate you are. Come, Kahlua." Barry led his slave away.

She watched them head toward the back. *I don't care what Barry thinks of me.* So why did it feel as if her self-esteem lay shattered on the floor?

"Man, your ex sucks and the woman? She's one malicious piece of work." Zuri's brown eyes were full of sympathy. "Did you live with her?"

Unable to speak, Valerie nodded.

"I wouldn't have lasted longer than a day." Natalia shook her head. "I'm glad you're away from them."

Linda patted Valerie's hand. "That's exactly what I was thinking."

Friends were a treasure. Valerie forced her voice to come out even. "Thank you."

Tucking her new top back in the bag, she rose. "Since I'm here to play, I probably should pursue that part of the program.

"Are you hooking up with the Colonel later?" Linda asked.

"I..." Valerie glanced toward him.

Head inclined, Ghost had all his attention on the beautiful young submissive who'd knelt for him.

Feeling another stab wound cutting through her, Valerie flinched.

She had no right to be hurt. Ghost was allowed to enjoy what-ever good...fucks...came his way. It wasn't as if they had any commitment to each other.

She was the one who'd insisted there be no relationship. If he took the redhead up on her offer, it was Valerie's own damn fault.

But this was why she'd tried to keep from getting involved. Because she never again wanted to feel like she was filled with jealousy. Feel so miserable she couldn't even pull in a complete breath.

Like now.

Stupid, stupid Valerie.

"No, I rather doubt we'll be hooking up," she told Linda, trying to sound indifferent. The snap of a whip and a scream caught her attention—and provided the excuse she needed. Because leaving the club right now would feel too much like Barry and Kahlua had driven her away. But she couldn't stand to stay here, attempting to ignore Ghost with the beauty. "I'm going to go check out the single-tail scene back there. Say hi to Sam for me."

Linda frowned, but nodded. "All right. We'll see you later."

"Sure." Holding her head high, she headed toward the other side of the room.

———

"There you go." Ghost seated the pretty redhead in the unclaimed submissive sitting area near the bar.

"Thank you, Colonel," she whispered, eyes downcast.

He smothered his laugh. "Much better. Now, remember what I told you."

Not waiting for her response, he strolled away. The beautiful woman wouldn't have trouble finding a play partner, although he doubted a serious Dom would be interested.

Most Dominants wouldn't mind a submissive asking for a scene...although the stricter Doms might take offense.

But when she knelt and begged after he'd refused, she'd gone too far. Rather than getting a play partner, she'd earned herself a lecture on manners.

Perhaps, someday, she'd discover a Dom didn't want someone who was completely self-centered.

Shaking his head, he headed through the room. He'd spotted Valerie sitting with Linda, but she wasn't there now.

Well, it was too early to take time off for a scene anyway. He'd watch for her, though.

He slowed to watch some wax play, pleased to see the Top was using a drop cloth and had a small fire extinguisher at hand. The young man stretched out on the table shuddered nicely with each drop of wax. Someone was having a good time.

As Ghost strolled past some younger members, they fell abruptly silent. A glance showed they were carefully not looking at him.

Discussing the new manager, perhaps?

Amused, he continued on. But by the time he reached the back of the room, he'd run into several other instances of the same behavior—and his amusement was gone.

Shades of déjà vu. This felt like Seattle after his reputation had been dragged through the dirt.

Mood darkening, he checked out the back rooms.

In the medical room, a gay submissive wiggled vigorously as he received an enema.

The fucking machine room was popular. Galen and Vance

were holding Sally between them. The submissive was sweat-drenched and exhausted.

The pet play members had taken over orgy central, and somehow there was a baby dragon in there, nipping at a kitten's paws.

The dungeon was busy, including someone getting thoroughly hammered on the sex swing.

He received more side-eye looks, and his gut tightened.

As he walked back through the main room, he could hear whispers. Stares felt like hot prickles on his back.

Time to find out what was going on.

At the bar, he spotted the two veterinarians, Jake and Saxon. Jake's submissive, Rainie, was arguing with them, her hands waving in the air. At any other time, Ghost would have smiled to see her. She had a personality as vivid as her colorful flower tatts and streaked hair.

He thought twice about breaking into an argument, but then she saw him and flushed. *Right.* Guess who was the subject of their conversation?

Catching the Doms' attention, he said, "Fill me in, please."

Jake hesitated.

"He's right, bro. He should know what's being said, and we need the truth." Expression grim, Saxon rubbed the back of his neck. "What I'm hearing is you left Seattle because you screwed up a scene and ignored a submissive's hard limits. She had a meltdown, didn't get aftercare from you, tried to commit suicide—and ended up in a mental hospital. Apparently, everyone, including her, blames you."

Felt like he was getting shot right in the gut. Again. First, a punch through the skin, then the shock, and finally the explosion of pain.

This same bullshit had swept through Chains two years ago. He braced his feet and sought his balance. "I see."

Jake's eyes narrowed. "You don't appear surprised. How much of that is true?"

"Some of it, actually, but—"

A scream from a nearby scene interrupted him. A bottom had gone hysterical. The screams continued, bringing back far too many memories of Faylee. The Top desperately tried to free the woman, and a flailing arm knocked him on his ass.

Hell. "Excuse me." Ghost hurried over to assist. The dungeon monitor, Sam, approached from the other side.

A while later, with the woman released and wrapped around her Top for calming, Ghost rounded up Peggy to clean the scene area.

"Of course, Sir. I'll get right on it." She beamed at him.

Such a sweetheart. After Z terminated the lazy young women Wrecker had hired, Ghost had been delighted when Peggy agreed to return.

"Thank you, Peggy."

All right. The disaster averted, now what to do about his own? He headed for the bar to give Jake and Saxon their answers.

A bright red skirt caught his attention, and he paused.

Valerie. And she was beautiful in that outfit. He'd hoped to see her tonight, but—now, what with the gossip, he wasn't sure what to do.

She'd seen him, though. Had she noticed his hesitation?

"Valerie, it's good to see you." Only it wasn't. He had a mess on his hands, and she was still a newcomer to the lifestyle and to him. He could hardly ask her to believe his word, to stand with him against the onslaught of gossip.

His mouth tightened as he tried to find the right words.

"Ghost. I..." Her brows drew together, and she took a step back.

So...she'd heard the rumors.

Her withdrawal wasn't a bullet to the gut, more like the slide of a dagger between the ribs, slicing into his heart. Hauling in a pained breath, he gave her what she obviously wanted.

What she needed.

"I have things to deal with right now, Valerie. I'm afraid I won't be able to join you tonight."

Her gaze dropped, hiding her reaction. Her face held the calm overlay she donned when she didn't want to share her emotions. The one he would normally call her on.

With persuasion and care, she'd normally give him everything.

But this time, when she said, "Of course. Perhaps some other night," he stepped back and let her pass.

As she walked away without a backward look, he felt as if he stood in Dresden as two thousand tons of bombs and incendiaries blew the city apart.

So...that was that, Valerie thought.

Ghost *had* found someone he'd rather play with than her. She had to give him credit. He'd had the courtesy to let her know so she wouldn't wait for him. So, she'd be free to find someone else to play with.

Very polite of him, wasn't it?

Like a wounded animal, Valerie stepped behind the screening plants in an empty sitting area. It felt as if she'd laced her bustier so tightly, her lungs were compressed, and she couldn't get any air.

Surely that was why her chest ached enough to bring tears to her eyes.

Bracing her hands on the back of a chair, she breathed through the pain, much like she did when Ghost flogged her.

Trying to turn the hurt into something else.

I guess the technique doesn't work for this kind of pain.

She knew better. These wounds were only cured by time and endurance. Her lips tightened. Wasn't it nice she was a pro at enduring?

She'd endured her parents, endured being eighteen and penniless, endured the fading and death of a marriage, endured Alisha and Kahlua.

Straightening, she swiped a finger beneath each eye, eliminating the few tears that'd spilled over.

She could endure this, too.

Another breath.

She tugged at her bustier and smoothed her skirt.

Another breath.

Better.

Ghost had headed toward the rear of the room. *Good.* She could leave without making him feel badly about her decision.

Yes, his rejection hurt—and maybe she wouldn't mind kicking him a time or two. In the balls. Nonetheless, it wasn't his fault he'd found someone he liked better. He'd been polite when he let her down. Kind, even.

At least, he hadn't dumped her the way Olivia had Natalia.

She blinked hard...because it still hurt...and headed for the front and escape.

Keeping a slight distance from the bar and the Masters there, she walked past a sitting area with two women and a man.

"Are you bullshitting me?" A screechy blonde in a pink negligee spilled her drink. "She attempted suicide because Ghost messed up a scene?"

What? Valerie almost tripped

"Yeah, but she didn't die." The Dom wore shiny black latex. And...she knew him. Who could forget his dangling Fu Manchu mustache? Dogget worked in the same realty as Barry's buddy, Scott Hicks.

Stalling, she fiddled with the clothing bag Natalia had given her.

"I don't remember anyone here attempting suicide." The second woman had green-streaked brunette hair and a soft voice.

"Didn't happen here." Dogget tugged on one side of his mustache. "It was a club named Chains in Seattle."

"Ohhh, maybe that's why he's in Florida, huh?" The blonde grew increasingly worried.

"No shit. Yeah, the so-called colonel ignored her hard limits and kept going until he reduced her to wanting to kill herself."

Ghost hadn't honored someone's hard limits? Valerie had a moment of doubt. Something *had* happened in Seattle that sent him here, and he'd said he had a scene go bad. It still bothered him.

No, she didn't believe what they were saying. He was far too honest. Honorable. And careful. Look at the way he'd negotiated everything first with her, then kept checking in, never doing anything he hadn't covered.

Dogget leaned forward as if he were trying to persuade the two women. "The Shadowlands owner sure shouldn't have fired Wrecker and put that incompetent bastard in. Ghost has fucked everything up and—"

"I like the changes," the petite woman with green-streaked hair interrupted. "And I know Master Z wouldn't put anyone in as manager who wasn't a good Dom. Ghost never seemed—"

"Shut up, Tabitha. You know nothing," Dogget snapped. "The asshole ignored her hard limits even though she was screaming at him to stop. He—"

Valerie struck the back of the leather couch so hard the sound filled the air—and made them all jump. "*Enough*. Ghost would never ignore someone's hard limits. If there is anyone in this club who is honorable, it is the Colonel."

Dogget scowled. "Jesus, you're Barry's ex. What the fuck would you know? You have no clue what—"

"On the contrary, I've scened with the Colonel; you haven't." She stared him down. "I don't know what bullshit you're trying to peddle, but you're not only lying, you're setting yourself up for a lawsuit, as well."

He turned pale, and his mouth snapped shut.

Bringing up lawsuits to a realtor? Easy score. *Heh.*

Now, should she give Ghost a call and warn him about this turn of events? She turned and...

Oh-oh. Perhaps she'd been a...bit...loud.

Every person on this side of the bar was staring at her—including several of the gold-banded Masters. Master Sam nodded to her. Arm around Gabi, Master Marcus was studying Valerie. Master Cullen was grinning.

Her face heated to the point she knew she must be dark red. No meditation was going to quiet her nerves tonight.

At least, the Masters would tell Ghost about the rumor-mill.

Valerie swallowed. Or they would once he finished scening with the redhead. The thought was like a drenching of icy water. Straightening her spine, she headed out the door.

"Yeah, Scott, we pushed the gossip big-time." Barry grinned at the sound of gleeful laughter over the phone. "The rumors are all through the club. Some members are planning to call the owner to get GI Joe's ass fired."

As the noise in his kitchen escalated to slapping sounds and screams, he muffled the receiver against his chest. "Jesus fuck, you bitches stop fighting. Alisha, fetch me a drink."

Damn, he missed Valerie. Kahlua and Alisha hadn't been nearly this bad with her around.

Putting the cell back to his ear, he heard, "You're a good friend, Barry. I owe you."

"No problem. That's what friends are for." Barry took the glass of whiskey Alisha handed him and started to fondle her breasts, but she moved out of his reach.

Great, what got up her ass?

On the phone, Scott was still complaining.

Barry scowled. "We won't be there long either. Can't afford the fees without the huge discount you gave us. Any chance you'll get the job back?"

"No way," Scott griped. "Grayson was a real cold bastard on the phone...the fucking asshole. The extra money was sure nice. My bitch-wife's a real tightass about what I spend. I don't suppose you have some you could spare?"

"Fuck no. I'm broke." Two more potential contracts had fallen through, all because he'd lost his temper with a nitpicky asshole client who wasn't satisfied with the work he and his crew had done. Who said he'd been drunk on the job.

Didn't take much to mess up a man's reputation.

A twinge of guilt ran through him...because he'd spent the evening destroying another man's rep.

Then he shrugged. Served Ghost right for stealing Scott's job —and being a stick-up-the-ass prick.

CHAPTER SEVENTEEN

In her bedroom, Valerie squinted blearily in the bright light. There should be a law the sun wasn't allowed to be so bright when she was in a crummy mood.

Bah. She blinked, trying to find a particle of energy. None. Her muscles, her bones, even her *hair* felt tired.

How long had she been awake last night?

Worrying about Ghost and those rumors had turned into thinking about making love with him and then into a misery-fest. Because she wasn't what he wanted, and it hurt.

She should have known better. Naturally, he preferred a prettier, sexier, younger woman.

And then, in front of an audience, she'd defended the guy who dumped her.

Did that make her honorable...or pitiful?

Just stop. Tossing the covers back, she sat up. She didn't feel bad about standing up for him. Their non-existent relationship was a separate matter from Dogget's smear campaign. Defending him had been the right thing to do.

Hoping to outrun her...ghosts, she went for a morning jog and let the cool, salt-laden air soothe her.

But not too much. Because she could hear the Colonel's deep rasping voice. *"Always maintain situational awareness. Move like a badass, not a victim—head up, shoulders back, look straight at each person."* She carried pepper spray in one hand, wore a personal safety device on her wrist, and had her phone in her pocket.

Each day, she changed her route, keeping to the more populated trails.

It worked. Although she'd spotted possible muggers in the past week, none tried to approach her.

I'm a badass.

After a long, hot shower, she did her meditation, then rewarded herself with a mocha coffee.

Settling down at the tiny balcony table, she tried to pretend she didn't miss having Ghost across from her and didn't miss reading the news on their devices, sharing interesting tidbits, and making their plans together for the day.

Her chest couldn't be aching because she was sad.

It was merely a nice heart attack, right?

Rolling her eyes, she turned her thoughts to less fraught subjects...like rumors.

Dogget was Scott's friend, and Scott was a vindictive creep. Could Scott be trying to destroy Ghost, who had tossed him out of the club and then replaced him as manager?

Gods, this was ugly. Because...Barry had always trailed after Scott like a street dog after the meat wagon. What were the odds her ex was also involved in spreading lies about Ghost?

And they *were* lies. Because she knew Ghost. Whatever had happened in the past, he hadn't behaved dishonorably. She could understand he might have made a mistake in a scene, but he was nothing like the monster Dogget had described.

She tapped her fingers on her thigh and scowled because Ghost might not defend himself. Not to his accusers, not to the club members. The idiot would be all honorable—and would lose. His enemies didn't play by the rules.

They'd lie. Manipulate. Cheat.

No, she wouldn't have it. Not if there was something she could do.

But if she was going to act, she needed more information.

Taking a sip of coffee, she studied the puffy clouds in the sky. Someone must know what had happened in the Seattle club.

As manager, Scott would've had access to all the files in the Shadowlands. She'd bet it was where he'd located information about Ghost.

But...records never gave the complete story. That would come from the people themselves. From people who'd been there at the time. She needed to talk to them.

How?

At the housewarming, hadn't someone been talking about a Seattle club named Chains? A Master had mentioned he'd known Ghost at that club and hadn't recognized him here because he'd shaved off his beard.

Wait, wait...right.

It was the Master named Max. He was one of Zuri's Doms.

There was her starting point. She reached for her phone.

Zuri was an excellent accomplice.

Disconnecting the phone call, Valerie grinned, then shook her head. *I hope I didn't get her into trouble.*

Sitting at her kitchen island, she checked the list in her planner. Phone number: check. The rest of the list had the topics to cover—and the possible request.

All right. Time to go to work. Pulling in a breath, she reminded herself she was good at this kind of stuff. It was a shame she'd never been a Girl Scout—she could have sold the hell out of those cookies.

Especially the Thin Mints.

I really could use a cookie right now.

With a huff of exasperation, she tapped in the numbers and then touched CALL. *Please, be a nice guy and answer a call from an unidentified number.*

After two rings, she heard a man's voice. "Drake."

"Hi, um, Master Drake. You don't know me, but—" Here she had to evade a bit, since Zuri had discovered the man's phone number by going through Max's hard copy of contacts. "Well, my name is Valerie, and I'm a member of the Shadowlands where Master Max Drago and Ghost are members. Ghost has run into a problem, and we—some of the submissives—would like to help him with it."

There was a silence on the line for a moment, as if the Dom was parsing through exactly what she'd said. "Well, this is unexpected." The voice was deep and smooth, like warm satin with a hint of a French accent. "And what exactly are you to Ghost, might I ask, Ms. Valerie?"

She choked and felt herself turning red. "I...we're, I mean"— she firmed her voice—"we're friends."

He made an amused sound. "I see. In that case, how may I be of assistance?"

That afternoon, Valerie hit the pause button on her laptop. The video playing on her television screen stopped. Even though she'd already watched the recording twice, her sense of outrage lingered. "Now you have it. What do you think?"

There was silence for a moment.

Her apartment was crowded with the women who'd been available to help.

On her living room couch, Gabi, Sally, and Rainie were crowded together. Jessica—so very pregnant—sat in one chair, Linda, the other. Kim, Beth, and Kari were cross-legged on the floor. Josie and Andrea had perched on the kitchen island stools.

They were all there because Ghost already had the support of the Shadowkittens.

Valerie paced across the room as everyone started talking at once.

"I *knew* he wouldn't have ignored someone's limits," Linda told Jessica, who agreed.

Valerie let them talk for a while before raising her voice. "People. I need ideas on how we can distribute this to the club members."

"Give it to Master Z so he can email everyone through the Shadowlands distribution list?" Rainie suggested. "Like a special newsletter?"

Valerie frowned. "I have a feeling Master Z would first ask Ghost what he wanted done with the video."

Jessica broke in. "He would."

"And Ghost would undoubtedly say no," Valerie finished. "Because it would...well, expose Faylee."

Linda nodded. "That would be my read on him, as well."

"*Dios*, men have the weirdest codes of behavior," Andrea muttered. "So...we go around him. *Them*."

"Can we send the emails off without involving Master Z?" Gabi asked.

Eyes turned to Jessica who scowled. "After firing Wrecker, Z changed all the passwords—everywhere—including to the Shadowlands email software. I can't get into it."

For some reason, everyone turned to Sally.

The brunette shook her head. "I promised Galen and Vance I wouldn't hack into anything without getting their permission first."

"And the first thing they'd do is consult with Z and Ghost." Zuri bumped her shoulder against Sally's. "I hate those kinds of promises."

"Tell me about it," Sally muttered.

Well, so much for the easy way. *I'm not giving up. Nope.*

"All right," Valerie said slowly. "What if we play the video for everyone at the club tonight? The members who see it will kill the rumors. Gossip can go both ways, after all."

There were nods of agreement.

Beth turned to Jessica. "How do we get people to where they could see it?"

"I can get the announcement chime to sound," Jessica said. "That'll get most of the members to gather at the bar."

Kim scowled. "There isn't any screen or TV in the club. And the walls are covered with floggers and paddles and stuff."

There was silence, then Josie laughed.

Valerie turned to her. "Idea?"

"Yes." The bartender waved her hand at everyone in the room. "But...if Master Z fires me, I expect y'all to come to my defense."

Smiles started to appear along with a chorus of agreement.

"Sure." "Absolutely." "Gratitude blowjobs will be given."

"What do you have in mind?" Linda asked Josie.

"When I was young, our church showed movies on a white sheet pinned to the wall."

Zuri shook her head. "All the whips and paddles and stuff on the walls would make a hanging sheet too lumpy."

"True." Josie agreed. "Which is why you need me. Remember all the chains fastened to the rafters above the bar? We can hook a sheet to them. But if you're trotting up and down my bar hanging a sheet, the first person Z will hold responsible is me."

Rainie grinned. "That'll work perfectly. Especially since everyone faces the bar naturally."

"I'll defend you, Josie. If nothing else, I'll play the pregnancy card." Jessica's bottom lip quivered almost as much as her voice as she said, "I...I was so upset to hear Ghost might leave. I begged them to help me, Master."

Kari snorted. "And if the mind-reading psychologist believes *that*, I have a nice glacier out in Tampa Bay to sell you."

As the laughter quieted, Jessica turned to Valerie, and her green eyes brimmed with tears. "It wouldn't be a total lie. Z feels guilty that he can't monitor the club like he used to. Having Ghost there lets him relax because he trusts the Colonel to care for the members as well as he could."

Kari got up on her knees to wrap an arm around the blonde.

Jessica looked around the room. "I don't want to go back to worrying about Z. We have to fix this."

Fury rose inside Valerie hard and fast, and she spat out a stream of Arabic.

"What did you say?" Gabi asked, grinning.

"Nothing nice." When all eyes were still on her, Valerie realized they weren't going to move on until she translated. Stubborn submissives. "I said the club is *not* going to lose Ghost because of the lies of a backstabbing, suit-wearing steer who smells like the bottom of a camel-herder's sandal."

The group burst out laughing.

Sally was giggling so hard, she sputtered. "Doc Winborne, you can spit out the *best* insults."

"Not even one curse word," Rainie said in obvious approval.

Andrea nodded. "That's what mine sounds like when I translate for Cullen."

As everyone settled back, continuing to refine the plan, sadness swept through Valerie. She was old enough to know the pain of losing Ghost would ease. Eventually.

Until then, it would hurt too much to see Ghost with others, so visiting the club after tonight wouldn't happen for a while.

But, maybe, she could keep these new friends even if she didn't see them at the Shadowlands. She'd hate to lose being part of this unique group.

With a bittersweet joy, she savored the feeling of belonging, then set it aside and picked up her planner. Time to make a new list. "All right, my fellow conspirators. Who has a white sheet? Who has a projector?"

In the Shadowlands office, Ghost set two papers on Z's desk. "Here is my resignation from the manager position and for my club membership, as well."

Z pushed the papers back toward Ghost. "Neither is accepted."

A trickle of amusement made Ghost cough. "I realize the submissives in the club consider you God; however, this isn't your decision."

"It should be." Z leaned back in his chair. "Finlay, rumors die, especially when unfounded."

"The flood of gossip will recede, yes." Ghost shook his head. "But doubts will remain. If I was merely a Dom, it wouldn't matter. But you can't have members distrusting the integrity of the manager—or the Masters. It's not good for the club."

"The club would survive." Z's gaze was uncomfortably percep-tive. "At the moving-in party, you appeared to have a rather lovely reason to keep your membership."

Ghost stiffened as pain knotted in his chest. *She'd turned and walked away.* "That...didn't work out."

"Are you going to let her go so easily?"

There was nothing easy about it.

But it was a valid question.

Ghost's jaw hardened. "No, I'm not. I plan to talk with her." Tonight, since he'd no longer have club duties to attend to. "She deserves the truth so she can make an informed decision rather than one based on lies."

It still hurt she could believe those lies.

He continued, "Resigning from the club and the job has

nothing to do with my relationship with Valerie. Leaving, though, is best for the club."

"I'm pleased you and Valerie will talk. I disagree about your resignation." Z tapped his fingers on the papers. "Nonetheless, as you said, it's not my decision. If you could be kind enough to remain in the position for another week, until I can find someone to step in, I would appreciate it. I'm uncomfortable leaving Jessica when she's so close to her due date."

Ghost eyed Z, recalling all too well the man was a psychologist. "I've heard Jessica talking about playing the pregnancy card. I hadn't realized a father-to-be could use it, too."

Totally unashamed, Z smiled slightly. "We all play the cards we're dealt." He folded his hands on the desk and waited.

Damn. Ghost sighed and nodded. "Of course, I'll stay until you find my replacement."

It would have been easier to simply walk away, but he owed this man a lot. If Z was worried about his Jessica, then Ghost would remain and handle the flack.

The Shadowlands was incredibly crowded. Had all the members swamped the club in hopes of more juicy gossip? As Natalia circled the bar, her fingers tingled with the need to slap their nattering faces.

But that wasn't who she was.

Her imagination was excellent—she *was* an artist, after all— but hitting someone? She wouldn't.

Not even in fun. She'd far rather be on the receiving end.

Having to work, she'd missed the meeting about Ghost and the rumors, but Sally had filled her in on the plan. Since they didn't need her to help, she was free to deal with her own problem.

"Hey, Natalia, want to play tonight?" The quietly intense

brunette was in her forties and a good Top, but Natalia wasn't in the mood for play. Not tonight.

Maybe not ever. "No, not tonight. But thank you."

Ever since she'd told Gabi, Valerie, and Kim about the breakup with Olivia, she'd been thinking about the months with the Mistress. They'd been so happy, yet everything had fallen apart. In the space of a few minutes.

It didn't make sense.

Olivia totally owed her an explanation.

And after that... Natalia felt tears burning at the back of her eyes.

Maybe it would be better to make a clean break, even if it meant losing her friends, too. Working for Linda, she might still see the Shadowkittens now and then.

Natalia swallowed against the lump in her throat. Olivia had gotten her the job, insisting she needed something more fun than working in a fast-food place.

She slowly walked another wide circle around the bar, remembering how her Mistress had wanted to see each new painting and how Natalia would be quivering inside, watching her face to see what she thought. Slowly, Olivia's eyes would light. Her smile would appear as she took in the colors, the lights...the feeling. She not only appreciated the craft, but she always caught the emotions Natalia'd tried to convey.

Why, why, why did you break up with me, Mistress? Why?

Natalia made another circle of the bar. She was waiting for the right time...and hoping to find some courage to go with it.

Some of the Shadowkittens were sitting in an area close to the bar. Gabi and Kim, Sally and Beth. Valerie, Andrea, and Rainie were there, too. For some reason, they'd pulled a rolling bondage table into the circle.

Sally waved for Natalia to join them, but her nerves were too jumpy.

She made another loop, passing Master Sam and Linda at one end of the bar.

Mistress Anne and Ben were near the middle.

At the other end, Kari and Master Dan were talking with Jessica, Master Z, and Ghost.

And then...

Mistress Olivia slid onto a barstool two seats down from them.

As the air in Natalia's throat clogged, she rubbed her sweaty palms against her jeans.

Now or never.

Never might be better.

Straightening her shoulders, she walked forward.

Is this what it feels like to walk to an execution?

She halted a few steps from Olivia. "Mistress."

Olivia didn't turn...because Natalia had whispered the word.

Kim had said, "*Make your voice loud enough that others can hear.*"

Sooo not easy. But she could do this. Her jaw set. Olivia had called her a Chihuahua once—small but mighty.

Tonight, she'd try for yappy, too. She pulled in a breath, and her voice came out loud with only a tiny quiver. "Mistress Olivia, I'd like to speak to you."

The Mistress set her glass down with a thud and turned. "I don't want to talk with you. I've made that clear."

Don't cringe. "You broke up with me and wouldn't tell me why. I want to know why."

When Olivia's mouth tightened with anger, Natalia's nerve started to break.

"Don't stop now." Gabi hissed from nearby.

"Finish the job," Valerie called in a firm voice.

Finish it. Mustering her own anger, Natalia fisted her hands at her sides. "I loved you, served you, did everything I could to make you happy. And then you told me to leave, with no reason. I deserve to know w-why." Her voice cracked on the last word.

But she kept her head high.

Flushed, Olivia stood. "Because you bloody well *cheated* on me, damn you. I saw the picture. I know." Hands in fists at her side, she sucked in a breath, then...did that Domme thing she did, taking control of her emotions.

She gracefully resumed her seat and turned her back on Natalia.

It was over, and Natalia had lost.

Because. Wait, what had she said? "*Cheated?*" Inside, anger grew, rising hard and fast until her vision blurred red. Her whole body shook with fury.

"Cheated?" Her shout held a hoarse quality she'd never heard before. "There can't be any stupid pictures because I never cheated on you. I've never cheated in my whole life! You're a *liar*."

Olivia thought she'd cheated. Could *believe* she'd cheated.

As her heart broke all over again, her throat closed, tears filled her eyes, and she ran for the exit.

She would *never* come back to this place.

Even as her ears still rang from Natalia's furious shouting, Olivia heard the little submissive sob.

And something cracked inside her chest.

Her mouth opened.

Natalia ran out of the club. Leaving the words she'd yelled hanging in the air. Reverberating in Olivia's heart.

"I've never cheated in my whole life."

Right up until Chelsey shared the picture, Olivia would have staked her life on her Latina submissive being the most honest person she'd ever met.

"Olivia?" Anne set a hand on her shoulder.

Olivia's voice didn't sound like her own. "I *saw* the picture...on someone's phone. Natalia with a Domme. A very"—she swallowed—"explicit picture."

"From prior to when she was with you, maybe?" Anne asked.

Olivia shook her head. "No. I could tell because of her hair. She'd never had bangs before, but I thought they'd be cute, so she had them styled after she moved in with me."

And it damn well hurt because the bangs had made her eyes look so big, and she was so pleased, and so was Olivia and—

On the other side of Anne, Ben cleared his throat. "Photos can be faked. Doesn't take too much work, either."

Olivia froze. "Faked?"

Two people slid onto the stools at her right—Ghost and Z.

Olivia turned to Z. "Was Natalia lying?"

His voice was gentle. "I think you already know the answer, *Mistress* Olivia."

She closed her eyes for a moment as dismay swept through her. Because everything inside her said Natalia had spoken the truth.

"However, someone lied." The Colonel studied Olivia with a hard, professional gaze. His anger was obvious but controlled. "I'm wondering who showed you the photo, and if they had a selfish reason."

Olivia shook her head. "Chelsey. She came to me and said—"

"Chelsey, hmm?" Ghost gave her a grim nod and strode away.

Walked away.

Probably disgusted with the whole mess. Olivia stared down at her drink. Took a sip. Could barely swallow it. Had she jumped to a horribly wrong conclusion? Had she destroyed something so wonderful without even questioning it?

All because she was a fearful git who'd been burned in the past?

Eventually, she realized Anne was speaking, "What exactly did Chelsey say?"

"She wanted to play, and I told her I was in a committed relationship, and she asked why I was committed when Natalia wasn't. Then she showed me the picture."

"Do you have a copy?" Ben asked.

"No, no, of course not."

"Mistress Olivia." Ghost's harsh voice broke in. "If the picture was so successful, I'm sure Chelsey kept it. Didn't you, Chelsey?"

Olivia turned on her bar stool.

Chelsey stood there, shaking like a leaf.

Ghost gripped the young woman's shoulder with one hand—and held a garishly decorated phone in the other. He must have taken Chelsey into the loo to retrieve the phone from her locker.

Olivia stared at Chelsey. "Show me the photo."

"It's not... I'm sure it's gone. I wouldn't have..."

With an annoyed sound, Ghost pressed Chelsey's finger to the phone's fingerprint scanner.

Chelsey made a sound and tried to back out of Ghost's grip. He growled at her. "Kneel."

The authority in his voice made Chelsey drop to her knees—and several other submissives struggled not to follow suit.

He studied the phone and swiped the screen a few times, then handed the phone to Olivia.

She winced. "Yes, that's the one."

Ben plucked the phone from her hand and studied the display, then angled it so she could see. "Look at the shadows down their bodies. You can see the light came from the right. But...notice the shadows on Natalia's face—like beside her nose? There the light comes from the left."

Olivia stiffened.

Ben magnified the photo, magnified it again, and handed the cell back. He hovered his finger over Natalia's neck. "See how the skin texture has disappeared. It's too smooth, and the pigment doesn't quite match. Someone tried to blur the line where Natalia's head was substituted for someone else's."

Olivia could see it now. "It's not Natalia," she whispered.

"No," Anne said firmly. "It's not."

Olivia stared at the kneeling submissive.

Chelsey had gone dead white. "I...Mistress, it's only because... I'm sorry, I..."

The anger filling Olivia was huge. Engulfing. Throttling it back, she asked Ghost, "Advice?"

He considered a moment. "Work things out with Natalia, and afterward, the two of you decide together what Chelsey deserves. Then talk with me"—he winced—"I mean, talk with Z."

The pain in his expression broke through her anger.

She'd heard the bloody stupid rumors about him and could guess the originator. *Wrecker.* The arsehole was out to ruin a good Dom who was perfect for the job of managing the Shadowlands.

"Natalia and I will figure it out," she growled at him, "and be back to talk with you. As for you, don't be a plonker and quit on us."

"Olivia—"

She held up her hand. "I have things to do."

The hardarse actually chuckled. "Yes, you do."

Turning her back on him, she pulled up "share" on the picture and sent herself a copy. Maybe it would keep Natalia from killing her dead.

After deleting the photo, she handed the phone to Chelsey. "You hurt two people very badly. Think on that for a while."

As she stalked away, she heard Chelsey break into tears.

In their staging area of a bunch of chairs close to the bar, Valerie stared as Mistress Olivia walked out of the Shadowlands. "Wow. What a mess."

As she'd known would happen, Ghost had stepped in. Of course he had. She'd heard the way he told Olivia to talk to Z— and oh, she'd wanted to go give him a hug. They had to make this right.

"What a mess." Gabi shook her head. "Natalia did good. When she goes in, she sure goes all in."

Rainie scowled. "Who else wants to knock the backstabbing, buttheaded bimbo named Chelsey into the next county?"

Sally's hand shot up.

And they all followed suit.

The Masters at the bar had returned to talking. *Perfect.* This was the time they'd been waiting for. Valerie pulled in a breath and rose. "All right, people. Let's get our show on the road."

"Yes!" Sally bounced to her feet. "Bar team, with me."

Gabi, Beth, and Kim followed her.

Valerie pointed at Rainie and Andrea. "Projector team, prepare for action."

Grinning, Rainie saluted. The two women opened the bag sitting on the bondage table and pulled out the projector and laptop.

Valerie picked up the microphone and tried to relax. This wasn't any different than lecturing at the university, right?

Wrong. Students didn't carry whips and floggers hooked to their belts.

Outside Z's office, she punched in the code for the sound system—*thank you, Jessica*—killed the music, and selected the button marked *Announcement chimes*.

The three melodic notes sounded once, then again, alerting the members to gather at the bar. People around the room started to move. Scenes that could be ended easily would stop.

On the left end of the bar, Linda slid off her barstool so Kim could use it to climb onto the bar top. At the other end, Kari rose to give Sally the same access.

Even as Sally and Kim pulled down the chains that dangled from a rafter above the bar, Josie set the long white sheet on the bar top. The two grabbed the sheet, secured each end to chains, and pulled the chains so the sheet rose into the air.

Still on the ground, Gabi and Beth fastened the bottom corners of the sheet to the embedded anchors in the bar top.

Valerie grinned. There was their display screen, nice and tight, hanging above the center of the oval bar.

Around the bar, the Masters watched, eyes narrowed. But neither Master Z nor the Colonel had moved. The conspirators had counted on the Doms being too curious to put a halt to everything.

Microphone in hand, she moved toward the bar so she could see it better.

Rainie gave her a thumbs-up. The projector was ready.

Her turn.

"Members of the Shadowlands." She decreased the mic volume slightly to keep the sound contained to the area around the bar and not disturb the scenes. "Many of you have heard the rumors about the Colonel. Before we start... Did you realize the people who started the rumors are good buddies with the previous manager?"

Even as the crowd near the bar grew, people reacted to what she said with either frowns or swearing.

Seeing movement, she froze.

Dogget and Knuckles, a muscled brutish friend of Barry's had spotted her with the mic and were heading straight for her.

Spit, now what?

Ghost noticed and—Master Z put his hand on Ghost's arm, obviously keeping him there.

"Relax, pet." On her left, Saxon patted her shoulder.

Ben took up a position on her right and grinned down at her. "Anne wanted to see where you're going with this."

In an uncanny choreography, the two men crossed their arms over their muscular chests.

She had guards.

Knuckles and Dogget stopped, then faded into the still-growing crowd.

Okay then. One calming breath later, she spoke into the mic. "Usually rumors should simply be ignored, but since this kind of slander was deliberately set up to affect your trust in the Shadow-lands manager as well as in the owner, a response seemed appropriate. The ones peddling their lies say Ghost ignored a submissive's hard limits and drove her to attempt suicide."

There were some shocked sounds. Perhaps not everyone had heard the gossip. Far too many heads nodded.

"We went straight to the source to get the truth for you. The submissive's name is Faylee—and this is what she has to say."

Valerie pointed to Andrea and Rainie.

The projector lit up, and on the white sheet over the bar, the video played.

Faylee stood in front of a wall of bookcases in what appeared to be an office. She was probably in her thirties, brown hair cut in a bob, wearing a lacey blue blouse and dark pants. She was slightly underweight but appeared healthy.

Her voice was a bit harsh and high-pitched. "I have no idea how to do this, but here goes. I'd always planned to apologize to Ghost if the opportunity arose, but this sure isn't how I planned to do it. Jesus Christ, don't you idiots realize what kind of a fantastic Dom you scored for your club?"

A low voice said something, the words undecipherable, and Faylee sighed. "Right, right. Sorry."

Aside from a few scene noises, the entire club had gone quiet.

"So, Valerie asked me to tell you what happened on—how do the mysteries call it?—the night in question. Here's the background, something I'm finally able to talk about." Hands clasped in front of her waist, Faylee pulled in a visible breath. "I was abused as a child. Raped, beaten, messed up. By my father. And most of my life since has been trying to cope with that in one way or another. I'm also a masochist. Pain gets me out of my head and lets me know I'm alive."

Valerie had heard this recording several times now—and it

didn't seem to matter. When Faylee's voice wobbled on the last few words, on "I'm alive", Valerie's heart broke all over again. She swallowed back the tears.

Faylee was saying, "So, back then—fuck, it's like two years ago —I wanted to try something new, not just a good flogging, but being restrained...to get past what my father had done to me. I picked a Dom I'd never played with but who was awesome. So careful and controlled I knew I'd be safe. I'd watched him play before, almost always with a woman his age, but he hadn't been in the club for maybe a year, so when he showed up, I jumped at the chance."

Valerie moved closer to the crowd, thinking to watch their reactions. Inevitably, her gaze shot straight to Ghost.

Master Z still held his arm, although they'd moved away from the bar, probably to see the screen better. Jessica stood on Z's other side.

Ghost's expression was unreadable in the dim light of the club, but the very stillness, the way he held himself conveyed...anger.

Valerie's stomach felt as if she had rocks in it. She knew he'd be mad...and she couldn't let it stop her. Even if they weren't friends any longer, this needed to be done. Jessica had called earlier to report Ghost had tried to resign.

Not going to happen. The club needed him...and he needed the club.

On the screen, Faylee shook her head. "When I...okay, I'll confess that when I totally begged, Ghost agreed to a pick-up scene. I didn't know where his usual submissive was and didn't care. I was..." She bit her lip. "It's hard to admit, but at the time, the only person I cared about was me. We went through the negotiations, and it was all good. But when he asked about my past, about emotional problems and potential triggers, I lied to him—and then spilled my drink to fuck with my body language so he couldn't tell."

Someone muttered, "That's messed up."

"I fucking hate liars," gritted out a Top with a whip on his belt.

Faylee laughed suddenly and pointed at someone in the room. "You should see Master Drake's face. He's furious with me."

She shook her head. "Ghost talked about aftercare, and I told him no aftercare. I said I didn't like it and didn't tell him I couldn't tolerate someone trying to hold me. He said he liked to call his bottoms a day or so later to check on them, but sometimes his job took him out of town, and did I have someone else if I needed help. I assured him I did."

"Yes, people, I lied again. I did have friends, but I would never let anyone know I was vulnerable. Or ask for help. Just...no."

Faylee started walking back and forth in the room. "So, Ghost restrained me, and it was fine until he used a whip, and I couldn't move—and you guessed it right? I had a panic attack. Screaming and crying and—hell, I don't think I even used a safeword, but he had me out of the restraints and got me calmed down. He's really good at that. Then he ignored what I thought I'd wanted and did aftercare. Wrapped me in a blanket, helped me drink a Gatorade, and, since I wouldn't let him touch me, he just sat next to me. And talked. About nothing special. Letting me know I wasn't alone. That I was safe. God, it was nice. But, being an idiot, as soon as I spotted one of my friends, I had her take me home."

"What a mess," Saxon said under his breath.

Ben grunted his agreement.

On the screen, Faylee walked across the room again. Her face was pale, and she was blinking back tears.

Master Drake said something, and she shook her head. "No, I want to do this. It's...harder to talk about than I thought it would be."

She faced the camera again. "See, it was my own fault the scene went bad and cracked open all the shit I'd buried. For years, I'd been depressed and not really living, only this time, I went into a total meltdown. I really wanted the pain to end, and I was so angry and confused." She snorted. "Alcohol and drugs—really not a good choice."

Valerie sighed, wanting nothing more than to give the young woman a hug.

"Okay, right about then, I realized Ghost never called to check on me, and suddenly, *everything* was his fault. My meltdown and the drugs and all the shit wrong in my life. I was higher than a kite when I called my friends to rant about Ghost and blame everything on him. And then I tried to die."

She showed the scars on her forearms. "Cutting deep felt so good, like I could feel something, only then I realized maybe I wasn't ready to die, and I called 911. The doctors admitted me into a facility, and that's when I got help."

She was back to pacing back and forth.

"I was in the facility for quite a while. Once out, I avoided my friends—because that's what addicts are supposed to do. I didn't return to the club for a long time. But when I did, I found out the damage I'd done."

Pulling on her hair, she stared into the camera. "The reason Ghost hadn't been in the club for so long was because his wife died. Lucky him, his first night back after a year, he was saddled with a lying, crazy person."

There was a soft murmur going around the club.

Z still had a hard grip on Ghost's arm. Ghost knew he could get free by punching the bastard—and he'd seriously considered it—but flattening his friend seemed excessive.

Still, watching a submissive essentially flog herself over something she couldn't have helped pissed him the hell off.

In the process, she was sharing more about Ghost's past than he was pleased with. *Dammit.*

Faylee wiped her eyes. "I mentioned he didn't call me a day or two after the scene. Sure, he'd warned me that might happen because of his job, but in my deluded self-centeredness, I just *knew* it was because he'd simply blown me off. Well, it turned out he was a colonel in the Special Forces and sent overseas, and when carrying one of his soldiers to a helicopter, he got his leg shot up. And amputated. *God!* After all the hospital stuff, he finally gets back to Chains and finds out I'd totally destroyed his reputation."

She shook her head. "If you're listening to this, Ghost, I'm so sorry. When I talked about this with my counselor, she asked me... Well, I realized I not only lied to you, but I was so fucking self-involved I never asked you anything about you. It was my fault I didn't know you were military. Or knew your wife had died. In my mind, you were only there to give me what I wanted. And that's not right."

Pulling in a breath, she motioned toward the other side of the room. "When I eventually talked with Master Drake, he'd already pretty much figured out what happened, and I offered to visit the club and put things straight, but Ghost had already left. The club. The city. Even the state. What I did to him was probably the last straw on two years of misery. In spite of that, he'd left a note with Master Drake to hand over to me, one full of encouragement. Cheering me on to get better."

When Faylee's eyes welled with tears again, Ghost's chest ached in sympathy.

"Now, apparently some dumb asswipes in your club are trying to start it all back up for him. Well, you bastards, don't you dare use me as part of your smear campaign. Ghost is one of the best Doms you'll ever find, and you should be damned grateful to have him there." She set her hands on her hips and glared at the camera.

Ghost shook his head. He'd only spent a brief period of time with her, yet...he was damned proud of her. Her own strength had brought her out of the darkness. She was no longer huddled around herself but had grown enough to think of others.

Near where he stood, the members were talking quietly—and angrily.

"Those rumors were bullshit, total bullshit."

"She's right—talk about a fucking smear campaign."

"Barry was the one who told me that shit. He was totally lying."

Ghost blinked. *Well, damn.*

On the screen, Master Drake walked forward, very European in a black silk suit. He had black eyes and black hair and a neatly trimmed, gray-flecked mustache. After setting a supportive hand on Faylee's shoulder, he turned to the camera. "I'm Drake—and I own Chains, the club in Seattle where this happened. Ghost, if the Shadowlands doesn't suit, I'd be more than pleased to have you back and even more pleased to acquire a manager. You club members, if you have questions, you may call me. If any of you bother Faylee, I will have the skin flogged from your body."

The smile he gave was a grim promise.

And the screen went blank.

Beside Ghost, Z chuckled. "I see Drake hasn't changed. He's always had a rather stringent attitude toward discipline."

"All too true."

Z gave Jessica a squeeze and moved her to stand beside Ghost. "Please watch over her for me, Ghost." He strolled toward the bar.

When Jessica curled her arm around his, Ghost realized Z had effectively pinned him in place. "Your Master is a sneaky bastard."

She grinned up. "Isn't he though? I'm not sure whether he went into psychology because he has a conniving personality or if it's what he learned from being a shrink."

Ghost snorted.

At the front of the crowd, Z was saying, "In case any of you are wondering, that was, indeed, Drake, who owns Chains. We've been friends for many years. In fact, we'd already discussed this incident before Ghost became a member here."

There were quite a few members with shame-faced expressions.

Z shook his head. "Gossip happens wherever people gather. However, when the talk becomes destructive to someone's reputation or potentially harmful to another person, I would request you let me or Ghost know."

A murmur of agreement came from the people.

"Now," Z's smile flashed, "if our Shadowkittens have no more to present, let's return to enjoying our evening."

Almost dancing with glee, Sally and Gabi walked over.

Ghost eyed them. "You pulled off quite an operation, ladies." When they grinned and exchanged fist-bumps with each other, he added the question he'd been considering since Valerie started talking. "Who put it all together?"

"Valerie did," Sally said. "She was the one who called Drake and talked to Faylee."

The awakening of hope was painful.

Gabi's head tilted. "You seem surprised, Colonel."

"Actually, yes. I thought she'd believed the rumors." If not, then why had she backed away last night?

"I didn't get that impression at all," Gabi said. "In fact, she reamed out a group of gossipers last night."

"She's the one who gathered us all together at her apartment to plan this," Sally added.

Valerie believed in him and had defended him. The feeling was indescribable—like he was back in Special Forces with his teammates to guard his six.

Beside Ghost, Jessica stiffened. He followed her gaze.

At the bar, Z was getting his toy bag from Josie. He slung it over his shoulder.

"Oh God." Jessica bit her lip. "He plans to play. Why do I think my night might involve more pain than pleasure?"

From Z's point of view, the Shadowkittens had completely

disrupted the usual club evening...without obtaining permission. Ghost asked gravely, "How involved were you in setting this up?"

"I was part of the group. Do you think being pregnant will save me?"

Betting she was the one who gave Valerie the code to the speaker controls, Ghost smothered a smile. "Perhaps."

Not a chance.

Ghost bowed his head slightly to the three women. "You have my gratitude. Thank you."

As he moved away, he looked around. He needed to thank Valerie, as well. And...ask her a few questions.

However, if she'd rescued his reputation in her capacity as a friend and believed there was no "them", she might well decide to slip out without speaking to him.

That wasn't going to happen.

CHAPTER EIGHTEEN

Valerie had restored the music, returned the equipment to the owners, and touched base with her conspirators who were in high spirits.

It was time to make her escape. Ghost was the sort of man who'd feel he had to thank her for her part in this. Talk about awkward.

After expressing his gratitude, he'd undoubtedly return to his new play partner. And that would hurt.

As she crossed the room, a muscular sandy-haired man stepped into her path. "Nice presentation, and I'd have to agree you've been very good. Do you want your spanking now?"

What?

She stared at him a second. Oh, *oh*! She had on the shirt she'd bought from Natalia. The one saying *SPANK ME I've been good*.

Chuckling, she shook her head. "I'm afraid I have to be elsewhere."

He tilted his head in acceptance and stepped out of her way. "Hopefully, some other time."

"Maybe so." She smiled and headed off.

Maybe someday the time would come. When the hurt died. A

pang of sadness hit. When she'd first come to the Shadowlands, such an offer from an attractive Dom would have made her night.

Now, it just made her regret the offer hadn't come from Ghost.

Get moving, woman. Detouring, she swung by the bar. "Thank you for the help, Josie."

Busy drawing a beer, the redheaded bartender chuckled. "It went a lot better than I thought it would."

"I know." Valerie blew out a breath. "Did you get into any trouble?"

"There was a moment. Z gave me a *look*, and I swear, I took a couple of steps back. But then he shook his head and simply asked for his toy bag."

"Thank the gods."

"Right?" Josie set the beer on a tray for a server. "I thought I was off free and clear, but before he walked away, he said Master Holt would instruct me on appropriate behavior."

"Uh-oh."

"I'll be fine." Josie grinned. "I daresay you might be getting the same sort of lesson from—"

"Doubtful." Ignoring Josie's frown, Valerie gave the bar a quick farewell tap. "You take care now."

As she headed for the door at a quick pace, a shriek, then giggling from the dance floor caught her attention. A "little" was banging a stuffie on the ground. Her Daddy Dom hauled her up and over his shoulder. When she kicked her legs, a reproving smack on her bare thigh drew a squeal that made everyone laugh.

So cute.

Hating to leave, Valerie turned back toward the door and ran right into someone. "Oh sorry, I wasn't watching where—"

"It's a very bad habit, pet." Ghost's deep, rough voice blasted through her defenses like a hot knife through butter.

He closed his hands on her upper arms.

"Ghost." She tried to step back, but his grip tightened.

Gaze on his chest, she said in a flurry of words, "I know, I know, you're grateful, so you're welcome. Now, I really do need to be leaving."

Silence. Then a low chuckle. He cupped her chin with a warm palm and lifted her head. "Look at me, Valerie."

Her heart thumped crazily in her chest. "*What?*" Good grief, she sounded as surly as her son at fifteen.

A smile eased Ghost's stern mouth as he moved his hand to curl around her nape. "I think it's time we talk." Even as she shook her head no, he added, "Or I can tie you down and role-play an interrogation scene to get my answers."

Play with him again. Every single cell in her body started to rejoice. "No, absolutely not. Are you crazy?"

Still holding the back of her neck, he studied her with a focused intelligence. "For someone who defended me so vigorously, you sound as if you don't trust me."

Oh no, she didn't mean to make him feel bad. "Of course, I trust you," she said hastily.

Amusement flickered in his eyes before his gaze turned razor sharp again.

Holding her unmoving, he stroked a finger over her lips, down her neck, and into her cleavage.

Her nipples tightened so fast and hard they ached.

On top of her shirt, he brushed over the lettering on the right and left of the V-neck. SPANK ME. "You wrote out your request right over your breasts. Nice."

She shook her head. *No.*

"Professor, I think we need a scene—one where I beat on your pretty ass until I get some answers."

Sadness filled her to overflowing. Her voice came out hoarse. "They won't be the answers you want."

His hand slid up from her nape to tangle in her hair, his grip almost painful. "That happens."

"I should go."

"I don't think so." His gaze darkened. "Say yes, Valerie."

She shouldn't. No, she really shouldn't.

But to be with him...one last time?

Her whisper was barely loud enough for him to hear. "Yes."

Sometime later, she realized the wonderful, amazing pain had paused. When had the world disappeared?

She blinked, trying to focus her eyes. Gleaming brown...a hardwood floor. *Right.* She was naked, bent over a tall, four-legged barstool. Her wrists were bound together to one of the legs. Her thighs were spread, and ropes secured her parted knees to the wooden legs.

Some unknowable time ago, Ghost had warmed her up and then started alternating between paddling her ass and flogging her. Hard enough she'd struggled to escape. Hard enough she'd cried.

And then the pain slid into a sensual golden space where each blow made the air sparkle. She turned her head and saw his legs. He was standing next to the stool.

"You make the prettiest canvas, pet." His fingers traced over her bottom in a ripple of heat like small wavelets. "Your skin turns such a nice red."

Three more blows of the paddle hit her bottom. How could sparkles feel so warm?

And then he went down on his haunches in front of her. He lifted her head slightly so he could look into her eyes.

"Now, let's talk a bit," he murmured in his gravelly baritone. His green eyes held hers in a steady gaze.

"What?" The word came out slurred, as if she was drunk. And she was—drunk on endorphins.

The sunlines next to his eyes deepened. "Normally, when we

meet, I get a hug and kiss. Last night, you stepped back. Because you'd heard the rumors..."

"What? Uh-uh. I never...didn't hear anything till I was leaving." Her mouth closed. She wasn't going to say that, was she? If he knew she hadn't—

"If it wasn't the rumors, then why didn't I get a hug?"

Her eyes closed, trying to shut him out. She shook her head as her mind started to focus again. There was no way she'd tell him it was because he'd found someone else.

"I see. Then we'll keep going."

Keep...going?

The *whap* against her ass stung like fire because she'd slid out of the warm fog, but as he continued, hard and soft, right and left, up and down from her upper thighs to her upper buttocks, the feeling of the stool beneath her disappeared.

Then he was flogging her, the heavy blows thudding hard enough to shake her bones, and somehow the floor turned all foggy, too.

Sometime later, he ran his hands through her hair. Touched her cheek. "Valerie, why didn't you want to be with me last night?"

Last night was a long time ago. "I was sad," she whispered.

"I hate seeing you sad," he said in a low voice. "Why were you unhappy, pet?"

"You found someone else to play with." The feeling swept over her again, the hurt of seeing him with the beautiful submissive. Tears filled her eyes.

"Did I now? But I had you, sweetheart. Why would I want someone else?"

Her mouth opened, and then she frowned. *What in the world am I saying?* She pulled at the ropes on her wrists, shaking her head.

And then the flogger was dancing over her back, sending a hot wave of desire through her. Somehow, she was rippling along on the tops of the waves. A harder blow made her gasp and squeak, and he laughed, a rough, amused sound. Pain and desire hit so hard she shuddered.

"Valerie."

She blinked. "Where did you go?"

"Oh, I had to beat on you a while. You were telling me why I wanted someone else besides you."

She was? Easy enough. "I'm not young, not beautiful anymore."

"Mmmph, neither am I."

"You're a man. Women are... We have to be beautiful." She tried to get her thoughts to work. "Or useful. Or we're worthless. Throw us away."

He was quiet enough she started to drift, pleased he understood.

"Did your parents think you were worthless?"

My parents. She wouldn't think about them; she wouldn't. Her mouth closed.

"There's an unhappy frown." He gripped her hair tightly, and the feeling of being controlled, totally under his authority, washed heat over her skin. "When they were mad, what did they say to you?"

A chill wind swept away the warmth surrounding her. "*With your looks, you better learn to be useful.*"

"*...never wanted to have a fucking kid, let alone an ugly one.*"

"For fuck's sake," Ghost said under his breath. "Those bastards."

"No, they—" Wait, what had she said?

"Shhh." With a palm under her cheek, he stroked her hair. "I heard your ex's slave is shit-talking you. I bet that's bringing back the bullshit you suffered as a child."

She wiggled, trying to focus on what he was saying. "What?"

"It's good to know what I have to fight." With a satisfied

chuckle, he kissed her. Slowly. Tenderly. "You thought I'd found someone younger to play with—and you backed away."

Her mind cleared enough to know she'd made a fool out of herself. But the truth was the truth. "I saw her, Ghost. How could you resist someone so pretty who drops to her knees in front of you?"

"Very easily, actually. Especially since she pulled some manipulative crap after I said I wasn't interested." He brushed his fingers over Valerie's cheek. "I lectured her about proper submissive behavior and left her in the subbie waiting area."

"But...she's young."

He snorted. "Not an enticement. I'd rather spend time with someone who grew up with the same music and movies and books. Who doesn't use a phone as another appendage."

She understood...because she had loved how Ghost understood the jokes and movie quotes she'd grown up with.

"I like that sex with you is more relaxed. You have experience, know what you like. Like to give as well as take. Like to explore."

She was starting to feel good. Really good.

"I want a woman who's lived a few decades. And as it happens, I like a soft woman under me." His voice dropped to a rumbling growl. "You are very soft, pet."

Oh.

He kissed her again. "Be warned, lass. We're going to work on the crap you absorbed from your folks."

"I...I learned what they said wasn't true." But then she let it affect her again. She sighed. "Or so I thought."

"That's all right." A corner of his mouth tilted up. "I'll have no problem punishing you any time I discover you thinking unkind thoughts about yourself."

A horrified squeak escaped her.

His smile widened. "Actually, let me rephrase; I'll enjoy the hell out of it."

Oh gods.

CHAPTER NINETEEN

Sixty...sixty-one... The next morning, Valerie lay on the carpet in her apartment and tried for another crunch. Her abs burned like fire. *I can do it...* Or not. With a groan, she flopped like a dead person onto the carpet. And *ow*. Her back and shoulders stung, too, because...flogger.

She smiled and wiggled her shoulders, savoring the light pain.

What a day and night.

Thank goodness she'd convinced Faylee and Master Drake to make the video. It hadn't been easy. Then again, she'd grown up supervising the self-important housekeepers in her parents' home, raised two children, and taught for years. She had skills.

There hadn't been any need to convince the Shadowkittens. The amazing group of women had simply rallied around.

Valerie sat up and put her arms around her knees. The actual presentation in the Shadowlands had gone off better than she could have dreamed. *Spit,* but she'd been tense, what with worrying how the members would react.

And how Master Z would react. She'd half thought he might shove her into one of the cages for disobedient submissives.

Mostly, she'd worried what Ghost would think.

Resting her chin on her knees, she thought about his face. When he saw Faylee and realized what was going on, his jaw had gone hard.

And her stomach had sank.

But as the members started swearing at Wrecker's lies, he'd been surprised. She'd known then he wouldn't be resigning and was going to be all right.

And...she'd realized she loved him.

Not that she'd admitted it to herself or him during his "interrogation"—no, she hadn't been thinking at all then.

But later, upstairs in his "quarters", when he'd been inside her, filling her, his green eyes trapping hers...then she'd known.

She was in love with him. With Ghost. With Dr. Finn Blackwood. With the Dom and sadist and manager of the Shadowlands.

Way to go, self. Didn't I tell you not to get involved with anyone? To stay out of a relationship?

Her jealousy should have been a warning to run, far and fast. But noooo, her heart operated independently of all her rules.

She tightened her arms around her knees as worry slid through her.

When Barry dumped her, it'd hurt so much, even though, by that time, their marriage felt more like roommates than lovers.

But with Ghost? Every time he spoke to her, laughed with her, touched her—her heart radiated with joy, and her emotions danced.

If—when—he walked away, it was going to shatter her into tiny pieces.

She breathed out.

Face it, woman, it's too late to flee. At this point, running away would simply mean she would hurt much sooner.

Might as well accept the inevitable. If studying the various religions had taught her anything, it was that one should savor each moment with one's beloved.

She could push him away—or cling obsessively—in fear of losing him to someone else or even to death. Or she could accept that change would happen and make the most of what she felt.

Because she really did love him.

For a few minutes, she simply indulged in the glory of the emotion. Of feeling alive and being able to give, to receive.

She'd never thought she'd feel this way about a man again.

The world really did hold miracles.

Eventually, she returned to earth...after remembering making love with him a few times.

And then she remembered their condom discussion after he'd returned from disposing of one and cleaning up.

She grinned. He'd been so sneaky...

"You know, a nice woman would take pity on a poor crippled veteran and let him stop using condoms."

She'd sat up and smacked him on the arm. "I don't believe it; you're using your leg as a guilt card."

"You use the weapons that are available." His sexy grin flashed. "Or the cards that are dealt. But, seriously, if you're all right with it, let's lose the rubbers. I know you were checked when you joined the Shadowlands—and I had one done last week. I left the results for you on the dresser."

"Last week?" she asked suspiciously. "Oh, don't even try to act innocent. You planned to have this discussion."

"Well, yeah." He ran his hand down her arm. "I know you're on birth control, and our test results were negative. I don't screw around—I consider us to be together."

Together. Such a lovely word.

With a happy sigh, she shook her head and...*spit on it all*, started back with the exercising torture.

Push-ups sucked. She managed two standard ones before surrendering and doing the rest of the push-ups from her knees.

Finished with her goal, she collapsed to the floor on her belly and let out a high, exhausted, "Woohoo!" Two real push-ups!

When she'd started, she could barely manage one from her knees.

Serious progress.

She felt good. And really, being streamlined, wrinkle-free, and young wasn't an achievable goal. Healthy? That she could do.

And that was what she *would* do.

Rolling over onto her back, she stared up at the ceiling. Last night, she'd been in floaty-land when Ghost quizzed her about why she'd backed away from him. But she did remember what she'd said.

It was true her parents had made her feel unworthy. Once in the States, she'd realized she was pretty. In the military and later, she took jobs where her worth wasn't measured in appearance. Where her sense of esteem had soared.

So, she'd been fine, right up until Barry and his slaves had sliced her self-image to pieces.

And she'd allowed it to happen.

She rolled her eyes. *I should have left when I realized he was all about Alisha and no longer interested in me.*

Ah, well, hindsight.

But the damage was done, and she still had some work to do to restore her internal balance. She needed to accomplish it quickly.

Ghost liked that discipline stuff way too much.

The late morning sun glinted off the puddles left by the night's rain. Such pretty sparkles. At any other time, Natalia would have been grabbing her paints. Today, though?

Glaring, she drove straight through the puddle.

And then felt like crying because…did puddles have feelings?

She was one hot mess.

Her eyes were red and puffy from sobbing fits all night long. Her toes hurt from kicking everything in sight.

Since she'd spent the night in a fellow artist's attic, her tantrums hadn't disturbed her friend's sleep. And she'd been able to cover a gift canvas with angry red and black blotches.

Her friend had seen the ugly mess, winced, and given Natalia a sympathetic hug.

As she parked her car outside her small duplex, she felt emptied. Her drama was done. The hopes she'd clung to were gone, too.

Olivia had thought she'd cheated on her. *God.*

It was time to move on with her life, somehow, rather than hoping Olivia would change her mind.

"Cheating." She shut the engine off. "Didn't she know me at all?" That hurt more than anything.

Swinging her purse over her shoulder, she headed for the house, gaze on the ground. The broken and uneven paving stones in the coarse St. Augustine grass required her attention, or she'd trip and break her neck.

At the last stone, she looked up and gasped.

In jeans and a sleeveless denim shirt, Mistress Olivia sat at the top of the three-step landing. Her elbows rested on her thighs as she watched Natalia with an unreadable expression.

Natalia stared at her. "What are..." *No.* She didn't want to know why the Mistress was here. "I'm sorry I caused a fuss at the club. Now, if you don't mind, please leave me alone."

Taking a step back, she gestured toward the street.

"No." Leaning forward, Olivia held out her phone. "Here. Check this out."

Natalia sighed. The display would probably show that Master Z had canceled her Shadowlands membership. Even though she planned to quit, her heart sank.

"Fine." Natalia checked the screen. It wasn't an email. Or a text.

It was a photo. Two naked women in bed. The one on top was using a strap-on on the other woman. The one on the bottom had her arms bound to the headboard, and...

"It's *me*." Natalia stared. "That *can't* be me. I've never... That can't be me, but it is."

Olivia ran her hand through her spikey pale hair. "It's a Photoshop trick, love."

"Why?" Natalia whispered.

Closing her eyes for a moment, Olivia made a growling sound. "When Chelsey told me you were cheating on me, I didn't believe her. Then she showed me this photo, and bugger it, Nats, I went barmy."

Chelsey had done what?

Olivia's hazel eyes, more brown than green today, gleamed with tears for a second. "I'm sorry. I can understand if you don't forgive me, but I wanted you to know how it happened. And to apologize. I'm so sorry."

Natalia felt as if her brain had broken. The picture. Chelsey.

Olivia.

Here. Apologizing.

What was she supposed to do? Her legs started to wobble, to buckle.

Olivia sprang up and caught her around the waist, then used both arms to hold her up.

Dropping her head against the Mistress's shoulder, Natalia breathed in the clean, warm scent, like a warm day in autumn. The arms around her were strong. The Mistress wouldn't let her fall.

"Sit, girl." After settling Natalia on the top step, Olivia tried to move back. And couldn't.

Natalia realized she was clinging. Oh God, she was so confused. "Sorry, I'm sorry."

Olivia snorted. "No, poppet, you're using my line." She shook her head. "I kicked you out and didn't even explain. Or let you talk."

She hadn't, had she. *Oh look, here's some anger that hadn't drained in my temper tantrums.* Natalia scowled at the woman she thought loved her. "I noticed. Why?"

Taking a seat on the lowest step, Olivia wrapped her hand around Natalia's bare ankle.

Natalia could feel the warmth, the calluses. Her Mistress's hand. The longing shook her deep inside.

"I..." With a sigh, Olivia shook her head. "I have no good excuse."

Natalia hardened her heart although her voice shook as she forced out the word, "Try."

Olivia's jaw tightened, before she nodded. "Fair."

Natalia waited. The Mistress rarely shared her past.

"It's like this, Nats. Every lover I've been with eventually cheated on me, one after we'd been together for three years. Since submissives obviously couldn't be faithful, I swore off monogamous relationships. Then I met you."

Natalia felt her breathing stop.

"We—we were so perfect together, and I trusted you. I knew you would never lie to me."

Oh God, no wonder. Natalia whispered, "Then Chelsey showed you that picture and told you I was like your previous girls. A cheater."

To Natalia's shock, Olivia's eyes reddened with tears. "I hurt you badly. I'm sorry."

Unable to answer, Natalia stared at her hands.

One evening, in the Shadowlands, Natalia had heard Ghost telling a new member that if a submissive was hurt, her Dom would feel like shit—because he'd failed in his duty to keep her safe.

How much worse was it if the Domme herself delivered the blow?

Lifting her head, Natalia looked at the Mistress—really looked at her.

Olivia had dark circles under her eyes, her hair was a mess, her clothing wrinkled. "Were you here all night?"

Olivia shrugged.

Yes, then, she had been.

The Domme's clothing was loose. She'd obviously lost weight in the last month or so. Her tan had faded. The lines in her face were deeper.

Natalia bit her lip. "Is it bad I can see I'm not the only one who's been unhappy since we broke up?"

After a sharp bark of laughter, Olivia shook her head. "I've missed you so bloody much." She pulled in a breath. "Every day."

Natalia almost didn't recognize the feeling swelling inside her.

Happiness.

She swallowed. Could...could they go back to... "Um. Want to come inside and explain how my face got in the picture? Maybe?" A quiver of hope ran through her.

The same hope appeared in Olivia's eyes.

Natalia leaned forward.

The kiss was soft, tender, questioning. Olivia pulled back far enough to whisper, "You shouldn't forgive me...but I love you so much."

"Well, I guess I could beat on you for a while." Natalia tried to smile, but she really, really hoped it would be the reverse.

A glint appeared in Olivia's eyes. Her voice was soft and level, as she said, "Yes, love. Let's go inside and see who beats on whom."

When Valerie had returned to Ghost's place later that day, he'd wanted to work out. Since she'd already done her own exercises, he gave her a self-defense lesson.

It was amazing how many ways there were to hurt someone.

After the lesson, her reward was to use the punching bags Ghost had hung in the weight room. She felt like such a kick-ass when she drove her fist into the person-sized sandbag. Although he kept telling her she wasn't putting enough muscle into it.

Men.

After her shower, she stayed commando and simply pulled on lightweight cotton drawstring pants and a scoop-neck, loose T-shirt.

In the dining room, Ghost stood in front of the arched window, watching the rain. Even with his back to her, he seemed to radiate authority. His hands were interlocked behind his back, callused palms facing her. An officer's stance.

He looked so...alone.

"Are you all right?" she asked softly as she took a seat on the couch.

He turned, and his eyes lightened. "I'm always better when you're here."

Couldn't he just melt a girl's heart?

He'd already set out a glass of wine and a bottle of beer on the coffee table, and he sat down beside her.

The tall windows were open, letting in the moist offshore breezes with a trace of perfume from the tropical flowers. The sound of rain was a soft pattering, accompanied by the low rumble of thunder. It felt so...right, simply to share a quiet evening with him.

He picked up her hand and curled her fingers around the wine glass. "I thought you might like this red."

The merlot was smooth and soft with a lingering plummy taste. "It's perfect." She took another sip, then frowned. "You sound hoarser than normal."

His laugh was rueful. "I was passing an accident where a pickup had smashed the rear of a sedan. The driver—a drunk guy in a suit—was bellowing at the other driver, a tiny woman who was probably about eighty. And...I might have yelled at him for a while."

"Of course you did." Laughing, Valerie shook her head, then eyed him. "I noticed you have some scars on your neck. Did your vocal cords get injured? Is that why you get hoarse?"

"Good guess. Back in my first days with Special Forces, I ended up too close to an explosion. Whatever hit me fractured my larynx. The vocal cords caught some damage, then picked up scar tissue, too. Could've been worse. I had good surgeons, so I have a voice"—he ran his hand over the scars on his neck and grinned—"and can still yell at assholes."

He really was amazing. The only response she could find was to trail kisses from his jaw and down his neck. The explosion could so easily have killed him.

Eventually, she settled back against him and drank some of the wine he'd brought out because he knew what she liked. "So, speaking of assholes, do you think Wrecker will give up on trying to get revenge now?"

Brows drawn, Ghost sipped his beer as he thought. "Difficult to say. The manager job is only part-time, so the loss shouldn't affect him much. However, if his ego is tied up in being a Dom, he'll hate having lost access to the club. All the clubs."

Gods, she really hoped Scott would leave well enough alone.

"Thank you again for what you did." Ghost took her hand and kissed her fingers.

She moved her shoulders. "I've been wondering. Why do you feel as if what happened with Faylee was your fault? I can see you think that."

His face went still. "Yes, I should explain."

At the pain in his voice, she ran her hand through his dark gray hair. Cut in a short no-nonsense style, his hair had the wavy softness of a sheep's fleece. "Ghost—Finn, you don't have to tell me any of this."

"No, if you're playing with me, you need to know I can make mistakes." A muscle flexed in his cheek. "Since I'd seen Faylee around, I knew she was a masochist and experienced enough to know what she liked. She said she was a pain slut and wanted to be restrained and whipped hard enough to leave lines—and it's not an unusual request. But when she asked to be pushed, I refused since pushing boundaries isn't something to get into with pick-up play. During the negotiations...hell, I was struggling with being there without Kelly."

How he must have hurt. Missing his wife and trying to move on. It'd taken him a year. Then Valerie blinked. "Wait... Do you feel guilty because you didn't catch her lie?"

"I should have seen it," he growled. "My head wasn't completely in the game.

Of course it hadn't been. And Faylee had pulled a sneaky trick with spilling her drink.

Ghost wouldn't accept her sympathy, so maybe she'd poke the bear instead to get him past this sticking point. "I guess Doms aren't allowed to be human. I suppose I should address you as Supreme Power?"

His eyes held surprise, then narrowed.

"That would be a fine start, yes." He set his beer down with a thump—all the warning she had before he yanked her, belly-down, over his legs. "Presumptuous mortal, you must learn to be respectful."

Three not-very-stinging swats hit her tender butt.

"Ow!" Only it didn't really hurt.

His unmoved expression indicated he didn't believe her in the least.

And she started to giggle.

With a grumbling sound, he sat her up and pulled her into his arms. "I beat on the woman, and she giggles. You're killing my ego." Chuckling, he murmured, "Fuck, I love you."

She froze, and her breath caught in her throat.

"Such an expression." He cupped her chin, watching her face. "Too soon?"

Breathe, Valerie. "You're serious?"

His eyes turned soft. "Yes, Dr. Winborne, I'm profoundly serious. I love you." His thumb stroked her cheek.

"But... I didn't want a relationship."

He chuckled. "Oops?"

Even as her heart swelled with joy, his unapologetic smile made her laugh. "I suppose if I say I still don't want a relationship, you'd say you'll wait?"

He tilted his head. "Sometimes patience is needed to win a war." He firmly gripped her hair and tilted her head back. "As it happens, I'm an expert at strategic planning."

His mouth covered hers in a slow, provocative kiss. One that left her boneless.

He pulled back far enough to look into her eyes. "Now, tell me the truth, woman."

The words left her in a long sigh. "I love you."

When his lips curved up, she blinked, tried to scowl, and laughed. "You... Yes, I really do. *uHibbuka,*" she murmured in Arabic. *I love you.*

"Thank you, *ya amar.*"

My moon—saying she was beautiful. She sighed and tilted her face for another kiss. And another.

Eventually, when she was purely boneless, he let her go.

"Now, let's discuss." He leaned forward and picked up his beer, then realized it was empty. His grumpy frown made her grin.

Without a word, he set the bottle back down. He rarely had more than one beer in an evening.

Still...how could she not offer another and have another chance to tease him? "Oh, my Supreme Power, let this unworthy one fetch you a fresh drink."

She said the whole thing without laughing.

His head turned as if on a swivel, and he pinned her with a

disbelieving gaze. "Again? I get the feeling my professor is craving an extended amount of discipline."

Her mouth went dry...and every nerve in her body sparked to life.

Ghost was surprised—and pleased—as Valerie's eyes dilated and red rose from her neck into her face. "Well, well, well. Far be it from me to turn down such an interesting request."

Her swallow was audible. "I...didn't request anything."

"But you did." He rose, took her hand, and pulled her into the bedroom. A twist of the wall rheostat set the Moroccan lanterns to a low glow. The light scent of sandalwood from the infuser drifted in the air.

Hearing the music, she tilted her head and smiled.

"I thought you'd enjoy it." He'd put together a very sensual Middle Eastern playlist, and now, over the hidden speakers came the rhythm of the *dumbek* with the clear tones of the *zumara* and *mizmar*.

Smiling, he pulled her soft shirt up and over her head, baring her upper body. Unable to resist, he fondled one breast, then the other. "I'm going to have so much fun with these tonight." Under his palms, the nipples bunched into delectable peaks.

In her wide eyes, anticipation warred with anxiety.

Perfect.

He backed her to the bed. A few days before, he'd stocked the big nightstand on his side with interesting toys for her. The Velcro cuffs went on her wrists. After checking the fit, he hooked them together in front of her.

"Now, I want you to sit here quietly and await the orders of your Supreme Power." *Supreme Power.* He'd known she had a quiet brat streak.

Tipping her chin up, he took another quick kiss, then pinched the tips of her breasts, watching to see when she reached the border of pain.

In a while, he'd take her to that edge...and keep going.

Sit quietly? Valerie stared at the Colonel. Was he insane?

From his nightstand, he pulled out what he called toys.

Who in the world came up with the notion a cane was a *toy*?

First came a long stick with a square of leather at the end—a crop. Then a paddle. After each, he met her gaze with a wicked glint in his eyes, as if silently asking, *Now, what might I do to you with this?*

The quivers deep in her belly moved outward until her fingers trembled.

"Stand up for me, please," he said quietly.

She wiggled off the high bed and let him pull her pants down, then help her step out of them.

From under the bed, he brought out a roll-topped black cushion. It was about a foot high and wide, and maybe two feet long—like an extremely narrow saddle. He set it on the bed near the edge of the mattress, picked her up, and helped her straddle it. She was facing the headboard, trying to figure out how it worked. Reaching only to the middle of her thighs, it was too low for her to rest her butt on it.

"We'll start with something entertaining." He gripped her nape and bent her forward until her ass was higher than her shoulders. Her wrists still clipped together, she braced herself on her elbows.

"You have the most satisfying ass." He caressed her buttocks between spanking her lightly.

A lovely heat began to spread over her body.

But then he pulled her cheeks apart. A slickly lubed plug pressed against her anus—and was firmly pushed inside.

"What—wait!" She jerked. It stretched the muscles there, burning, and feeling...just plain wrong.

As she tried to rise, he set his hand between her shoulder blades, holding her in place. "I did read over your limits list, lass. Weren't anal plugs on the list?"

Oh spit. She had checked the item as a *wanted to try*. "Yes." Grumbling—mostly at herself—she tried to relax and was unable to ignore the way the thing felt inside her. Invasive...and disconcertingly erotic.

"Let me know if becomes distressing." He stroked down her back and gave her hair a light tug. "You can sit up."

Helping her rise—and didn't that plug feel weird when her weight rested on it?—he lifted her arms and fastened her wrist cuffs to a chain dangling from the black arches that were part of the steel canopy bed frame. Rather than letting her sit back on her heels, the position kept her kneeling up in a straight line from her knees to her hands. The cushion was still between her legs.

"Mmmph, yes. You're unbelievably beautiful in this position, lass." Resting a callused hand on her shoulder, he stood beside her.

The satisfaction in his gaze made her very aware of how she must look. On her knees. Naked. Arms bound over her head.

"Close your eyes, please." He tied a blindfold around her head.

"What? No." She would have removed it—but her arms were restrained. "Ghost..."

"I thought it was Supreme Power." The amusement in his voice was all too obvious.

She was going to regret teasing him. Because this wasn't a pick-up scene...and they'd been together long enough he wouldn't have a problem pushing her.

The blindfold was definitely a push. Not being able to see changed...everything. She was far too aware of the cuffs around her wrists, of her raised arms—and how she was now totally unable to defend herself. Her skin felt every waft of rain-cooled air from the open windows.

She was already damp in anticipation of he'd do next.

"You're such a good submissive, waiting so patiently," he murmured. Before she could react to the sweet—or scary—compliment, he curved his hand around the back of her head and then his mouth covered hers, taking her, possessing, eroding any sense of resistance.

Pulling back, he cupped her breasts with warm callused hands. Fondling, then squeezing, pulling and tugging on the nipples.

Her breasts swelled until the skin felt too tight.

Running his hands over her, he stroked and fondled...everywhere, making it clear her body was his for whatever he wanted to do.

Heat surged through her in waves at the knowledge.

The cushion kept her knees apart, and his fingers easily found her clit to tease it lightly. She could feel how slick she was. "It seems you're ready for more. Probably not for how much more you'll get perhaps."

She stiffened. What did—

He cupped his hand over her mound—to brace her, she realized a second later, when his other hand swatted her ass. The blows fell lightly at first, then hard, and he rubbed away the sting between each set of blows.

Such a lovely burn—and somehow the blindfold made her even more sensitive.

Stopping for a moment, he gripped her hair, tilting her head back so he could kiss her, his mouth rough, then startlingly tender. "Ready for more?" he whispered.

She swallowed.

He didn't wait for her assent. "Let's see if you like this paddle." A second later, the wooden paddle smacked against her bottom, and the sting barely had a chance to bloom before he struck her again and again. With each blow the plug inside her shifted, stimulating new nerves, even as the pain grew, sweeping everything away.

Her eyes filled with tears that pooled and dampened the blindfold.

He stopped, his warm hand on her cheek, as he kissed her hair. Giving her a chance to safeword, she knew, but the pain was like a waterslide, pulling her downward to the depths.

His hand rubbed her bottom for a minute, increasing the wonderful burn.

"Now, we haven't played with the crop yet." He stroked the leather down her back and over her butt before starting in with a light tap-tap-tap sensation. Not a bad feeling, really.

The crop moved up and down her ass, then he increased the strength, hitting with a few light ones, then a heavier one that made her squeak.

The sting was shocking, leaving behind a deeper pain as if her skin was welting.

Still standing beside her, he went over the same area, and soon, her ass felt as if it was on fire. A volcano of shimmering sensation reached deep inside her, feeding into lakes of desire.

But then...

He stroked the leather end of the crop over her breasts.

"Wait...uh-uh." She shook her head, even as he started tapping, creating an almost slapping sensation in circles around her breasts—then hitting right on her nipple.

Ooooh, that was horrible. Wonderful. How could she feel tense, even as she was sliding away?

In between circles, he ran his hands over her burning breasts, hurting her—rousing her unbearably.

"Now I have you warmed up, we can move to the good stuff." His voice ran over her almost like his hands, warm and sensuous.

The odd cushion between her lower thighs shook, before something pressed lightly against her clit.

A second later, there was a loud hum. Ghost set his hand on her ass and pushed her forward—right into a vibrator.

Only this wasn't a pleasant bouncy vibrator like the one she owned. Her modest vibrator felt like a dirt bike compared to this gigantic Harley-like effect.

How in the world did a vibrator on her clit make the anal plug vibrate, too?

Too much. Tugging against her restrained arms, she managed to move her hips back only enough the overwhelming sensations decreased...slightly. She sure couldn't keep from squirming as the vibrations took effect.

"Yes, very nice, pet."

Then the paddle hit her ass, driving her forward, pressing her hard against the vibrator. He continued, blow after blow, each strike sending a shock of pain through her ass that somehow met the intense pleasure of the vibrator right on her clit.

Her body tightened, the pressure coiling within her, driving her toward an orgasm.

With a low chuckle, he squeezed her breast, set a hand on her bottom, and pushed—holding her right against the vibrator.

Every nerve in her lower half clenched in a shimmering ball of tension and exploded outward in a huge climax. The anal plug added a whole different sensation, and wave after wave of pleasure shuddered through her.

His low laugh held a dark pleasure. "Very pretty. Let's do that again."

What?

The crop hit her bottom, her burning bottom, and the riptide of sensation pulled her loose and took her away.

Ghost was deep into Topspace, feeling as if unseen ropes connected him to Valerie. Her skin was sheened with sweat, her face and chest flushed to a dark rose color. How many times had she come? He'd lost track somewhere on the way to a dozen.

But, damn, he'd never seen anything as beautiful as she was when she came, immersed in the cycle of pain and pleasure. Her breasts were red and swollen and might have a light bruise or two.

Her ass, though, would show quite a few more.

She should never have told him she enjoyed seeing his marks on her.

He closed his fingers in her hair and pulled her head back so he could kiss her.

"No more, please." Her voice, raw from coming, had reached a sexy low contralto.

"One more. I want to be in you when you come this time, pet."

She swallowed. "I can't."

"Lass, you have to," he said gently, "because I won't give you the choice." He cupped her breast, squeezing gently.

A shiver ran through her, his beautiful submissive. Bending to his will.

He kissed down her neck, tasting the salt on her skin, and nipped the top of her shoulder. In his palm, her nipple bunched into a peak.

All right then.

Leaving her hands restrained, he turned her and the magic wand mount, so her knees were on the edge of the bed, facing away from him. He moved her wrist cuffs to a different hook on the overarching bedframe, which forced her to lean forward. "There, just right."

Freeing his dick—and fuck, but it felt good—he slicked the head in her very wet folds, then entered with a hard thrust.

"Oh, oh, oh." Her husky cry of pleasure made him grin.

Damned if the anal plug, slim as it was, didn't make her beautifully tight.

After flipping the switch on the magic wand, he started to

thrust. His movement forced her forward onto the wand—and he could feel the thing vibrating all the way through her. Nice.

Her body went stiff. "Noooo."

Relenting, he retreated enough she'd only touch the vibrator when he thrust and would get a break when he moved back.

She wouldn't need much to send her over again. Her cunt was already clamping down on him as she aroused again.

With one hand, he teased a swollen, undoubtedly painful breast, tugging on the abused nipple, as he increased his speed. She was slick and hot around him, her body quivering delightfully as he drove her into the vibrator and back.

"Gods, oh gods," she gasped—and she came, tightening around his dick like a hot fist, hard enough the rhythmic clenching ripped his control apart.

The pressure tightened in his groin, ran like scalding liquid through his balls, and overwhelming pleasure filled him. Bending his head, he wrapped his arms around her as he came and came.

Valerie felt like a total limp noodle as she watched Ghost finish preparing for bed. He'd already gently sponged her off before tucking her under the covers.

Sitting on the mattress, he took off his odd peg leg walker, then slid into bed. "Come here, lass." He pulled her up against him, setting her head on his shoulder. He was so warm she didn't mind when he tossed the covers back. "I'm surprised you're still awake."

"I can't believe the things you did to me," she muttered. And, okay, she really loved hearing his deep laugh.

"Professor, I thoroughly enjoy doing things to you."

"You're such a damn sadist."

"Yes." He stroked down her waist, curled his hand over her ass and squeezed, laughing at her hissed curses.

She earned another squeeze for calling him a son of a dirty, stinky camel.

Life was easier when no one knew Arabic.

"By the way, did you notice the new mirror in here?" he asked.

"I did. It's really beautiful." It was huge—probably three feet wide by six feet high with a dark frame of ornate metal inlay work. The black and gold finish matched the hanging Moroccan lanterns in the corners. "And perfect with your décor."

In shades of blue and black, his bedroom was a beautiful blend of clean lines and luxurious fabrics, rich tapestries and rugs. An Arabian night's dream in the current century.

"I'm glad you like it." He brushed her hair out of her face and kissed the top of her head. "Maybe it will make up for the two new rules that go into effect in the morning."

"What rules?" She lifted her head to eye him suspiciously.

The glint of laughter in his eyes was unsettling. "Rule one—you'll be naked whenever you're here. And when you leave, you'll wear the underwear I buy you."

"Excuse me?" *Like that would ever happen.* Valerie shook her head. "Two glasses of wine and a lot of orgasms are totally insufficient preparation for this kind of order, Colonel."

His deep, open laugh sent quivers through her, and then he caught her chin, keeping her head up. Trapping her gaze. "Because of the damage your ex and his nitwits caused, you were going to walk away from what we have together, pet. That's unacceptable."

It felt good to hear him insult them, but... She swallowed. "Yes, what they said made me feel...ugly...but how will being naked help?"

"Covering up isn't helping you, lass." He pulled her against him, his arms comforting. "My experience—losing part of my leg —is different, yet similar. It took quite a while before I could stand to see myself in the mirror, before I could accept that my body wasn't the same as what I wanted, but it's mine, and I'm not less of a person. Simply different, which is okay. Some people like who I am and how I look—and some don't. And that's okay, too."

She huffed. "You're like sex on a stick, and I'm old and flab—

"Stop." He picked up something from the bedstand and swatted her thigh.

"Ow!" It stung like a line of angry bees had nailed her. "That didn't feel good at all."

When she tried to rub her stinging thigh, he held her hand away from it. "You told me you know you have a problem because of those assholes. Can't you trust me enough to let me help?"

She trusted him. She *did*.

And maybe being called on her disparaging thoughts might help. Would help. Oh effing hell. "I'll hate it, but I guess being switched for disparaging comments is all right."

Not able to meet his eyes, she glared at his chest. "The naked stuff, though..."

"I know it'll be difficult, sweetheart, but it goes with the rest." He stroked her hair. "Although I can't say it's going to be a problem for me. I love seeing you naked, and I'm really looking forward to seeing you in the lacy red undies I bought you."

"You won't when you see what I—" Her mouth closed with a snap, because she'd seen him touch the gods-benighted switch.

"Excellent response time you have there, Professor." He cupped her cheek, kissing her lightly.

With a sigh, she set her forearm on his stomach and gazed down at him. "Why couldn't you have been an accountant or pencil-pusher? I'm not sure I'm up to all this military discipline."

"Discipline is fun," he said solemnly, although a crease appeared in his cheek. "At least from this side of the paddle."

Her lips twitched because he totally meant it. "*Riiight.*"

"And if you're walking around bare-ass naked, it means we'll be having sex a hell of a lot more often."

She blinked. *Actually, that sounded rather nice...*

When he burst out laughing, she hit him.

And regretted it...

CHAPTER TWENTY

W ednesday morning, Ghost walked out of the bathroom. *Jesus.* "If I have a heart attack, pet, I'm blaming you."

Bending over, Valerie was doing a shimmy to settle her gorgeous breasts into the royal blue bra he'd purchased for her. "What?" Brows together, she glanced over her shoulder at him.

She hadn't turned on the lamps, relying on the dawn light coming through the tall arched windows. The glow danced over her skin. Hair the color of caramel swung loose. Her full, heart-shaped ass was...right there. Her breasts were pushed together, begging for his hands.

Within two steps, he'd closed on his quarry and pulled her upright and against him. With her back against his chest, he turned so she faced the full-length mirror. His arm across her pelvis kept her ass pressed against his already hard erection. He curved his other hand around her throat.

Her eyes had closed.

"No, pet. Look at yourself. At us," he growled. "Woman, you're sexy as fuck."

She opened her eyes, and he smiled at her flush. The way she aroused so quickly was a delight.

With his foot, he shoved her legs apart and slid a hand under the pretty thong to cup her pussy. "You're slick for me."

"Ghost...no."

"Such a weak protest." He squeezed one breast, increasing the pressure until he heard her breathing catch. Until he felt even more wetness against his palm. "I found a ripe peach in my bedroom...and I'm going to pluck it from the tree and enjoy every bite."

To illustrate, he sank his teeth into her shoulder, pleased she'd wear the mark of his teeth all day.

And then he stripped her and satisfied them both.

CHAPTER TWENTY-ONE

Olivia had chosen her attire with an eye to what was coming. Black leather pants, black bustier, black leather jacket, knee-high black boots. Her hair was spiked, her makeup strong.

Natalia, the little brat, had laughed and decked herself out in an adorable pink tank and lacy briefs.

Leading the way into the club, Olivia glanced around. "It's busy tonight."

Natalia gave her a pleased nod. "About like it was before Wrecker drove off all the nice members."

So it seemed. "Has it been a month since Ghost took over as manager? Time really does fly, doesn't it?"

Standing near a scene, Alastair spotted them and nodded a greeting. The tall Master was wearing a dungeon monitor vest...as was the younger Dom beside him. One of Ghost's changes. She'd helped teach the first DM class last weekend and was pleased with the quality of Doms he'd chosen. Interested, experienced, intelligent, responsible. Later tonight, she'd put in her DM time and would have what Ghost tended to call "recruits" following her.

Last weekend, she'd given a demonstration on Florentine flogging along with some instruction on when it was useful. Too many Doms learned because it was flashy—instead of understanding it was merely one more technique. In this case, one to be used for the rather delightful effect that continuous rhythmic sensations could have on a submissive.

She half-smiled...because Natalia had started to drift into subspace illustrating exactly what Olivia had been saying.

As they headed for the bar, Natalia returned a silent wave to a couple of submissives. A group of Doms gave Olivia chin-up greetings.

Yes, the Shadowlands had returned to being the friendly place Z wanted for the community.

Ghost studied them as they approached, and his lips quirked. "Olivia, if Chelsey pisses herself at the sight of you, you get to mop the floor."

Aaand that was all it took for Natalia to break down into giggles. "I said about the same thing to the Mistress."

"Natalia." Olivia shook her head. "I can't have you laughing—"

Her normally quiet submissive giggled harder—and Ghost grinned.

Olivia grabbed her hair firmly enough to make her gasp, hard enough heat rose in the liquid brown eyes.

Don't get diverted by thoughts of sex. With a bit of work, she kept her voice hard. "Girl, are you going to behave or should—"

"She can sit with us, Mistress Olivia," Gabi called from a nearby conversational area. "She'll be able to watch without having to be involved."

Olivia turned to Natalia and raised an eyebrow.

"Yes, please, Mistress." Laughter gone, Natalia pulled in a breath. "When Chelsey is actually here, it's not going to be funny at all and..."

And Natalia would probably end up in tears. Olivia pulled her tenderhearted submissive into her arms. Over the past twelve days, they'd done as Ghost asked and discussed consequences for Chelsey. They'd arrived at a plan.

Ghost had agreed, arranged for several other Masters to be here as witnesses, then told Chelsey when to show up. If she wanted to remain a member, she'd be here.

Olivia looked around and realized Ghost was surrounded by Masters: Sam, Anne, Vance, Marcus, Cullen, and Alastair. Their submissives were seated with Gabi.

Olivia gave Natalia a squeeze and murmured, "All right, love, sit with the submissives."

Natalia turned her face up for a kiss—and got one. Then she hurried over to the submissive group and tucked herself up against Ghost's Valerie. Gabi moved in closer on the other side.

Olivia smiled. Her love was as buffered against what would come as she could possibly be.

Friends could become closer than family, couldn't they?

And a lover could be...everything. She drew in a slow breath of happiness.

Cullen moved over. "I'm surprised you didn't decide to simply kick Chelsey out of the Shadowlands."

The other Doms halted their conversations, turning to listen.

"We talked about terminating her membership," Olivia said. "But starting fresh somewhere else wouldn't force her to deal with her actions."

"Interesting," Marcus said. "What's your reasoning?"

"I'm from an exceedingly small town. Everyone knows everyone—and their history. If you mess up, for years afterward, you'll have your nose rubbed in what you've done. People watching to see if you've changed, if you were sorry, if you worked to regain the trust. Peer pressure can be a force for good as well as bad."

Max nodded. "Our town in Colorado is the same way."

Olivia's gaze fell on Natalia. How wonderful it was to have her back.

And they'd been miserable for over two months solely because of the jealous woman who was now walking up to the bar.

Chelsey saw Olivia and stopped dead. After a second, she continued forward until she halted in front of Olivia. "Mistress Olivia." Her gaze met Olivia's for barely a second, then she dropped to her knees. "I'm sorry."

Not nearly sorry enough.

"Chelsey, explain to me—and everyone listening—why you're here to be disciplined."

Chelsey gripped her hands together in front of herself. "I... changed a photo and—"

"I cannot hear you, missy," Sam growled.

The submissive swallowed and spoke louder. "I found a picture of two women together in bed, and I photoshopped Natalia's head onto one woman's body. And then I lied to you, Mistress Olivia, and said Natalia was cheating on you."

"Holy crapping doo-doo," someone said from farther down the bar.

"Yes. That is what you did. Here are the consequences." Olivia kept her voice steady and firm. "This incident will be added to your Shadowlands record and visible to whoever wants to play with you."

Chelsey went pale.

Yes, she'd now get to live with the effects of screwing up in a small community.

What Chelsey wouldn't know was the record would also contain a suggestion to the Dominants to observe this submissive for lying—and to reward honesty.

"After six months, if the Colonel feels your behavior has improved, he will wipe it from your record. We will all be watching you, Chelsey." Olivia paused and her voice lowered. "Your lies hurt me and Natalia—and damaged you, as well. Because, at heart, you're a good person, and I cannot imagine that you haven't felt ugly inside about this."

Chelsey burst into tears, confirming Olivia's belief.

She waited long enough for the young woman to be able to listen, then added, "This is your chance to fix what you damaged. Work on your character. Become the honorable, honest person I know you can be. Then you will have made things right with me and Natalia—and the club."

Olivia stepped back and paused. *Bloody hell.* The girl was in no shape to leave right now.

"I got this," Ghost murmured. Ignoring the submissive's tears, he lifted her to her feet, then put a notebook and pen into her hand. He set her on a barstool at the end of the bar and Olivia heard him say in a low voice, "The journal is for you. For the next hour, set down your thoughts on what you've done, how it made you feel, and what actions you're going to take to do better."

Despite her tears, Chelsey gave him an appalled stare.

"No one will read what you write. But you will sit here and work on your task until the bartender says your hour is up. Then you may go home."

He glanced up, and Josie gave him a mini salute.

"Am I clear?" he asked Chelsey.

"Yes, Sir," Chelsey whispered. "I understand." She took a better grip on the pen and opened the journal.

When Ghost returned to the group of Masters, Olivia nudged him. "You are such a bloody professor."

He grinned. "It'll give her time to settle down, so she'll be safe on the road."

"Good thinking." Olivia sighed. "Thank you."

"Part of the job." His gaze was on Natalia, who looked a bit shaken. "A suggestion?"

Olivia eyed him.

"Saxon commandeered the orgy room for a pet corner again. Why don't you turn your subbie into a kitten and let her play pounce until she feels better?"

"It's, actually, a very good suggestion," Olivia said slowly. She turned to Alastair and Marcus. "It would be even better if Natalia had a couple of buddies in there."

"I do think that is a fine idea," Marcus said in his slow Southern accent. "Gabrielle makes a most adorable puppy."

Alastair grinned. "Uzuri had buyer's meetings all day. Being a kitten would be particularly good—and she can release some of her irritation by bouncing off a clueless puppy."

Marcus just laughed.

Olivia shook her head and gazed at the Dominants who'd come to support her. "When we all stopped coming to the Shadowlands, I hadn't realized how much I missed you all. I'm glad we're all back together."

The smiles she received showed they felt the same.

Then her adorable submissive wrapped her arms around Olivia and batted her innocent brown eyes. "*Mew, mew, mew?*"

Of course, the submissives had been listening. Olivia burst out laughing.

CHAPTER TWENTY-TWO

Sleeping in, sex, then a nice workout were excellent ways to enjoy a Sunday. After finishing his push-ups, Ghost sat on the mat to watch Valerie working the big sandbag.

After two weeks of being naked, she'd grown comfortable with her body—at least around him. So now, she was wearing a tank and shorts.

Punch, punch, punch.

He frowned. She was barely denting the bag. Still.

"Put some effort into it, Dr. Winborne," he called.

Lifting her shirt to swipe sweat off her forehead, she gave him a nice glimpse of her stomach. *Nice.* Since they'd started working out, she'd put on some muscle, but she still had a beautiful roundness to her belly. So damn bitable.

She turned back to the bag for more punches.

No. "The power comes from your toes, growing in strength all the way up. Turn your hip into it and let loose."

She did try, but she still wasn't committing to the all-out effort it would take to flatten an opponent. Sure, her punches would hurt. But in a real fight, she needed to do more than inflict some pain.

Ah, well, he'd keep working on her. Emotionally, she was a strong woman, but also had a gentle spirit. Hitting someone with all her strength went against her very nature.

"Go ahead and take the first shower," he suggested. "I still have some sit-ups to do."

She laughed and patted her damp shirt. "I definitely need a shower. And I'm blaming you for at least part of why I do."

"Lass, it's not my fault you're too sexy to resist in the morning."

"You're male. You think wake-up boners mean *anything* is sexy in the morning."

"Ahh." There was some truth to what she said. However... "You're confusing available with sexy. If I'm starving, I'll eat whatever I can find—even porridge. But I'd far prefer a big meal of bacon and eggs, which is always amazing, even when I'm not particularly hungry."

He flashed her a smile. "You, woman, are always sexy...any time of the day. I see you naked, and boom, there I am"—he wrapped his fingers around an imaginary hard-on— "pitchin' a tent. Popping a chub. Sporting a woodie."

She flushed. Had she and her dickhead ex never talked about sex? Even after almost living here for a month, she still easily flustered.

The sadist in him totally enjoyed turning her red.

"You're so bad. I'm going to shower and you"—she pointed at him—"you stay here and finish your workout."

It was almost a dare, but he was still content from a vigorous bout of sex this morning, and his dick liked a bit of recovery time. He wasn't eighteen any longer, after all.

Instead, he finished off his sit-ups, then tidied up the living room to cool off while he waited for her to finish.

He liked that the room now showed someone lived here. The coffee table held his notes for the military history book he was writing and his latest crossword puzzle. E-readers sat on the end tables, since Valerie also preferred reading to television watching.

He tucked her embroidery stuff back into its basket and shook his head. Although she often meditated in the garden, she used her cross-stitching as a mindfulness exercise.

No wonder she radiated peacefulness.

The shower shut off, and, giving her a few minutes, he finished cleaning the room.

Hearing her in the bedroom, he leaned against the doorframe to savor the scenery. "So, what's the plan for today?"

Startled, Valerie jumped, dropping her dress.

As she bent to retrieve it, his dick hardened. "Damn, I love your ass."

And he really liked how she looked in the underwear he'd bought her. The tiny briefs were more lace than substance, and the deep blue contrasted beautifully with her fair skin.

If she didn't have anything planned—

Rather than using a bra, she pulled a blue sundress over her head, then captured her breasts in some sort of built-in rigging.

No wonder women had less trouble with bondage than men; they'd been doing it for years.

As she tied the laces at the back, she glanced over her shoulder, noticed where his gaze was focused, and laughed. "You, sir, are insatiable. I have grading to do, a test to prepare, and I need to visit my apartment. I haven't been there in a couple of days, and I'm out of clothes."

Her place. Joining her, he ran his hand down her bare arm. "Valerie, why don't you move in with me? You're practically living here anyway."

Her mouth dropped open.

Interesting. Why did the suggestion come as such a surprise?

"Lass."

"Wait. Just wait." She took a couple of steps back.

The way she retreated from him was concerning...even frustrating.

Rather than responding, he moved back to the doorway. "Can you tell me why you appear to be upset?"

She pulled in a breath. "I... It's too soon, okay?"

Irritation prickled his nerves. "Not everything needs to be on a time-table. I love you. You love me. Yes?"

"Those are feelings, Ghost." She tried to run a brush through her hair, the bristles caught, and she spat out. "*Al'ama.*"

It was a mild curse, the Arabic equivalent to "damn". But she wasn't one to curse often, although, he had to admit, a bout of vigorous sex—and his hands—had rather thoroughly tangled her hair.

He studied her for a moment. "Feelings are usually involved when people move in together."

"I suppose." She moved forward, then stopped, obviously expecting him to get out of the doorway.

He didn't move.

Her color rose. "There's more involved than merely feelings. Like being practical and looking forward and...and—" She sputtered to a stop.

Hmm. "You're rarely at a loss for words when you're comfortable, which makes me think there's something else at play here."

"I'm simply not...not ready, okay? I don't want to give up my apartment, my place. Even if it's more work to run back and forth." Her face had flushed.

"Do you still think I'm going to...to replace...you like your husband did?"

Her expression changed, flattened until no emotion showed at all.

She did think that.

"Seriously?" Anger sparked inside him. His jaw tightened until it hurt.

After a second, he stepped out of the doorway to let her out.

"I'm... I know you're not like him, but"—she shook her head —"I know, but I still—"

"What...exactly...can I do to reassure you?" Despite his efforts, he could hear the frustration in his voice. Because he'd been basking in a glow of happiness, and she'd been worrying he was going to... What, dump her? Go after some youngster? "Let's talk about what you're feeling."

"I don't think so. No." Rather than caving in, she turned to glare at him as she crossed the living room.

"Valerie."

"I'm really sorry if my worries don't conform to your timeline, Colonel. Feel free to give me a detailed schedule, and I'll get back to you."

Snatching up her purse and sandals at the kitchen door, she walked out.

Not slamming the door, no, not his professor. But it closed with a very decided sound.

It was good to know she could stand up to him—and it was also as annoying as hell. Because she'd walked out in the middle of their discussion...argument.

Fight.

Yeah, he'd fucked up quite nicely.

Early in the evening, Valerie ran a finger around the rim of her glass of sangria, half-heartedly listening to the other women around the round table. The upscale bar was crowded with tourists, probably there for the "happy hour" drink special.

She wasn't much in a happy hour mood, but Linda had called and talked her into joining some of the Shadowlands submissives.

What a messed-up day.

Earlier in her apartment, she'd started a list of the pros and cons of giving up her place. Then, annoyed, she'd abandoned it and instead scrawled Finn's name at the bottom of her F list. Because he was an item that definitely needed work.

Effing man.

After enjoying the momentary satisfaction, she'd done her grading and finished preparing the tests for the remainder of the year. Cleaned her apartment. Did the laundry.

Being angry with someone was more energizing than a potful of coffee.

So was being angry with herself.

She certainly could have handled the discussion about her apartment in a more reasonable fashion. Instead, she'd stomped away—no, *fled*—like a child.

Even worse, she wasn't sure what to do at this point. Should she stay away? Or show up as usual with her suitcase. Could she even assume he still wanted her there?

Or at all?

A burst of laughter brought her attention back to her friends.

Really, Valerie, this wasn't the time to be stewing.

And who could stay in a grumpy mood when Zuri had brought fuzzy kitten-ear headbands for everyone to wear?

Caving into peer pressure, and honestly, unable to resist, Valerie had donned a band, fluffing her hair enough her ears pricked up just enough to be seen.

She checked her image in the tiny mirror from her purse and laughed. "I'm too old for this and not a cute person."

"Yet you look adorable," Linda confirmed and took the mirror to check her own ears...and grinned. "We're both cute."

"However, this costume party stops with ears," Valerie said firmly. "No whiskers."

Andrea snickered. "Be grateful it isn't a Master dressing you up. Cullen likes seeing me as a cat, and he *always* adds a tail."

Valerie frowned. "A tail. Like with a belt or—"

Across the table, Gabi broke out laughing. "*Or*, Valerie, very *or*. The tail is attached to a plug that goes into a very uncomfortable place."

"Good grief." Valerie's buttocks tightened in protest.

Gabi waved her hand. "Right after I'd joined, Marcus dressed me as a cocker spaniel— floppy ears, fuzzy mittens, and a *tail*, and made me crawl on top of the bar. The Doms lined up to give me orders. *Sit. Bark. Down.*"

A nearby tableful of tourists went silent in shock.

Valerie started to snicker. "Too loud, Gabi."

Following her gaze, Linda sputtered with laughter, setting Gabi off.

Shaking her head, Jessica pointed her finger at Gabi. "Woman, you are cut off."

"Of course, you'd say that, oh Miss Preggie, who isn't allowed anything alcoholic," Gabi sniffed.

Jessica frowned. "Why do you say Miss *Preggie*, and I hear Miss *Piggy*?"

"Don't let Master Z hear you calling yourself fat, or you'll be a very pink-assed preggie," Sally pointed out.

Valerie stared. "Z would...um... swat you for putting yourself down?"

"Oh, girl, you have no idea," Jessica said ruefully. "A good Dom won't try to change who you are, but all bets are off if what you're doing or thinking makes you unhappy."

"Yeah, they're all over that shit." Sally scowled.

"But you're both beautiful," Valerie protested.

"Jessica's lessons were about how she feels about her size. Me?" Sally wrinkled her nose in annoyance. "My Demon Doms wanted me to *talk* about my feelings."

Andrea held up her hand in a show of unity. "For me, I wouldn't ask for help. *Mi señor* got so frustrated he had me sold to a sadist during a club auction. It forced me to learn that lesson."

Cullen auctioned his submissive? "Well, *gods*."

Without exception, they all had half-rueful, half-pleased expressions.

Even Linda.

Valerie raised her eyebrows at her friend but didn't speak. Sometimes people didn't want to talk about their personal life.

"It's all right to ask," Linda said with a smile. "Sam helped me overcome the belief that being a masochist is wrong."

"Valerie, I get the impression you've earned a Dom correction or two," Gabi asked gently. "Want to share?"

No way.

Or...maybe yes?

Yes.

"Turning fifty was rough, partly because my husband's slaves had been calling me ugly and old. And their opinion ended up being how I saw myself."

"We need to bitch-slap Kahlua for her," Sally muttered. All the nods of agreement totally made Valerie's night.

"I can see how your experience would leave you with a challenge." Gabi nodded in understanding. "Most of us remember insults far longer than compliments."

"Exactly." Valerie rolled her eyes. "Ghost says I have to make it through the next club night without any thoughts or comments about being old and unattractive."

"Ooooh, good luck." Jessica shook her head in sympathy.

"It could happen. Maybe." Between her own work and Ghost's help, Valerie really was a lot more comfortable in her skin these days.

"All us humans have insecurities, you know." Gabi wiggled a fried cheese stick to make her point. "Even our Doms. Often enough, they think they need to be strong for us and won't share when they have problems."

"You nailed it," Zuri said. "That's Alastair, especially if one of his kid patients dies."

"And Cullen when there's a bad fire," Andrea agreed.

"And Z," Jessica said under her breath.

"Or they have old wounds to set them off. Like previous bad relationships, losses..." Gabi said.

And got a vigorous nod from Natalia.

"Sometimes their jobs get to them," Sally said. "But shooting my Master Grumpy Pants and Master Frownie Face with ice water worked pretty well."

Valerie choked. "That would be so unwise."

"Right? Sally, my dear, if you spray Master Sam with ice water, I'll be happy to watch. From a distance." Linda glanced at Valerie. "Because there's pain and then there's *pain*."

"So, I have discovered," Valerie agreed.

"Totally. No ice water for sadists," Natalia said with a grin, "or evil Mistresses."

"Speaking of evil Mistresses..." Sally pushed Natalia's glass closer to her. "Have some lube, sister, then spill the deets. How are you and the Brit doing? You've been, like, missing in action since the other night."

Natalia flushed, took a gulp of her drink, then smiled at Gabi and Valerie. "First, thank you. For the advice."

Sally's eyes narrowed. "What advice? I know about the Chelsey photoshopping scam—the bitch—but what advice?"

"We told Natalia to confront Olivia at the bar," Gabi smirked, "when either Z or Ghost were there, preferably both."

"Ooooh, so brilliantly evil." Jessica snickered, then frowned at Natalia. "But you ran out without finishing the fight. What happened then?"

Natalia tsked at her. "Don't you know curiosity killed the cat?"

"Personally, I always thought Mr. *Curiosity* was framed," Valerie muttered—and after a second, the Shadowkittens whooped in laughter.

Andrea leaned forward, grinning at Natalia. "You're not going to escape, girlfriend."

Slightly worried, Valerie watched Natalia's expression, then relaxed. The young woman was pleased to be pushed into sharing.

"So, after I left, well, I was all mad and everything, and I didn't even go back to my house until the next day, and she was sitting on the steps waiting for me."

"Oh, *boo*," Zuri murmured in sympathy and reached across to pat her hand.

"I was all cold and told her to leave, only she showed me the photo. A Domme with *me,* and we were on a bed and obviously fucking, and I...I couldn't find any words." Natalia shook her head. "I mean, I *know* I was never with the woman in the picture, and I still thought for a minute that person was me."

"And?" Sally prompted.

"Mistress apologized, and we talked. And we made-up." Natalia sighed and her smile took over her face.

"Ah-huh. They had makeup sex," Sally muttered.

"It's totally the best," Zuri agreed.

Makeup sex. Valerie felt her shoulders slump as she remembered how she and Ghost had fought. Makeup sex could only happen if a couple actually made-up.

"Sometimes, it's the best..." Gabi scowled. "Sometimes, the sex involves handprints."

Natalia giggled and nodded. "I had trouble sitting down for two days."

"*No.*" Shocked, Valerie straightened. "The breakup wasn't *your* fault."

"The breakup wasn't." The brown eyes filled with mischief. "But my poor Mistress felt awfully bad about what happened and was being so nice. Really, way too nice to tolerate. So I kind of on-purpose set her off and..."

"You, woman, are a subbie after my own heart." Reaching around Andrea, Gabi fist-bumped Natalia.

"So...we have Natalia and Mistress Olivia back together."

Jessica grinned at Valerie. "And if Ghost is going all Dom on your ass does that means you two are together?"

Valerie's heart sank, and she shook her head.

Everyone frowned.

"What happened?" Natalia wailed. "You two are a perfect fit."

"We had an argument this morning. Well, maybe it was a fight?"

"A big relationship-ending fight or one of those *you-brew-coffee-wrong* ones?" Jessica asked.

"An *I-want-you-to-move-in* versus *I'm-not-ready* fight."

"Ohhh, one of those." Natalia shook her head in understanding. "Some people get serious way too fast. We call them *u-hauls*, the ones ready to move in after only a couple of dates."

"The Colonel wants you to move in?" Gabi asked with a wide smile.

Valerie nodded. "And the idea is simply crazy. My divorce still seems awfully recent."

"Then you two didn't really have a fight," Jessica pronounced. "More like a scheduling conflict."

"It felt like a fight to me," Valerie said in a low voice. "He was really unhappy, like I'd rejected *him* instead of his offer to move in right now."

And she wouldn't hurt him for the world, except...the thought of not having her apartment if she needed it was too scary.

"Men can be idiots," Andrea agreed.

"*Chica*, that's sexist." Natalia shook her head. "*Dominants* can be idiots."

"There's the truth," Zuri said, and agreement ran around the table.

Linda turned to Valerie. "Which one of you walked out on the other one?"

"Me. I did. And I've been feeling like a sulky teenager all day, actually."

"You left." Gabi gave her a serious look. "According to the

Unwritten Book of Relationships, the one who stomps out is the one who has to crawl back and start the apology session." She polled those around the table. "Am I right?"

The vote was unanimous. So were the comments.

"You did him wrong, girl. You'll have to go back first."

"Sorry, Valerie, it's up to you."

"It's going to burn, but woman-up."

Valerie's grumping, "You all suck" only got laughter.

Her eyes narrowed. If she had to suffer, so would they. She leaned forward, her voice rising, "I'm going to tell your Masters y'all compared their dicks to gummy worms, baby carrots, and triple-A batteries."

Sally spewed her drink across the table.

Hands over her mouth, Zuri was giggling.

Beside Valerie, Linda choked. She was looking at the table of tourists. "I think they're shocked stupid," she whispered.

Valerie felt her face turning red. "Um...oops?"

A fresh outbreak of laughter went around the table, even from Jessica who was completely sober.

"You know what's even worse?" Linda's question brought mostly silence. "Remember how Gabi whines about handprints going with makeup sex?"

Valerie eyed her warily. "Yes?"

"Her Master Marcus isn't a sadist." Linda patted Valerie's shoulder in overt sympathy. "Ghost is."

Oh...spit. "I think I need another drink."

Sunsets in Florida were far more spectacular than in the Pacific Northwest, Ghost decided. In the screened pool enclosure, he sat on a bench while Olivia installed a new security camera she wanted him to test.

Overhead, reds and oranges streaked the sky. A brief afternoon shower had left behind scattered clouds to reflect the colors of the setting sun. First the disturbance, then the beauty. Sounded like a recipe for life.

He could only hope the disturbance this morning would conclude so well.

Earlier, he'd worked awhile in the Shadowlands office. But Valerie had planned to help him dig through Wrecker's disastrous bookkeeping...and he kept missing her.

She hadn't returned.

After switching to his amphibious prosthesis—one he could get wet—he swam laps for a while, then tossed the inflatable double lounge into the pool to float on.

When Olivia showed up a while ago, he'd pulled on shorts and a T-shirt and let her in.

Ghost reined in his thoughts and studied the woman. "You're looking good. Happier."

Her tech focus interrupted, she eyed him. "I was miserable without Natalia. I still can't believe I was such a bloody idiot."

"The picture *was* damning."

After screwing the last bracket in place, Olivia sat on the opposite bench to pack up her bag of electronics. "I knew she wouldn't cheat, and still, after my previous lovers, I didn't think anyone would be faithful. Ugly past experiences, you know?"

Ghost frowned. "Past experiences..." If the past could derail a confident woman like Olivia, how much worse would they affect a sensitive person like Valerie?

Glancing around, Olivia said carefully, "From the rumors in the club, I'd expected to see Valerie here."

He winced. "Good aim, Olivia."

"My comment wasn't intended to be painful, Ghost. I like the two of you together. You fit well."

"We do—and there's the problem." He rubbed his neck. "I wanted her to move in and pushed too hard."

"Yes, you did," Natalia said as she came around the screening shrubbery and entered the screened pool enclosure. She dropped down beside her Mistress, then glared at Ghost. "You made her feel really bad, Colonel."

The imp had some courage...and an aim as deadly as her Domme's. "I regret pushing her. I forgot her divorce wasn't very long ago."

"I think I understand why she might hesitate to fully commit," Olivia said.

Ghost frowned. "Go on, please."

"You and Valerie both had long marriages, right, Colonel?" Olivia put her arm around her submissive, pulling her closer.

He nodded.

"You lost your wife to death. Which is horrible but didn't affect how you thought of what you had together." Olivia shook her head. "Valerie's marriage ended because her beloved turned on her and dumped her for younger women. What she sees is her judgment has proven bloody bad. Even if you don't turn out to be a bastard, you might simply change your mind. I can see how she'd hesitate at losing her last safety net."

"Yes, I reached the same conclusion." He sighed. "Right about the time the door closed after her."

Tonight, at her apartment, he'd see if she'd open that door to him—and if she'd forgive him for being a pushy fool.

At the Shadowlands, Valerie parked her car, grateful she'd kept her alcohol intake under control so she could drive. Master Marcus, who'd picked up Gabi and Natalia, had offered her a ride, but she'd wanted the time alone so she could think. In fact, she'd taken a long detour before finally heading here.

Moving in with Ghost wasn't an easy decision, especially for her right now. And he'd been obviously frustrated with her. And sometimes it was *really* annoying when he analyzed her like a...a damn Dom.

Only, fine, it was especially annoying when he was right. Like today. He'd realized the reason she clung to her apartment was because she still didn't feel secure.

She rested her forehead on the steering wheel. Although she was working on those fears, they wouldn't magically disappear, which meant he'd simply have to deal. Normally, they did well at talking to each other. Unlike Barry, Ghost listened to her. They should be able to work out a compromise now.

Right?

How angry was he going to be?

Through the windshield, she eyed the third-story landing. Maybe she should have had another drink.

As she slid out of the car, Natalia and Olivia stepped through the gate in the fence.

Natalia ran over to give her a hug. "He's sitting by the pool and feeling all mopey. Go for it."

"Thanks." Valerie brightened. At least she wouldn't have to climb those steps and wait at the door. "Wish me luck then; I'm going in."

Natalia giggled and ran back to her Mistress.

The two were wonderful together.

The gardens were quiet as Valerie walked past the lanai and to the secluded pool area.

There he was. He was sitting on a bench, forearms on his thighs as he watched the water splashing into the pool. The Colonel, who was usually so very alert, hadn't even noticed her. He seemed...sad.

Her heart gave a painful squeeze.

Straightening, he turned and spotted her. His green eyes sharpened, and in one sweeping look, he evaluated her posture, her mood, probably even her alcohol intake.

He rose.

"No, sit." She opened the screen door and crossed to him. "I'm sorry."

"An interesting approach." His lips tugged upward. "What... exactly...are you apologizing for?"

Her breath huffed out. Doms were annoying. Couldn't he just assume she was sorry for everything?

Only she wasn't—and he probably knew it.

"Join me, Professor." He tugged her down to sit beside him on the bench.

"I'm sorry I lost my temper and left."

"I like your temper. But walking out?" His gaze was level, his voice even. "You surprised me."

She winced.

"Lass, I'm glad you didn't cave in and agree to something that bothers you. I didn't take into account your past." He smiled slightly. "As Olivia and Natalia pointed out."

They'd spoken up for her? How sweet was that?

He stroked his hand down her arm in a warm caress. "I'm sorry for pushing you. I hope you can forgive me."

She stared at him, then hauled in a shaken breath.

"Valerie, what?"

"I...I wasn't expecting you to apologize or be reasonable. Only, I know you are, but I was braced for you to be angry." Because Barry would have been.

His eyes narrowed slightly. "One more example of how the past can linger and bite a person on the ass, hmm? I'm not your ex, pet."

"I know."

"You do—in your head. It might take time to know it in your gut. Not your fault and not my fault. It's nothing but fact." He leaned forward and kissed her gently. "Which is why you are right to wait before giving up your apartment, and I was wrong to push. If you need a place to escape so you feel secure, that's fine."

Her muscles started to unknot.

A hint of humor appeared in his deep voice. "I'll try to make my bed appealing enough that you're in it more times than not."

All the tension drained right out of her.

He ran a finger over her lips and smiled slightly. "Since Natalia arrived upset with me, I had a feeling you'd been with her." He plucked something out of her hair—the kitten ears—and his lips quirked. "It appears you were with, perhaps, a clowder of Shadowkittens?"

Didn't it figure he'd know what a group of cats was called? Valerie snorted. "Yes."

"Knowing that bunch, you've had a nice start on me as far as alcohol consumption."

"Not by much." She wrinkled her nose. "Not compared to the others." Because they had drivers.

When he reached behind her to untie the sundress laces, every remaining drop of alcohol in her system started to bubble in delight.

"So, your judgment isn't impaired. Excellent." He tugged the top down, exposing her breasts. "Because...you did walk out on me in the middle of an argument."

Well, he had a point. "It *is* why I apologized."

"I've always found it best to deal with a submissive's guilty feelings immediately." The glint in his green eyes sent anxious arousal rocketing through her.

She edged away from him by an inch. "I'm not feeling all that guilty."

"Then consider this a prelude to makeup sex." His fingers tangled in her hair as he took her mouth in a hard, wet kiss.

Her bones started to dissolve—which was surely the only reason he was able to yank her stomach-down over his lap. "I do love these sundresses you like to wear," he murmured and flipped up the skirt.

His hand came down on her ass with a hard slap.

. . .

Some time later, Ghost was lying on the two-person-sized inflatable lounge that floated in the pool.

Kneeling between his legs, Valerie had her hot, wet mouth wrapped around his dick. She had an extremely clever tongue, an abundance of enthusiasm, and he was going to lose control all too soon.

The sight of his beautiful submissive on her knees was more erotic than anything on a porn channel.

"Stop, before you send me over." Gripping her long hair, he gave a tug. "I'd rather be inside you."

Her tongue swirled around him one last time before she lifted her head.

The cool evening air swirled around his wet cock.

She braced her hands on his thighs, her breasts wobbling delightfully. Her lips were puffy from his kisses—and an excellent blowjob. Her makeup was streaked from the tears she'd shed during her spanking and the trip into the pool.

She was gorgeous.

"Are you sure, Colonel?" Her eyebrows lifted. "I'd hate to be sent to the guardhouse for slacking off on my duty."

In the past, he'd noticed how, each time she climaxed, her voice grew huskier. Which meant, right now, she sounded sexy as hell.

Smothering a smile, he gave her a stern look. "I'll have no slackers on my watch, so you may soldier on...once you climb on top of me."

"Yes, *Sir.*" Her enthusiastic response made him grin.

Light from the solar lamps around the pool glowed on her damp skin. The only sounds came from the frogs and crickets, the melodic splashing of the stream, and the lap of water against the float.

The lounge rocked in the water as she carefully crawled up to straddle his hips—and his cock strained upward in search of its target.

She stopped.

"Put me inside you," he said softly. "Then stay still or there will be consequences."

To clarify, he squeezed her undoubtedly sore bottom and enjoyed the sharp inhalation of pain. Although she always got off on being spanked, he'd done a very thorough job of it today.

In fact, when he'd finished, her skin had been so hot he'd tossed her into the pool. Her scream had warmed the cockles of his sadistic heart.

And the names she'd called him had earned her having to suck him off.

Now, once she'd settled her knees on each side of his hips, she gripped his shaft and lowered herself onto him.

Her cunt was as hot and wet as her mouth, and damn, he wanted to thrust.

Not yet.

Watching him carefully, she stayed perfectly immobile on her knees.

"Very nice, pet. Lace your hands behind your lower back." Ah, he really did love making her vulnerable to him.

When her arms were out of his way, he cupped her breasts, squeezed—and enjoyed the way she clenched around his dick.

Valerie could feel herself shiver as Ghost teased and tortured her breasts until the painfully erotic sensations were zipping southward, straight to her pussy.

Don't move. Because her ass still burned from the spanking.

Oh, but she wanted to start lifting, moving up and down. He felt simply amazing inside of her, stretching her, filling her.

Taking his time, he played with her breasts until she couldn't help wiggling on top of him.

"No moving, lass." As if he'd been waiting, he rolled her

nipples between his fingers, tightening painfully until her toes curled with the heady sensations.

Despite coming so many times already, the full feeling of his cock inside her and his rough fingers on her breasts created a slow throb of need.

"Ghost," she whispered and could hear the plea in her voice.

"Do you, perhaps, want my fingers somewhere else?" His face was in the shadows, but she could hear the laughter in his words.

Reaching a hand down, he slickened his fingers in the wetness beside his erection and slid right over her clit.

"Ah!" At the burst of exquisite pleasure, she jumped.

With a tsking sound, he pinched her nipple in reprimand.

She couldn't stop squirming as too many sensations assailed her. His thick cock inside her, the pain from her breast, and his clever fingers that still rubbed her clit on one side, then the other.

The ball of nerves felt as if it had swollen to an aching, sensitive tightness.

"Let's see how obedient you can be, my professor," he said softly. "Hands on my shoulders—so we don't end up in the drink."

The float bobbed as she moved. Thank goodness it was so wide. Carefully, she leaned forward and braced herself on his shoulders.

"Now let my hands guide the up and down." He moved his hand from her breast to squeeze one well-spanked ass cheek.

Ow, ow, ow.

His fingers over her clit pressed harder. "Up, please."

She lifted her hips, and the slow slide of him leaving her body felt sooo good.

His hand on her bottom tightened and brought her down, filling her with his thick shaft. He did it again, pressing on her clit to make her lift, squeezing her butt to make her drop down onto his cock again. "There you go; that's the idea."

Caught between a hand on her clit for pleasure and one on her ass for pain, she was kept rocking on and off his shaft.

Slowly. Too slowly.

Trying to speed up earned her a hard swat to her ass, and two hands gripping her sore ass cheeks, forcing her to move the way he wanted.

Pain was a hot liquid swirling through her lower half, bringing every nerve to a bubbling need.

"Please," she whispered. "Please, faster, please."

In the darkness, she saw the white flash of his teeth. "All right, pet. You've been good, so take the rest at your own pace."

Gods, yes. She gripped his shoulders for leverage and started slamming down on him, harder, faster, and oh, she loved when he put his fingers back on her clit, stroking and sliding until everything thrummed inside her. Until she was gathered on the razor's edge of need.

Every muscle strained to the quivering stage—and he slapped her ass even as he pinched her clit and sent her over the edge.

Great shuddering contractions of pleasure blasted through her and exploded again with his next swat on her bottom.

And he gripped her nape and her ass, holding her tightly against him, his shaft jerking inside her as he took his own pleasure.

Panting, she pressed her face against his neck, breathing in the lingering scent of his aftershave. Her heart was still slamming against her ribs as her muscles went limp, leaving her sprawled over him.

"The other submissives were right," she murmured, "makeup sex is amazing."

And the Colonel really was a sadist.

When he wrapped his arms around her and burst out laughing, contentment filled her. There was nowhere in the world she'd rather be than right here with him.

CHAPTER TWENTY-THREE

Making the rounds of the Shadowlands, Ghost was damned pleased at the change in the atmosphere.

Having better music helped. After requesting input from the members, he'd created new playlists, starting with dance-friendly, moving to aggressively rhythmic scene music, and ending with sensual tunes for quieter scenes and socializing. Tonight, however, he'd added interludes from *Star Trek* movies and the TV series.

To counteract Wrecker's over-macho bullshit, Ghost had chosen a nerdy theme—a Federation Starfleet Celebration.

Star Trek done kink-style.

"Port windows" on the walls overlooked a black, star-filled galaxy. Scene areas resembled different areas of the Enterprise.

Ghost entered the back hallway. On the right, he saw Dr. McCoy's medical clinic was extremely popular.

To his left, what used to be the office room was now the Situation Room. A young man dressed as Data was bound to a chair.

As two men in fleet uniforms entered the hallway, they nodded at Ghost. The Dom had a chief medical officer insignia. His boy wore Captain's rank.

Ghost's eyebrows lifted. "You're keeping the captain under your thumb, Doctor?"

The Dom laughed. "Ever since I was a kid, I wanted McCoy and Kirk together...with Bones in charge."

The very submissive Kirk dropped his gaze under his Master's slow smile.

Ghost grinned at the Dom. "In that case, beat on Captain Kirk for me, will you? If I'd pulled some of the crap Kirk did, the military would've booted my ass out."

"Colonel, it'll be my pleasure." Chortling, McCoy led the poor captain away.

After finishing his walk, Ghost swung by the bar and stopped beside Z. "Admiral."

"Captain. Excellent theme night." Z tapped a finger on his chest and gave Ghost a narrow-eyed look...because his black uniform jacket held an overwhelming fruit salad of military medals and ribbons. The brightest ones Ghost could find in the costume store.

"It actually wasn't my idea. Sally, Josie, and Holt wanted a sci-fi night and bribed me by saying they'd do most of the decorating."

"They did a fantastic job." Cullen was dressed as Q, complete with black headgear and a fulsome red robe. "You're going to get requests from the *Star Wars* fans, next." He set a cobalt-blue drink in front of Ghost.

"What the hell is this?"

"Buddy, don't you recognize Romulan ale? Sure, it's outlawed in the Federation, but hey, so is half of what we do here." Cullen grinned. "Josie and I researched recipes. It's blue curaçao, vodka, seltzer, and a squeeze of lemon."

Ghost tried a sip. "It's damned good."

He spotted Saxon approaching. Saxon's blond hair had disappeared under an odd cap. The bandana around his neck, leather bomber jacket, and red raggedy shirt didn't come across as futuristic at all.

"Who is he supposed to be?" Cullen asked.

"Ah, he's Zefram Cochrane who invented the warp drive in 2063," Josie called as she leaned past Cullen to grab a bottle of gin.

Although not Black, she was dressed as Guinan, the bartender on the Enterprise, wearing dangling earrings, a long, elaborate mahogany dress. Her distinctive Guinan-hat looked like a beret turned into a flat-topped, flying-saucer. She wasn't Whoopi Goldberg, but she'd caught the style.

"Right, I knew that," Cullen muttered.

Z's eyebrows went up. "I believe Cochrane caught a feline in his spacecraft."

Stepping up to the bar, Saxon had his hand wrapped around a young woman's nape. She wore cat ears, painted-on whiskers, a fuzzy shirt, and a long tail.

And if a cat could cringe, this one was.

Ghost nodded at Saxon and asked, "Does your kitten have a name?"

Realizing she had Ghost's attention, the young woman hunched even lower.

"Spot, of course," Saxon said.

Ghost had to wonder how many Spots—Data's famous cat— were running amok in the area he'd sectioned off for pet play.

"Did...Spot...misbehave? Your feline doesn't appear to be happy," Z commented.

Recognizing Z, the kitten let out a dismayed squeak.

"I told her to meow at a Dom in the pet play area, and she chickened out. Her punishment is to work for an hour." Smiling evilly, Saxon called, "Got room for another barmaid, Josie?"

Josie was pulling a beer at the other end. She eyed Saxon and the kitten in his grip and half grinned. "Let Q decide where she'll work. He's in charge of the waitstaff tonight."

Cullen's laugh rang out. "Okay, Spot. You work the section from the very front to the back wall, but only on this side of the bar. If a conversation is intense, don't interrupt, simply pause for a few seconds in case they want you."

She nodded and almost whispered, "Take orders, pick up empties, and clean up?"

"No, tiny cat." Saxon handed her a pad and pencil and frilly apron. "Since there's more than one of you working there, *you* are only taking orders. Now get to work."

She fled.

Chuckling, Saxon told Cullen, "She and her friend joined the club, but she's too shy to meet anyone. If given the option, she'd spend the entire hour cleaning—and not talk to anyone."

"We can always use more volunteer waitstaff," Cullen said.

"Great," Saxon said. Then, if Spot doesn't panic, can you... suggest...she sign up for more volunteer hours?"

"Be my pleasure, buddy."

"Nicely done," Z said to Saxon.

"Part of the job," Saxon said, heading away.

Ghost exchanged pleased glances with Z. Master Saxon had impressive skills and power, and he'd always helped with dungeon monitoring and teaching. Now, he'd upped his game to protecting the entire community, especially the submissives.

Excellent.

In a secluded nook out in the Capture Gardens—or what had been designated, the "Pleasure Planet", Olivia nuzzled her submissive, then bent to give her another long kiss. Soft lips, warm body, big heart. "I love you, girl."

Natalia wrapped her arms around Olivia's neck as she kissed her answer.

It was a few more minutes before Olivia was ready to move again. "Come, love, it's time to get back inside."

"Yes, ma'am."

The night was beautiful, the moon edging toward full. Scattered clouds sent shadows dancing across the grass. The fountain's melodic splashes blended with the faint music from the club.

"Did I mention you are rocking my *Star Trek* world?" Olivia murmured. "Ever since I hit puberty, I've wanted to fuck Deanna Troi."

Natalia burst out laughing. "That sounds so wrong."

As Olivia helped her submissive back into the form-fitting long dress, she fondled the sweet breasts, still swollen and red, first from the lash, then from Olivia's mouth.

Olivia tugged at the pretty nipples and smiled at Natalia's squeaks.

What a brilliant night it had been. Especially the role-playing.

"Deanna Troi, I'm quite pleased you transferred to my ship." Olivia pulled on her black pants. "I do hope you noticed my command is much more...hands-on than your former captain's. I'm also far stricter than Captain Picard."

"No kidding." Natalia's giggle held an adorable post-sex huskiness. "Mistress...Um, Captain Janeway, I promise to behave...um, obey all your orders."

As if to emphasize her willingness, she helped Olivia don her turtleneck and then the red and black uniform top. "There. All dressed, Captain."

Olivia shook her head and finger-combed her hair straight back. Janeway had no sense of style.

At least she wasn't stuck with a Deanna Troi look.

Puffing up her hair in front, Natalia re-settled her jeweled hairband and fluffed out the long waves in back. "You know, I always wondered if Janeway wasn't into girls."

"Janeway is *totally* into girls." Olivia pulled Natalia against her, curling her hands under the cute round ass. "Especially this one. Only this one."

Natalia's eyes filled with tears.

Olivia felt her world slow.

Because this was the right time. In the soft moonlight, outside of the club where they'd met, played, and fallen in love. Where their friends had helped them make up.

A breath brought her the scent of Natalia's sweet spicy perfume—and she found some much-needed courage. Stepping back, she went down on one knee. With one hand, she pulled the box from her pocket and took Natalia's hand with the other.

"I love you, Natalia Rosales. Those months without you were bloody awful. It felt as if I was living in a desert. But now, I know past any doubt, you're the one I want to share my life with. I can't promise you our life will always be roses, but I can promise no one will work harder than I will to make you happy."

The hand in hers was trembling. Joy dawned in Natalia's big brown eyes.

"Love, when I look into the future, I see us working together, raising children, growing old until there we are, in rocking chairs, with grandkids playing around us." She managed to pull in a breath and then another one. "Natalia, will you live with me, grow old with me... Marry me?"

She opened the box and showed the ring. Held it out silently.

Natalia wasn't the kind to play games, to draw out suspense. Sobbing, she dropped to her knees and latched on with both arms so she could bury her head in Olivia's neck.

And the muffled words made Olivia's world explode in happiness.

"Yes, yes, yes."

Having dressed at her apartment to keep Ghost from seeing her in costume—although he'd bought her dress—Valerie parked her car in the parking lot. Stepping out, she studied the Shadowlands.

It remained an oversized stone mansion with glowing black-iron sconces. *How disappointing.*

"Valerie, don't tell me you're still worried about walking in alone?" Linda was approaching from a few cars away.

"It's not that." Valerie motioned toward the building. "Considering Sally's enthusiasm in decorating, I expected the place to be a giant white starship."

"Master Z would have a *fit*." Laughing, Linda joined her.

"So, where's Sam?"

"He was signed up for early dungeon monitoring and is already here. And I'm late, since a shipment came in for the store, and I wanted to shelve the stock before I left."

"Ah, the joys of owning a business."

Linda laughed. "Yet I love it."

As they walked up the sidewalk, Valerie smoothed down her very tight dress, started to think about how it showed every bulge, then reminded herself of her goal for the evening. No self-disparaging thoughts or statements.

Ghost had warned her there would be *consequences* for any slip-ups.

In the entry, the slender security guard at the desk had a Vulcan's pointed ears and wore a *Star Trek* uniform. He held up one hand in the Vulcan greeting. "Live long and lustily."

Linda widened her eyes. "My dear Spock, how your attitude about sex has changed."

As the guard laughed, Valerie smiled. When young, she'd watched reruns of the classic *Star Trek* shows. Later, she and her children enjoyed the newer series and the movies.

Tonight was going to be so much fun. As she signed in, she told the guard, "Your costume is great."

"Thanks." The slender guard grinned. "The manager gave me tomorrow night off so I can show it off and participate inside. Somehow, he figured out I'm a Trekkie."

"Ghost seems as perceptive as Master Z," Linda said.

"Love your dress, by the way," the guard told Valerie.

"Thank you." Coming from a *Star Trek* fan, the compliment

meant a lot. "I'm glad it works." A present from Ghost, the red vinyl dress was skintight through the torso, flared slightly in the skirt part, and ended only a few inches below her ass—because the females' crew uniforms on the original Enterprise were all about the minidresses.

The long sleeves ended with narrow, gold wrist cuffs to show her rank as a lieutenant.

The neckline was so low-cut it had barely left room for the *Star Trek* delta insignia.

"You look fantastic." Linda's lips quirked. "But if you take a deep breath, your breasts are going to pop right out of your dress."

"Great, now I'm going to worry all night." Valerie tugged at the neckline. "Are you sure it's Sam who's the sadist?"

Laughing, Linda led the way in.

"Wow, I didn't expect all this." A few steps inside the door, Valerie almost got a crick in her neck from trying to take it all in.

There were aliens everywhere, especially on the dance floor. Some of the Ferengi appeared ready to start an orgy on the spot.

"This place is packed." Linda had a wide smile on her face. "Tabitha told me there'd been no theme nights since Z went to Europe. I think everyone must have missed them."

The enthusiasm was contagious—as was the sense of welcome. "The club feels different."

Linda's smile widened. "You noticed. Yes, this is what it felt like before Wrecker. Oh, not all the time, but people tended to be...well, friendly."

"The bullies made the atmosphere ugly." Valerie checked out the room. "Because the nice people—like me—don't realize we have to step up and take them to task, even if it means being rude. I've learned something about the dangers of being too polite."

"I think we all did."

Valerie's gaze caught on a short brunette. "Is that Sally?" The first scene area past the dance floor was the bridge of the Enterprise. Instrument panels made a semi-circle around the captain's chair.

Linda gave a low laugh. "The poor baby."

In a short-skirted uniform, Sally was tied to a seat at the navigation station.

"Stop chattering, ensign." In the captain's chair, Master Vance scowled at her, then asked his partner, "What do you think, Mr. Spock?"

Master Galen stood near an instrument panel. Pointy ears and slanting eyebrows added to his black hair and black eyes made him into a perfect Vulcan. "Captain, I fear Ensign Sally has been possessed by an Organian. According to my calculations, a beating of exactly ten point two minutes should exorcise the alien and drive it back to its planet."

Sally squeaked. "Wait. No way—no, Captain! I'm not, you can't..."

"I'm sorry, Ensign," Captain Kirk gave her an oh-so-sympathetic shake of the head. "Sacrifices must be made if we're to ensure the safety of the crew."

Sally was still pleading as Spock and Kirk led her away.

Another group with what looked like Chekov, Sulu, and Kirk moved in. Chekov's uniform pants covered a very big bulge.

"No, no, no," Valerie murmured to Linda. "I can see Kirk as being a kinky perv, but not sweet Chekov."

"It's mind-bending," Linda agreed, then motioned to their right. "Those two picked the perfect characters."

Mistress Anne was dressed as the Borg queen and wearing a bald cap to hide her hair. She had a grip on Ben's shirt and was dragging him toward a scene that resembled an evil engineer's workshop.

"A man's pride 'n' joys shouldn't be turned into machine parts," Ben protested in a low growl.

"Resistance is futile, boy." Anne's smile was evil. "I will ensure your weak human testicles will remain operational for centuries to come."

Valerie put her hands over her mouth to muffle her snickering.

"I'm so glad I'm female," Linda choked out, then brightened. "There's my Sam."

"Off you go. Tell him hi for me." Valerie made a shooing motion. "I'm going to check out the rest of the place and let Ghost know I'm here."

So much to see.

Interested glances came her way, adding to her high spirits. Then again, how many of them were simply hoping her breasts would fall out?

"Nice boots, lieutenant," one Dom murmured with a nod at her high black boots.

Pleased, she smiled at him. Maybe her legs had a bit more jiggle than in the past, but they were still shapely.

And Ghost claimed the jiggle made spankings even more fun for him. How could she argue about that? She'd happily let him spank her each and every day of the week.

"Valerie, just who I wanted to see." Kari approached with Master Dan. The hard-faced cop hadn't dressed in costume, but Kari wore a mini-skirted uniform much like Valerie's. Only Kari's clothing wasn't made of vinyl. "Hey, love the uniform. Can you even breathe?"

"No. Needless to say, it was a present from the mean manager." Valerie waved her hands in the air. "Would you believe it's to remind me he's the only one who gets to squeeze my—"

Dan grinned.

Spit, had she actually said that in front of a Dom?

"Squishing the girls is really mean." Kari beamed at Master Dan. "I'm so glad you're only a bit into the owie stuff."

He wrapped an arm around her. "You're a lucky subbie." He turned to Valerie. "Think how good it will feel when he peels you out of it."

Her face heated. Because he said if she had any dents from the uniform, he'd use clothespins on them. On her *breasts*.

She pulled in a breath. "Kari, did you need me for something?"

Kari nodded. "Did Natalia tell you about her gallery showing at—"

"Val, babe." Barry grabbed her shoulder. "Jesus, you look fantastic." His gaze ran up and down her body, lingering on her breasts.

Revolted, she yanked free and took a step back. "Did you need something?"

"You, babe. I need you." He reached for her again.

She retreated another step.

"I miss you. A lot."

There were no words.

"What?" The furious voice announced Kahlua's arrival. "You're asking the hag to return?"

"Shut up, slave," Barry snapped, then his smile returned. The tender, gentle one she had fallen for, had loved. "Come back home, Val. To me. I need you."

For perhaps the first time in her life, she studied him with impartial eyes. After being around the Masters, around Ghost, she could now perceive his handsome outer shell covered a weak inner character. He was far more interested in himself than in others.

He wanted her back...and as long as she provided what he wanted, he'd "love" her. If and when he found someone better, he'd lose interest. Even worse, once again, he'd chip away at her confidence to keep her off balance and from leaving.

The question wasn't *would she return;* it was how had she been so blind for so long? A sense of loss mingled with her anger.

Because in the beginning, they'd been friends. Sometimes, people didn't change for the better.

"You don't need that old biddy." Kahlua latched onto Barry's arm. "You have me. She's going to be toothless in a year or two."

Old biddy. Toothless. A momentary doubt swept over Valerie, then she laughed. "Are you really so insecure you have to keep recycling those pathetic insults? How sad, Kahlua."

The young woman stiffened in indignation.

"You don't have to worry." Valerie turned her attention to Barry. "We're divorced. That's final, and I want nothing to do with you."

"But babe. You love me."

"Hmm." She tapped her chin. "No, actually, I'm in love with someone else."

Kahlua sneered. "As if anyone would have you."

Another second's doubt. Was Kahlua right?

No. No she wasn't.

"I would have her." Ghost wrapped a thickly muscled arm around Valerie's waist and drew her against his rock-hard body. "I *do* have her. And I know how to treat the woman I love."

Kahlua's mouth dropped open.

Barry's face flushed with anger.

"Ghost, this is my ex-husband, Barry, and his live-in, Kahlua. Barry, this is the manager of the Shadowlands, Ghost, and our friends, Master Dan and Kari."

Barry's jaw thrust forward—and for a moment, she thought he'd lose his temper.

But he reined it in. "Yeah, right. Have a nice night then." He shot her a glare, gripped Kahlua's arm, and stalked toward the bar.

"That went well," Kari murmured. "Not."

Ghost eyed Dan. "You let the asshole put a hand on Valerie?"

"I didn't realize it was unwelcome until she jerked free. If he'd touched her again, I'd have cuffed him. I wouldn't let your woman come to harm."

"Sorry." Ghost pulled her closer. "I didn't like seeing him grab her."

"I hear you. Then again, sometimes it's good to face old lovers and deliver the hard truths." Dan gave Valerie an approving nod before grinning at Kari. "Right, pet?"

"Yes, *Master*." Obviously irked, the short schoolteacher poked Dan in the side.

Valerie almost laughed. It seemed she wasn't the only one who'd had a relationship go sour.

Ghost kissed the top of her head. "Are you all right?"

"I am." She leaned into him. "It did feel good to close the door on the past, but I totally appreciate the rescue. Really. It might have turned ugly."

"I can't think of anything I enjoy more than rescuing you." His gaze held a warm promise as he cupped her cheek. "Anytime, anywhere. I got you, lass."

He could make her heart overflow.

Unable to speak, she pressed a kiss into his warm palm instead.

And that earned her a kiss, a long, possessive, hungry kiss.

When he released her, she took a step back and took a moment to study him.

He wore black jeans tucked into black boots, and a long-sleeved gold tunic with the Star Fleet insignia. His iron-gray hair and ingrained military posture gave him an authority far more authentic than any actor's.

It certainly didn't hurt that his tunic was tight enough to show ridged abdominal muscles. *Mmm.* "You look better than Kirk ever did."

"Good to hear." Ghost grinned, then motioned to the room. "Have you all noticed how many sadists came as either the Borg or Klingons?"

Valerie laughed. "Mistress Anne is a Borg."

"And Edward went for Klingon. Interesting." Dan eyed Ghost. "Considering you're a sadist, I'm surprised you showed up as Kirk."

"It was the deal I made with Z. If I wanted him as Fleet Admiral, I had to show up in a captain's uniform."

"I'd take bets he wore a black dress uniform," Dan said.

Ghost nodded. "You'd win."

Kari snickered. "He's all about the black."

Seeing the slight quirk of the Colonel's lips, Valerie asked. "What did you do?"

"I provided his insignia and medals." Ghost's eyes crinkled. "He now has the most colorful chest in the galaxy."

Even after the drive home, Barry was still fuming. *That fucking bitch.* He stormed into the house with Kahlua sulking behind him.

"Jesus, I need a drink." Spotting Alisha, he snapped out, "Get me one now."

She was too slow, so he grabbed the bottle and poured, then gulped it down.

Kahlua started telling Alisha about seeing Valerie at the club but changed the story so she sounded like hot shit.

He scowled. "You acted like an idiot."

Her mouth snapped shut in the middle of insulting Valerie.

"And you're dressed like a skank."

Wailing, she ran into the bedroom.

Valerie hadn't looked sleazy; she never did. Even tonight with her tits almost popping out, she was still classy.

And he'd forgotten how much he liked her big breasts. Real breasts—Kahlua's cheaply bought bazookas were almost as hard as rocks.

The sobbing from the bedroom didn't diminish.

"Fuck, I'm tired of the noise." He poured himself another drink.

When Valerie lived here, the place had been clean. He had a good meal every night. And they had money. "She needs to come back."

"Valerie? You asked her?" Alisha asked slowly. "What did she say?"

"Said no." His mouth went tight. "She hooked up with the bastard who robbed Wrecker of his job."

The asshole had not only taken the manager job, but he'd stolen Valerie. He was in too good at the Shadowlands to be ejected, but if he thought he could keep Valerie... Barry scowled. Not going to happen.

He needed to find a way to make his wife see reason.

"So she's not coming back. You know, that sucks. We're like really out of money." Alisha scowled. "The cable got shut off, and I can't get any of my TV shows."

"Yeah, well, it's sad shit, 'cause I don't have any money coming in right now." Another contract had been broken because he'd fallen behind on getting the work done. And his insurance was raising his rates because there'd been too many accidents at the job sites. They said he was negligent.

Barry eyed Alisha. "Maybe you should get off your ass and get a full-time job, huh?"

"And maybe you should stop drinking, so you can bring in what you used to. Valerie was right."

Rage rising, he slapped the sneer right off her face.

"Or maybe not." She walked away from him and into the bedroom.

After repairing her tear-streaked makeup in the Capture Gardens' side entry, Natalia followed Olivia through the clubroom. Her legs felt wobbly.

How many orgasms had the Mistress given her after giving her a ring? Wasn't it awesome Natalia had been allowed to give her fiancée almost as many?

Fiancée. What an amazing word. Happiness fizzed in her veins.

"Mistress, I totally deserve a strawberry daiquiri." Natalia gazed up at Olivia through her dark lashes. The Mistress was always teasing her about her puppy-dog eyes. She should put them to use. "Puh-leeze, Captain Janeway?"

Olivia touched her cheek with such gentle fingers Natalia's heart simply melted. "I believe we can accommodate you, Counselor Troi."

Josie wiped the bar top in front of them. "Captain Janeway, it's good to meet you. I've been an admirer for years." Observing appropriate protocol, the bartender only smiled at Natalia. "What can I get you two?"

Natalia settled onto a barstool and folded her hands on the bar...because she couldn't help marveling at her amazing engagement ring. Small diamonds swirled around a deep red, round-cut ruby. The combination was so much warmer than a plain diamond solitaire. So very perfect.

"Oh, my sun and stars, Natalia!" Totally abandoning D/s protocol, Josie grabbed Natalia's hand. "What a gorgeous ring! Are you two engaged?"

Olivia grinned. "Yes, we are."

Josie's delighted scream caught everyone's attention. "Mistress Olivia and Natalia are engaged!" Then she winced. "Uh, sorry, Mistress Olivia, I shouldn't have—"

"It's good," Olivia said, cutting her off as club members surrounded them.

"Do you have a date picked or any plans?" Josie asked. "Will you have a big wedding? Natalia's family lives in Tampa, right?"

Natalia grimaced. Her family? Talk about awkward with a side-helping of ugly. Maybe she and the Mistress should have discussed this while they were outside. "Um, we'll probably go with very small and private."

Olivia turned and gave her a long perusal. "I rather thought you'd want a big, splashy wedding."

The Mistress had remembered.

On their first evening at Olivia's, they'd been in her pool, sharing a giant inflatable lounger, drinking wine, and describing their childhood dreams. Natalia said she'd wanted the white gown, friends and family, the walk down the aisle. The whole spectacle.

The dream had died the day she'd introduced Olivia as her girlfriend. That was when her family realized she wouldn't accept their choices for her schooling, her career...or her partner.

Natalia shook her head. "We don't need a bunch of people there."

"Girl." The Mistress's hand closed over hers. "We're going to talk about this some more. Don't think we won't."

Natalia sighed. Olivia always knew when she was evading.

"Whether you have a big or small wedding, congratulations." Ghost said.

Beside him, Valerie was beaming.

"Indeed, congratulations, Mistress Olivia. Natalia." Z said.

Natalia smiled at them all as Olivia responded.

Jessica abandoned Z to edge her way to Natalia's other side where she could admire the ring. "It's absolutely stunning. Good job, Mistress Olivia."

"Thank you, love."

And Natalia leaned closer to Jessica. "You're going to pop any minute, girl."

"I know, right? I'm so ready. But my due date isn't for another week, so I should be able to make your showing."

Natalia's eyes pooled with tears. "You don't have to. It's a small gallery and—"

"Pfft, of course we're coming." Jessica glanced at Olivia. "Will your family in England fly over for a wedding here? Or will you have it there?"

Natalia winced. Jessica had missed Natalia's pronouncement of small and private.

"I rather think we'll have it here with our friends," Olivia paused and added, "then I'll drag my sweet subbie home to England to meet the family."

Olivia's family? Oh no. Natalia squeaked like a trapped mouse. And her evil Mistress laughed.

The announcement of Natalia and Olivia's engagement had been a fantastic climax to a solidly good theme night.

Smiling, Ghost captured his own submissive and steered her into a sitting area sheltered by tall foliage. A perfect spot to have a word. Or two.

But first... Tangling his fingers in the heavy silk of her hair, he took her lips. The way she melted against him told him she trusted him as a Dom. She loved him as a man.

Her body didn't lie.

He had a feeling she wouldn't lie verbally, either.

"Since the evening is about half over, it's time for an assessment." Ghost ran a finger down her cheek and under her chin so she'd meet his gaze. "How many thoughts or verbal self-put-downs did you catch?"

She had the most luminous blue eyes he'd ever seen. Warm and open and...

Unable to resist, he kissed her again.

Her slightly befuddled expression when he finished made him grin. Damn, but he'd be happy to call it a night and take her to bed.

But no, this evening was for her. Well, mostly. Torturing her a bit was going to be fun.

"Valerie? Disparaging thoughts?"

"Well." She bit her lip, thinking. "Maybe one thought when I first arrived. A couple of times with Kahlua's insults, but I pushed them away and moved on. I have to admit, it was a relief to see her and my ex head out the door."

"Of course it was." Because from what he'd seen, the two

would make her feel as if she'd stepped onto a battlefield. She'd shown courage in being so honest. He crossed his arms over his chest. "Thank you for sharing with me. I think punishment for the thoughts along with a reward for not letting them linger. Yes, a combination sounds appropriate."

Her expression turned wary.

"If you hadn't told me the truth, you would have spent the rest of the evening naked."

She took a step back.

"I appreciate your honesty, sweetheart, and your dress will stay on...but open." He unzipped the front completely, from neckline to hemline, and the edges fell open.

"Jesus, woman, you really are beautiful," he growled. Cupping her breasts, he found her skin warm and slightly damp from the unforgiving vinyl. Her nipples responded to his fingers immediately, turning into perfect hard peaks.

Her lips were puffy from his kisses, her hair tousled from his fingers. She looked like someone who should be tossed onto a bed and ravished.

He couldn't.

Fucking manager job.

But...her punishment would be a delightful diversion.

Gripping her forearms, he set them behind her back and locked her thin wrist cuffs together.

Straightening, he studied her face.

Ah, there were the first hints of nervousness, something any Dom would savor. And any sadist would enjoy what he was about to do next.

He pulled the first set of silvery chains from his right pocket.

"A necklace?" she asked.

"Mmmph, let's call it body jewelry." When he untangled a tweezer clamp from the chains, her apprehension visibly grew.

Nice.

Her velvety nipples were still jutting perfectly. He fastened one clamp on the left, tightening it until her entire body tensed. "Breathe, pet. Another."

Savoring her submission to his will—and the way her lips pressed together, and her neck muscles stood out—he waited.

There. She started to relax.

Smiling, he clamped her right nipple and sent her onto her tiptoes as he tightened it.

Her pupils dilated, and she moaned. Her voice was pure sexy sin.

He had to reposition the hard-on tenting his jeans. He kissed her gently, then rougher, before whispering roughly in Arabic, "I love the way you react when I hurt you, the way you slide right into arousal."

Oh gods, he saw her too well. Knew her too well. Even as the cool air brushed her heated skin, her clamped nipples pulsed in time with her heartbeat. The chain between the two clamps hung between her breasts. Another chain dangled straight down with another clamp at the end.

Surely not.

"Now." The wicked pleasure in his eyes sent quivers through her. "This one is going to drive you mad, pet."

He sat on the coffee table and guided her to stand in front of him. "Legs apart, please."

No way.

His gaze met hers, held hers. And somehow her feet moved to a wide stance.

"There's a brave lass." He pulled a packet of lube from his pocket and squeezed some on his fingers. "Let's get you nice and erect, hmm?" His slick fingers rubbed up and down on each side of her clit.

The incredible burst of pleasure made her knees shake.

"Now the fun part." With the silicone-ended tweezers

touching each side of the base of her clit, he slid the tiny ring up to tighten the ends.

"Ohhh!" As the pressure grew, she instinctively jerked back—and was stopped by his hand on her ass. Her protest emerged as a husky whine.

Sitting back on the coffee table, he had a slight smile on his firm lips. Head tilted slightly, he studied her...and slowly, the pressure on the sides of her clit transformed into the pounding bass drum of arousal.

"Very pretty." He rose and pulled more chains from his pocket. A thin silver collar went around her neck, and the attached chains fell in pretty loops over her breasts. Another set fastened around her waist, spilling in more loops over her lower belly and crotch.

Whenever she moved, cool, silky metal brushed across her hot skin.

"Almost done. Perhaps something colorful would be pretty, don't you think?" He attached a red crystal weight to each nipple clamp.

Ohhh. The edgy pain on her breasts stoked her fires higher.

With a merciless expression, he did the same with the clit clamp. The weight bumped against her labia with every movement—and tugged on the increasingly sensitive ball of nerves.

"Ghoooost, no."

"Now you know what we're doing, I'll give you a choice." He curved his hand around her nape, his gaze serious. "Since I can't leave yet, we're going to walk around the club. You can either wear your unzipped dress with—or without the jewelry. Of course, if you annoy me, you'll be completely naked."

Her mouth dropped open at the threat.

Fine, she wouldn't annoy him. However, what about the other options? Try to walk with clamps on her breasts and, so much worse, her clit?

However, the jewelry gave her some covering, at least.

Without the chains, her breasts and pussy would be on full display.

Her brain went into a meltdown, unable to decide.

His smile widened.

"You really are a sadist."

"You say that as if it's a bad thing." When he tugged on the nipple clamps, then the clit one, sensations sparked across her nerve endings like fireworks.

She could feel the dampness growing between her legs as the pain slid into a heady carnal desire. "I don't suppose we could simply go upstairs and play?"

He chuckled and traced one looping chain over her hip, her mound, to the other hip. Like the wake after a speedboat, he left a trail of heat behind. "Seems to me you have a punishment to serve first."

"Next time, I'm going to lie," she muttered.

Laughing, he motioned her to walk with him. Beside him, but on her own. Leaving her to face all the stares.

And people *did* stare.

Dammit, it felt as if her clit was poking out for everyone to see. Like it was ten times the size of normal. Rather than checking, she held her head high.

Ghost headed toward the bar. "Let's get you a drink before we wander through the rest of the club."

He chose a spot near the small replica of the Enterprise. Over her head, small planets dangled from the ceiling rafters.

Although Cullen had disappeared, probably to play with Andrea, Josie was still bartending. "Hi, Colonel—or I should say Captain. What can I get you tonight?"

"A Coke for me, please, and a Romulan Ale for Valerie."

"Coming right up," Josie said.

Valerie smirked. He'd have to release her hands so she could drink.

On Ghost's other side, a white-haired Dom in long, heavy robes assisted an equally aged woman onto a barstool.

The Dom turned. "Ghost, how are you this evening?"

"Gerald, it's good to see you." The men shook hands.

Ghost set his hand on Valerie's shoulder. "Martha, Gerald, this is Valerie."

"A pleasure, Miss." Gerald gave her a formal nod.

Martha had a totally sweet smile.

"Interesting." Gerald studied her dress—and chains—before giving Ghost a laughing look. "You have a wicked streak in you."

"Here and I thought I'd been very charitable." Ghost grinned. "If she's a good subbie, I won't have to lead her using the leash."

What leash? Valerie glanced down and stiffened. A length of chain ran between her clit and nipple clamps. If he pulled on it...

She wasn't sure if she'd yelp or *come*.

Even as embarrassed warmth swept into her face, her nipples bunched tighter, adding to the pain of the clamps.

"You found an attractive discipline method." Gerald turned to his wife. "I'm going to get you some chains, maybe in a darker color. They'd be lovely on you."

"Yes, they would."

When his wife beamed in delight, Valerie considered her. Martha was dressed as Lwaxana Troi—Deanna's mother—in a bold jewel-encrusted dress with her shoulders exposed and plenty of cleavage.

Her breasts certainly weren't perky, her face was wrinkled, her round belly also sagged.

Yet the way Gerald watched her said none of that mattered. He still desired his wife's body. From Martha's confident expression, his opinion—and her own—were all she cared about.

I've been an idiot. She could remember when she turned thirty-five and had been amused at the angst she'd felt in her twenties over everything—her appearance, dating, making love.

At Martha's age, would Valerie look back on *this* year and be equally amused?

Achieving Martha's serenity would be a worthy goal to strive for.

"Ghost, my dear. Sam and his Linda are joining us for dinner in two weeks on Sunday. You must come and bring your woman." Martha winked at Valerie. "Just good company with all our clothing on."

Valerie broke out laughing because the dress code was exactly what she'd been wondering about.

Smiling, Gerald harrumphed. "Back in our day, we enjoyed the kink parties, but now, we're happy to play here."

"Same," Ghost agreed. He accepted the drinks from Josie with a quiet thanks. After putting a straw in the blue-hued Romulan ale, he held it to Valerie's lips.

He wasn't going to release her wrists? When she scowled, his mouth twitched with his amusement.

"You're letting your subbie glare at you?" In a gray, hooded Vulcan robe, Nolan helped Beth—who wore a skintight T'Pol catsuit—onto a stool, then took the one beside her. "Sets a bad example for the newbies."

Ghost huffed a laugh. "I'll tug on her leash for every second of disrespect."

Oh spit, not the leash.

Valerie slapped on such an angelic expression that angels probably circled her haloed head.

"Nice." Nolan slapped Ghost's shoulder and grinned at Beth. "I'm liking the potential of those chains—and clamps."

Beth gave Valerie an appalled look before saying in the sweetest tone, "My wonderful, kind Master of the Universe would never want his ever-so-respectful submissive to endure such pain."

The mean-looking Dom had a great laugh. "Nice try, li'l rabbit." He glanced at Ghost. "When you get a chance, email me where you bought them."

CHAPTER TWENTY-FOUR

The mild evening air held hints of coffee and cigars, garlic and onions, and Ghost pulled in another deep breath. The historic district of Ybor City was much like New Orleans' Bourbon Street. Done Cuban style.

"The school year is almost over." He smiled down at Valerie.

"Tomorrow. Finally. I'm looking forward to the break before summer school starts." Her face went soft as she added, "And I'll have time to spend with the children—and Luca."

"Did Dillon get back?" Her son had spent a few months setting up a manufacturing plant in China.

Her face lit up. "I forgot to tell you. He texted yesterday he was back. And planned to spend a few days recovering from jet lag and doing laundry."

Ghost gave her a tug on her hair. "Knowing you, you're dying to go stock his kitchen and do his laundry."

"Well, mmm, yes?" Her expression was rueful. "But he's very proud of his independence and being a man now, so I won't."

Ghost took her arm to bring her to a halt so he could watch her instead of the street. "Valerie, are you ever planning to tell your children about me? The two of us?"

"I... Yes." She exhaled, then rested her forehead against his shoulder. "I'm being foolish, I know. I guess I'm scared at how they'll react, since they still want me and Barry to get back together."

He rested his hand on her nape, wishing he could fix everything for her. But this battle was hers to fight. "They might not give up their hopes until they realize you've moved on."

"Which means my stalling is having the wrong effect." Straightening, she smiled up at him. "You're right. I need to stop being a coward and let them know."

"You're not a coward, lass, merely cautious." Because her asshole parents and husband had ripped her loving heart open. Her children had damned well better not do the same.

"They're good children. They'll understand." She bit her lip for a moment. "I'll have them over this weekend and tell them about you. You're going to be gone anyway."

A bunch of his Special Forces buddies were gathering at Eglin Air Force base to celebrate a friend's retirement from the service. Since it was over a six-hour drive, he wouldn't be back until the wee hours Sunday night.

"I'm going to miss you, you know." He dropped a kiss on the top of her head and started moving again.

"Me, too." As they stepped off the curb to cross the street, she eyed his leg. "How does your new prosthesis feel? You're not limping today."

Rather than being embarrassed she noticed when he limped, he appreciated her concern. "The microprocessor and hydraulic ankle make it better on stairs and rough ground. It's heavier than a basic carbon foot, though."

"But you like the zing of cutting-edge technology."

"Well, yeah, I'm a guy." He grinned at her huff of laughter.

Inside the art gallery, he picked up a flyer about the four emerging, modern-impressionist artists. "Despite being Tuesday, they've drawn a good crowd."

"Natalia must be so excited." Valerie studied the milling people. "I hope there are more collectors than family and friends."

He spotted discreet "Sold" tags on many of the paintings. "I don't think you need to worry."

"Worrying is listed somewhere in the "friend" manifesto."

"Then it's good you have that item covered." He gazed down at her. "You know, I rather like the New Yorker style on you—black pants, black blazer."

She chuckled. "It's in bad taste if your clothing competes with the art."

He ran his knuckles over her shimmery blue shirt. "This matches your gorgeous eyes."

Her cheeks turned pink. "So Hailey said. It was a Yule present."

Would she still flush from a compliment after they'd been together a few years? Smiling, he bent to capture a quick kiss.

Yeah, he really loved this woman.

They were good together—all the time, not just for the sex and scenes. He looked forward to their quiet evenings...and also when they went out. She'd been with him for university events, faculty lunches, and evenings with other couples like Linda and Sam.

Everything was more enjoyable with her companionship.

It appeared she felt the same way about him, since she was with him every evening and night. Gradually, her clothing was filling in the spaces he'd emptied for her.

She still had her apartment—her security blanket, she called it. On her own, she'd obtained a recommendation for a counselor from Gabi and was working through her parents' neglect and how her ex's slaves had resurrected the issues.

Last weekend at the Shadowlands, she'd been much more comfortable with her body. And, even though aging had bothered her, she'd never disliked or questioned *who* she was. She liked herself.

He did, too.

"So, let's check out the art." He guided her through the brightly lit gallery, detouring around the clusters of people. Some were holding small plastic cups of wine. A few should obviously have stopped with one cup.

As they worked their way through the paintings, her smile grew. "I love the impressionist style."

He nodded. "Monet and Pissarro are near the top of my list. But modern impressionism might be even better than the pioneers."

"Hmm. Because there are more colors available, maybe? Or perhaps it's because no one tells them they have to confine themselves to a certain style."

"That might be it." He stopped in front of one of Natalia's paintings. From the long, high pier, he'd guess it was Naples Beach, a popular spot for photographers. Natalia's painting held two dark figures sitting in the sand, leaning against each other, silhouetted by the light on the water.

A moment in time. And a universal feeling.

"Who hasn't watched a sunset with a lover?" Valerie murmured.

"I think our quiet Natalia will go far." Ghost tilted his head and grinned. "Although she might choose to flee, instead."

Near another of her paintings, Natalia had been cornered by an older man. He was gesturing with his wine in a way that showed he might have already had a few.

"Time for a rescue, Colonel?" Valerie asked.

"*De Oppressor Liber.*" *To free the oppressed*, the Special Forces motto, seemed quite appropriate.

"Natalia, your paintings are stunning." Valerie swooped in, cleverly maneuvering herself between the young woman and the pompous fool.

The man's expression darkened. "Hey, I—"

"Natalia, it's about time we found you," Ghost growled, deliberately sounding irritated.

The man took a step back...and decided he needed more wine.

Valerie patted Ghost's chest. "I love your sadist voice."

"And your timing." Natalia rolled her eyes. "He was telling me why I'd chosen the subjects I used."

Valerie snickered. "Mansplaining, hmm?"

"Totally. I didn't realize I had repressed sexual urges when I painted a great white heron in the Everglades."

"Ah." Ghost gave her a serious look. "It's good to learn these important details about your motivation."

When Natalia's mouth dropped open, he chuckled. "And if you share his theory with your Mistress, I'm sure she'll help you with the problem."

Natalia broke into giggles, leaning on Valerie for support. "Thank you for the rescue. Some of these people are...well, really enthusiastic."

And a bit much for the quiet artist. Until her Mistress arrived, they'd better stay close enough to break her free when needed.

"Where's Olivia?" Valerie was obviously on the same wavelength.

"One of her clients had a break-in, and the police wanted the security camera recordings. Since she's boss of the security firm, she has to deal with it. She texted to let me know she was stuck there for a while."

"Did she now?" At Valerie's raised eyebrows, Ghost explained. "She never used to let anyone know when she'd be late, and she's almost always late."

"She doesn't like me worrying," Natalia said, "so she texts now."

Of course. To keep from stressing *Natalia*, Olivia would make the effort. Stressing out her fellow Dominants, however, wasn't a concern. Ghost almost laughed.

"Nattie!" A group of people advanced toward her. Brown hair, brown eyes, familiar features. Natalia's family had arrived. Three men wore tan coveralls with the logo of a local windshield repair service.

Arm around Valerie, Ghost backed away.

"Mama!" Natalia hugged an older woman who was babbling congratulations. The rest of the family was studying the people and paintings.

The two women close to Natalia in age studied one of her paintings, then read the tag. And exclaimed.

Ah, yes. Ghost had noted the gallery had gone for transparency and included the price on each info tag.

The two young men who weren't in coveralls joined them. "The red dot means it sold. Damn, that one's sold, too. Look at those prices!"

The men in coveralls went over. Their surprised exclamations didn't hold the same tone of pride as the first group.

Valerie stiffened. "They didn't realize she's any good?"

Joining them, Olivia obviously overheard. "It's partly denial because some of them don't want her to be any good. The entire younger lot works for her uncle who owns some auto glass repair shops. Since she excelled in school, he's pushing her to take accounting courses and deal with the licensing, taxes, employees —all of it."

Frowning, Valerie studied Natalia. "She doesn't seem as if an office job would make her happy."

"She hates numbers. And managing people." Olivia shook her head. "All she's ever wanted to do is paint. To create. But they keep trying to shove her into a narrow little box."

Ghost set his hand on her shoulder. "She escaped. With luck, tonight will make that clear."

Unappeased, Olivia growled under her breath.

"I doubt she would want to lose her family, even if they don't understand her. Although tonight might help." Valerie nodded at Natalia's mother.

Olivia followed her gaze, undoubtedly seeing the woman's pride in her daughter. The mother smiled at Olivia.

Olivia nodded back and said reluctantly, "*Some* of them might have figured out how amazing she is."

Valerie gave the Domme a sympathetic pat on the arm and pointed out, so very tactfully, "Isn't it nice she has you to help set boundaries with them."

After a second, Olivia chuckled. "There's the difference between you and my Nats. You don't have a problem with nudging someone in the right direction."

Ghost smiled slightly and murmured to Valerie, "You really do have an amazing talent with people."

"I know." Her eyes lifted, holding a warmth for him alone. "But can I admit I love hearing you say that?"

Because her marriage had been a wasteland, empty of compliments and approval.

He kissed her forehead. "Both of you are excellent at management, but, after seeing Natalia's paintings, I'd say she's found her own way to steer people where she wants them to go."

Because the shy submissive's works were all about connection. To the world of nature—and to each other.

"I'm so proud of you. Did you see how many of your paintings are sold?" Natalia's oldest sister whispered.

"I'm trying not to check," Natalia confessed and hugged her, then her other sister and two big brothers. How cool they'd all dressed up. "I'm glad you came."

She glanced at her uncle and his two sons and wished they'd stayed home. They were still dressed in their work coveralls.

She shouldn't have been surprised or embarrassed by their disrespect.

But she was.

Hands stuffed in his pockets, Uncle Bartolo was checking out the room. "You got yourself a nice hobby, Nattie. But nothing you can make a living at, not like managing a business." He gave her a patronizing look. "Get on back to the business classes so you can be of use to the company. To your family."

Here? He was going to push his weight around *here*?

Smoldering resentment sparked into anger, and she tried to tamp it down. "No, thank you. This is what I do."

"Yeah, then you'll need a guy to keep you from starving." Tadeo was the most obnoxious of her cousins. "Leonel still wants to date you, even if you are a fancy *artist*."

She wanted to slap the smirk off Tadeo's face. Her whole family knew she wasn't interested in men. Knew she dated only women. Knew she was seeing someone.

And she was done with this bullshit.

"Actually, dating Leonel won't be possible. Olivia and I are engaged." She held her hand out to show her ring.

Her mother's mouth dropped open, but Natalia's sisters squealed and hugged her and admired her ring. And then her mother joined right in.

That was so very wonderful.

Her brothers managed to reach in to give her a squeeze, then one smiled over her shoulder. "Hey, Olivia. Congratulations, and um, welcome to the family."

Olivia? Natalia spun and squealed. "You made it!" She launched herself, knowing her Mistress would catch her.

Arms closed around her, holding her tightly, and she felt Olivia's cheek against the top of her head. "Of course, I made it. I wouldn't miss your first opening for the world. Everything looks fantastic. Congratulations on your success, love."

When Olivia stepped back, Natalia took her hand.

Her mother stepped up, smiling—and hugged Olivia. "I have another *hija*, now. I'm so pleased."

Grinning at Olivia's flummoxed expression, Natalia kissed her mother's cheek, then giggled, because her sisters were all sentimental and teary-eyed as they hugged Olivia, too.

"Seriously?" Her cousin's sneering voice made them all pause. "I don't get the lesbian shit. Nattie, how can you know you're gay if you've never slept with a man?"

"Good point." Stepping away from Natalia's sisters, Olivia studied him. "I do have to wonder, Tadeo, how can *you* tell you're straight if you've never slept with a man? Or...have you?"

Natalia pressed her lips together because what answer could her cousin give? It took him a second to figure that out. He turned a furious red.

As her sisters snickered, one of her brothers knocked the idiot back a step, and the other snapped, "Give it up, idiot. She made her choice. A good choice."

Natalia's mouth dropped open. Her brothers were backing her up?

Her uncle scowled. "I don't hold with gay marriage."

"In that case, I'd suggest if a gay person asks you to marry them, you should probably say no," Valerie pointed out ever-so-politely.

A snorting laugh escaped Natalia, and she plastered her hands over her mouth. A lot of others weren't nearly so discreet, though.

"I must point out"—the authority in Ghost's gravelly voice put every submissive in the room on alert—"anyone who isn't stuck in the last century simply calls it marriage."

Uncle Bartolo's mouth snapped shut.

Because who would argue with the Colonel?

"Olivia, Natalia." Valerie linked arms with them. "Let's go check out the paintings and talk about wedding dates."

So tactful. She was trying to get them away from the harassment, but her cousin wasn't going to stop. "Jesus, Nattie, you gotta give this bullshit up. No one will come to your wedding—if you could even find someone to perform the ceremony."

His rudeness shocked everyone.

"Indeed." Master Z's smooth voice broke the silence—and was so cold Tadeo shriveled at least a foot.

Natalia turned.

Master Z was wearing the tailored dark suit Jessica said made her mouth go dry.

On his left, his mother, Ms. Grayson, looked like European royalty.

On his other side, Jessica was in a beautifully billowy, maternity gown that matched her green eyes. Unlike Master Z, she was obviously spitting mad as she glared at Tadeo.

Uh-oh. It couldn't be healthy for someone so very pregnant to get so angry.

Master Z tilted his head at Olivia and Natalia. "It would be my honor to be your officiant and marry the two of you."

Natalia swallowed. "Ma—um, Dr. Grayson, it..." She glanced at Olivia who winked and nodded.

Natalia managed a breath. So much for a small civil ceremony. "We would like that very much, Sir."

"All right!" Uzuri swooped in to hug her, then beamed at Mama and Natalia's sisters. "Can I help with the planning?"

"But of course." Mama smiled. "We'll have fun, won't we, girls?"

Her sisters bounced up and down in delight.

Fun? Mama was insane. Natalia remembered well when her oldest sister married. It'd been pure chaos.

"Perfect," Jessica said. "We have someone to perform the ceremony and the planning is started."

"Witnesses will be required." Madeline Grayson tilted her head. "If Zachary is performing the service, I do expect an invitation."

Natalia had no words. None. That was Master Z's *mother*.

Olivia chuckled. "Madeline, we'll be delighted to have you there."

Cheers came from all around them...as well as orders: "You'd better invite me, too."

"And me."

"Do you need a volunteer flower-kitten?" Rainie called. "Or puppy?"

The Shadowkittens had arrived with their Masters.

Anyone who hadn't been at the club last weekend now took the opportunity to congratulate and hug Olivia and Natalia.

Mama was watching Master Z's mother who... Natalia's eyes widened. Mrs. Grayson had bought one of her paintings and was telling the gallery owner she wanted it for her visual arts center in Sarasota.

"What center?" Mama asked.

"She owns the Grayson Center for Visual Arts in Sarasota. It has one of the best collections of modern impressionism in the country." Natalia had loved going there as a child—and had been completely stunned when she learned who Master Z's mother was.

"I'm sorry I wasn't more supportive of your art, *mija*." Mama put an arm around her for a quick squeeze. "I'm proud of you."

Off to one side, Tadeo scowled at them, then yelled something nasty.

Almost as loudly, Rainie made a high-pitched *voom-voom-voom* sound. "That's what motorcycles with tiny motors sound like. All squeals and no power." As everyone stared at her, she smirked and patted her crotch. "Just like some guys and their tiny equipment."

After a shocked moment of silence, Natalia's brothers and sisters, then the Shadowkittens, howled with laughter.

If her cousin had any comment, it was drowned out completely.

A second later, her brothers grabbed Tadeo and force-walked him out the door.

"I owe your brothers some drinks," Olivia murmured in Natalia's ear.

Even as the congratulations continued, the gallery owner put a red "sold" dot on another of Natalia's paintings.

CHAPTER TWENTY-FIVE

After ending her phone call, Valerie raided Jessica's fridge and made up a tray with iced tea and some of the cookies people had brought. Such a light white kitchen with gray granite countertops and suspended chandeliers from the coffered ceiling.

Carrying the tray, she passed the family room. Cushy soft furniture and warm-hued Brazilian cherry wood flooring made the room cozy. Master Z's mother, Madeline, was reading a picture book with her granddaughter.

On Madeline's lap, Sophia enthusiastically *mooed* her accompaniment to whatever farm story they were enjoying.

Madeline looked up, her silvery-gray eyes the same disconcerting color as Z's. "How is Jessica doing, Valerie?"

"She's holding up well." Valerie shook her head. "Considering how far apart the contractions are, it's going to be a while."

Poor Jessica. Being in labor...well, it sucked.

"Of course it will be." Madeline's mouth pursed. "I believe the designer of female bodies must have flunked out of the engineering program."

Laughing, Valerie headed through the house to return to Jessica and Beth, her sandals tapping on the pale marble flooring.

In the glass-enclosed Florida room, the ceiling fan was assisting the breeze from the cranked-open tall windows

Valerie set the tray down on the marble-topped table and handed a filled glass to Jessica.

Beth accepted hers with a soft thank you, then frowned at a streak of mud on her forearm. "Whoa, I'm a mess." The slender redhead had been working on a landscaping design for the yard and was still in her tank top and overall-shorts.

"I'd want you here, even if you were covered in mud," Jessica said. "I'd go crazy if I didn't have all of y'all here to keep me busy."

When Jessica had whined at Master Z that she needed diversions, he'd recruited the Shadowkittens bunch. They were all taking turns to visit during the beginning hours of labor.

Valerie settled into a wicker chair next to Jessica and glanced around the room. "I like your sunroom. It's very serene." With all windows and white trim, the room was filled with light. The bright blue Mediterranean tile floor, foliage plants, and blue-and-white chair cushions added color.

"That was the plan." With one hand on her belly, Jessica gave a short laugh. "I'm not sure it's working today. I can't believe I probably still have hours to go!"

"One moment at a time." Valerie settled in the chair beside her. "You can get through this moment. Don't look at the future."

Beth nodded.

"Right. Thank you." With a sigh, the blonde relaxed before drinking some tea.

"Was your call from one of your children?"

Recognizing Jessica needed a diversion, Valerie nodded. "My son, Dillon."

"You have a boy and girl, right?" Jessica asked.

Valerie nodded.

"I don't know what I'm having. We already have one girl, and Z's never said if he wants a boy or girl." Jessica's eyes filled with worry. "What if he wants a boy? Guys always want boys, right?"

"I have a feeling Master Z will love whatever baby you two made," Beth said. "No matter what sex."

Valerie couldn't give Jessica the same reassurance. Barry had been disappointed to not have two boys. "Z would probably want you to ask him rather than be knotted up with worries. At least, that's Ghost's preference."

"Those two are way too much alike," Jessica grumbled. "And now I'm going to have to ask him. Because you pointed it out."

Valerie snorted. "Sorry."

"Is your son all right, Valerie?" Beth asked.

"He is. He wanted to confirm he'll come to dinner this Sunday. Both of my children will be there."

Beth frowned. "Why do you seem worried?"

Jessica raised her eyebrows, her green eyes bright with interest.

"Because I plan to tell the kids I'm dating." Merely the thought made Valerie tense, and she took a sip of her drink.

"Dating? Is that what it's called?" Jessica sputtered a laugh. "You're not going to say you're living with a kinky sadist called the Colonel—and having hot sex every time you turn around?"

Valerie choked on her iced tea.

"Jessica, you went through something like this with Z's boys. I bet he didn't tell them what he was doing with you," Beth chided as Valerie tried to clear her airway.

"He better not *ever* mention the stuff we do," Jessica muttered.

Beth grinned at her, then asked Valerie, "How long have you been divorced?"

"Since January. The proceedings were quick since the kids are grown." Valerie swallowed down the bitter memory. "And Barry had spent our savings on his slaves. I didn't want to argue over anything else; I just wanted out."

"And you've been *dating*"—Beth shot a grin at Jessica—"Ghost since near the beginning of March, right?"

"About then, yes."

"So it's not like you jumped into living with him after a week or two. But they won't know that. Did they take sides in the divorce?"

Valerie stretched her legs out. "I think they're trying not to, but Barry..." She blew out a breath. "I never realized how cleverly he makes himself seem like the good guy. Back when the kids were young and we'd make rules for them, he'd act as if the rules were *my* idea and would give in if they begged. It always seemed like *I* was the hardass. I bought all their presents—because he didn't want to—but he always acted like *he'd* chosen them."

"Owww." Setting her tea down with a thump, Jessica suffered through a contraction. Finished, she glared. "You should bring your ex here. I'd love to smack someone around right about now."

Valerie laughed. "Don't tempt me."

Beth grinned. "I think I understand. Your children are trying to be reasonable about the divorce, but your ex is playing to their sympathies. I bet you haven't told them about his slaves."

"Whyever not?" Jessica snapped. "Sorry. But wouldn't hearing about the other women make them see the light?"

It appeared everyone knew about Barry's slaves. Valerie almost laughed. Linda had warned her that what one Shadowkitten knew, the rest soon learned. "Barry asked me not to tell them, and honestly, I didn't think the slaves would live with him very much longer. It's not like there's any love between them. It's more of a support-us-and-we'll-give-you-sex deal."

"All the more reason to tell the children," Jessica said.

"I get why you don't. Bringing up the topic would be embarrassing—and humiliating." Beth's eyes were full of sympathy. "But...just saying...if your ex is twisting the children's emotions so cleverly, he's probably really good at manipulating you, too. Making you feel as if his *needing* other women is all your fault."

Beth totally got it. Valerie's throat clogged for a moment, so she nodded.

"I didn't even think of him messing you up, too. Your ex really *is* a bastard." Jessica grimaced and held her stomach. The contractions were finally getting more frequent. "Is that why you held off on moving in with Ghost?"

Valerie laughed. "Everyone talks about how snoopy Master Z is. I think you might be worse."

Beth grinned. "She has you nailed, Jessica."

"But you're here to keep me diverted," Jessica whined. "Talking about relationships is the *best* distraction."

"She has a point," Beth said. "And I kinda want to know, too."

The two of them were something. Valerie shook her head.

But she didn't really mind sharing. In the Shadowlands, they'd seen her at her most vulnerable. "After I was away from Barry, I could see all the ways he'd made me insecure. Everything I was proud of—like writing a book or getting my doctorate—was accomplished in spite of the obstacles he'd put up. With Ghost...I didn't want to end up with that happening again."

"Makes sense." Jessica tapped her fingers on her chin as she thought. "But I can't see the Colonel being anything like your ex."

"No, I don't think he is." Although, admittedly, every now and then, she worried.

Bending slightly, Jessica whined and went through another contraction. This one was a bit longer. Sweat beaded on her upper lip.

"Looks like you're going to have your baby today." Valerie reached out to hold her hand. "Soon, you'll have a lap for Sophia to sit in again."

Jessica's eyes filled with tears. "I've missed having her in my lap." Across the room, her cell phone dinged with a message. She tried to stand but didn't make it out of the chair.

Laughing, Beth rose and handed it to her.

Jessica glanced at the display. "Speaking of children..."

Seeing Valerie's confusion, Beth said, "Z's boys are grown, and they're worried and texting every hour or so to check on Jessica."

Jessica rolled her eyes. "They went from hating me for daring to be with their father to liking me, and now they're as overprotective of me as Z is."

"See?" Beth said. "The same thing will eventually happen with your children, Valerie. I can't imagine them not liking Ghost."

Valerie nodded. She could hope, right?

It must be around midnight, Zachary thought, as he wiped Jessica's face with a cool cloth. Despite the air conditioning, he felt as if he was in a sauna. As if he'd been in a firefight for hours.

Except...in this battle, his Jessica had been doing all the work. *Labor* didn't come close to describing the trauma of birthing a baby.

At the foot of the bed, Fay, the midwife, was humming along with the soft music of Clannad.

Although their friends were outside, he couldn't hear them—he'd had excellent soundproofing installed before moving in—and he'd been able to reassure Jessica they couldn't hear her when the pain grew too much for her.

Sophia would be in bed by now. She was going to be so excited to have a baby brother or sister. Every day, she'd been patting Jessica's stomach and asking if her baby was ready to come out and play.

Jessica's hand clamped down on his as she went through another contraction.

He waited for what seemed like an eternity before she relaxed. She was exhausted, dammit.

He kept his voice low, trying for encouraging rather than strained. "Almost there, kitten."

Her green eyes flashed at him, and he tensed, but then she laughed. "I know. I'm so ready to push."

"Are you now?" It seemed the swearing portion of labor was

over. Sophia's birth had given him occasional nightmares about the hellish period called *transition*. He'd undoubtedly have new ones after tonight.

"Agreed. You've made your ten centimeters." At the foot of the bed, Fay smiled. "Push now, Jessica."

Jessica's hand tightened around his in an unbreakable grip. Her head lifted, and her neck muscles stood out with the strain as she groaned and bore down.

"Perfect. This child is going to have dark hair." Fay looked up. "Want to catch your baby, Zachary?"

Torn, he turned to Jessica. "I can stay here, or I can play catcher. Which do you want?"

Her lips tipped up. "I'd like to tell our son or daughter you were there from the first moment. Go."

Heart overflowing, he kissed her and went to help their child into the world.

A few minutes later, he held a baby girl, white-patched and pink, and he could feel her already wrapping herself around his heart. How had he forgotten how tiny a newborn was? How much of a miracle?

When Fay nodded, he laid the baby on Jessica's now flaccid belly, letting the bond between them begin.

Sitting on the edge of the bed, he kept one hand on the newborn, needing to feel the reassurance of her chest moving.

Still pale but content, Jessica turned her head. "We did good, huh?"

"We did." He touched his forehead against hers. "Thank you for our daughter. She's perfect."

"Zachary." Interesting. She rarely used his given name.

He could feel the surge of determination from her and tilted his head in inquiry. "Tell me."

"Did you want... Are you disappointed this baby is a girl?"

She would worry, wouldn't she? "Jessica, I'm pleased," he murmured. "I'd *hoped* for another girl. How about you?"

The crease between her eyebrows disappeared and she relaxed, then kissed him. "Me, too. Now we have two sons and two daughters. We're balanced."

It'd taken a while for his grown sons to accept Jessica, but now they adored her and treated her somewhere between a mother and a beloved big sister.

Being Jessica, she simply thought of them as hers.

"I love you, kitten. More than I can say."

On Z's patio, Ghost waited on a carved wooden bench with Valerie beside him. Word had gone around the Shadowlands community that Jessica was in labor. Couple by couple, they'd gathered to lend silent support.

"How much longer?" Cullen muttered. "This can't be good for a woman."

Anne chuckled and smiled at Ben before blowing a raspberry on her son's bare belly. "Having a baby too quickly isn't all it's cracked up to be. Trust me."

Ghost shook his head. After Wyatt's birth, Ben had told him about how fast the labor had gone. How terrified he'd been.

"Yeah, but Z said she started this morning, for fuck's sake." Cullen scowled. Which was why Valerie, as well as the other Shadowkittens, had been in and out of Z's house all day.

The Doms had been here off and on, too, although they'd stayed outside...and worried. The thought of petite Jessica being in pain was unsettling, especially for those who'd known her the longest.

As one of her first friends in the Shadowlands, Cullen was taking it especially hard.

Finally, Z emerged from the house, and his expression promised happy news. "The midwife won't let me do a show-and-tell—she's very strict." His smile flashed. "We have a daughter, Aubrielle."

A cheer ran around the group.

"Jessica wants me to thank you all for being here—and especially for the diversions over the course of the day." He chuckled. "She would have told you herself, but she's already asleep with a well-earned rest."

Cullen's big laugh boomed out. "You're not in much better shape." He poured Z a shot of Glenlivet and handed it over.

Ghost agreed with Cullen. Z looked as if he'd spent the day humping a heavy pack over rough terrain.

"I fully intend to join her shortly." Z took a sip of the drink. "Honestly, it's terrifying to see her in so much pain and not be able to help."

Ben grunted. "I hear you."

"It doesn't get better with practice. Leah's birth was actually more stressful." Stretched out on a lounge chair, Dan patted the diapered butt of his second child—his six-month-old daughter—who'd fallen asleep on his chest.

"That's not reassuring."

Ghost considered Ben's reaction and bent to whisper in Valerie's ear, "Check Ben's face. What do you want to bet Anne wants a second baby?"

Valerie's muffled laugh sounded like a kitten's sneeze, and Ghost grinned.

Z held up his glass. "Thank you again for the good wishes and support. Now, I want you slackers to get to work and provide playmates for our girls. Benjamin, you and Anne are not off the hook."

Laughter broke out as people took the opportunity to slap Z on the back, shake his hand, or give him a hug.

Seated in a patio chair, Linda grinned at Valerie. "I'm so glad I'm past childbearing and rearing, aren't you?"

"It's such a relief to have them all grown up. And even better when they present you with a grandbaby." Valerie pulled out her phone to show off her latest picture of Luca.

Ghost was anticipating meeting the fabled grandson—as well as Valerie's son and daughter. It was time.

Hopefully, it would go well. Since Hailey and Dillon still had a father, they might well be displeased Ghost had replaced the bastard in Valerie's life.

Anne clapped her hands together to get everyone's attention. "Since we now have a date and sex for the betting pool, I'll check the entries and pay out tomorrow."

Ghost exchanged disgruntled looks with Sam. Neither of them had come close.

"You mean *today*, Anne. Would you believe it's after midnight?" Cullen pulled Andrea to her feet. "Time to clear out so the Graysons can get some sleep."

"I don't know about the rest of you, but I'm still revved up," Saxon announced. "There's a bar on the highway back if anyone wants to continue celebrating."

From the hum of interest, Saxon wasn't the only one still wide awake.

Ghost considered. Today and Friday were free of classes since exams would begin on Monday. He tugged on a lock of his woman's gorgeous hair. "Since we can sleep in tomorrow, want to go?"

"You're as wide awake as Saxon, aren't you?" Valerie grinned. "Sure, let's go."

Yeah, he really did love her.

"It wasn't fun." The small neighborhood bar was almost empty. The sounds of men playing pool in the adjoining room wasn't enough to drown out Josie's husky voice. The others around the table were quiet. "I was all alone, in labor, no one to hold my hand. And so scared."

Valerie's eyes prickled with tears.

Josie had only been a teen when her son was born—and she had been kicked out of her home. That must have been simply horrible.

Valerie shook her head. Maybe Barry had turned out to be a jerk, but he'd held her hand for both their children's births. "You ended up with a wonderful child, though."

Josie's smile was tender. Proud. "Carson is amazing, yes. It was worth every bit of misery to end up with such a great kid."

Valerie knew how she felt. Hailey and Dillon were amazing too. And no matter how much time passed, she'd never forget the joyful moment of holding Dillon for the first time. Of hearing Hailey's tiny cry and the wonder of touching those tiny fingers and toes. Or the unsettling, unexpected grief that she and the baby were no longer sharing a body.

And how love had shaken her like a leaf.

Oh dear, now she was missing her children so badly. She turned. "Ghost, we need to go visit—"

The chair beside her was empty.

Hmm. It appeared all the Masters had disappeared from the two tables they'd pushed together. Only the women—Josie, Andrea, Kim, Gabi, and Sally—remained.

A quick glance around the small bar revealed a slouched-over man at the bar, an older couple at a table in the center of the room, and a serious lack of Dominants.

"What's so funny, Valerie?" Andrea asked.

"When we started talking about labor and delivery, our squeamish Masters staged a retreat."

As everyone laughed, Josie grinned. "I saw them sneak out, probably to admire Holt's new bike."

"What new bike?" Kim's expression held worry. "Did he break his Harley?"

"Did he *ever*." Josie made a face. "Some aggressive New Englander was tailgating him—in a downpour, no less. Holt drove onto the shoulder, but the flooding hid a huge pothole. He was going slow enough he only ended up bruised, but his bike got twisted up."

"Poor Holt." Sally shook her head. "Other states get daffodils in spring; we get potholes."

"I'm glad he's all right," Gabi said. "Did he mourn his bike?"

Valerie grinned. Of course, the social worker would worry about Holt's feelings.

"Not for long—because Carson really wanted to help him shop for a new bike." Josie snorted. "And now all I hear are biker terms: displacement and flickability and farkles. My nerdy boy wants to be a biker."

Everyone grinned. Valerie had heard Josie's twelve-year-old was brilliant.

"Speaking of sons, are any of you going to obey Master Z and give his children playmates?" Valerie asked.

"Us." Kim raised her hand. "I tossed my birth control last week, actually. Although we've only been married a year, he's been my Master for over three years now. We're ready."

Sally rolled her eyes. "You're the only one I know who would think a Master/slave relationship is less stressful than getting married. Would you believe my Demon Doms and I have been married for two years now?"

The brunette was positively glowing. Valerie also noticed the glass in front of her. Water. "*Aaand*, is there something you want to share?"

Sally burst into giggles and pointed at Valerie. "Ghost is going to have trouble with you; you're too smart."

Gabi stared. "Wait...wait...wait. You—you're pregnant?"

When Sally's huge grin confirmed it, there were squeals of joy, and she was smothered with hugs.

Resurfacing, she said, "I know y'all are dying to ask, but we don't know or care if the father is Galen or Vance. However, when the time comes to make a second baby, the first baby-daddy will be celibate during *those* days of the month."

Gabi snickered. "Won't that just go over well."

"By the way." Sally held up her hand in a gesture for silence. "My Doms and I aren't the only ones making like rabbits." She cleared her throat. "Andrea?"

Andrea turned red, then beamed. "Me, too! We're now past the three-month mark and were going to tell you next week."

Her smile was huge as she collected hugs from everyone.

"I bet Master Cullen is all pumped up," Gabi said as she sat back down.

"He really is." Andrea was flushed with happiness. "And he keeps patting my belly."

Valerie couldn't hide her snort. "No wonder he almost panicked with how long Jessica was in labor."

They all laughed.

In the parking lot, Saxon held his phone to his ear, waiting as his vet tech pulled up a post-surgery poodle's weight and current vitals.

At a distance, the other Masters had circled Holt's bike and were teasing the firefighter about riding a *donorcycle*.

Holt's new Harley was a classy bike, but Saxon wasn't interested. For a brief period in his younger years, he'd joined a motorcycle club. His delusions of being a rebel had died a quick death. Hell, he hadn't made it past prospect status.

His tech came on the phone and a minute later, Saxon was able to stuff his cell phone in his pocket and rejoin the group.

"A problem at your vet clinic?" Ghost asked.

"Yeah, I did surgery on a poodle hit by a car. He's on IV pain meds, but the rate needed to be increased."

"You have a good tech to have seen the dog was hurting," Holt said.

"He has a gift with animals. Jake and I want him to go to vet school." They'd fund his tuition. It would be a shame for the teen to be deterred for lack of money.

Marcus glanced at the door of the bar. "Do you suppose it's safe to return?"

"Doubtful," Holt said. "I tell you, labor and delivery stories can get gory."

"Jesus, that first one sounded worse than combat," Ghost muttered.

Raoul tilted his head. "Do you hear them cheering?"

Saxon grinned. "Probably the latest prank Sally pulled on her Feds." The feisty brunette was endlessly creative.

"Ahhh, maybe not a prank." Galen glanced at Vance.

"Our Sally is probably sharing our news." Vance's face lit. "We're having a baby in around six months."

"All right!" Pleased for the two, Saxon slapped Vance's shoulder and shook Galen's hand.

The rest followed.

Cullen cleared his throat. "Andrea and me—same thing. About the same time."

"Well, the Deity of Reproduction is sure putting in the overtime." Saxon gave Cullen a one-armed hug.

As the uproar died down again, Raoul eyed the fathers-to-be. "Did you get Z's order for babies sooner than tonight?"

The fathers-to-be laughed and denied it.

"Or," Saxon held up a hand, "did he maybe lock you in the second-floor private rooms until you'd accomplished the deed?"

"Hell, don't give Z ideas," Holt said. "Some of us aren't ready for babies. Not yet anyway."

"My thought, as well." Marcus nodded at Holt. "We'd best avoid the second floor. If his Sophia is requesting playmates, Z will ensure she gets them."

True enough. Saxon tapped the seat of the motorcycle as he considered. Because, in all reality, if tiny Sophia demanded something, he, too, would do his best to get it for her. She was the cutest imp he'd ever seen.

"A warning, men." The Colonel crossed his arms over his chest. "If Z orders me to lock you in, you won't be released until, as Saxon says, the deed is done."

Grinning, Saxon joined in teasing the non-fathers-to-be and tried to ignore the nagging ache in his chest.

No one was giving him grief since he had no one to be locked in with. That was his choice, of course. He didn't want to be hitched to anyone.

But, dammit, he loved babies.

"So, you and Ghost are pretty much living together now, hmm?" Gabi lifted her eyebrows at Valerie as they left the restroom and walked down the narrow hallway toward the bar.

Valerie had to laugh. Gabi was as curious as the rest of the group. "Pretty much, yes. I still have my apartment, though. It's kind of like my security blanket, I guess."

Gabi nodded. "Sounds like you found a good compromise. You'll let it go when you're ready."

Valerie stepped out of the hall into the main barroom. Their group across the bar still lacked any men. Wimpy guys.

In the center of the room, the lone bartender was mopping up a puddle where the older couple had been sitting. They must have spilled a drink.

"Let's avoid the wet spot," she said and won a sputter of laughter from Gabi.

As they made their way around the side of the room, Valerie glanced through the wide opening into the room that held two pool tables and several people.

Valerie smiled at Gabi. "It's been years since I played pool. I wonder if I could talk Ghost into a game."

"Marcus likes—" Gabi's brows drew together. "Is that girl old enough to be with those guys—let alone in here?"

Seated in a chair, the young woman was rocking back and forth, trying to stand. Once on her feet, she staggered sideways.

One of the pool players caught her around the waist and ran his hand over her breasts.

"Uh-uhhh. Don't," the girl slurred.

And...a girl, she was. Not twenty-one. Probably not even eighteen.

With a sinking sense of déjà vu, Valerie recognized Scott. Her mouth tightened. Time to call the—

Gabi yelled out, "How old is that girl, Wrecker? She sure isn't of age."

Scowling, Scott stepped away from the pool table. He spotted Valerie, and fury darkened his face. "You fucking *bitch*. Cheating on my friend with asshole Ghost, and what kind of a pansy-ass name is that?"

The other three men turned. One was Piers, the big Dom who'd tried to punch Ghost—and who Ghost had tossed out of the club.

Beside him was lanky Dogget. The pointed ends of his mustache dangled past his jawline.

Brown-haired, over-muscled Knuckles slapped his pool stick down on the table.

None of them appeared remotely sober.

From the bar room came the scraping sounds of chairs. The other women had heard Gabi's shout.

"We gotta get out of here," Dogget told Scott. "Get *her* out of here."

"Shit." Scott grabbed the girl with an arm around her waist.

"Uhhh." The girl batted at his arm. Whether drugged or drunk, she was only half awake.

"We can't let them take her away." Gabi took a step forward.

"Gods." Valerie tried to think. This was a train wreck about to happen. She turned and saw the other women gathered in the wide opening to the pool room. "Sally, call the police."

"On it."

A glance into the main room showed the skinny bartender had fled behind his bar and was making his own phone call. There'd be no backup from him.

"Gentlemen," Valerie looked at the four *effing* men. "The young woman is incapacitated. We'll take care of her—and you can leave."

"Yeah, we can, can we?" Knuckles sneered and grabbed the girl's arm hard enough to make her cry out.

Arm still around her waist, Scott half-dragged the girl, making straight for the only exit to the room—the opening where Valerie and the women stood.

"Get the bitches," Dogget said. "Piers, enjoy yourself, yeah?"

This was getting out of control. Valerie felt her heart thumping like a pile driver. "Scott, Dogget. A bar fight won't be good for your professional reputations."

Scott's lips lifted in a snarl. "Like I care. My wife's getting a fucking divorce."

Oh, spit. His wife owned the realty where he worked—she wouldn't keep him on. Probably not Dogget either.

Scott's eyes were bloodshot, and he stank of a long drinking spree. "You cunts fed Grayson your bullshit and got me fired."

"Hey, there's the cleaning spic." Knuckles pointed at Andrea, who'd joined Gabi.

"Fuck, all of 'em belong to those high-and-mighty asshole Masters?" Pier lunged forward, grabbing Sally—pregnant Sally—who pulled back instinctually.

Valerie met her gaze and snapped, "Go get the men," and kicked Piers in the balls.

Folding in half, he shouted in pain.

And Sally was free.

"Go," Valerie shouted. As Sally fled, Knuckles lunged for her

—and Josie booted his knee out from under him, giving Sally time to dart outside.

Recovering, Piers charged Valerie.

She braced, punched, and was shocked when her fist hit her target—his neck.

He staggered back.

Valerie glanced over.

Andrea had an arm around the young girl, while Gabi and Kim blocked Scott and Dogget from them.

A sound made Valerie dodge sideways into the main room. She barely avoided Piers' fist. *Again*. Gods, she really *wasn't* hitting hard enough.

He swung at her.

She ducked, kicked his knee, and barely slowed him down.

He punched, and she blocked with her forearms, but the power of his blow knocked her sideways. Fear filled her. He was way too strong for her.

A cry came from her right. Josie was on the floor. Knuckles lifted his foot to stomp her.

Valerie kicked a chair at him that hit his leg. As he reeled sideways, a fist slammed into Valerie's shoulder.

Agony swept through her, and she let out a yell.

Piers roared in triumph.

Off balance, she lurched a step, hitting a table with her hip.

Sucking in a breath, she pushed upright and lifted her fists to defend herself. Pain stabbed through the arm Piers had punched. Gods, was it broken?

Not. Giving. Up.

Her mouth tightened, and she set her feet.

The bar door slammed open. The Masters charged across the room and attacked the effing bastards.

Cries of pain and shouts filled the room.

When Piers turned away to defend himself, Valerie let out a breath of relief.

"Try me, asshole," Vance barked, facing off against Piers.

A step behind him, Ghost snapped out, "No. He belongs to Valerie."

What?

Without waiting for Vance's reply, Ghost rammed a fist into Piers' jaw, sending him back a couple of steps. The man swayed, half-dazed.

"There." In Arabic, Ghost snapped, "Now, lass, hit and knee him like you *mean* it."

She wanted to protest, to whine, *"I'm done, I'm hurt, I don't want to.*

But she'd flubbed everything earlier and knew it.

She stepped forward. Gritting her teeth, she swung from her toes, twisting her hips, and punched Piers in the belly with all her might.

With a horrible grunt, he folded in half. As his head went low, she rammed her knee into his face.

He went down like a toppled tree.

And *owww*, her knee felt as if it had hit a brick wall.

"Nicely done." Ghost gave her a nod of approval. "Now you understand what I mean about not pulling your punches."

"Hell, now that's a Green Beret for you." Saxon stood over Knuckles, who was out cold. "Never waste a teaching moment."

Ghost winked at Saxon and stepped over Piers as if the man wasn't there. "Now, my Professor, let me see the damage."

His voice was calm, but his expression was cold, his eyes furious.

"Ghost..."

"Shh, it's all over." His gaze swept over her. Fingers gentle on her chin, he turned her face from side-to-side, then grasped her shoulders to—

She flinched.

"Your shoulder?"

The area was one big throbbing mass of pain. "The left."

He unbuttoned her shirt far enough to pull it down. The shoulder joint was red and starting to swell. After running his fingers over her skin, he pressed in painfully. "Bruised to the bone, I'd guess, but it's not broken. We'll ice it down."

When he drew her against his hard body, she sighed and started to shake. His hold tightened. "I've got you, lass. I'll always have you."

It was exactly what she'd needed to hear. To feel. His deep voice, his strength. Her refuge.

He rubbed his chin on the top of her head. "I must say, you did very well."

With a half snort, she rested her cheek on his shoulder. She really had done okay. And he'd helped her to do even better.

The Colonel would never hold her back from being the best she could be—or fail to be her support, like now.

Holding her tightly, he stroked her hair.

"I love you so much," she whispered.

"Mmmph." The acknowledgment was a rumbling sound deep in his chest. "I love you too."

She lifted her head long enough to check the others. Every submissive was getting similar treatment.

From where she was sandwiched between her two Doms, Sally gazed at Valerie. "Thank you."

"Josie helped. But I think you totally owe me." Valerie smiled. "And in a few months, I'll demand my reward—cuddle time with a baby."

Galen's grateful, dark eyes met hers.

Vance lifted his head. "All the cuddle time you want, *Aunt* Valerie."

Sirens sounded from outside, and a few seconds later, two uniformed police officers burst through the door.

All the bad guys were already down.

Valerie called out, "Those four men had this young lady with them. I doubt the girl's of age—she's was trying to tell them no but is either intoxicated or drugged. He"—she pointed to Scott—"tried to drag her out of the bar against her will."

The uniformed officer scowled at Scott, then nudged the other cop. "Isn't he the asshole we're on the lookout for around the schools?"

Valerie saw Ghost's lips twitch before he bent and murmured, "Dan and Max put out a warning. In case he went for younger ones."

Andrea, who still had an arm around the girl, gave her a shake. "Chica, how old are you?"

The girl blinked, obviously dazed. "Sixteen. I'm sixteen now."

The officers' expressions hardened.

As Ghost guided Valerie back away from the mess, she eyed Scott.

Lost his job, divorced. Now this. There were times when karma moved slower than a snail...but not this time.

CHAPTER TWENTY-SIX

What a shitty life, Barry thought as he walked into his house. His crew had bitched all fucking day about having to work on the weekend. Like it was Barry's fault they were so far behind on the kitchen remodel?

Total bullshit. The counters had been late. Not much a contractor could do about that. Yeah, so maybe when Valerie did the scheduling with her fancy project software, there hadn't been so many foul-ups. So maybe he should've ordered the countertops sooner. And had the plumber timed better.

Paperwork and organizing crap weren't his thing. He worked with his hands, for fuck's sake.

He reached the middle of the living room and realized no one had greeted him at the door. Used to be Kahlua and Alisha would be naked and waiting for him to walk in.

When had they stopped?

The house was silent enough to hear the crunch as he walked over spilled potato chips. Jesus, the place was a mess.

Kahlua was probably out partying with her friends. He'd told her not to, that slaves stayed home, but she didn't always obey.

Alisha, though, didn't like going out. She'd even refused to join the Shadowlands when he and Kahlua had. She'd rather stay home.

No supper made. Fuck. He opened the fridge. Empty, aside from his beer. Fucking great.

Without Valerie, the fridge was empty a lot—and now, he'd have to listen to his slaves battle over who would go shopping. He popped the top on a beer and took it with him to the bedroom.

Opening the closet door, he tossed his shirt in the laundry hamper, then spotted a gap in the clothing hung on the rod. His stuff was there. So was Kahlua's.

Nothing of Alisha's remained.

He crossed the room.

Alisha's designated drawers were empty. He turned in a circle in the room before the realization sank in.

The fucking bitch had left him. Without even talking.

Yesterday, he'd told her she needed to increase her hours as a janitor. After all, she was only working twelve hours a week and then keeping the money for herself. That was bullshit.

When he said Valerie's paychecks had gone into the shared bank account, she mouthed off and said Valerie wasn't here.

He probably shouldn't have hit her. But, hell, she'd gone and rubbed his face in it that his wife had left him.

Stewing, he drank his beer, feeling his guts twist with resentment. With anger.

Twenty fucking years he and Valerie had been married. And she'd just walked out.

Leaving him in the lurch. Leaving him this shitty mess.

He finished the beer and threw the can at the wall.

It was all her fault. And she needed to get back here to fix it.

He was gonna make that happen; damned if he wouldn't.

CHAPTER TWENTY-SEVEN

On Sunday evening, the timer rang in Valerie's kitchen. Leaving off mashing up avocados, she pulled out the baking sheet from the oven.

The aroma of butter and sugar filled the room, making her mouth water.

Even better, the strips of Scottish shortbread were a light golden-brown and simply perfect.

Her man was going to get a treat tomorrow. He deserved one.

She'd never forget the way he'd had her punch and kick Piers as a teaching exercise to improve her fighting skills. He could easily have taken Piers out himself and been the big hero. Instead, he'd been thinking of her.

And later at home, he'd iced her arm, made her tea, and cuddled with her.

Being on the receiving end of caregiving still left her feeling odd. As if she was slacking off. But when she'd protested, he bluntly stated he loved taking care of her, so she'd better learn to accept as well as give. Because good relationships had a give and take.

Maybe because she'd been missing him all yesterday and today, she'd been thinking about that. About what they had together—and how they both put time and energy into the relationship.

He bought her sexy undies and fetishwear because she enjoyed wearing them...and he enjoyed removing them. She helped him with the Shadowlands paperwork because shared work lightened the load.

He picked her flowers from the gardens; she made him the sweet cookies he loved.

In the evenings, after he took off his prosthesis, she served as the go-fer when needed. In the mornings, he cooked breakfast and tidied the kitchen, because she didn't deal well with life before coffee.

Tomorrow morning for the start of exam week, the best self-defense instructor in all the world would get shortbread, hopefully like his mama made in Scotland. She sampled a corner, and the buttery sweetness almost melted in her mouth.

Yum.

Pleased, she returned to making guacamole. Her children loved Mexican food, so she was making an enchilada casserole for Dillon's welcome home meal.

And, after they caught up on everything, she'd upset their balance by telling them about Ghost.

With her free hand, she patted her tightening chest. *Relax, Valerie.* Why was she letting herself get worked up this way? Her children were in their twenties, not teenagers. Her being with Ghost might come as a shock to them, but after a moment, they'd realize she couldn't be expected to live like a nun forever.

Of course they would.

She mashed the avocados harder, grateful she'd decided to cook for them. It gave her something to do with her hands.

In her small kitchen, Valerie studied Hailey and Dillon who'd perched on the tall stools on the other side of the island.

Rather than digging in with their usual big appetites, they were nibbling at the nachos she'd set out to hold them over until the chicken enchilada casserole finished baking.

Her introverted daughter was always quiet, but gregarious Dillon was also subdued today, although he'd given them a lovely summary of his time in China.

She studied him for a moment. He had her coloring with thick, dark blond hair, blue eyes, and fair skin, but had Barry's big-framed body. He'd lost a few pounds while overseas, but not enough to be of concern. The faint crease between his eyebrows was more worrisome.

She'd stalled long enough.

"I know you both asked how I'm doing these days"—don't mention Barry—"and actually, I'm doing better than I'd expected. I've, uh, even started dating again."

Dillon stiffened and glanced at Hailey, whose face had gone still.

They didn't speak at all.

Okay, okay, she'd known this wouldn't go over well, not when the children still hoped for a reconciliation.

Valerie clasped her hands together. Despite the warmth of the oven behind her, she felt cold. "Anyway, the man I've been seeing —his name is Finn. He's also a professor at the university, and I'd like you both to meet him. Maybe the next time you—"

"Is he who got you the job there?" Her son's expression turned hostile.

"What? No, I didn't meet him until—"

"Why would we want to meet the man who you were...were cheating with? He sounds like a real bastard to me," Hailey said.

Dillon scowled. "I didn't believe Dad when he told us about this guy—and about you."

At their furious expressions, she felt her breathing start to go strange. Tight bands wrapped around her chest. "Your father and I have been apart since last November. He doesn't have anything to say about who I date. Or about anything I do."

"He should," Hailey said, straightening. Her eyes were...cold. Disgusted.

"You were married for over twenty years, and you tossed him aside like he was garbage. Left him." Hailey's voice rose. "Did you know he started drinking? Because of you?"

This was...this was wrong. Lies. But Hailey had always been a daddy's girl, had idolized Barry. And Valerie had reinforced her children's belief in him, covering for him, propping him up as needed to keep from ruining his bigger-than-life image.

She'd been a fool.

"He was drinking before I left." Valerie kept her tone quiet and reasonable.

"Yeah, I bet he was. Because he was trying to hold onto a marriage, hoping to be loved by someone who didn't give a shit about him."

"Hailey, that's not—"

Dillon interrupted, his tone ugly. "He let you go, figuring you'd get your head on straight and return to him. Because he loves you —although, fuck, right now, I don't know why."

The words shot through her like knives, and her mouth went dry.

Her son, her baby, scowled at her. "I can't believe you cheated on him; you're sure not the person I thought you were."

"Th-that's not true, Dillon. I never—"

"Don't even try to lie to us; Dad told us how it was." Her son pointed a finger at her. "You need to go back to him and make it work. Put some effort into it this time."

"Honey, we're divorced. There were reasons I left him—and I'm not going to return to your father."

"Yes, you fucking are." Dillon's voice rose to a shout—the kind of angry volume that had silenced Valerie since before she'd even learned to talk. "Or you can just write yourself out of my life."

Somewhere in the back of her mind, she could hear her parents shouting at her. *You can just leave, Valerie. Leave and don't come back.* Because they hadn't loved her.

Didn't her children love her at all? Taking a step back, she tried to find her backbone. Find the words to fix this.

She needed to speak, to tell them what had happened. But her words had dried up like desert sands.

When Dillon stood, so did her daughter.

Valerie pushed air through her throat, managed to find her voice. "Hailey, you don't believe—"

"You screwed around on Dad, the best guy in the world. How could you, Mom?" Hailey shook her head.

"And he still wants you back." Dillon snapped. "I couldn't believe it, but he does."

"You need to fix things, to go back where you belong." Tears filled Hailey's eyes. "Or...or you won't see me or Luca again."

The horrendous threat hit Valerie like a hammer to the chest.

Her children walked out, Hailey closing the door gently behind them.

"No," Valerie whispered. And her heart snapped in half.

CHAPTER TWENTY-EIGHT

How had everything gone so wrong? Valerie sat behind the desk in her small classroom as her students finished their essays. *Don't think of Hailey and Dillon. Of their cold faces as they walked away from her. Not now.*

Her eyes still felt hot and swollen despite her bathing them in cold water before coming in.

Because she'd cried—oh, how she'd cried. When she was young, she'd been sure older people could handle anything. Adults never became upset, never cried their heads off.

Or spent hours thinking of the different things she could have said, how she might have found the right words to turn the disaster around.

Or would become so *angry*. At Barry, the lying bastard, but also at Hailey and Dillon.

How *dare* they not listen to her? How could they possibly think she'd lie to them or cheat on their father?

After a glance at the wall clock, she sighed and scrubbed her hands over her face.

How much of this is my fault? My doing?

She'd always felt parents should support each other, stand

together, for the children. That it was good for the kids to see their parents as strong and honorable, worthy of emulation.

So when Barry was inconsiderate or forgetful or inconsistent, she'd fixed his mistakes, covered for him, or made excuses.

Because she'd been too insecure to initiate uncomfortable conversations and demand he pull his weight, she'd *enabled* him.

She'd been a fool.

It'd taken Finn to show her how honesty and openness should form the foundation for a relationship.

Gods, she wished she could stay home and try to come up with solutions to this mess. But it was finals week. She had a duty to her students.

Finally, the class period was over. Filing out, the young men and women gave her worried looks. Jamail hesitated for a second, obviously wanting to show his concern, but Valerie shook her head at him.

Maybe she wasn't holding up as well as she'd hoped.

In the hallway, Queenie confirmed her worry. "You look like shit, woman. How about I give you a ride home?"

So blunt. So Queenie. "Thank you, but I'm not sick. Just..." She shrugged.

Queenie's eyes narrowed. "Problems between you and your soldier-professor?"

The accuracy of the guess made Valerie take a step back. "In a way. It seems we've hit a rocky patch."

"Want me to—"

"No, it's not him. My children and ex are displeased."

Queenie scowled. "Don't let the past decide your future."

Her future. Yes, she had a future. "I...that actually helps." Valerie pulled in a breath. "Thank you."

"You can handle this." Queenie patted her shoulder.

As they parted, Valerie could only wish she had the same confidence.

What was she going to do?

A few minutes later, she realized she'd walked to Finn's office and was simply...standing...in the doorway.

One hip resting on the edge of his desk, he was talking to a student. Laughing about something. The sound of his deep voice eased some of the tension inside of her.

And made her heart hurt worse.

Seeing her, he stopped, warmth filling his gaze. Then his eyes narrowed as he studied her.

He turned to the student. "Work on the project today and we'll see how you do."

"Sure thing. Thanks, Dr. Blackwood."

The young man headed out, and really, she should too, because...this wasn't the time. Why had she even come here? She needed to save this talk for later.

"Sorry, Finn." She took a step back as he crossed the room.

He took her hand, pulled her into his office—and closed the door.

"What the hell happened, lass?" he murmured, pulling her into his arms. "Did someone die?" His voice was so gentle, so concerned. The man didn't shout, even when angry.

He wasn't the storm; he was the mountain. Winds might batter at him, but nothing would move him.

He was her place of shelter. Her sanctuary.

"You're shaking, sweetheart." He stepped back and cupped her chin. "Talk to me."

"It's the children. I had them over last night and tried to tell them about you, only they—Barry told them I cheated on him before the divorce and—and they believe him."

"That bastard."

"They said I have to go back to him—or they won't see me again. Or let me see Luca."

.   .   .

360

What the hell? Ghost tried to tamp down the anger rising inside him. It wasn't easy, not when his woman—*his* woman—trembled. Her color was dead white.

Okay, think, Colonel. Because she sure wasn't. "Valerie, your kids don't have the right to order you to return to your ex. No one can make you go back to Barry. You're divorced."

"I know that, of course, I do." She pulled back. Away from him. "But...families do split apart over divorces, divide into sides. And they think I'm a liar. A cheater."

He said carefully, "Children often overreact over things like this. We've both seen it happen, haven't we?"

She paused. "Y-yes."

"You can't let them dictate your life for something they want. They'll get over it and—"

"I...don't know if they will. You didn't see their faces. Hear them." She laid her hand over his chest and stared up at him.

The skin around her eyes was puffy. She'd been crying. Fuck him, but she'd been crying, and he hadn't been there for her. "Lass...are you really planning to do what they want?"

Tears filled her eyes, but she shook her head. "No. But will it —can you forgive me if I stay alone until I figure out how to handle this?"

He cupped her cheek, wiping away a tear with his thumb. "There is no forgiveness. You must do what you need to do. Don't you think I could help?"

Her lips curled up slightly, even as more tears brimmed in her eyes. "You could help, except if I'm with you, all I'd be able to think about is how mad I am they'd threaten what we have. And I can't be mad or let myself burn bridges behind me. Not with my children."

Fuck.

"It annoys me you're making sense rather than flinging yourself in my arms and asking me to fix this." He hugged her close, relieved at how she hugged him back so tightly. "Take the time you need, and call me or come over when you're ready. I'm not going anywhere."

Unlike her insensitive children.

"Thank you." She pulled back. "I just need to...to think. To find a way to get through to them."

Going up on tiptoes, she pressed a kiss to his jaw and walked out, leaving only the light scent of jasmine behind.

A minute later, a tap on the door made him look over.

"Z. What are you doing on campus?" Ghost could hear the lack of welcome in his voice and couldn't find it in himself to care. How the fuck was he going to—

"Was that our Valerie I saw with tears on her face?" Z's expression was as grim as Ghost felt inside.

"Yes. It was." *Tears*. God, she was breaking his heart. "This isn't a good time—" He stopped himself. Actually, Z might have some ideas.

Ghost straightened. "Let's walk. If I stay here, we'll get interrupted by students."

"All right." Z laid a folder on the desk. "Jessica asked me to drop off the contracts for service companies for the house and grounds. They should have stayed with the mansion but were packed by mistake."

"Ah, fine. Thank you." Ushering Z out, Ghost locked the door. "How's the baby?"

"She's doing quite well, thank you." Z's gray eyes lightened. "She's beautiful—far quieter than Sophia was her first few days, so of course, Jessica and her mother are trying to decide which relative Aubrielle takes after."

Ghost held the outside door for Z. "I believe inheritance guessing is a mandatory sport after a new addition to the family."

On the campus grounds, the air sweltered as storm clouds from inland piled into a dark mass. Students huddled on benches, frantically studying for their exams.

"Valerie doesn't seem the type to upset easily," Z prompted.

"She's not." Ghost felt the muscles in his cheek flex. "It seems her children handed out an ultimatum. Said she has to return to her ex-husband or not see them or her grandchild again."

Z stared in disbelief.

"I haven't met her kids." Although Ghost had been looking forward to getting an introduction. Before this bullshit. "I have no idea if they'd follow through."

"It's quite a threat."

"Z, she dotes on her children and grandbaby. He's only two."

"What did you suggest she should do?" Z asked, mildly.

"I said they couldn't force her to return to the asshole." Ghost felt anger rise again. "Then she told me about the threat."

"And now, she's in a no-win situation."

"She wants some time to think. But it leaves her without my support." And he found that impossible to tolerate.

"Ah." Z tilted his head back, studying the black clouds. "Can she work through this on her own?"

"I'm not sure." The rising wind carried the heavy scent of ocean. "She is the calmest, most rational person I know. However, her parents were unloving assholes. Their verbal abuse and cruelty left scars, and her divorce..."

"Insecurities do tend to resurface with the trauma of a divorce." Z nodded.

"Exactly. And last night, her children essentially said their love comes with conditions." Ghost's hands closed into fists before he forced them open. "It's a shit show."

Z's mouth tightened. "She didn't need more wounds. Especially that kind."

Ghost considered the psychologist. "Suggestions?"

"Can I assume you're not going to give her up without a fight?"

Give her up? It'd be a cold day in hell. "I love her; what do you think?"

"Excellent." Z gave him a faint smile. "However, I can understand how she would have difficulty arriving at a reasonable decision if you're present. She probably can't see past an either-or solution."

Meaning she could have Ghost or her children, not both. "Roger that."

"I suggest we find a couple of people who understand what she's going through and can help her see a way out of the trap."

What she was going through? Her children had turned on her. Such a mess couldn't be common. No one he knew...

Ghost stopped walking. "I know someone."

Ghost had once told Valerie that in the military, he'd go running any time his emotions started to slip out of control.

Since her emotions had passed uncontrolled and were headed straight for meltdown, she donned her jogging outfit.

In the first few minutes of running, her legs didn't feel as if they belonged to her. As if she wasn't even in her body.

As her blood warmed, her heart and lungs and muscles started to work together.

By the time she'd reached a mile and turned back, the pandemonium in her head had cleared, leaving peace behind.

She ran harder. Her shirt clung to her as sweat trickled down her back and dampened her sports bra. Her shoes slapped the trail with a mesmerizing rhythm.

Suddenly, a vagrant darted out of the bushes to block her way. "I need cash, lady. Gimme cash."

He'd shattered her brief period of tranquility—and rage engulfed her in a wave of heat. "*Seriously?*" Her voice rose to a shout. "Get out of my way, or I'll *decimate* you."

"Jesus, lady." He backed away so hurriedly he fell on his ass.

And she ran on.

She'd won.

That battle.

But she was in another fight—a war with her ex-husband she hadn't even realized was happening.

The thought eroded her mood until, by the time she reached her apartment, she was fighting back tears—and fury. Again.

How could Dillon have spoken to her like that? How could Hailey have threatened to keep her from her grandson?

They were her children, who she loved with all her heart. She'd carried them, birthed them, nursed them. She'd fought for them and taught them. Cried when Hailey had first said, "Mama." Stayed up all night whenever one of them was ill. Read stories to them every night, helping them sound out the words so they'd been able to read even before kindergarten.

And now...

The pain was overwhelming as if each rib in her chest had cracked under the blow. She cried in the shower—and then pounded her fist on the wall because she'd raised them better than this.

Wet hair in tangles, dressed in cut-offs and a loose T-shirt, she folded down in her tiny meditation corner. The scent of frankincense drifted through the air. A gull cried from outside as thunder growled in the distance. The scent of moist air from rain over the Gulf of Mexico swept in from the open balcony door.

She set her open hands on her thighs and pulled in a slow, deep breath. If nothing else, her life had taught her how to handle pain. How to reach tranquility so reasonable solutions could be found.

Emptying her mind, she let the world fade away.

That evening, she was ready to think calmly about the mess. It would take a lot of thought to sort out this tangle. There were too many players involved. Too much hurt and anger.

She mustn't react without careful consideration.

Hoping to get more information, she'd tried to call Hailey. Her daughter didn't answer. Texts received no response.

Frustrated anger made her want to do something equally childish, like texting, "Never call me again. I have no children."

Although momentarily gratifying, a final break wasn't the solution she wanted.

Now, what was she going to do?

A light tap on the door lifted her hopes. *Hailey? Dillon? Finn?*

Without checking the peephole, she yanked open the door—and her spirits fell.

Linda and Olivia stood together.

Linda's expression held sympathy. "I'm sure you were hoping to see repentant children, but you're stuck with us. May we come in?"

"I'm sorry. Of course." Valerie motioned them in. "You mentioned my children. How did..."

Linda moved her shoulders. "Ghost sent me."

Simply hearing his name warmed her. "I see."

"And Z sent Olivia."

Valerie's eyes widened. "Master Z?"

"It seems he saw you leaving Ghost's office and asked what happened," Linda said.

"Of course he asked. The man's a snoopy shrink as well as a Dom." Olivia moved into the kitchen. "My mum believes hot tea will improve any disaster. May I make us some?"

Valerie blinked. "Ah...certainly. There's a selection in the corner." The Domme looked determined—and tea would be good, since it appeared they planned to stay awhile.

After setting a large tote bag on the counter, Olivia filled Valerie's electric tea kettle with water from the dispenser and set it to boil. She took a moment to examine the tea collection, then nodded in satisfaction. "We have the same tastes, don't we?"

Since Olivia appeared comfortable brewing tea, Valerie went

to the living room and picked her notepad and cardigan off the sofa. She gestured to Linda. "Please, make yourself at home."

Linda sat down. "So, I know you'd mentioned your children are adults. How old are they?"

"Dillon is twenty-four and single. Hailey is twenty-five, married, and my grandson recently turned two." Valerie felt as if a boulder was sitting on her ribcage. "If Ghost talked to you, then you know my children said if I don't return to Barry, I'll never see them again."

A snort came from the kitchen. "Our so-called loved ones know where to jab in the knife, don't they?"

Linda sighed. "They do. The trick is to be smart enough to reach them before they cause too much damage. To us and themselves."

Too late. The damage is done.

Linda pointed to a chair. "Sit, before you collapse."

"How old are your children, Linda?" Valerie sank down onto the chair.

"My son graduated from college last year and works in St. Petersburg. My daughter has another year to go."

Olivia brought out three steaming mugs of tea. "Here we go."

Valerie took a sip, then another. "This has more than tea in it." Along with the orange Pekoe tea, there was a healthy shot of spiced rum, a touch of honey, and... "Cognac?"

"Best hot tea grog ever." Olivia settled in a chair with her own mug.

Linda sampled. "Very nice."

After a second, Valerie rose and brought out the cookie tin of shortbread she'd made for Ghost. "Alcohol and sugar—universal remedies, right?"

"Bloody right." Olivia nibbled on a shortbread strip and smiled her approval. "Z suggested I talk with you. I've been through something similar—someone withholding affection to get their way."

Olivia didn't have children, did she? Valerie gave her a confused look.

"My father decided a lesbian daughter would destroy his standing in town. If I wanted to be in the family, I needed to marry a nice young man. Otherwise, I had to stay away."

Linda stared. "That's horrible. How old were you?"

"Eighteen, done with sixth form, and thought since I was an adult, it was time to stop hiding who I was."

Olivia's brown eyes held so much pain Valerie wanted to cry for her. Leaning forward, she took the woman's hand. "I'm so sorry. I can't even imagine how such an ultimatum must have hurt."

"Yes." Olivia's English accent grew stronger. "We all know that pain, don't we? The hurt of someone saying we must behave according to their rules, or their love will be withheld."

Valerie closed her eyes as the words hit home. That was... exactly...what Dillon had said. "What did you do?"

"I told him he and the family could piss off, and I left. I ran all the way to the States." Olivia tilted her head down as if her tea was the most interesting thing in the world. "Leaving my mum and siblings, my friends...it was hard."

Valerie blinked. "When my parents and I had a final falling-out, I mourned them—even though they never loved me. It must have been so rough on you. Did you ever hear from them again?"

"That's what I wanted to share." Olivia cupped her hands around her tea mug. "I waited a couple of years and called, but Dad answered the phone and was furious. Said I was breaking Mum's heart."

"What a jerk," Linda muttered. "Laying his guilt on you."

"I almost gave in. But the lifestyle is full of people who have suffered because of narrow-minded idiots like my father. Not all of them lose their families." Olivia moved her shoulders. "I thought...maybe, just maybe...not everyone in my family felt the same way. Some might have been silent because Dad is overpowering. Some might not have even known what had happened."

"You went back," Valerie guessed.

"I did and found he hadn't told anyone about his ultimatum. Everyone thought I'd simply up and left."

Linda gasped. "Why, the bastard."

"Yes. I explained why I left—and explained some more. After they realized I wasn't lying, Dad was in for it." She snorted. "He slept at my uncle's place for a month before Mum let him come home."

"Serves him right." Valerie wanted to reach across the ocean and smack the guy. "How awkward is it when you visit now?"

"Not at all bad. A couple years ago, my uncle had a heart attack and decided he, too, was done with hiding and came out of the closet. My father was properly horrified to learn his brother and the farm manager had been lovers for years."

Valerie glanced at Linda, and they both snickered.

Olivia smiled. "Almost losing his brother woke Dad up. Last time I was back, he apologized and had moved from being a complete prat into an ally. I'm rather proud of him, in fact."

Valerie sat back and sipped her tea. Grog. Whatever. The heat of the drink with the slight buzz of alcohol was comforting.

So was the presence of friends.

Olivia had come simply to offer...hope. She'd been cut off from her family, yet what seemed final hadn't been. People and their opinions could change.

And love could survive.

Valerie considered Olivia. "I take it Z knows about your past?"

"He was the one who encouraged me to return." Olivia snorted. "I cursed his name with every mile closer."

Linda chuckled. "I wonder how many of his patients do the same. So, for me... A while back, Sam told Ghost what I went through with my children."

"Sadists of the world—unite," Olivia murmured.

Valerie pulled in a breath, knowing she wasn't going to like what followed.

When Linda hesitated, Olivia stepped in, "Linda's kids discovered she'd visited a BDSM club before she was kidnapped to be a sex slave. They acted like visiting a kink club justified her being grabbed. And *then* they learned she was sleeping with a sadist."

Even as Valerie's mouth dropped open, Linda rolled her eyes. "Very succinct, Mistress Olivia."

It sounded like a nightmare. "Gods, I can only imagine how badly that went over."

Linda pointed a finger at her. "See? You get it. The only reason they didn't call me a whole lot of ugly names was because Sam was there. I was so angry I kicked the lot of them out of my house. And after doing that, I wasn't sure I'd ever see either of them again." Her eyes reddened.

Valerie slid over on the couch to put an arm around her. "But it worked out. Didn't it?"

Please let it have worked out. Linda never seemed sad when she spoke of her children.

"It did. Sam took it on himself to force them to listen to everything I hadn't shared with them. I'd thought some realities were too difficult for them to bear." Linda's gaze met Valerie's. "I was wrong. If our families don't know the whole truth, how can they separate lies from facts—or make the correct decisions?"

Oh.

"I see where you're going with this." Valerie rubbed her hands over her face. "Thinking about how angry Dillon and Hailey were and what they said, I know Barry told them some really ugly lies."

Linda nodded. "I'm afraid so."

"But to fight back, I'd have to ruin their belief in their father." Valerie sighed. But he'd done just that to her, now hadn't he? "Actually, I'm not sure I can even convince them I'm the one telling the truth."

Her heart quailed.

"It's not my decision, but my opinion is you should try." Olivia's mouth tightened. "You have something else to consider. Lies or not, what your children are threatening isn't right. It's called emotional blackmail."

"Blackmail?"

Linda nodded. "When toddlers and teens don't get their way, they use the 'I hate you, Mommy,' And it really stings, doesn't it?"

"It does," Valerie whispered. Perhaps it hurt her even more because she was particularly vulnerable to love being withdrawn.

Her jaw set as she realized the ugliness of what Barry had created. "If my children said they found my behavior repellent and wanted to distance themselves, it would be one thing. But they're withholding their love to get their way. Or, in this case, my ex's way."

Linda nodded.

Valerie turned to Olivia. "The same as what your father did with you."

"You see it now."

"My Sam..." Linda folded her hands in her lap. "He'd say a parent shouldn't let a child get away with emotional manipulation. Because such behavior would sabotage their future relationships."

"Your Master is a hardass." Smiling slightly, Olivia glanced at Valerie. "And, although quieter about it, so is the Colonel."

Ghost did have convictions about honesty. And about protecting her.

Valerie's next breath came easier. Although honoring her fears by staying away, he'd found her help. Because he loved her.

And she loved him.

Should her children be allowed to dictate who she loved and where she lived?

No.

No more than she would order them around.

And if they would erase her from their lives without listening to her, she'd truly done a horrible job of raising them.

But she wouldn't judge, not at this point. First, they needed the facts. "Before I can combat Barry's lies, I'll need to get the children to see me. They aren't even taking my calls."

"Brats," Olivia's eyes narrowed. After a minute, she said, "I doubt they'd be able to resist reading a certified letter."

"Perfect. As for getting them to see you in person"—Linda smiled cynically—"shame and remorse are feelings that should be spread around, don't you think?"

Valerie considered. "In other words, they're not the only ones who can appeal to emotion."

"Exactly." Linda nodded. "We parents are masters of the art of the guilt trip."

Olivia tilted her head. "After sending the letters, you might let them stew for a few days."

"I don't have much choice. This is finals week followed by commencement." After a heartening sip of grog, Valerie pulled her notepad forward. "I think I know how to do this."

By the time Linda and Olivia left, she had the letter.

My children,

You've listened to what your father had to say about my various "crimes" and apparently, have convicted me without a hearing.

I believe I should have an equal chance to speak.

After all, I heard what you, Dillon, had to say after Hailey insisted you tried to drown her in the pool.

I let you, Hailey, speak your piece when our neighbor said you'd deliberately run over her grandson's tricycle.

When your father insisted you'd both stolen his wallet and run up his credit cards, did I immediately convict you?

Dillon, when your coach kicked you off the team for drinking, did I listen to all sides and then dig up the information to prove you were innocent?

When Dillon told me that you, Hailey, had been shoplifting, did I call the police—or instead, ask you about it?

I demand the same fairness I gave you. I want you to meet me on neutral ground and simply listen to what I have to say.

Please meet me at noon, Sunday, at Lettuce Lake Park near your favorite playground.

Mom

CHAPTER TWENTY-NINE

You're getting old and set in your ways, Colonel.

The next evening, Ghost sat outside and worked on his floggers. Beyond the pool of light, the world was pitch black except for brilliant flashes of lightning. Over the sound of rain pounding on the lanai's roof, thunder boomed and growled.

Unable to settle comfortably inside, he'd brought out the leather impact toys from the armoire as well as his bag. After cleaning and conditioning the toy bag, he started on the floggers.

One by one, he conditioned the leather falls and lightly brushed the suede ones. The fragrance of conditioner and leather filled the air.

Memories came and went. This lightweight flogger had been Kelly's favorite. One made of heavy buffalo hide had made an older masochist very happy. The Latigo leather was his favorite for intense sessions. Valerie liked the regular-size moose leather.

He reached for another flogger. Really, he should be grading the last few essays he'd brought home. But his students' work deserved his complete attention...so this wasn't the time. He'd tackle the papers first thing in the morning.

Damn, he was tired. Last night he'd slept alone—and badly.

All today, her absence and his worry about her had fragmented his calm.

He loved waking up with her in the mornings, her soft body against his. Discussing the upcoming day over coffee. Teasing her into hitting him during her self-defense lessons—and seeing her worry when she landed a good punch. The woman didn't have a cruel bone in her body.

She had enough service submissive in her she liked to cook for him, and if she was in the kitchen, well, she drew him like a moth to a candle, so he'd be there helping. They both ate healthier than when they'd lived alone. Kelly had disliked cooking. Now, he was discovering how fun it was to partner someone in the kitchen. Or to make her breakfast, since, God knew, the woman wasn't at her best in the mornings.

Last night, he'd put together a sandwich and called it good.

Normally, she'd be with him here on the lanai. Enjoying the rain. Comparing notes on their days. Talking about everything. She was not only as smart and educated as he was, but her different view of life made for fascinating discussions on politics and economics and history.

Yeah, he missed her.

Finishing the last flogger, he cleaned off his hands in the lanai sink, then sank back down into his chair.

Dammit, he wanted to be with her. Nevertheless, if she needed time to think, that's what she'd get.

But what if she needed him now? Would she be comfortable calling him...or would she be uncertain if he'd still want to be with her?

He shook his head. *Nice attempt to convince yourself to go see her, Colonel.*

His logic didn't fly. Earlier in their relationship she'd been insecure, but what they had now was damn solid. He'd won her trust.

He'd give her the time she needed.

Not even five minutes later, he saw something move beyond the lanai.

"Finn." Carrying a plastic bag, Valerie opened the screen door and stepped out of the pouring rain.

She was drenched, her green button-up shirt and khaki pants clinging to her. Her religious necklaces were around her neck—a crucifix, a pentagram, an Allah medallion, and a Shinto Torii gate. She was his favorite kind of quiet rabble-rouser.

And she was here.

"Valerie." He rose.

Even as he moved forward, she dropped her bag and met him partway. As he closed his arms around her, he felt as if he could finally take a full breath. "I missed you," he said gruffly.

She was hugging him as hard as he was her. "Me, too."

After a minute or so, he realized she was shaking, and he pulled back. "You're soaked, pet."

"I noticed. I got you all wet, too. Sorry." Bending, she opened the plastic bag, pulled out a covered wicker basket, and handed it to him. "I came with a Happy May Day—or Beltane, if you will —offering."

Drawing the red napkin back, he stared. Jesus, she'd made him cookies. All his favorites. Including shortbread. He picked up the note she'd tucked in the side. *Thank you for sending Linda.*

"You're welcome." He cupped her cheek. "If this is what I get when I send you reinforcements, next time, I'm sending the entire Shadowkitten clowder."

"All of them? Gods, I'd probably be home with a hangover instead of here." She looked past him at the pile of leather strewn over the table. "Is there a reason you have floggers out here?"

His floggers were all nice and conditioned. Be a shame to waste all that effort. He smiled slowly as his dick stirred.

"Valerie..."

"Uhhh." Valerie had no idea how much time had passed. But she was still restrained outside on the lanai.

Naked.

The stubborn Dom had ignored her protests—not about being flogged, but about the naked *outside* part. At least, he'd been nice enough to lock the gate from the parking lot.

Nonetheless, the wrought-iron lanterns on the stone mansion wall gave off way too much light.

After securing her between the lanai posts, using those eyebolts he'd pointed out so long ago, he'd said he wanted to introduce her to his floggers. All of them.

She'd eyed the table covered with his toys and told him a handshake would be sufficient introduction, thank you very much.

Laughing, he'd started.

He had a *lot* of floggers.

The soft ones had been so sexy.

Some had thinner leather and others were long and heavy enough to drive the breath from her with a blow. Some made her whine with the evil stinging sensations, and gentler ones he first used on her back and ass, then her breasts.

Gods.

"Valerie. Are you with me, pet?"

"Hmm?"

His so-very-masculine laugh made her lift her eyelids.

He stood in front of her, dressed only in his jeans and boots. The muscles in his arms and chest were pumped to iron from flogging her. The light from the lanterns showed his faint smile. "It was a rough day—I'm glad you were able to escape it for a while."

She blinked at him and realized he was right. When her skin started to burn, her worries had disappeared. When the pain turned into bottomless liquid heat, her thoughts had poofed away like magic. "Thank you?"

He chuckled. "I'm going to play with you a little more and then fuck you for the makeup sex part of the agenda."

Oh, she was way ahead of him on that part since she'd come right after he'd used the nastiest flogger on her. He'd called it her reward.

But...getting off again would be fine. So fine. She licked her lips. "Okay."

Leaning forward, he cupped the back of her head, leaning down to murmur, "Lass, I wasn't asking permission. Merely giving you an idea of what will happen next. You're naked and all tied up —the only way you're getting out of this is to safeword."

Shivers coursed over her skin at the easy authority in his deep voice.

Stepping back, he held up a shiny steel Wartenberg wheel, so the light glittered off the pinwheel-looking device. The multiple disks were covered in sharp spikes.

Her eyes widened. "I...um...Ghost?"

"Let's see if you like this, pet."

Her arms were raised in a V position, with her wrists tied to high anchor points on the posts. Her legs were secured apart. The rain hadn't let up, and occasional gusts of wind blew droplets of rain through the screen and across her hot skin.

Bending, he ran the wheel lightly up her left thigh, creating a sensual tickling sensation. He did the same on the right leg, working his way up in swoops and swirls, bypassing her groin.

"It tickles," she whispered.

"Does it?" His grin came and went so fast she almost didn't see it. A warning tingle ran down her spine. That had been his sadist smile.

He ran the wheel over her stomach, making big circles and letters, and, really, it was prickly, tingly fun.

Things changed when he circled behind her to make the same circles, using the same pressure, on her back.

Only...her flogged skin was already hot and sensitive, and the device felt almost like tiny razors. She hissed and arched. "*Oh, spit.*"

"Breathe, lass." His hand was cool and soothing as he stroked over where the wheel had gone.

A breath, another.

"Now, this is the letter I," he murmured, tracing the devious device down the unflogged skin over her spine.

It felt surprisingly good, and she realized she was sliding back down into her happy place as all of her senses focused on where the torture thing was headed.

"Here's an L." The wheel ran down her flogged skin on the left and crossed to the right.

Her back arched at the burning line.

"And a U." It went over her scapula and down, across and back up. Such glorious, amazing pain that wasn't pain now, but a billowing slide of sensation. "Ooooh."

ILU. What was he spelling?

Oh, oh, he wasn't. "I love you, too." She laughed, her voice hoarse.

Then the spiky pinwheel ran over the already burning skin on her buttocks adding a shocking burst of pain. Up and down and across it went, until all her ass ignited into a wonderful roaring fire.

Her legs were moving, trying to dance her bottom out of the way, even as she pushed her butt back for more.

"Mmmph, let's see if you happen to like this elsewhere. Somewhere even more fun."

Earlier, her head had grown so heavy she'd rested it against her upraised arm. Now, she opened her eyes as he walked around the posts to stand in front of her.

His eyes held the glint she'd learned to respect. To fear as much as she could fear someone she trusted and loved.

Still...

Her ass cheeks burned.

He started at her neck, using the device so very lightly it merely tickled. Moving downward, it went across the tops of her breasts.

Her breasts were still swollen and hot from the suede flogger, and the pinwheel traced lightly around each in a sensuous circle.

Then it changed as he spiraled in, pressing harder, the sharp pain sliding into a heavy line of heat.

With his other hand, he touched between her legs, his fingers sliding in her wetness. He teased her clit until she tried to go up on her tiptoes, even as the device slowly circled one nipple and then the other.

The exquisite pleasure on her clit somehow joined the piercing sensations on her nipples until she couldn't tell which sensation was pouring into her.

And the pain and pleasure boiled over, rolled over her, and flattened her as she came and came. Her scream echoed off the stone building.

"That did sound nice. I'm not sure whether you were screaming in pain or from coming." His low laugh sent a tingle through her as he guided her across the lanai...and when had he freed her from the restraints?

Her heart was still pounding, and her breathing was too fast as he bent her over the back of a heavy patio chair. The cushion was cold against her stomach as he pushed her legs apart. "Don't move, pet."

His voice was deep. Commanding. And she could hear his pleasure at what he'd done to her. What he planned to do next.

A thrill ran through her. Sex with him was unlike anything she'd ever had before.

She could hear him unzip his jeans. The harsh denim rubbed

her tender ass cheeks as his erection pressed at her slick entrance. He eased in slightly, gripped her hip, and penetrated her in a long, hard thrust.

Pleasure exploded through her at the intimate invasion. "Ah, ah, ah."

"Very nice." Chuckling, he bent over her, his chest against her back, his cock plunging even deeper.

And then he closed his hands on her tortured, sensitive breasts...and squeezed.

Pain—pleasure—pain poured through her in erotic waves.

He rubbed his callused palms over the pinpricks left by the Wartenberg wheel, and she squeaked. When he rolled her swollen nipples between his fingers, her body responded, contracting around his shaft as she squirmed beneath him.

Laughing with a sadist's enjoyment, he tugged on her nipples with each hard thrust.

And the floodwaters of sensation closed over her and drowned her in pleasure.

CHAPTER THIRTY

Sunday had finally arrived. As Valerie headed for the playground, anxiety about the upcoming confrontation slowed her step.

She paused for a calming breath. The scent of the surrounding swamp was thick in the air. Only a few puffy clouds broke the deep blue of the sky. So much anxiety filled her it seemed wrong for the sun to be shining.

You can do this, woman.

She straightened her shoulders.

Alongside the Hillsborough River, Lettuce Lake had always been one of her family's favorite parks. As a mother, she'd appreciated the shady playground when the children were young. Years later, they'd traverse the boardwalk to look for alligators. Eventually, there'd been canoeing and kayaking.

Her heart hurt. They'd been a happy family, hadn't they?

With a sigh, she crossed the lawn. She'd deliberately come late, hoping her children would have time to talk. To think.

Even to worry...because her fear for what would happen was broken up with pure anger.

She'd never spanked them. What a shame it was too late to

start now.

There they were, standing by a picnic table.

In tan shorts and a short-sleeved shirt, Hailey wore her long brown hair pulled back in a no-nonsense braid. Ready for business.

Her husband, Rom, sat at another picnic table, close enough to hear, distant enough to not be part of the conversation. He held an eReader.

Valerie's grandson was sleeping in a stroller beside him.

Her stomach clenched. Had Hailey brought Luca as a form of emotional coercion?

No, she'd give her daughter the benefit of the doubt.

Across the table from Hailey was Dillon. He wore cut-off jeans and a T-shirt...and an obviously bad attitude.

Valerie sighed.

Finn had offered to come with her, but she'd refused. His presence would have sparked more conflict. But she sure felt awfully alone right now.

And wasn't that a sad thought when she was walking toward her children?

"Mom." Dillon's mouth was set in a line, his jaw jutted out.

Yes, she'd already been tried and convicted.

Hailey's gaze was troubled, but the way she held herself said she continued to believe Barry's lies.

Valerie's heart broke even more. Didn't they know her at all? Maybe she should walk away from it all.

No. She wouldn't let the bastard steal her children from her. Not without a fight.

Rising, Dillon crossed his arms over his chest. "I don't know what you hope to accomplish by this. We've heard everything that happened."

"I'm sure Barry said a lot." She kept her tone mild because she'd always try for peace before war.

When Hailey started to speak, Valerie held up her hand.

"Here are the ground rules. This is my time, so I get to speak without interruption. When I'm finished, I'll take questions. Is that reasonable?"

They hadn't forgotten their lessons on fairness and grudgingly nodded.

"Good. First of all"—her temper rose so hard and fast she almost choked—"I have never, ever cheated on your father. Never."

Dillon's face turned red. "You're lying. He said—"

"Be. Quiet." Valerie pointed at him. "This is my time to talk. Not yours." She imitated the authoritative snap Ghost put into his orders. "Sit *down*."

Huh. It works.

"This is what happened before I left and why we're divorced. I apologize in advance for offending you at the news parents have a sex life."

Hearing Hailey choke, Valerie barely suppressed a hysterical laugh. Gods, she was shaking already. She shoved her hands into her shorts' pockets.

"After you two moved out, we were trying to put some life back into a marriage that had turned...quite frankly...boring. We joined a BDSM group and were experimenting with some of the kinky facets of the lifestyle."

Hailey's eyes went wide.

"With each other, mind you, no one else." Valerie eyed her self-righteous children and couldn't resist. "I discovered I rather like being spanked."

This time it was Dillon who choked.

"Your father uncovered a different desire. He wanted to be served, or I should say, he wanted to have a slave. To that end, he found Alisha. She's in her thirties and was thrilled to live with us and serve Barry."

Hailey whispered, "No way."

"Truth." Valerie wrinkled her nose. "Since Barry wanted so

much to try it, I agreed. Very reluctantly."

"You liked her, too?" Dillon asked slowly.

Well, at least he wasn't a homophobe like Natalia's relatives. Valerie shook her head. "No, I didn't. It might have been different if I was interested in women, but I'm not. I allowed her to live with us to please Barry."

"You let another woman live in your house? And sleep with Dad?" Hailey whispered.

"Yes. It gets worse, though." Valerie could hear the bitterness in her voice. "After three months, I told Barry a three-person relationship wasn't working for me. Rather than telling Alisha to leave, he brought in *another* woman."

At the silence, Valerie looked at Hailey. "Kahlua is about a year older than you."

Dillon shook his head. "I don't believe a word—"

"Be *quiet*," Valerie snapped and was gratified to see Hailey shoot him a glare.

"Alisha works a few hours a week at a part-time job. Kahlua does nothing. Neither of them cooked meals nor kept the house up—so I ended up being the housekeeper. My hard-earned salary went to feeding and clothing them and to the expensive gifts your father gave them. If I'd liked them at all, maybe things would have been different. Instead, they spent all their time running me down until I felt like"—her voice cracked, and tears welled in her eyes— "like the ugliest, oldest, most worthless person on this earth."

She spun, trying to regain her composure. As she wiped her cheeks and blinked away the tears, she saw...Finn.

Beside Rom at the other picnic table, he rose, obviously ready to go to war. She could hear his low curse.

Straightening her spine, she shook her head. *My fight.*

He stood for a moment, then slowly resumed his seat.

She drew in a breath. He'd come to support her. His presence gave her strength like nothing else would have done.

I can do this.

When she turned back around, both Dillon and Hailey were standing, their expressions appalled.

"Mom," Hailey whispered. "I've never seen you cry."

"If I needed to cry, I did it in the bathroom or bedroom, so I wouldn't upset my children." Anger put the rest of her thought into words. "But it seems I won't have any children, so what's the point in trying to be strong?"

Hailey stepped back as if she'd been struck.

"Dad said"—Dillon swallowed—"you dumped him for some pervert. And he'd forgive you and take you back. That he needs you back."

"Dillon, he's trying to support two unemployed women without my salary. Of course, he wants me back." As her patience faded, she pulled papers from her purse and tossed them onto the table. "Since one of your parents is obviously lying, I brought our credit card reports from the last three years. You can see what we normally spent before the arrival of the slaves. You can also see when expensive clothing and jewelry store expenses appear. That's Alisha. When those expenses double again and the liquor stores show up, those are Kahlua's purchases. She loves her alcohol."

"But Dad said he started to drink because of you," Hailey objected.

Valerie snorted. "Early in our marriage, when Barry started drinking like his alcoholic father, I told him if he wanted children, he had to agree to abstinence. It's why we never had alcohol in the house."

Hailey's eyes narrowed. "You don't have a problem?"

"No. But I didn't want him to be tempted, so I abstained to support him." Valerie shook her head. "Kahlua wouldn't. Instead, he joined her, and the drinking started to affect his work. And his behavior."

She realized she was rubbing her cheek when Dillon's gaze focused on her hand.

Her son stared. "He *hit* you?"

"It was the last straw, yes."

Chin trembling, Hailey picked up the credit card reports. "These stop in November."

"That's when I started divorce proceedings, canceled the card, and separated our accounts." A movement caught her attention.

Barry was stomping across the grass toward them.

Wasn't that wonderful? "I take it one of you mentioned this meeting to your father?"

Hailey went red. "Sorry. I thought if he talked to you when we were here..."

Her soft-hearted daughter.

"I'll tell him to leave," Hailey said.

"No." Valerie searched deeper for courage. "Let's get everything out in the open."

Barry stopped at one side of the picnic table and scowled at her. "What lies are you telling them, babe? Or are you saying you'll get your ass back where you belong?"

"Sorry, Barry, but you have enough women at the house. I won't return."

"Then you'll lose your children and your grandchildren." He made a sweeping gesture. "Tell her, kids."

Yes, it was obvious he'd set this whole thing up to get his way. Olivia had been right about how manipulative this was.

"Dillon." Valerie turned to her son. "Do you know what emotional blackmail is? It's when a person threatens to withhold their affection to force a person to do what they want."

She turned to Hailey. "For example, if Rom cheated on you, you'd want to leave him, I assume."

Hailey looked appalled but nodded. "Of course."

"What would you do if I said you had to stay with him, or I wouldn't love you or be your mother any longer?" When Hailey's mouth dropped open, Valerie nodded. "That's emotional blackmail."

"Hey, now..." Barry's protest trailed off.

Because dismay and distress had filled her children's expressions.

"Shit. That's what we did. What we said." Shame filled Dillon's expression. "God, Mom, I'm *sorry*."

"We did." Hailey glared at her father. "We did because you *instructed* us to, Dad. You lied to us and then told us what to say to Mom." Her eyes filled with tears. "I believed you, and I was so upset for you, and I couldn't believe Mom would cheat on you, but you swore she did."

She launched herself at Valerie.

Valerie caught her—and here was her little girl, no matter how old she was, back in Valerie's arms, crying on her shoulder. Choking out broken words, "I'm sorry, Mommy."

The world started to right itself.

"Jesus, Dad, that's totally dick behavior," Dillon snapped. "You fucking lied to us."

"Your mom needs to come back to me," Barry whined and swayed slightly. "You know how much I love her."

Valerie studied him for a moment. His face was flushed, eyes slightly glazed. His words had been slurred. "You're drunk."

"What? It's barely noon." Hailey took a step back. "You *are*."

Dillon crossed his arms over his chest. "So, where's Alisha. And *Kahlua*? Jesus, there's a name for someone who likes to drink."

"Yes, Dad," Hailey said. "I think we should meet your new women."

"I don't have any new—"

"Don't bullshit us, Dad," Dillon snapped.

Valerie sighed at how much like Barry his son sounded.

"Yeah, well, Alisha left when the cable company cut..." Barry's voice trailed off, and he blinked.

Valerie sighed. He really was drunk.

"And Kahlua?" Hailey asked. Her expression turned cold as she realized how thoroughly he'd played them.

"Over there." He motioned back where he'd come from.

Valerie shook her head. Of course, Kahlua had come. "She's the blonde in the halter-top."

"Fuck me," Dillon muttered. "She's our age—only I have better taste."

Seeing she had been spotted, Kahlua smirked and strutted over, hips swaying like a metronome.

"Gag me," Hailey whispered.

"Honey." Kahlua latched onto Barry's arm and shot Valerie a spiteful look. "These must be your wonderful children."

The shrill voice was like fingernails on a chalkboard.

"Right." Barry's expression was uncertain. "Kahlua, my son, Dillon, and my daughter, Hailey."

"It's so good to finally meet you." Kahlua gave them a wide smile.

Dillon shook his head. "I can't say the same."

When she scowled, he ignored her. "Dad. When I was sixteen, you told me alcoholism runs in our family, and it'd be better if I never drank. I believed you. Now, you're sure setting a hell of an example of how alcohol can ruin a person."

"What?" Barry shook his head. "What do you mean?"

"I mean drinking is fucking up your life. You're an alcoholic, Dad, and you need help."

"I need your *mother*," Barry said stubbornly. "That's what you're supposed to be doing. Getting her back for me."

Valerie's heart almost broke. In the beginning of their marriage, he'd been a good father. A good husband. The middle hadn't been awful, but then came a midlife crisis, stupid decisions, and drinking. "You don't need a wife, Barry, you need Alcoholics Anonymous."

Hailey stared at him. "After I was suspended in high school, you and Mom told me to consider who I hung out with. You said good friends would pull me up and help me be the best I could be —and bad friends would drag me into the gutter."

She eyed Kahlua and scowled. "You should check the friends you're keeping, Daddy, because from where I stand, you're a manipulative liar and a drunk, and I'm ashamed of you."

Barry's face flushed with shock, then anger. His fist came up, but even as he took a step forward, he staggered. He realized Dillon was staring at his *fist*, and he stopped dead. "Fuck me. I'm drunk."

"Hailey..." His voice wavered.

Crying in Valerie's arms, Hailey shook her head.

Valerie glanced over at the other picnic table. Finn had his hand on Rom's arm, keeping him there...and both men stood in front of Luca's stroller.

"Jesus, Dad." Dillon looked disgusted.

Barry's expression changed, and he whispered. "What have I done?"

"Master," Kahlua whined. "They're just being pissy. Don't listen to—"

He peeled her hands from his arm. "I'm...I'm going to stay with friends for a few days. It's time for you to move out, Kahlua. Take all the alcohol with you."

And he walked away.

Settling Hailey on the picnic table, Valerie hoped against hope Barry might return to the man she'd known.

Face reddening with fury, Kahlua watched her meal ticket leave. Then she charged at Valerie, shrieking, "You fucking bitch, this is all your fault, you old hag."

Fingers in claws, she swung at Valerie's face.

Automatically, Valerie blocked the arm, stepped, and...no. Rather than punching as Ghost had taught her, she smoothly tripped the woman, sending her to the soft ground.

The slave might have been a factor in Barry's turning to alcohol, but she hadn't forced him to drink. She was a horrible, vindictive person, but pounding her into the ground wouldn't solve anything.

Kahlua pushed to her feet. "Bitch. You're all assholes. All of you!" She staggered away, cursing them loudly.

"Holy shit, way to go, *Mom*," Hailey said in awe.

Dillon stared. "Where did you learn to do that?"

From behind Valerie, someone cleared his throat.

She turned to see Rom with the stroller.

Beside him, Finn nodded at her. "Very nice block. Poor follow-through."

"I couldn't hit her."

"I'm not surprised in the least." His chuckle ran along her nerves like a warm stroke of his hand.

Hailey and Dillon stared at him.

Well, no turning back now. Deliberately, Valerie moved closer and smiled up at him to let him know how much his presence meant to her.

How much she loved him.

A corner of his mouth tilted up, and he put his arm around her.

She leaned in. "Finn, I'd like you to meet my family. Hailey, her husband Rom Romano, Luca, my grandson—and my son, Dillon. And you all, this is Dr. Finn Blackwood, a professor at my university."

"It's good to meet you," Finn said, totally at ease. "She's very proud of you, you know."

Hailey gave him a rueful sigh. "Up until this week, maybe. I take it you know what's been going on."

"I'm afraid so." His smile was still as charming as the first time Valerie had seen him. "How about I treat you all to lunch? There's a good Italian restaurant across the street, and we can get to know each other."

To Valerie's delight, both her children nodded, and then Luca woke up.

"Gammy. My Gammy," he crowed, holding his arms up to her.

Yes, the world was right again.

CHAPTER THIRTY-ONE

Ghost had never envisioned the private gardens teeming with half-pints, but such was life with a soft-hearted woman who'd mother the world.

Last week, when Beth and Nolan's sons whined they never saw Sophia anymore, Valerie had decided Ghost should have a get-together for the Masters with children...and any other Masters and their subbies who wanted to come.

The question should have been who *didn't* want to come.

Shaking his head, he left the crowded lanai to see what was going on in the gardens.

Off to the right was the pool. Stepping inside the screened enclosure, he stayed well back to avoid the tsunami of splashing.

In the pool, Kim and Raoul were playing ball tag with a batch of Marcus's underprivileged teens. The boys were good kids despite some looking like advertisements for a tattoo and piercing business. Appearances could be deceiving.

Kim's big German shepherd lay in the shade near the pool, watching intently. If Kim looked as if she was in trouble, the giant furball would jump in to save her.

A couple of the newer boys furtively checked out Ghost's prosthesis—which was visible since he was wearing shorts.

For social events, he tended to wear jeans or pants. Although he didn't particularly care what adults thought, he didn't like the thought of upsetting children. But Valerie had said it was too hot for pants—and children were more adaptable than he gave them credit for.

The two boys in the pool realized he'd seen them checking out his leg. One flushed. The other one grinned. "You should paint flames on the silvery part."

The pylon was the metal shank between the socket and the shoe. Ghost laughed. "I'll let the prosthetics designers know."

Yes, Valerie was right about tough, resilient kids.

At the pool's shallow end, Gabi and Marcus were playing with energetic Sophia, who wore water wings. Who would have thought such a small person could splash so effectively?

Something bounced lightly off his back. He spun to see a bright red and yellow inflated ball rolling away.

"Yay!" In the pool, Kim did a victory dance.

"She got the Ghost!" The teens were cheering so exuberantly, a laugh escaped him before he assumed a suitable frown.

After all, a submissive had attacked a Master.

Obviously in agreement, Raoul shook his head at Kim. "Chiquita, such behavior to a Mas—ahem, the person who invited us—is most disrespectful." The reproving words might have had more effect if Raoul hadn't been smiling.

"Oh dear. I'm deeply sorry, Ghost." Kim's penitent expression wasn't even close to believable.

"Raoul." Ghost crossed his arms over his chest and looked stern. Because he'd had years of suppressing laughter while reprimanding new recruits. "After the party, please convey my dissatisfaction with your woman's *very* insincere apology."

Grinning, Raoul snagged Kim around the waist. "Of course, my friend. I will be happy to do so."

There, that should ensure the couple would have an interesting evening.

Chuckling, Ghost tossed the ball to Kim's opponent and continued his stroll.

In the blue-flowered contemplation garden, Uzuri, Rainie, and Jake were talking with Olivia and Natalia. The newly engaged couple was snuggled together on a loveseat and positively radiated contentment.

Made a man feel good.

Farther into the gardens, he spotted Saxon.

The big blond veterinarian was jogging slowly. His search-and-rescue, border collie-lab mix bounced happily beside him. "Yo, Ghost. Your woman was looking for you."

"Ah, thank you. I'll—" He stopped when Saxon glanced to the right and slowed.

"I see Saxon!" Seven-year-old Connor sprang out from a clump of bushes. "Get 'im, Grant."

Charging from the opposite side, Grant tackled Saxon.

"Ooof!" The man helpfully fell over—and Connor piled on, too. Thrilled with the fun, the fluffy black-and-white dog danced in and out, licking faces and hands.

The children—and the giant Dom—were laughing so hard Ghost doubted any of them could breathe.

Kids, dogs, and Doms were an unbeatable combination.

Grinning, Ghost headed back to the lanai to see what Valerie needed.

Ah, Hailey was here. The young woman was sitting beside her mother, talking animatedly.

In the three weeks since the blow-up at the park, both of Valerie's children had dropped by a few times. Probably to get reassurance they hadn't irrevocably ruined their relationship with their mother.

Valerie had, of course, forgiven them.

And they'd accepted she'd essentially moved in with Ghost.

He grinned, remembering their questions about the mansion. Hearing the downstairs was used by a *private* club, they'd hastily abandoned the subject. It seemed the concepts of *parent* and *sex* were mutually exclusive.

Spotting Hailey's husband, Rom, near the food table, Ghost veered in his direction.

"Gose!" From under the table, Luca ran over, bounced off Ghost's legs, and put his arms up.

Laughing, Ghost picked up the pocket-sized squirt and tossed him in the air. Giggles filled the air—and when Luca laughed, everyone within hearing smiled.

Including Valerie.

"How are you, lad? Have you been a good boy?"

Luca slapped a hand on his tiny chest. "Good."

"In that case, you deserve a cookie, hmm?"

Rom grinned. "Being a grandparent sure beats being a dad. No one yells at *you* for handing out cookies."

A grandparent. The title set up a warm feeling in Ghost's chest, and he glanced at Valerie.

Her eyes were warm and pleased. His generous woman was happy to share her family with him.

Was it any wonder he loved her?

He smiled at her and then settled down to the serious business of helping Luca select the perfect cookie.

A sugar cookie with bright red frosting won. After giving the boy another one to take to Gammy, Ghost tossed a few broken pieces to the two exhausted dogs sprawled under the table. A fluffy black-and-white pooch was Rainie's, the one that resembled a giant terrier was Cullen's Airedale.

Had all the childless couples brought their pets as kid-substitutes for Valerie's children's day gathering? Sneaky maneuver.

Leaning against a post, Rom nibbled on a cookie. "Thanks for letting us break into your party. Hailey... She needed to talk with her mom for a few minutes."

"Problems?"

"Not really. It's—"

Rom was interrupted by the shouts of glee as Connor and Grant charged through the door and onto the lanai.

"You got another little kid!" Grinning, Connor asked Ghost, "Who's that?"

"He's Luca, Valerie's grandson."

"Can we play with him?" Grant motioned to the designated toddler area where balls and trucks dotted a large, plush rug.

Ghost saw Rom nod permission. "I know you two will be gentle with him, so yes."

"Hi!" Connor ran over to the two-year-old. "Wanna play trucks?"

That's all it took.

Grabbing Connor's hand, Luca dragged him over to the rug.

"Well, damn." Rom exchanged disbelieving glances with Hailey. "He's usually real timid."

Ghost chuckled. "Connor's a charmer. His brother, Grant is quieter but careful. He'll keep your boy safe."

"I see that." Rom smiled. "Nice. Usually whenever we try to have a conversation with someone, Luca's underfoot and wanting attention."

"Since he's not..." Ghost eyed Hailey. Like the two teenagers who'd snuck into the Shadowlands, Hailey looked as if she wanted to sit on her mom's lap. "What unsettled your Hailey?"

"We were here to visit a buddy who busted his leg jet-skiing, and"—Rom's mouth tightened—"stopped by to see Barry." Rom held no respect for Valerie's ex.

"Ah. How is he doing?"

"Better, actually. Kahlua is gone. He's sober and attending AA meetings." Rom shook his head. "Since he trashed his rep as a contractor, he found a job with a remodeling company. Seems happy. Said he'd always hated the business part of being a contractor."

Ghost considered that for a moment. "What do you want to bet Valerie handled the paperwork and scheduling?"

"No bet. Your woman did a hell of a lot more for him than he ever admitted." Rom snorted.

Hmm. "And now he's come clean?"

"Yeah." Rom grimaced. "I gotta say, it was nice to see him off the pedestal Hailey had put him on."

Ghost tilted his head. Now there was an aspect he hadn't considered before. "Difficult to live up to?"

"No lie. She just figured out today how much her mom did to prop him up. Not only for his job, but for the kids, too. And the bastard never reciprocated. She built him up; he, pretty subtly, ran her down."

"She dimmed her brightness to let her husband shine." Ghost turned to study his woman.

Since she'd generously helped him out with the Shadowlands paperwork, he'd treated her to a spa day yesterday. She'd returned with fingernails and toenails a glowing blue that matched her eyes. Her skin was silky and perfumed...and far past his ability to resist.

He'd tumbled her right into bed and kept her there for hours.

Today, her lips were still slightly swollen. Beard-burn had pinkened her neck. Her tawny hair was pulled back into a tail, but escaped tendrils danced over her sunburned cheeks. When her daughter said something, her husky laughter bubbled out.

Maybe Valerie had dimmed her light for a while. Today, she was shining brighter than a midday sun.

After talking for a while, Rom checked his phone. "We need get going. If Luca doesn't get to bed on time, he'll be cranky tomorrow."

After giving Valerie a kiss on the cheek, Rom collected Hailey, then Luca who called, "bye-bye" to everyone in the area.

Ghost sat down beside Valerie on the swing and put his arm around her. "Are you all right?"

"I'm good, really." With no hesitation, she leaned against him, her gaze on the groups of people talking on the lanai. "I'd thought we'd have three or four couples, at most. This is crazy—but it's fun, isn't it?"

"It is." He indulged in stealing a kiss because sitting with her was like entering a bubble of peace—something to be cherished by an old soldier.

Trotting over, Grant grinned at Ghost. "Luca's a cool kid. As fun as Sophia."

"You should call us when he comes here," Connor stated. "We can keep him busy so you can talk with the grownups."

"That's a very nice offer," Ghost said gravely. "His father said you guys are very good with Luca."

"We're practicing," Connor said.

"I see." Ghost considered the two boys. "And for what are you practicing?"

Grant's grin was wide enough to show his missing two front teeth. Could a kid get any cuter? "We're practicing for our new sister."

Under Ghost's arm, Valerie's shoulders were shaking as she tried not to laugh.

Sitting at a nearby table, Nolan had heard them. "We've met a young lady—all of four years old—who will stay with us next week, and, if we're good together, she'll join the family."

"We'll be good," Connor assured his adopted father, then grinned at Valerie. "Mama wanted to talk to you. Did you talk?"

"You know, we haven't had a chance. Do you know where she is?" Valerie asked.

"Back there." Grant waved at the gardens.

"I'll show you." Connor held his hand out.

Chuckling, Valerie gave Ghost a quick kiss, then took the small hand. "Lead on, my man."

Ghost was totally unsurprised when Grant took her other hand. She could lure children in faster than a candy store.

As they left, Nolan told Ghost, "You have a hell of a woman."

"Agreed. And you have great kids. It'll be interesting to see them with a sister."

"Oh yeah." With a rueful expression, Nolan rubbed his neck. "We wanted to wait another year—gave them a dog instead—then Kari and Dan's girl came along, and they remembered they wanted a sister."

Kari and Dan's two children were both adorable.

It'd be interesting in another fifteen years when all these girls reached dating age. It'd take a brave kid to ask out the hardass cop's daughter. Or Z's girls, for that matter.

Or...Nolan with a daughter? God help them all. "I look forward to meeting your new addition."

"We won't be the only ones adding on. I hear Sally and Andrea are pregnant."

"So I hear." Ghost's smile faded as he considered the ramifications to the Shadowlands. "Hell. Scheduling is going to be a nightmare."

"A nightmare is being optimistic." With a tired grunt, Saxon dropped into a chair beside Nolan. "You're screwed, dude."

"I do not need bad news," Ghost growled.

"Sorry, not sorry." Unfazed, Saxon laughed. "Most of our Shadowkittens are in the thirties range. Means when their buddies have babies, they're gonna get the urge." He opened his fingers to mimic an explosion. "And then...baby boom."

"Not helping." Ghost gave the vet a dour stare.

Smirking, Saxon held up his hands. "Hey, I'm innocent. I'm not getting anyone pregnant—I'm single."

"You are, aren't you." The question was why. The Dom had skills and charm, made a good living, and the submissives called him the Viking god.

"Whoa, dude. Uh-uh, I've seen what happens when Z gets that expression—hell, speak of the devil." Faster than George

Washington had fled from New York, the Viking god exited the lanai.

"There was a quick retreat." Chuckling, Z settled into the chair Saxon had emptied. "One does have to wonder why our Saxon hasn't found the right woman."

Nolan barked a laugh.

"No, one doesn't." Ghost shook his head. "I'm content being club manager, Grayson. I'm not stepping into your village match-maker shoes."

"Understood." Amusement in his gaze, Z watched as Saxon disappeared into the gardens.

Ghost grinned, recognizing the look. The poor veterinarian was doomed.

CHAPTER THIRTY-TWO

From the brightness of the room, it was morning. Rolling over, Valerie reached out to the other side of the bed.

Empty.

Her brows drew together. Although it was Monday, her summer school lecture wasn't until this afternoon. Ghost wasn't even teaching.

So, what happened to sleeping late—and making love?

I've been cheated.

Grumbling, she slid out of bed. The party had run late, and when she'd finally headed to bed, Ghost and Saxon had stayed out on the lanai, talking about the Shadowlands. She had no idea when her man had finally come in.

After a long yawn, she shook her head tentatively. Well, all *right*. She had no headache and no hangover. Ghost's advice had worked. As she was heading in to bed, her protective Dom had reminded her to drink a glass of water and take aspirin.

Because he loved her.

As she picked up the clothing she'd tossed onto her dresser, she uncovered the planner she'd brought from her apartment.

Opening the book, she studied her *effing* list:

Fitness: She flexed her biceps. Her muscles had certainly worked well when punching Piers. Maybe she should feel guilty, but no...she still felt like a badass.

Friends: She smiled, thinking of how Linda and Olivia had shown up at her place to help. Of the Shadowkittens gatherings. Of the wonderful time she'd had last night.

Family: Wasn't it funny how the mess with Barry had brought her and the children closer? Now, Finn was talking about taking her to Scotland to meet his mother and half-siblings. The thought of a bigger family was...nice.

Finances: Good enough and would improve when she let her apartment go at the end of summer. Because she was ready.

Fun: Got that one covered.

Friskiness...and Finn: She scowled. Those two items were definitely problematic. Her Colonel had taken himself right out of her bed this morning.

Well, she knew how to fix any lack of friskiness. Although Ghost had rescinded the *naked-at-all-times* rule a while back, she hadn't forgotten the lovely side effects to a lack of clothing.

Smiling, she took a quick shower, then used the lotion from the spa. Ghost had enjoyed the scent of it so much she still had bite marks on her butt.

She tousled her hair, tossed it back, and strutted out into the living room.

"Colonel, I woke up and—" Her voice strangled in her throat.

It wasn't Ghost who sat at the dining room table—it was Saxon.

The big blond Master had a cup of coffee in his hand. He lifted an eyebrow and took himself a leisurely perusal of her very naked body, then glanced at the kitchen where Ghost stood. "I must say, I've never seen a more attractive advertisement for giving up the single life."

Oh gods. She gave Ghost an outraged look, saw his eyes crinkle, and fled back to the bedroom.

She fumbled for clothes in the dresser. Honestly, what did one wear after a total mess-up? She pulled on her briefs and was fumbling into a bra when Ghost came up behind her.

"Oh, now, I don't think you need to put anything on just yet, lass." He took the bra and tossed it on the bed.

"Stop it. You have *company*." And didn't *that* sound irritable?

"He'd already finished breakfast when you came out. He's gone." Ghost pressed a very thick erection against her ass. "You know what seeing you naked does to me, woman. There is a penalty for getting me into this condition."

He gently bit the muscle at the top of her shoulder, then whispered in Arabic in his deep harsh voice, "And you knew what would happen when you waltzed out, showing me everything you own. Everything I intend to enjoy."

"I think you're mistaken." The huskiness in her voice made the protest completely ineffectual. Because she had wanted exactly this.

"It's time for some give and take." He moved her a step toward the bed, murmuring, "You are going to take everything I give you, orgasm after orgasm, until you beg me to stop."

As his powerful hands squeezed her breasts, everything inside her started to melt.

His unshaven cheek rubbed against her ear as he whispered, "And I'll take your heart and give you all of mine in return. I love you, lass."

Her legs went weak. "I love you. So, so much."

"Yes, you do." His laugh was deep and satisfied. "We're going to have a wonderful life together."

"We are."

She should add a new item to her list—*fulfillment.*
Got it covered.

NOT A HERO

"I couldn't have asked for a better start to a new and absolutely ADDICTING romance series! I was only left with one question...how quickly can I get my hands on the next one?!" ~ Shayna Renee's Spicy Reads

In the Alaska wilderness, four streetwise boys became men—and brothers

Now the crazy ex-military survivalist who plucked Gabriel and three other boys from an abusive foster care home has died. But the sarge leaves them a final mission: Revive the dying town of Rescue.

Gabe is done with being a hero

Wounded in body and soul, the retired SEAL simply wants to remain holed up in his isolated cabin. He sure doesn't want to be chief of police in some defunct town. Nevertheless, he has his orders.

Audrey needs a place to hide

After the Chicago librarian discovers a horrendous crime, she wakes to an assassin in her bedroom. Injured and terrified, she flees, covering her trail every inch of the way. New name, new ID. *New home.* As Audrey learns to survive in Rescue, she begins to fall for the town...and the intimidating chief of police who protects it.

Can the shy introvert and the deadly police chief find a life together?

Despite the discord in town, Gabe is finding his own peace... with the quiet young woman who seems to have no past. She's adorable and caring and so very lost. But how can he trust someone who lies to him with every breath she takes?

In no hurry, Gabriel MacNair strolled the business section of Main Street—two blocks—reached the end, and headed back on the other side.

It'd take a while to get his footing here. Get to know the place. When visiting Mako, he'd only come into town to pick up groceries.

But police work was police work, no matter the size of the town.

He'd been a police lieutenant in LA. Led a merc squad. Fuck knew, he could handle paperwork. Didn't mean he looked forward to dealing with an entire station's budget.

He glanced at the store he was passing, saw it was Dante's Market, and entered. The owner was a Vietnam vet, and the reason why Mako had chosen Rescue as a place to live.

Not spotting Dante, Gabe glanced around.

Only one person was in the store, a white adult female perusing the cookie section. She had stunning hair. The thick, wavy tangle was every shade of gold and reached halfway down her back. About five-five, she wore jeans and a flannel shirt bulky enough to disguise her curves.

Before he could speak, she picked up a box of cookies and tucked it into her purse.

Well, fuck. Disillusionment washed through him. Even here, people were no good. Odd, he hadn't realized how much he'd hoped for different until that desire was crushed.

He cleared his throat.

She spun, saw him, gasped, and began backing away down the aisle. Hand on her throat, she looked so terrified, he almost had a moment of pity.

Or not.

Staring at the man, Audrey retreated as fast as she could...and he came toward her. *Oh God.*

He blocked the narrow aisle completely. Her heart began to pound painfully inside her rib cage. She glanced over her shoulder at the back door, but the locked door would take time to get open.

She turned to face the man. He was frighteningly big. Over six feet tall, with short brown hair. The beard shadow was darker than his outdoorsman's tan. Harsh lines bracketed his unsmiling mouth, and he looked...threatening.

Could the hitman or his people have traced her?

A glance didn't reveal Spyros; the man was alone. Besides, she hadn't left a trail. People disappeared all the time into remote Alaskan towns.

No, she was safe here. Surely she was. "Wh-what do you want?"

He crossed his arms over his chest—a very broad chest. "It's simple. Hand me everything you stole, and then we'll go down to the station and have a chat."

Have a chat? She wasn't going anywhere with him. The rest of his sentence registered. *Station...* Oh my God, he was the *police.*

She stared at the badge on his black fleece-lined jacket.

Wait, what did he mean "stole"?

"I didn't steal anything." Fear blossomed anew. Although her photo ID looked real enough to her, it wouldn't hold up to a police background check. She took a step back.

His eyebrows lifted slightly. "I saw you. Bring your purse up to the counter."

Outrage swept through her, vying with anxiety. "I'm not stealing. Dante said I could take whatever I wanted to eat."

"Mmmhmm." Disbelief was obvious in the man's deep voice. "Let's ask him."

Audrey crossed her arms over her chest, imitating the man. "He's not here."

When his gaze pinned her in place, she saw his eyes weren't black—they were midnight blue and brimmed with skepticism. "He wouldn't leave his store unattended."

"He asked me to mind the register."

"And steal the goods?"

"Listen, sheriff—"

"There are no sheriffs in Alaska. Call me Chief."

"Chief." Oh, she was so screwed. He wasn't merely a small town cop, but the Chief of Police. She swallowed. Where was Dante? Shouldn't he be back by now? "Chief what?"

"MacNair. And you are?"

"Juliette Wilson." She'd done her homework. Wilson was almost as common as Jones, Johnson, and Smith. Juliette was a popular name, too.

"Wilson, huh?" His mouth flattened in a cynical way.

The door opened. As Dante moseyed into the store, relief filled her.

Only a few inches taller than she was, the wiry grocery store owner had receding white hair and a thick white mustache and beard.

He saw her, and his bushy brows pulled together. Turning to Gabe, he snapped, "Yo, buddy, leave my girl the fuck alone."

When the chief turned toward him with a scowl, Dante blinked. His face lit. "It's Gabe, isn't it? I'll be. You're really here?"

The chief didn't even notice Dante's delight. "Ms. Wilson here was stuffing her purse with groceries and says you left her to mind the place." The cop's deep voice held enough sarcasm to fill a lake.

"Heh, working in L.A. done made you cynical, boy." Dante might've left Oklahoma behind a long while back, but the southern twang in his voice remained.

"She told the truth?"

"Yep, she sure 'nuff did." Dante stepped behind the counter and set down a travel cup and white paper sack from the coffee shop. "She's working now and then in exchange for one of my rental cabins and some groceries. Room and board, you might say. Keeps me from having to close up every time I want to leave the store."

Audrey's muscles began to unknot.

"I see." The chief glanced at her, and his sharp gaze lingered on the yellowing bruises on her face. His suspicions didn't appear much abated, although he said, politely enough, "I'm sorry to have bothered you, Ms. Wilson."

"Quite all right. I can appreciate how guilty I must have appeared." If she'd been a criminal, she'd be running from him as fast as possible.

To her relief, he nodded and joined Dante at the front.

After the two men shook hands, Dante glanced over. "Julie, how about you unpack those boxes of cereals?"

Yes, she totally needed something to keep her hands busy. "I would be delighted."

"You shopping or walkin' your beat," Dante asked the chief.

"There's no food in my cabin, but I'll shop later." The chief shrugged. "I wanted to see what I had to deal with here."

"A lot, boy. A lot. Get yerself settled in and then we'll talk." Dante's smile widened. "You might check on your brother across the street. There was a shit-ton of swearing coming from over there."

Pretending not to listen, Audrey blinked. The man had a brother. There were two of them in this town. *What an awful thought.*

"No surprise. He hates paperwork." The chief's lips didn't move, but the sun lines beside his eyes crinkled.

Oh. Dear God, the man would be lethal if he ever really smiled. She realized she was staring.

He noticed. His eyes narrowed, and his face hardened. Even though Dante's explanation should have placated the cop, he obviously didn't trust her at all.

A chill washed through her because she knew she must have looked guilty as hell.

ALSO BY CHERISE SINCLAIR

Masters of the Shadowlands Series

Club Shadowlands

Dark Citadel

Breaking Free

Lean on Me

Make Me, Sir

To Command and Collar

This Is Who I Am

If Only

Show Me, Baby

Servicing the Target

Protecting His Own

Mischief and the Masters

Beneath the Scars

Defiance

Mountain Masters & Dark Haven Series

Master of the Mountain

Simon Says: Mine

Master of the Abyss

Master of the Dark Side

My Liege of Dark Haven

Edge of the Enforcer

Master of Freedom

Master of Solitude

I Will Not Beg

The Wild Hunt Legacy

Hour of the Lion

Winter of the Wolf

Eventide of the Bear

Leap of the Lion

Healing of the Wolf

Sons of the Survivalist Series

Not a Hero

Lethal Balance

What You See

Standalone Books

The Dom's Dungeon

The Starlight Rite

ABOUT THE AUTHOR

Cherise Sinclair is a *New York Times* and *USA Today* bestselling author of emotional, suspenseful romance. She loves to match up devastatingly powerful males with heroines who can hold their own against the subtle—and not-so-subtle—alpha male pressure.

Fledglings having flown the nest, Cherise, her beloved husband, an eighty-pound lap-puppy, and one fussy feline live in the Pacific Northwest where nothing is cozier than a rainy day spent writing.

www.ingramcontent.com/pod-product-compliance
Lightning Source LLC
LaVergne TN
LVHW020929100825
818316LV00031B/471